Pink

A CHRISTMAS ROMANCE NOVEL

BY

monica collier

RED PRESS CO.

Published by
Red Press Co., Inc.
http://redpressco.com

Library of Congress Control Number:
2021940654

ISBN 9780998589930 Hardcover
ISBN 9781737400318 Paperback

Printed in the United States of America

Cover photo by Amy J. Coe

Look for other books by Monica Collier
Unwritten: The Extaordinary Life of Caroline Blaine, Book 1
Unbecoming: The Secret Life of Caroline Blaine Continues
Kissing Hollywood: Divorce Was Only The Beginning

monicacollier.com

Because of Jamie

Hello reader!

Thank you for choosing my book.

It's been many years since I introduced you to my first protagonist, Caroline Blaine. She is always at the forefront of my mind because I have more tales to share with you concerning her. Spoiler alert: you'll see Caroline in these pages, although she is not the focus of this novel. Even if you have not read Unwritten and Unbecoming, this book is a stand-alone adventure including Caroline and company.

I held a small writer's retreat in the Autumn of 2010. Because of a writing prompt from Jamie Cat Callan's Writer's Toolbox, "She was wearing the wrong shade of pink," this novel came forth. The story has been simmering in my mind for years. At the time, my family spent Christmas in Charleston, South Carolina. I looked forward to spending time in the city throughout the year and especially at Christmas. Take note of the main character's surnames as they are old family names in the history of Charleston. The city remains special to me. I urge you to visit and soak up all Charleston has to offer.

If you are not already familiar with my work, you'll find an ode to military service between the pages somewhere, if not blatant, honoring the past and present sacrifice for those who serve. In this particular novel, mental health after trauma is addressed along with profound loss. If you or a loved one is struggling, whether or not it is service-related, please reach out for help. You are loved. You have something to contribute. You are not alone.

There are numerous named locations in Franklin, North Carolina, New York City, and Charleston, South Carolina. These are mentioned for their contribution to our culture and the impact they have on our daily lives. Look for them and see how many you recognize. Are they your favorites as well? Tell me.

Finally, I cannot express what it means for a reader to give me the sacrifice of their time to read my work, review my material, and recommend my book. If you want to see more books from me, or any author, always follow the three R's: Read, Review, and Recommend. Tag us on social media. Post a photo of the book where you are reading. Don't worry about a detailed review. Just a short review helps other readers to find this book. I need your help as it is crucial to the success of this book.

Thank you for supporting me all these years. I appreciate your help in making this book another bestseller for me. I hope you grow to love Charlotte Rose and Ethan Cooper as much as I do and embrace them as you have Caroline Blaine.

God bless!

xoxo,

Monica

1

Change In The Late Autumn Air

With less than two weeks before Thanksgiving, and her own plans to leave town for New York City, Charlotte Rose wasn't up to a clandestine operation. "I never know whether to panic or smile when I see your number come up on my caller ID, Captain Blaine. How are you? Calling to wish me happy holidays? What will it be this time? Repairing boards for missiles, or sneaking me into a country that despises us?" Charlotte held her breath, willing the call to be of a friendly nature and not the latter.

Captain Caroline Blaine, commanding officer of the United States Naval Intelligence arm ARES, had to laugh because Charlotte's sentiments were spot on. "Stand down, Pink. I just want more of the white half-sheets on felt paper for Isabella's stationery box and to order this year's Christmas cards. I sent you an email with the design

I want this year. I can't get the cards I'm after in Italy, and yours are the best. Are you going to let that breath out now?"

Charlotte exhaled loudly into the microphone of her cell phone. Her body relaxed for a split second before she pulled the curtain over the French doors aside. "You're not creeping outside my porch, are you? You know that used to freak me out."

"I'm still in Italy, don't worry." Caroline shook her head in amusement.

"That's good to know. Thanks for the heads-up on Admiral sourpuss. I didn't waste any more time than I had to last week in Washington." Charlotte let the curtain fall back into place. Her mid-morning cup of coffee was growing cold on the kitchen counter.

Captain Blaine was multi-tasking, reading a situation report handed to her by a yeoman, then a flight manifest. "You're welcome. Isabella wanted me to tell you that her friends at school adore her Scottish Terrier stationery. She's nearly out of the note cards and the half sheets. That's why I called. I'll give it to her for Christmas. She asked me for a fountain pen yesterday."

"I'm glad she likes the Scottish Terrier stationery so much. That's my best seller, along with the peonies. I'll make sure you have it by Christmas for her. I'm heading to New York next Tuesday to find a home for the boutique, finally."

The flight manifest for Savannah, Georgia, listed a man Captain Blaine's team was watching. "I'll not keep you. It's getting late here, and I know you have many things to accomplish before leaving town. Since you are leaving the family business, I'll have to get to know your brother better for when I might need his help. I'm happy you're embracing your dreams, Charlotte. Benjamin would be pleased you're moving on. Dream big, just remember one never really leaves this business. Bye."

Noon had flown by with the clock now rocketing toward one in the afternoon. The gray November sky made it difficult to discern the exact time of day. The clouds were thickening, obscuring a bright blue sky. Cardboard boxes were open, waiting silently on the closet floor for their quarry to be folded up and placed inside. Two hours had passed since Charlotte began to remove the last vestiges of her late husband's belongings from the house. She had saved his clothes for last. Benjamin would have wanted someone to benefit from the wear left in his wardrobe. Her New Year's resolution last year, this year as well, was to donate his things to a local charity. Nearly two years had passed by in a blur. She would have to hurry up if there was any hope of getting everything in the car and donated before darkness fell in the mountains of Western North Carolina.

Charlotte cradled a fresh cup of Earl Grey as she sat staring up from the floor at the right-half of the walk-in closet. The morning's business and phone calls prevented her from getting too emotional about today until now. There were still days when she would pull one of his shirts out and wear it in the house. For a while, after his death, the clothes continued to smell like him. Now they smelled mostly of dust. Grieving was never an easy process. Friends and relatives had lent their advice on the subject, but she decided to go with her own timeline for moving on. They could continue with their tries at matchmaking. She would be the one to determine when it was time to let someone else into her world. Was she even capable of that?

The empty teacup sat on the floor, now abandoned. The last article, a long sleeve Stewart dress plaid flannel shirt from L.L. Bean, hung on a wooden hanger. She remembered him wearing it on cold days. Winter in North Carolina was far different than those Benjamin had experienced growing up in Israel. His first encounter with snow was in college at MIT. Charlotte smiled at the thought of him seeing snow for the first time in his life. He had shared that memory with her every time it snowed, wherever they were, during their fifteen-year marriage. They both adored snow.

She pulled the shirt from the hanger, wrapping herself in the soft, mostly red fabric. The plaid clashed severely with her pink cashmere sweater. The boxes were now full. The black Sharpie she had used to scribble her married name on the end, David, was running out of ink. Her family had insisted she resume her maiden name of Rose as she carried the title of President for Rose Aerospace and Defense, a Department of Defense contractor. Seeing David on the end of the box brought a smile to her lips. When they had first married, she corrected everyone's pronunciation of the name to DAH-VEED. How she missed Benjamin David!

The used-up marker was tossed in the trash. Her fingers began to twirl the small silver snowflake charm that hung around her neck. The necklace was a gift from the first year they were married. A single tear ran down her cheek as she let go of the snowflake. The last few years hadn't brought much snow to Franklin, North Carolina. Charlotte didn't know if she was grateful for that or not because of the memories the frozen precipitation would always evoke.

Her phone began to buzz on the nightstand across the room. She hurried over to answer, recognizing the New York City number immediately.

"Hello, Racheal." Charlotte held the phone away from her head, waiting on the Bluetooth portion of her hearing aid to kick-in.

"Hi. I wanted to call and check on you." Racheal continued to speak softly. "I know this is a hard day for you. Texting like we usually do just didn't seem appropriate."

Charlotte lifted the sleeve to her cheek, wiping away another tear that had escaped. "I've done pretty well. I've only cried three times today." She let an odd laugh escape her lips. "I'll just make like a yeast roll and rise above it. Pardon me while I commit a heinous act of using my sleeve to wipe my face."

Racheal's face softened into a smile for her still-grieving friend. "I think I can forgive you that tiny infraction on good manners." She signed papers absently as her assistant, Barbara, pointed to where. "Did you email me your flight information?"

"I forgot. I should arrive before lunch on Tuesday if we accidentally take-off on time. I'll send you the details, I promise. Then you can pass them along to Lewis, so he can pick me up." Charlotte pulled Benjamin's shirt off, tossing it into the laundry hamper. She was keeping that one.

"Great. I can't wait to see you again. New York City is a different experience this time of year. You've always visited in the Summer." Racheal laid her pen down as Barbara hurried from the office, a thick stack of signed papers grasped tightly in her hands. "We can go shopping. I can take you to the parade..."

Crowds, crowds, crowds, she thought. "I can stay inside to design your new letterhead, Mrs. Partner!"

Racheal giggled into the receiver. "And then there's that. We're going out to celebrate after you arrive. I can finally introduce you to my long-time friend. You're both southern, and you're both widowed."

"We will celebrate, but please don't try to set me up. We've been over this. And all of this is contingent on you having the time. I've been to New York many times. I'll be fine on my own until we can paint the town together." Charlotte's mind went into overdrive about choosing foods off of menus that probably weren't kosher. They'd be eating out mostly because Racheal didn't cook. Then there was the thought of being out in crowds. Her breathing sped up. She would not allow herself to have a panic attack on the phone over mere thoughts. "First, I have to get this house in order before I leave or my brother's family is going to think a tornado came through here. Mom is still giving me a hard time because I'm missing Thanksgiving with them, even though I'll see them all at Christmas in a few weeks in Charleston." Charlotte noticed the time as she passed through the hall, into the kitchen, placing her teacup in the dishwasher. "I gotta go. The church's thrift shop closes at five on Friday. I'll call you this weekend, and we can talk more."

"Better call late Sunday. Gabriel is supposed to be back from Boston tomorrow. I haven't seen my hubby in a week."

Charlotte's face colored. "Gotcha! Will do. Bye."

Minutes later, the back of a borrowed Rose Aerospace and Defense van was full of boxes and down the road. Her thoughts drifted as she raced toward town. William, her younger brother, would be arriving the day before Thanksgiving with his lovely wife, Jennifer, and her nephews, Tyler and Lee. They always stayed at her house. She'd miss them this year. The boys would be heading off to college soon. Their long Summer stays with her before returning to Seattle for school by September were something she had always cherished. At least she'd see them soon enough at their intimate gathering for Christmas. Christmas. Another holiday season was creeping up quickly. Another holiday without Benjamin. Another reminder of his death occurring during Hanukkah. Would the holidays ever get any easier? She prayed this one would be different somehow because, deep down, Charlotte adored the Christmas season.

The van rolled into a parking space in front of Perk-Up, on Main Street, in Franklin. Charlotte wanted to pick-up her favorite coffee roast to have in the house for her arriving family. Alison Pantaleo, the owner, was hugging her wiggling toddler, Josh. She handed him over the counter to her husband, Carey, kissing both of them quickly.

"Thanks, honey. I'll see you later." Alison smiled and waved at Josh, his chubby arm rising to wave back excitedly. Charlotte Rose was pulling the door open to enter, the bell jingling on the door. "Hello! Time for some more beans, Charlotte?"

"Hi! Yes, please." Charlotte stopped in her tracks to hold Josh as Carey walked toward her, near the door. Josh stretched out his arms toward her, smiling and trying to talk. Her heart skipped a beat. "Oh, you're growing so fast."

Carey passed him over to her. "Yes, he is, too fast. How are you?"

"I'm fine, thanks. Heading to New York next week to catch-up with an old college friend. Are you prepping for another season of Cleremont?"

Charlotte cooed over Josh, telling him what a handsome little boy he was and repeatedly raising him up in the air. He let out giggles, squeals, and unintelligible babble each time she'd lift him. She smoothed his blonde hair lovingly and handed him back to Carey. Josh wanted down, squirming and fussing, but Carey held him firmly.

"Yes, I've been in Asheville all day, meeting with the director of photography at Biltmore Estate. Period television shows are interesting to work on. I'm happy to be back behind a camera for a while. It's demanding, but the pay is excellent. I don't miss Hollywood. I wouldn't trade the life I have here with Alison and Josh for anything." Josh finally laid his head against Carey's shoulder and yawned. "I'd better get this one home. He's exhausted. Nice to see you, as always, Charlotte."

"You too, Carey." Charlotte finally made it to the counter. "How's the day been?"

Alison taped the bag of now ground coffee beans shut. "I'm tired but great. Josh usually sleeps through the night, but not last night. And I was up late, talking to Alex. She and Parker are flying in the day before Thanksgiving, so we can catch-up and spend some time together. Once Cleremont's production gets going, I'll lose my husband and her for a while. I'm excited about seeing her again. She said they were stopping in New York for a few days to see Parker's uncle, Charles Grey, before that. Who knows, maybe you'll see her since your friend Racheal works for his firm. You should give her a call while you're there if you have time."

"Maybe. The only thing I've seen of her in a while is the name Alex Casey, producer and or director, on the Convergence credits. I'm glad she's happy and doing so well."

"Me too and that handsome hubby, Parker. Can I get you anything else?" Alison punched the total into her register.

"That's all. Thanks so much. I like this Farmhouse roast. Get some rest tonight."

"I will. Thanks." Alison tried to smile just as a yawn got the better of her.

Charlotte noticed the town Christmas tree was already up across the street as she went back to the van. She put the coffee in the passenger seat and headed to see her friend Jane Elliott at her home bakery, on Garnet Creek, in West Franklin. Charlotte had been craving her Paradise shortbread cookies. She wanted to pay her for the Thanksgiving desserts that were ordered for her family, even though she wouldn't be there to indulge. Lights were already on in some windows as she passed the clock tower in the square. Franklin was always decorated so well, and early, due to the weekend festivities that started the day after Thanksgiving. She'd be missing them this year, but new adventures awaited her in New York City. The question of whether or not she could shake the panic attacks that often gripped her in large crowds remained in her mind.

Once more at home, the freshly ground beans were placed in the ceramic coffee canister, beside the French press, on the kitchen island. So much to do and only a few days to do it. She'd have to pack after the house was ready for her brother and his family. Charlotte picked up the phone to call William and see if her brother's home had sold yet in Seattle. The last offer had been countered this morning.

"We should hear something soon. Have you told Mom and Dad that you really are leaving the company?"

She ran a pale hand through her shoulder-length blonde hair. "I haven't yet. They just think I'm going up to spend some quality time with Racheal for now and take a break while you're on the east coast to handle things. I wanted to make sure I can find the right space for the stationery boutique in New York first. If I can't,

I might just have to open it in Charleston. I found a great place on King Street. And then there is the matter of finding myself a place to live. I don't want to rock the boat with Mom and Dad until I know for certain that I'm leaving. I'm just not sure if it will be New York or Charleston."

"Sis, you've been doing what Mom and Dad expected of you since you could walk. Once the house sells, we're moving back there. You and I have been over this already. Jenn and I will buy the house from you and give you the clean break you need. If you don't do this for yourself, you're going to always regret it. It's what Benjamin would have wanted for you, too. It's what I want for you. You're great at what you do for the company. No one can charm an Admiral like you when we're negotiating Navy contracts. Somehow, I'll manage. The company will be just fine with me at the helm instead of you."

"Pray for me, William, that I'll have the courage to make this change, and I'll find the right place for the boutique." Charlotte stared out on Rose Creek through the french door before she let the curtain go. The valley was dark, dotted with a few lights from homes. She stepped too close to the contact sensor for the alarm on the door, and her hearing aid screeched. "Sorry."

William pulled the phone away from his ear at the painful sound until it abated. Since she began wearing the devices after the explosion that injured her and killed Benjamin, he'd grown accustomed to the noise on occasion. He wished she didn't have to depend on hearing aids at forty-two but was glad she could hear again. "It's okay. How have the panic attacks been lately?"

Charlotte drew a sharp breath. "I haven't had one in about a week. I was checking out of the Adams House, in Washington, over a week ago. I had one sitting in the cab heading to the airport. We were stopped at a light. A large transfer truck was parked, and the driver slammed the trailer door shut. Loud, sudden noises usually are the worst triggers. I'd not had one the entire trip, then bam!"

"Did you get your Black Spruce essential oil out and inhale it?"

"Yes, I did. Caroline was right; it does help." She opened up her calendar app on the MacBook, still open on the kitchen island from this morning's work. "Before I forget, the Saudi Arabian Foreign Minister and I had a long chat yesterday. The GE engines they're shipping over for repair should be ready to go back by the first of the year, barring any unforeseen issues. If you need me to speak with him while I'm in New York, let me know. The Marine detachment there is waiting to move those planes until then. We can't get them in the country as easily without the Minister's help."

"We're all going to miss your language skills. I speak enough of Arabic and Farsi to get myself into trouble."

"You're going to have to take a language program and get better, that's all. I learned it while I was married and traveling so much with Benjamin. If you use it, like I do, you'll learn it. Hebrew came that way too. You're better with German than I am because you were there for a while in the Army."

"You're right. Rosetta Stone, here I come! But I can't do what you do with electronics. I don't have a Masters Degree in electrical engineering."

She laughed, "You speak nerd just fine. I'm going to go. I borrowed a van from the shop to haul some donations this afternoon. I need to return it. Let me know if the house sells."

"I will. Talk to you later. Have fun in New York."

"I will. Give my love to Jennifer and the boys. Bye." Charlotte grabbed the keys to the Sprinter. The conversation with William had lightened her mood considerably. Now to get through the weekend and all that remained before leaving.

"Nancy? When you get a moment, I need to see you, please."

Ethan Cooper released the button. No sooner than his finger lifted, his assistant of eighteen years appeared in the doorway.

"You look worried, Nancy."

Her left eyebrow raised as a Long Island accent cranked up. "Thanksgiving is nearly here, and don't get me started on how much you love Christmas, Mr. Grumpy Pants. Yes, I heard the music in the elevator on my way up from the library and the copy room. I'll have them change it back to the classical station until after Thanksgiving. That's all I can do."

Ethan smiled, "Thank you, Nancy."

"You're welcome. Did you return your mother's call?"

He sighed, looking up, replying through clenched teeth. "Not yet."

"She can't bite through the phone, remember that." Nancy laughed, "We have plenty of time, weeks even. Your Dior tuxedo will come back from the cleaners the day before the event. Your shoes are being repaired and shined. Marcus has the limos lined up for that night. Your family table has been taken care of, like I take care of it every year, to exacting specifications set by you and your mother. The gala fundraiser will go smoothly again this year, even though you're changing the format. You'll raise millions, like you always do, to support the arts in New York City schools. The new liaison with the art gallery will be here next Tuesday to finalize the pieces you'll have for auction. You have a meeting with her at three. It's all taken care of and on your calendar. You can call your mother back and tell her so. Of course, you're going to have to explain why you don't have a plus one, again. I won't take the heat for that one."

He chuckled, "I love you, Nancy." His face remained pulled up in a coy smile. "Marry me."

"I did, years ago. We had a quiet Hamptons wedding, made all the New York tabloids. You put me up in a penthouse, on Park Avenue, in the lap of luxury, and only see me on holidays because of your work schedule. Oh, wait! I dreamed that. I'm too old for you." She grinned back at him from under her half-moon spectacles, resting near the tip of her nose, a dangling chain, keeping them anchored, safely encircled her neck. Soft wrinkles around her wise blue eyes were apparent only when she smiled. "Now call your mother. I'll call about the music, and then I'm going home. Don't stay here all night."

"Night, Nancy. See you Monday."

With that, Nancy turned, disappearing back to her desk. Her perfectly coiffed white hair could barely be seen over the countertop on the high desk enclosure surrounding her office domain. Ethan's glass door was still open. He could hear her speaking. She was on the phone taking care of the music. He pursed his lips, looking at his desk phone. He always dreaded talking to his mother. Conversations with her never ended on a good note, nor did they begin on one either. He rose from the desk to pour himself a drink. He needed alcohol before dialing her in Charleston, South Carolina. The bourbon's allure wafted to his nostrils as he peered out on the lights over Manhattan from the thirty-seventh floor of 601 Lexington Avenue. His tired reflection in the glass stared back at him. The hand-stitched gray suit he wore appeared black in the glass, along with his eyes.

His fingers didn't seem to want to grasp the phone when he sat back down. A loud knock broke his silent stand-off with the phone. "Perfect timing, Racheal. Come in."

She eyed his left hand. "That's a large glass of bourbon you're cradling. Pondering a case or avoiding a phone call to your mother?"

"Unfortunately, the latter. Have a seat." He cleared his throat and took a large draw from the glass. "What brings you to my office?"

"I signed off on the hotel merger. Barbara messengered it to Cassidy."

"Great. That's one deal I'll be happy to see close and off our plates. Carter is going to be a happy man." Ethan raised his glass. "How very rude of me. Would you like a glass yourself?"

"No, thank you. I'm heading to the King Cole Bar with two of our top associates to meet Cassidy's crew for drinks and dinner soon. Then we can put this baby to bed. Underwriting took their time on that merger. I'm just happy we have terrific assets in our associate pool with all the research required on that deal. Mr. Carter gets prime New York City properties, and Cassidy gets to avoid bankruptcy."

Ethan drank more of the amber liquid. "You handle the associates and the other partners very well. I should have made you a partner a long time ago. If I had known how easy it would make my job…"

Racheal laughed, "Thanks for having faith in me, but I had to put my time in here first, like everyone else."

"Stephanie told me if I didn't hire you I'd live to regret it. She was correct." Ethan polished-off the glass. He looked over to the left corner of his desk at the photo of himself, with Stephanie in his arms, Central Park covered in snow for the background. It was still his favorite. "She always knew best."

Racheal rose, walking behind the desk to stand beside him, placing her left hand on Ethan's shoulder. She knew where he was looking. "I miss her every day. I can't believe it's been fifteen years since I worked with her in the DA's office. Steph was the best ADA they had. She always loved this time of the year. They're putting up the final decorations in Herald Square for the parade. I noticed it yesterday." She paused, drawing a breath, then exhaling so she wouldn't tear-up. Ethan always became withdrawn socially and uncharacteristically grumpy this time of year. Racheal decided it best to move this along. "I'll make sure this deal goes through for the firm."

"Thank you." Ethan grew quiet. He thought about another glass of bourbon. "Let me know if you have any issues with Cassidy's bunch."

"I will. Enjoy your weekend. Get out of here." She walked toward the door. "My friend is coming to town next week. I know you prefer to keep the company of bourbon, but I'd like to finally introduce the two of you."

Ethan let a chuckle escape his lips. "Don't go there, Rae. No setting me up with your friend."

"You guys would really hit it off. She's southern too." She exhaled loudly, "Alright, fine. Go easy on that bourbon until you've had some dinner, okay?"

"I have to call my mother about the gala fundraiser. I make no promises."

Voicemail. Great. At least he wouldn't actually have to speak to her. Ethan began to leave a short message for his mother. He loosened his tie, gray with subtle raised dots, and waited for the tone.

"My apologies for not calling sooner. I've been otherwise engaged today in legal matters..."

The direct line from his partner, Charles Grey, was lighting up on the Cisco phone. He ended the message for his mother and pushed the button for Charles.

"Good evening."

The smooth British accent cut cleanly through the phone line. "Good evening, Ethan. I was in hopes I could catch you before you'd gone for the weekend. My nephew, Parker, and his wife, Alex, will be stopping by next Thursday. I've drawn up a new contract for their production company to renegotiate with the network regarding Cleremont. I'd like you to take a look before they arrive. I want you there in the meeting when all parties are present in the coming days if you're agreeable. Parker has asked for you since we are both listed as their managing agents and firm of record. "

"Of course. Let me know the time. I'll have Nancy calendar it."

"I will when I've planned my schedule with them. I'm retiring for the evening. Good night. I'll return to the office next Thursday morning before they arrive."

"Enjoy the house in the Hamptons, Charles. Give my best to Ina. Good night."

Ethan admired how Charles could get away to relax and leave business alone. He had yet to grasp the practice for himself. Of course, he was the other half of Grey Cooper and Associates. Could they both be gone at the same time? Should they? What did Ethan have to get away from? The large apartment overlooking Central Park was something he had worked hard to acquire, but the place was lonely when it was just him. At forty-five, things were supposed to be different. Racheal was only thirty-eight and seemed to have a zest for her work and life, balancing the two. He admired both

Charles and Racheal for that. Something was missing. In truth, it had been missing since Stephanie's death.

The buzzing cell phone in his pocket brought his attention to immediate focus. His younger sister, Jane, was calling.

"Hello, Jane. Nancy printed off your itinerary. It looks like you'll be here in plenty of time for the parade."

"Hi. Yes, we will. The boys are very excited about the parade and about seeing their uncle."

Ethan looked at his calendar on the computer screen. It was packed. "I'll do my best to schedule some time with Nancy so that I can see you all.

Jane snorted, "So let me translate. We'll get five minutes with you, in your office, if we come and see you."

"No! I'll move some appointments around. I promise. I want to see the boys and you."

"The last time we visited, we saw you for less than half a day. Forgive me if I sound unbelieving. Oh, mother said she hadn't heard back from you. She wanted me to convey her regrets over missing time with all of us."

Ethan let a loud laugh escape. "Like she would ever come up and actually attend the parade with us. I haven't seen pigs fly yet."

Jane grinned, "She wouldn't be caught dead standing on the sidewalk watching. Someone might bump into her favorite fur or step on her Louboutin's. Oh, the horror of wearing real shoes and standing on a sidewalk of crowded commoners. How did we ever survive childhood?"

"The poor housekeeper raised us when we weren't at Aunt Effie's, that's how. I think of Mrs. Icey, fondly, every day. I cannot say the same for mother."

She laughed, "True. We need to stop this. Mother is going to be mother, snob that she is. I won't keep you. Thanks for answering. I miss you. The boys do too."

He grinned, "Miss you. I always answer when it's you. Everything alright with you and the hubby?"

Jane paused before answering. "I still think Colin's cheating again. He keeps denying it, but I'd be stupid to ignore the signs for the third time."

"I'm sorry, Jane. I really am. You'd think he'd have more respect for you and his marriage. Is he still going to counseling with you?"

Her face scrunched up. "No, he stopped going. I still am, but it takes both of us to make a marriage work. He hasn't been interested in me for a long time. If I can prove he's cheating, again, I don't care what mother thinks it will do to our family's reputation at Saint Phillips. I cannot keep doing this. I'll divorce him, and she will just have to live with it."

"I don't blame you. I'm here if you need to talk. Anytime."

Jane beat the steering wheel with her hands. "Oh, come on! Is this light ever going to change?" She hit the gas as soon as the green light flashed. "Sorry. I'm running late to get the boys from music lessons. I know you're here for me. Thank you. I feel like I bother you too much with this."

"You're never a bother. You and the boys are the only family that I claim. And Aunt Effie's house is there if you need it. It's more than enough house for you and the boys. I'm not there to use it. I don't know why she left it to me."

"You were her favorite. I was already married when she died. She couldn't stand her kids. And bless their hearts; they've both left this world too soon from their extravagant lifestyles. Drugs are the modern-day scourge of society."

"Agreed. She always supported my whims of art, playin' music, and goin' to Harvard. Mother and Aunt Effie were nothing alike. You'd never know they were sisters." Ethan heard his southern accent pick up a bit. It always became stronger whenever he spoke with his sister, who still lived in Charleston. The accent had faded since he'd been in New York for so many years.

"I'm gonna go, for real. I've still got to grab some dinner. I have no idea where Colin is tonight. He's not been home in three days. I'll talk to you soon. Love you."

"Love you. Bye." Ethan put the cell phone down. He resolved that he would clear some time in his schedule to see his sister and her two boys while they were to be in town. If things were to change for himself, he would start with his priorities for family to find more balance. Work could wait, couldn't it?

2

Of Bourbon and Bacon

The plane had landed with a bang in New York City, literally. One of the wheels on the landing gear was stuck. Charlotte had managed to keep herself calm by deep breathing and using the Black Spruce essential oil. She employed the same technique while negotiating the luggage carousel, the cab line to leave the airport, and the enormous crowds everywhere she turned on the sidewalks as well. Usually, her panic attacks were initiated by a sudden loud noise. This day was a cacophony that would crescendo with each passing moment.

The city seemed intent on pressing the air out of her lungs. Her heart was beating loudly in her ears echoing through her hearing aids. To add to her panic, the key code for Racheal's apartment building wasn't working. After three tries, a maintenance man came up to the glass door. He pressed a button on the entry system. Charlotte noticed the name on the system, Rose, her family's company.

"Can I help you?" A Bronx accent tumbled out.

"The code I have doesn't seem to be working. I'm staying with Racheal Maxwell. Were the codes changed recently?"

His voice came through the intercom crisply on the chilly, late Fall day. "This morning, for all the residents. Unless you have a working code and you're on the list to get in, you're not getting in the door or on the elevator."

"But what am I supposed to do? I just need to put my luggage away, so I'm not late to meet-up with Ms. Maxwell. Is Mr. Lyons in the lobby?"

"That's your problem, lady: no code, no list, no entry. I don't know you. I'm not letting you inside. Come back at four. Mr. Lyons comes on duty then."

Charlotte's frustration was growing. "Let's call Ms. Maxwell, then, shall we?" Charlotte pulled out her phone and placed the call on speaker. Her heart was still beating wildly as the call rolled to voicemail. The man glared at her before walking away from the door. She dialed the office and reached Barbara.

"Racheal Maxwell's office, Barbara speaking."

"Hello, Barbara. This is Charlotte Rose. May I speak with Racheal, please?" Charlotte looked up to an empty door. The man was gone.

"She's in a meeting, Ms. Rose. May I take a message?"

"The code she gave me for her building isn't working. According to the maintenance man, the codes were changed this morning. I thought I was on the list. I know one of her building's attendants, but he doesn't come on until four. I'm stuck outside, with three large suitcases, looking like a tourist. I don't want to become the next statistic for the NYPD."

"I see. As it so happens, I have a new code for you, texting it now. You are on the list if the doorman could be bothered to look. Her driver, Lewis, is heading there now to help. He would have picked you up at the airport, but he was otherwise detained."

"Thank you, Barbara."

"You're welcome. If you prefer, I'll keep you on the line until Lewis arrives. I know Racheal is most excited to have you here. She had her schedule cleared this afternoon, but legal matters-"

"Arose. Yes, I understand. I wouldn't want to impose on you any more than I have. Thank you again, Barbara. I'll see you shortly when I come to the office. Goodbye." Charlotte knew Barbara was busy. She spotted a bench nearby. Racheal had warned her to pack heavily for changing temperatures as the weather was always unpredictable. It could be warm and breezy one day and snowing the next this time of the year. She didn't want to irritate the doorman by just letting herself into the building; the entry system was a breeze to get into if you knew how. And she knew how because she had helped to design it.

She resigned herself to suffer the cold breeze in a soft pink pea coat. The wind whipped at her gray pantyhose and charcoal pencil skirt as a black Mercedes sedan slowed to a stop. The dirty streets had a smell of their own, creeping up her nostrils on the breeze.

Lewis Griffin popped out of the car with a smile and a Starbucks cup. His familiar face was comforting to Charlotte. "Don't you just love New York in the Fall! Ms. Maxwell said to bring hot coffee because you wouldn't be dressed for this weather. Here, wrap your fingers around this." Lewis exchanged the coffee for a suitcase handle, plopping the large carry-on bag across the top securely. With so many years of experience and gentle patience, Lewis always knew how to make you feel at ease.

Charlotte smiled and squeezed her eyes shut in shame. She dragged the other piece of luggage behind her. "She knows me too well. So do you. How are you, Lewis?"

"Just dandy, thanks. Let's get you inside, doll." They shared a quick hug. With a suitcase handle in his left hand, he hauled out a key card with his right and touched the coated plastic key to the flat surface of the metal lock next to the door. "They may have changed the codes for that keypad, but the keys still work just fine."

As they walked inside, Charlotte looked around the lobby for the man from earlier. "Mr. Lyons isn't here yet. The man who came to the door wasn't about to help me with anything. I had forgotten how 'helpful' everyone is here."

"Carl? Oh, isn't he a peach? He's new. Stanley must have gone to the bathroom. He's new too." Lewis stopped at the front desk, next to the elevator. The lobby was tiny, with barely enough room for them to stand without bumping the elevator with her luggage. "Oh, here he is. Mr. Stanley, may I introduce Mrs. David-"

"It's Ms. Rose." Charlotte blushed to match her coat. "My apologies for cutting you off, Lewis."

He smiled back at her, "Like I said, Mr. Stanley, this is Ms. Rose. She's staying with the Maxwell-Rodriguez's for a bit."

Mr. Stanley nodded in acknowledging Lewis, reaching for her hand.

Charlotte shook Mr. Stanley's hand, smiling at him. "Pleased to meet you, Mr. Stanley."

She was looking him in the eye, smiling, shaking his hand like he was somebody. He knew then he liked her. "Likewise, Ms. Rose. Let me know if I can assist you while you're here."

"I will, thank you, and it's Charlotte."

Lewis stepped into the elevator with her, rolling the luggage along. They hopped off on the seventh floor. "Glad to be back in town?"

"I am." She paused, carefully choosing her words. "There's just something about New York City. Dad always said if I didn't move to Charleston, South Carolina, I'd move to New York."

"Well, we've been missing you for over a year now. Racheal is a great lady, but I don't have as much fun with her until you're in town." Lewis smiled at her. "Let's get you back to the office so you two can have a late lunch. It's almost two."

After showing her identification, she was issued a badge at the security desk. Lewis bid her farewell for now. Charlotte headed for the elevator bank in the center of the high rise, along with many others, bound for greater heights. She thought the elevator was never going to stop as it climbed higher and higher. Finally, they arrived on the thirty-seventh floor. She had expected Christmas music to be already playing in the car, as it was everywhere else she had been today. To her surprise, Bach settled in her ears. Just as his Brandenberg Concerto number four crescendoed again, the doors opened to white marble tiles on the floor in high contrast to the elevator car's dark floor. They extended half-way up the wall to her right; above that, the firm's name in black lettering was back-lit brightly. Her charcoal heels clacking on the floor and echoing with each step ceased at the main lobby desk. No one noticed the added noise to the light roar.

Three receptionists were fielding calls and managing the traffic entry into the firm, buzzing people in through a gate on one side. Others breezed through the other side, touching their badges to an entry system. The only sounds to be heard were men's footsteps, ladies' heels, muffled voices, and answered calls. The exact words rang out with each call, answered on a wireless headset.

"Grey Cooper and Associates. How may I direct your call?" Finally, one of them lent their attention to her. "May I help you?"

"Charlotte Rose, here to see Racheal Maxwell."

The gate on the right buzzed for entry.

"Have a seat. Someone will be with you in a moment."

Charlotte walked through and sat down in a plush leather chair. There were many of them along with a sofa, all full of individuals, waiting for someone. She joined them, listening to their conversations. It was only a moment until Racheal's brilliant and beautiful paralegal Barbara came out from a nearby hallway to greet her.

"You made it. Ms. Maxwell will be pleased to see you. She said to put you in her office until the meeting has concluded." The elegantly dressed black woman was pleased to see to her, flashing her gorgeous smile.

Charlotte followed Barbara quickly through one hallway, then down another until they popped out at a secretarial pool. She looked at the name on the glass door as Barbara led her into Racheal's new office.

"Wait here," Barbara commanded, "she will be with you when she can. Can I get you something to drink while you wait?"

"Hot tea or coffee, please, if you're getting some for yourself as well."

Barbara smiled, "I was about to get some hot tea. How do you take yours?"

"A little honey, if you have it, please."

"Yes, ma'am." Barbara disappeared, returning a few moments later with a Grey Cooper branded white mug. "Let me know if you need anything else."

"I will, thank you."

Barbara sat down, mulling Charlotte over. She had a very slight southern accent, noticeable only on certain words. Her manners stuck out most of all. Hardly anyone at the office used please and thank you. Charlotte was always kind.

Plants were everywhere, some with long vines down the sides of a tall bookcase. This office was different in a fundamental way; it had a great view of Manhattan. The glass outside wall led the eye into the buildings surrounding the structure. The taxis and traffic below streamed by people who were not discernible on the sidewalks, only their movement. Racheal's westside view wasn't a main thorough-fare. A few doors down, the corner office had the best view facing south, as far as Charlotte could tell.

Time crept by. It was now three in the afternoon. Breakfast had been many hours ago, in the dark, at the Asheville Airport. Rumbling couldn't be ignored any longer. Charlotte pulled herself off a sticky note from Racheal's desk and used a pen to scribble a note.

Gone to grab some lunch across the street. Text me if you want me to bring you something. 3:05 Love, C

"Enough! Conrad, listen to what Racheal is trying to tell you. This has already been settled. If you had read the disclosure, you'd know it included all five properties here in New York and your considerable debt accrued through the unfinished remodeling. You came out smelling like a rose. Be glad Mr. Carter is so generous. There will be no more haggling for a meaningless title in his com-pany. The deal is done. You're done. Now, if you please, we've all worked through lunch listening to your unnecessary babbling for the last four hours. We have messages to return and our client's business to attend to. You and your counsel can show yourselves out. Good day, gentlemen."

Six members of the firm followed Ethan from the glass-enclosed conference room on the building's west side. They dispersed into the hallways as he headed across the firm to the large corner office, a few doors down from Racheal's. Another conference room separated them.

Ethan pinched the bridge of his nose as he stormed into his office. Racheal followed him inside, not knowing if a dressing-down was coming.

"I need a drink." He headed toward his bourbon rather than his desk. "On second thought, I need air." He spun around. "Go back to the new deal for the Napa properties. I don't want him pulling this nonsense again. If Conrad Cassidy wants to play hardball, we're going to beat him at this game before his cheap suits hit the court. Mr. Carter trusts us to have his back. I don't have to tell you how much this deal is worth to our firm, Racheal. I want to see the new wording for the California buyout on my desk tonight and the new packages by morning." He tried his best not to sound too terse with her.

"Yes, sir. I'll handle it." She turned to walk out of his office. It was going to be a long night with the associates. Charlotte would have to amuse herself.

"Racheal." Ethan cleared his throat.

She waited.

"Don't let Cassidy make you flinch. You're here because you've earned it. You've handled the New York deal very well, just like I would have. Now lock it up with the California portion. You've got this." He smiled at her.

"Thank you." She smiled back at him.

"No. Thank you." Ethan left his office and spoke with Nancy regarding messages and a delayed appointment with the art gallery's new representative.

After answering Nancy's questions, he rode the elevator down to the ground floor. His stomach grumbled as he exited the lobby. He could call his car service and go somewhere or walk across the street to the usual haunt, The Boxwood.

The English boxwoods gracing the windows out front, for the restaurant's namesake, were covered for winter. Inside, the dark bistro and bar were sparsely populated before dinner. The bar was abandoned entirely. Happy hour it seemed wasn't so happy today.

The couple sitting one table over from Charlotte quietly talked, so quietly in fact, she could hardly make out a word even with bionic ears. As she sipped her glass of Pellegrino and lime, the world inside The Boxwood went completely quiet. It was only when the server returned, who was also the bartender, and began speaking to her, that she realized her hearing aids needed to be turned back up. His lips were moving, but there wasn't much sound.

She motioned with her finger for him to wait a moment. The devices had been adjusted while inside the law office lobby, as the noise was too much for her.

"My apologies. I can hear you now."

He smiled at the pretty blonde, not expecting her to be wearing hearing aids. She was too young for that. "No problem. I just wanted to tell you that your order is coming up. Would you like something else to drink?"

"I'll eat something first. For now, I'll stick with this." She poured the rest of the Pellegrino into the glass and handed him the empty bottle.

With her hearing aids turned up, she could clearly hear the couple's conversation now. It was in Farsi. They were discussing where to visit next. The wife wanted to see Tiffany's before heading to their hotel. She pouted about his work schedule during their visit. The husband kissed her hand and promised her a romantic carriage ride in Central Park before leaving this time. She was unsure of how far away they were from Tiffany's.

Charlotte spoke up, in Farsi, and told them they weren't far at all. "You're very close to one on Greene Street. The next is on Fifth Avenue."

The wife's reaction was priceless. "Thank you. See! I told you we weren't far. Now can we please go?"

The husband seemed more taken with Charlotte's answer in Farsi than actual directions. "How is it that you speak Farsi? It is not common here."

Their conversation continued as Ethan Cooper walked in. New York was a true melting pot. You never knew who you would run into or what you would hear each day. He was struck by a beautiful blonde, sitting alone, chatting away with a couple in what he guessed was a middle eastern dialect. The blonde woman had a stunning smile. Her porcelain face could light up a room. He intently listened as he waited on Todd to return from table duties, setting a plate before Charlotte. There were never many servers between shifts, and dinner service didn't start until five. The bartender knew precisely what Ethan wanted, as he was in at least three times a week.

A glass of straight bourbon was placed before Ethan without a word and Todd continued about his duties. The couple settled their bill with Todd, speaking to Charlotte once again before leaving. Ethan stared into the glass before him, letting his mind go blank. The woman made a noise of absolute pleasure that intrigued him and became an instant distraction. His eyes darted to her. She did it again. What on that plate could elicit such an utterance?

Charlotte took another bite of her bacon, lettuce, and green tomato sandwich. The restaurant was now empty, save for one man sitting at the bar, nursing a glass of bourbon. He kept looking over at her. She didn't realize her pleasure of tasting bacon again was so distracting to the gentleman. Then again, she had dropped her napkin on the floor, and now the aioli was running out on her hands.

Ethan could not stop being a voyeur to the woman's obvious joy regarding her menu choice. The last sigh, almost a moan, brought a smile to his face. The sounds were stirring his curiosity and passions.

He raised the glass and finished the drink in one swallow. "Another bourbon, Todd, and one of whatever she's having."

The bartender spun around, his face frozen in shock. "You want a BLT?"

Ethan's head rolled back with laughter. "On second thought, just give me the bourbon, and hand me a napkin." A moment later, he rose from the bar with his glass and a napkin. He strolled over to the woman's table and handed it to her.

"Thanks. Sorry, I'm disturbing you." Charlotte laid her half-eaten sandwich down onto her plate.

"It's no trouble. You looked like you could use a napkin." He grinned at her. Her face was lovely. Long eyelashes hung over striking brown eyes. Rosy cheeks and pink lips framed her face. He noted her voice; she was southern. How charming! The wool coat laying beside her on the bench seat revealed a Burberry plaid lining. She was impeccably dressed, right down to the pearls around her neck. Ethan was intrigued.

"I usually don't eat a meal without wearing some portion of it. I appreciate the gesture." She wiped the garlic mayonnaise from her fingers. He was wearing an expensive handmade suit and a tie that cost more than a bottle of vintage Dom. "How's the bourbon here?"

"It's not Woodford Reserve, one of my favorites, but I'll take it. You like bourbon?" The woman had been listening to him as well while he sat there and ordered his second drink.

Charlotte smiled, hoping she wasn't wearing aioli on her chin right now. His light brown hair was perfectly groomed, along with the rest of him. Vivid dark blue eyes and the longest eyelashes she had ever seen peered back at her. "*Good* bourbon."

Ethan turned his head away from her. "Todd, a *good* bourbon for the lady." He looked at her once more. "I'm keeping you from your meal, my apologies. I just had to know what the fuss was over here."

She licked her lips nervously as he continued to study her. "I haven't had bacon in about twelve years."

"Twelve years? Why on earth would you go that long without bacon?" He couldn't fathom the thought. He ate bacon almost daily.

Todd brought the glass over to them, setting it down on the table in silence. "Do either of you need anything else right now?" Both indicated no, and he disappeared to watch the two of them instead. Ethan only spoke to the staff usually, ignoring the patrons and never to someone he didn't know.

"Have a seat." She motioned with her hand.

"Ethan." He sank into the chair opposite her.

"Charlotte. And I haven't eaten bacon in twelve years because my husband was a Messianic Jew. He liked to keep kosher. I gave it up for him. He knew I loved it, so I like to think he's looking down, right now, smiling. He's probably laughing at my antics, in fact."

The amused look on Ethan's face over the bacon faded. Her last words were quite sobering. "I'm sorry."

"It's okay. Thanks. This bacon is ringing every food bell I have. It's crispy. That goes nicely with the fried green tomato on the sandwich too."

"Bacon has to be crispy. I will not stand for floppy bacon!"

Charlotte raised her bourbon glass towards him. "Thank you for the drink. Here's to crispy bacon!"

A toast was shared.

Ethan had settled into their conversation and ordered a vegetable plate. Charlotte observed his proper manner of eating. Napkin tucked in the lap, each bite of cooked greens chewed while the fork was placed down. He was left-handed. Then the pinto beans disappeared in the same fashion, the cornbread square on his plate missing only one bite. The sides were for the evening meal, but Ethan was obviously treated very well here by the staff. He knew them all by name as servers filed through, setting up the tables for dinner service.

"Todd, tell Chef he needs to work on the greens and beans. They're good, but they're missing something. And the cornbread is moist, but it's sweet. That's just wrong."

Todd laughed from behind the bar. "I'll do that."

Charlotte was curious. "What exactly are they missing?"

"It's a pork fat thing."

She smirked, "I see. Ham hock or salt pork? I know exactly what you mean."

"I'll bet you do since you're southern."

She smiled again. "I'm from Western North Carolina. How does a New Yorker know what's missing in collard greens and pinto beans?"

"Hey now, I'm southern too. Don't let the mostly missing accent fool you. I might have lived here for twenty years, but I know that cornbread should not contain sugar."

"You're absolutely right. If it has sugar, it's a cake."

Todd was very amused listening to the two of them. He'd never seen Ethan carry on like this with a stranger. He seemed relaxed and enjoying himself. Todd was glad. Ethan hadn't been the same since his wife died. "Sugar in cornbread is not a Yankee thing."

"It is where I come from." Ethan meant the comment playfully, and Todd knew it. The cornbread was abandoned on the plate. "By the way you're dressed, I'd say you're in town on business."

"By the way you're dressed, I'd say you're taking a break from business." She smiled, awaiting his reply.

He nodded slightly, affirmatively. "Touché."

"I am in town on business. If it all works out, I'll be here until the week before Christmas. I plan to make the most of it. Business is important while I'm here, but I have some living to catch up on."

"So do I." Ethan wore a wistful expression. "You referenced your husband earlier. How long has he been gone?"

"Almost two years." Charlotte sighed, "I figured he wouldn't mind if I had some bacon today."

"I lost my wife, Stephanie, five years ago. Some days are easier than others. Everyone tells you to move on because that's what they would have wanted. You don't move on. You just learn to function again, a day at a time, without them. The hole is still there."

"Exactly." Charlotte sipped the glass of bourbon thoughtfully. "I lost Benjamin during Hanukkah."

"This must really be a tough time of the year for you then, with it coming up soon." He didn't want to mention his own pain at hearing Christmas music because it evoked Stephanie's memory.

"Tough because he's not with me. I won't let his loss dampen what the season means. He really wouldn't want that. Benjamin knew how much joy Hanukkah and the Christmas season brought me. If I let what happened to him change that…then they've won. I won't stand for that." Charlotte finished her words passionately.

Ethan fingered the top of his glass, then let it go, digesting her words carefully. He was letting Stephanie's death affect his enjoyment of Christmas and winter. He truly did enjoy both. "Who's they?"

Just as Charlotte was about to reveal more, Ethan's cell phone buzzed in his right breast pocket. She waited patiently as he retrieved the phone, glanced at the screen, and replaced it.

"My apologies for rudeness. My three o'clock has become my four-thirty." He folded his napkin, leaving it on the table. "Todd, I need the check, please." His attention once again focused on her. "I cannot believe my good fortune in meeting you today, Charlotte. I've thoroughly enjoyed our chat. Unfortunately for me, duty calls."

"I've enjoyed it as well. Maybe I'll see you here again."

"Perhaps."

"I hope the four-thirty goes well since it was my good fortune they were tardy." She flashed a genuine smile at him.

He rose to give Todd his credit card at the bar, a few steps away. Her smile could have melted his resolve to return to work. He drew his favorite Parker pen from his suit to sign the slip and stepped toward her once more. "It's getting chilly out there. Stay warm." He raised his lapel as he was without a jacket.

"You too, Ethan."

And with that, he was gone. Charlotte felt a loss at his departure, and she couldn't explain why. Moments later, Todd returned.

"Can I get you anything else?" He waited.

"No, just the bill."

"It's been taken care of. Stay as long as you like. Please come again." Todd walked away to his bar.

Charlotte exhaled and grinned. Despite the rocky start, the day hadn't been so bad after all. A meal shared with an endearing stranger: a well-dressed, proper, bourbon and bacon-loving southern gentleman. Ethan wasn't someone she'd soon forget.

Charlotte rolled over onto her back. It was still dark outside. The incessant noise and light from the street below had kept her awake most of the night. Despite often staying in hotels, New York City had a level of noise that was unrivaled by any other city she knew. The wailing sirens and blaring car horns were something she never had to endure back home in North Carolina. Her closest neighbors in the valley below her house were cows, and she liked it that way. She was wide awake.

She crossed the floor of the SoHo apartment to look for coffee in the kitchen cabinets. Racheal had come in late. They both went to bed about one in the morning. Since a case had Racheal's attention until further notice, Charlotte was on her own. That was fine because there was work to be done, as always. She had real estate scouting to keep her busy between Rose Aerospace calls and filling orders for stationery. Maybe she would go back to The Boxwood this afternoon and try another meal. There were several empty storefronts near there anyway. She had noticed them upon leaving yesterday.

The clock on the wall oven read five seventeen. No wonder she felt rough. After several minutes of searching, no coffee was found nor a pot to brew it in. Charlotte opened the fridge. Meager contents, consisting of half-full water bottles and a few take-out containers. The freezer was devoid of any content. The cabinets didn't yield any food items either. There was a salt-and-pepper shaker set with a grocery store's logo on them sitting near the sink. The set seemed to be the only condiments in the entire apartment. Apparently, Racheal still held the same dietary whims of her college days when Charlotte had met her. Racheal didn't cook. And if Charlotte was a betting woman, the oven served the same purpose it did in the first New York cracker box Racheal and Gabriel had as closet storage.

Charlotte pulled the oven door down. Bingo! Shoes. Good thing she didn't try to cook anything last night. Manolo Blahnik's and Christian Louboutin's would have been on the menu upon preheating. At least this apartment had a kitchen and a small dining table, along with an actual guest bedroom. The rent had jumped from three thousand to over five thousand each month. The last visit was so abbreviated there had been no time for enjoying the new digs, framed with large windows. Great apartments weren't easy to find in Manhattan. At least this one had a lobby, a front desk, and wasn't an eight-story walk-up because the elevator didn't work.

Racheal opened the bedroom door to find Charlotte sitting on the sofa, laptop open, typing away. "Morning! How long have you been up?"

"I got up about twenty after five. How do you handle this traffic noise and all the sirens?"

"Oh! Poor thing. Did you even sleep at all?" Racheal grabbed a bottle of opened water from the fridge.

"Not really." She closed the laptop, setting it aside.

"It's seven. Get dressed, and we can get some coffee. There's a bakery on the next block. I get something there every morning, and Lewis always brings me coffee when he stops to get his."

"And maybe some food to eat while I'm here?"

"Sorry. I always eat out. No one has time to cook here. I meant to grab some things before you arrived, but I've been busy with a hotel merger. I want to get this tied up so we can spend some time together. Thanks for being such a good sport about this."

"I'm perfectly fine. You, on the other hand, need to learn how to use an oven for something other than extra closet space!"

Racheal laughed out loud. "You know I don't cook. I guess the oven works. I've never tried it. Cook if you want to. I'll even give you some money on provisions. There's a Dean & Deluca a few blocks from here. You used to keep me fed in college. I'd have starved in undergrad if my older friend hadn't have looked after me. Can you make us one of your quiches? I used to really enjoy those."

Charlotte leveled her with a look and an exhausted smile. "But first, coffee."

"Yes, coffee."

"Thanks for bringing me back to the apartment yesterday afternoon and bringing me a late snack to munch on while we caught up. It wasn't much of a supper for you."

Lewis glanced sideways at her. They had dropped Racheal off at the office at 601 Lexington Avenue and headed back west to Soho. Whenever Racheal wasn't in the car, Charlotte always rode in the front with him. "You're most welcome. You look like hell, lady. Didn't you sleep?"

She laughed, "Not really. Can you swing by a grocer before we make it back? Racheal doesn't have anything in the apartment whatsoever!"

"Well, you knew that would be the case. I should have taken you somewhere last night when we came back. That's why I knew I'd have to bring you something over. I know just the place."

Lewis stopped a few blocks away from Racheal's apartment. It was a small facade, but once inside, the store kept expanding. Fresh organic produce, kosher meats, fresh-baked challah bread, and cheeses of every kind greeted Charlotte as she browsed. Lewis walked down the aisles with her, talking. Charlotte spent more time with Lewis, usually, than she did with Racheal when she visited. As a result, the two of them had an easy friendship.

"Oh, look at this goat cheese. I know just the thing for this. Grab a bunch of your favorite salad greens and one small shallot, Lewis! We're going to have brunch soon."

"Feed me anytime, doll. And then you're going to take a nap, correct?" His chin dipped slightly, hazel eyes peering over round black frames, waiting on her reply.

"I will. If I don't, I may fall over." She grinned, "Or maybe I'm just dehydrated."

One piled-high buggy later, and out the door they went.

All the purchases were put away and the fridge relieved of the used contents. Two cases of bottled water were now occupying shelves of the refrigerator, along with vegetables, meats, cheeses, fresh butter, condiments, and fruits. The poor thing was probably as full as it had ever been. Lewis carted the trash down to the hall chute and relocated ten pairs of shoes to the master bedroom floor while Charlotte whipped up kitchen magic. She pushed the button on the oven panel to set the temperature to three hundred fifty degrees. It came on.

"Well, what do you know? It does work." Charlotte smirked at Lewis upon his return.

He read the paper to her as she worked, the top of the pages hiding some of his shining bald head. Lewis had never married and enjoyed his single life at fifty-five.

Racheal had received every kitchen item that Williams-Sonoma would allow on a wedding registry ten years ago. Gabriel had remarked once about donating most of it to a thrift store because it was never used. The knives in the block, resting at the back of the granite countertop, still had plastic pieces holding them in place. She had gifted them to Racheal along with a few cookbooks in hopes it would spark some interest. *Apparently not.* Charlotte rooted around in cabinets to find a nine-inch cake pan and used it to hold a quiche made with chopped artichokes, goat cheese, and roasted red bell peppers.

A simple vinaigrette was made while the quiche cooked. Lewis washed the greens and plated them. Brunch was enjoyed at nearly eleven. Charlotte cleaned up the kitchen after Lewis departed. He was needed at the office to drive Racheal and another associate somewhere. She sent him with a plate for Racheal and a note that read: *Quiche, as requested.*

"I think a nap is in order." *Did I really just say that to an empty apartment?*

Charlotte pulled a fresh bottle of water from the fridge. After she had consumed a third of the bottle, a noisemaker app on her phone was turned on. There wouldn't be another night spent here without something to combat the outside noise. Thanks to the app store, that problem had been solved on the car ride back to the apartment earlier. She would know nothing but the softness and warmth of the guest bed until one-thirty that afternoon.

Ethan was about to order another bourbon from Todd when Charlotte entered The Boxwood. If she hadn't been sporting the same soft pink Burberry wool pea coat, he wouldn't have noticed her quiet entrance as easily.

"We meet again." Ethan flashed a wide smile at her from the bar. "I only came over for a drink, but if you're going to sit and eat, I might be compelled to join you."

Charlotte secretly hoped he'd be here. She wasn't exactly sure why. There was that smile again, deadly to her resolve for any resistance. There he stood, at the bar, fixing his eyes on hers. "Hi there. Happy Wednesday! I was looking at some shop space up the block and noticed how hungry I am. I was thinking of asking Todd if I could try the supper sides like you did yesterday, but I see there's sole meunière on the board."

"Todd?" Ethan waited.

"Have a seat, same table as yesterday, if you like. I'll go see if the sole can be ordered now since it's only three-thirty, and that's tonight's special."

Ethan and Charlotte walked a few steps to the same table they had occupied only yesterday. His heart skipped a beat as he gazed at her face once more. He truly was glad to see to her. The meeting with the art gallery curator had been an unmitigated disaster because all he could think about was the woman he'd met prior to the appointment. The curator would be choosing her favorite pieces, not what Ethan's mother's choices would have been. And somehow, he'd accidentally agreed to donate a piece he'd painted himself. It would be sold along with all the other donated works as well as sculpture, pottery, and photographs. Nancy had overheard the mess of a meeting and graciously saved him from his continued blubbering. Ethan neglected to tell her why he was in such a funny state. Little did Nancy know, that state was sitting across from him now.

Charlotte removed her coat, placing the folded article on the bench seat next to her. She was wearing a pink blouse today and a winter white pencil skirt. Her nude heels practically disappeared on her feet. She had long legs that had drawn Ethan's eye before they sat down. He unbuttoned his suit jacket, another perfectly cut handmade suit in a lighter shade of gray today paired with a Hermes silk, Faconnee H tie of nearly the same color.

She licked her lips before speaking. "You like gray, don't you?"

"It's neutral. I do wear it often, I suppose." He smirked, "You like pink, don't you?"

"I do. It's my signature color."

He laughed and exaggerated a southern accent, "Just blush, not bashful?"

"Only blush. I don't think I could get by with bashful too. I'm not as brazen as Shelby." She bit her lip and laughed a little. *Did he just reference Steel Magnolias?*

Todd returned, "The Chef says, 'Of course, he will make it now.' It may take a little longer as they're finishing the prep for tonight."

Ethan barely noticed Todd standing there.

"Sole for you as well? Did you eat lunch?" She waited on his reply.

Did she just asked him a question? He needed to answer. "I had a late breakfast at my desk. I'll eat sole with you, gladly." He didn't want to seem too excited about seeing her again.

"Two dinner specials then, coming up shortly. Would the lady like something to drink?" Todd smiled at her.

"I'll have what he's having." She titled her head to the side and smiled.

The bartender acknowledged her with a head bob. "Another one for you too, sir?"

"Yes, please. Thanks, Todd."

There was a moment of silent stares between the two. Todd felt like a third wheel, walking away quickly.

"I need to say thank you for my lunch and the drink yesterday."

"You're welcome. My pleasure, really." He swallowed the last of the bourbon in his first glass before Todd returned with a fresh drink. "You ordered the sole meunière. No bacon today?"

Another grin across the table from him.

"Not today. Have you had sole here before?"

"No, but I remember the first time I ate sole meunière. I was in France on business. My client had taken me to Normandy for the day. He ordered lunch for us. There was so much butter in the copper pan when the waiter sat it down on the table in front of me. The sole was practically floating. It was still sizzling when he expertly pulled the bones away and left the filets for us to eat. The taste was quite heavenly, so light, flaky, buttery, with a squeeze of lemon. Oh! What a memory, indeed!"

"That sounds delightful. What else do you remember eating there?"

Ethan paused for a moment. "Mussels in white wine sauce for dinner that night. So much garlic and lots of butter. I think I was sweating garlic after we finished. The coq au vin later that week was also memorable."

Todd brought their bourbon and left with Ethan's empty glass.

Charlotte grinned, "How could you not like any of that? Especially the coq au vin, since it has bacon in the recipe."

"That's right!" He picked his glass up to toast her. "Once again, to bacon!"

Still grinning, she lifted hers. "To *crispy* bacon!"

"You know I remember our housekeeper, Mrs. Icey, keeping a jar in the kitchen with rendered bacon fat. She used it to cook with." He had a faraway look in his eyes. "That woman taught me how to cook and to appreciate good food. She practically raised me and my sister, Jane. Thanks to her, we both had a food education. Learning to cook horrified my mother. I can still hear her saying, 'We have servants for that.'"

"Cooking is a great skill to have. My parents kept a bacon grease jar on the counter when we were growing up. Both of my parents cook. They taught me and my younger brother, William. We never had a housekeeper. Mom brought her low-country Charleston-style cooking. Dad had his raised-in-the-mountains style. I appreciate both styles because of it. Is your sister here in New York too?"

"No, Jane returned to Charleston after college in Savannah. To my mother's chagrin, she works too. She has two boys, works for another interior designer, and has a husband I'm ready for her to divorce." He rolled his eyes. "But we won't get into that. Your mother is from Charleston?"

"She is. Her maiden name was Dreyton. It's my middle name. She still has lots of family there and an old home place that isn't really livable anymore. I think my parents will retire there one day and fix up my grandmother's house again. It looks like a bad memory from the seventies, Harvest gold appliances and all."

"I know the Dreyton family name. My family has a strong heritage in Charleston too. My Aunt, Effie Mae Ashley King, had her hands in rice, tea, and a distillery. She was an enterprising woman who tried to use her part of the family assets to bless other people and their business efforts to foster growth in the area. My mother on the other hand…"

"I take it you two don't see eye-to-eye."

"She thinks it's preposterous for me, or my sister, to want to work. Mother's been living off of our family's inheritance and feels it's beneath us to work. She thought her sister Effie was a disgrace for working to invest the money in the community for a return. According to her, we're supposed to be social pillars in the community, attending church at St. Philips and organizing fundraisers for the less fortunate. Mother doesn't approve of my sister's life, nor mine. And she lets us know that every opportunity she gets."

"I beg your pardon, but she sounds like a snob."

"She is, but I love her anyway because she's my mother. I just don't understand her. Neither did my Dad; God rest his soul."

"You know what they say. You can pick your friends. You can't pick your relatives."

Ethan laughed, "That's true." He didn't want to talk about his mother anymore. "You mentioned you were looking at space up the block."

"I was. There are three empty spaces within two blocks from here. One of them is a corner unit. I called the listing agent on the sign. I'm supposed to meet her tomorrow morning. Only the corner unit is actually available. Apparently, the other two units I saw yesterday already have contracts."

"Oh, yeah. The corner unit used to be a dry cleaner. Real estate moves fast here."

"So I'm noticing. I have to start the search for an apartment, too. The same agent is supposed to help me with that as well."

"If she doesn't, let me know. I can help with that. And I'd be happy to look at the lease if it goes that far."

"I'd appreciate that. Thank you."

"Of course." He smiled, "What kind of business are you opening?"

"A stationery boutique."

"Really?" He was intrigued. "It just so happens I might need your talents then. My own business stays in constant need of a great stationer."

"I'd be honored to help then. I don't have a card yet, for up here. This will have to do." Charlotte pulled out a piece of paper from her bag as she didn't want to give him a Rose Aerospace and Defense business card. She was digging for a pen to no avail. "I can't seem to find my favorite pen."

"Allow me." Ethan pulled his own from his breast pocket.

She grinned, "Parker stainless jotter. Great pen." The pen was pulled across the paper. No ink would come forth. She gently shook the pen and tried again. Nothing. Charlotte twisted the two pieces apart. Black gel ink came out on her hands. The inside of the enclosure was full of liquid.

Todd walked up with their plates. "Sole meunière, for the bourbon drinkers." He sat the plates down, noticing the ink covering

Charlotte's hands. "Wow! That's a mess. Let me get you some paper towels. The ladies' room is past the end of the bar."

"I'm so sorry, Charlotte. I feel terrible. You have ink all over your hands." Ethan's face was drawn into a grimace.

"Nonsense. I'm just glad it didn't leak in your pocket. The ink would have ruined your suit." Charlotte used the paper towels Todd fetched to wipe her hands. He threw away the used towels and the leaking gel insert. The pen pieces were covered, inside and out in ink. She picked up the pieces with her smudged hands, observing the gummed-up ink in each piece.

"I have refills at the office for this, but I guess I better just throw it away. One of my favorite everyday pens is now a loss." Ethan wore a forlorn expression.

"I can fix this." Charlotte knew Todd was at the bar, running hot water to bring a towel for her hands. "Todd, will you bring your alcohol pads from your first aid kit in the kitchen, please? If you have a bottle of alcohol, bring that instead."

Todd returned with a bottle. "How's this?"

She eyed the plastic bottle. "Perfect, it's ninety percent. Can I have a highball glass too, please?"

The top, bottom, and spring from the Parker jotter were soaking in alcohol during their meal. Charlotte had also used some of the alcohol, taken to the ladies' room, to remove the ink on her hands. Thirty minutes later, Todd returned from the bar with the pen pieces, now devoid of ink, rinsed of alcohol, and wrapped up to dry in a towel.

"Now you can take the parts back and reassemble your pen with a fresh refill." She smiled brightly at him while unwrapping the pieces, dropping the spring inside them. With a few twists, she handed the clean pen over to Ethan. "Good as new."

"Thank you, my dear lady." A sly smile appeared on Ethan's face. "You didn't think you'd be saving a pen today, did you?"

She laughed, "If we couldn't have found alcohol, we could have used the butter left on our plates."

Laughter was shared between the two.

Nancy couldn't believe her ears when Ethan finally returned to work at the stroke of five. He was whistling.

"I don't know where you've been or what you've been up to, but you need to do it more often. I haven't heard you whistling in years."

"Sole meunière at The Boxwood with a new friend." Ethan grinned at her, strolling right into his office.

"And does this new friend have a name?" She waited, handing him three urgent messages.

"Charlotte." Ethan wore a look of happiness as he picked up the phone to return the first message.

"I see." Nancy smiled, glad to see some light back in his eyes. "I'm going home if there's nothing else. See you tomorrow."

With all the excitement over saving the Parker pen, Charlotte had neglected to write down her number. Ethan was consumed with work until after nine, realizing then he had no way to contact the mystery bacon-loving-stationer-in-pink. After inserting a new refill in the pen, he said a silent prayer that she would return to The Boxwood again on Thursday. He was about to leave when his cell phone rang. He didn't recognize the number and let it go to voicemail.

As Ethan was walking in the door of his apartment, he played the message on speakerphone.

"Mr. Cooper, this is Detective Frederick Togo of the NYPD. We haven't spoken in some time. I wanted to reach out to you. Some new evidence has come to light regarding the events surrounding your wife's death. I'd like to meet with you and discuss this. You can call me back at this number or call the twelfth precinct at…"

Ethan stopped listening when Detective Togo mentioned Stephanie's death. There would be no waiting until tomorrow to call him back. He shook off his suit jacket, crossed to the sofa, sat down, and pulled up the call log. In only two rings, the phone was answered.

"Mr. Cooper."

"Yes, thanks for reaching out, Detective."

"I never know who is listening on these things, so I'll be brief. I need to meet with you. When are you available?"

"For this? Anytime. You tell me."

"I'll be in lower Manhattan all day tomorrow. Chief's meeting in the morning at one PP. You free after lunch? I'll give you a call when I get loose. That work for you?"

Ethan had been waiting for this call for years. "Just let me know. We can meet in my office if you like."

"Somewhere quiet without so many ears. I'll call you tomorrow."

"Okay. Give my regards to my former father-in-law, Commissioner Fairchild. Thanks. Goodnight." He hung up. There wouldn't be much sleeping on his part tonight.

3

Location, Location, Location

Thank you for getting us out the door on time this morning and well-fed. Lewis was the happiest I've seen him in a while." Racheal pulled off her heels beneath the large walnut desk. It was open in the front and back, with just a few cords from the computer dangling toward the floor. She was rolling her feet across a green spiked ball. Heels made her feel pretty, but they could be murder on your feet.

"It was the truffle butter on the eggs. You're welcome." Charlotte was reading the Times and sipping her coffee. When they had stopped on the way in, Charlotte insisted they pick up chai for Barbara as well.

"Explain something to me. How did you know Barbara liked a dirty chai?"

"I noticed her sipping from a cup the other day marked as such." Charlotte kept reading.

"Oh! I feel foolish. I never look at the side of her cup. I just bring her the same coffee she's ordered before when Lewis or I are out on a run."

Charlotte put the paper down. "I strive to take care of the people that work with me the way I would like to be treated. Working with anyone means paying attention to the details and asking the right questions."

"That's true. I've always been the one fetching and trying to play catch-up for someone else. I have to place myself into a different mindset now that I'm a boss too." Racheal bit her lip.

"Partner. You're partnering with everyone here to get the job finished together. Don't be bossy." Charlotte wrinkled her nose up in silent laughter.

"I love you!" Racheal rolled her eyes, laughing quietly with Charlotte. "You've always said you get respect if you give it. You were right. I had to earn it here just like in the DA's office."

"I've watched you with the Associates since I've been in here. They respect you. You've been in their shoes and not so long ago. You know how they feel, Rae."

"I treat them better than most of the other partners. Some of those guys are just mean for no reason. I always feel badly for the paralegals and associates when the other partners mistreat them. I hope Barbara has never felt like I've mistreated her. I've only had her as an assistant for a couple of months."

"She has your back. Make sure you have hers, and you'll be fine." Charlotte sipped more of her coffee.

"Speaking of having your back. You better scoot if you're going to hoof it up the block to that building and meet your Realtor." Racheal looked over to the clock on the interior wall and then to Charlotte. "It's almost eleven."

"Ack! You're right. I don't want to be late. See you later this evening." Charlotte jumped up, pulling her coat and bag from their resting place in the other soft leather tufted armchair.

Charlotte was making her way toward the entry gates at the reception area. At the end of the second long hall, a couple was walking toward her. In her rush to dig through her bag and find her cell phone to call the Realtor, she missed the familiar face. In the noisy atmosphere, the voice saying her name was lost. Alexandria Casey, known to her friends as Alex, motioned to her husband, Charles Grey's nephew, Parker Grey, about ears. Parker didn't realize exactly what Alex was trying to convey.

His equally smooth as his Uncle's London accent came out. "What's wrong with her? Didn't she hear you?"

"I don't believe she did. Alison said she has hearing aids now. Let's see if we can stop her at the elevators."

"She's in quite the rush, love. We better get on." Parker made it out of the entry ahead of his wife just in time to grab hold of Charlotte's shoulder.

She spun around to see Alex fully and squealed just before a hug was shared in silence.

"Trying to act like you don't know me, Charlotte?"

"Never. Alison told me you'd be here before flying to Asheville and then on to Franklin for Thanksgiving."

"We were coming down the opposite hall toward you. I called out, but I guess you didn't hear me."

Charlotte's face drew up in a scowl. "No, I'm sorry. I didn't. I wouldn't have turned down the opportunity to rub elbows with the woman who's bagged half a dozen Tinsel Town Telly awards in the last few years. The hearing aids really help me, but if I'm in a place that echoes or has a certain noise threshold, I cannot discern voices at times like the reception area. Congratulations on the awards to you and Mr. Grey."

"Thank you." Alex squeezed Parker's hand and blushed. "I'm a very lucky woman. Charlotte Rose, may I introduce you to my husband of five years, Parker Grey."

Parker stepped forward to shake Charlotte's hand. "Lovely to meet you, Charlotte."

"And you, sir." Her accent was similar to Alex's on particular words. "I was in the coffee shop before I left and ran into Carey as he was leaving with Josh. He's growing so quickly."

"Alison sends us pictures almost every day. It'll be nice to be in the same town again for a bit. We start filming Cleremont, at the Biltmore Estate, the first week of January."

"I used a recipe in your cookbook this morning for truffle butter on scrambled eggs. It was a huge hit!"

"Thank you." Alex blushed again.

"I miss your food at the tearoom. Everyone does. Lillie seems to be enjoying life more only working part-time at Crabtree's General Store. She's got herself a new fella too."

"Really? Oh, that's wonderful! I know how devastated she was after Nig passed away." Alex's face reflected compassion on Lillie's loss.

"And Jane Elliott, our favorite Garnet Road baker, is enjoying a booming business. You have to stop in and see her while you're in town. Order ahead of time. She stays busy."

"Does she still make those lavender shortbread cookies?" Alex could almost taste them.

"She does, but you have to try her Paradise shortbread. It's now my favorite. I send her gift baskets out to clients. They're always a hit."

"I'll order some Paradise shortbread! Thanks, Charlotte!"

Parker had this goofy grin on his face.

Alex was giving him a questioning look.

"Dear, I'm sure Charlotte has a schedule to keep, and we've given her pause long enough. Although, I must say, I could stand here and keep listening to the two of you talk. Alex has been in L.A. with me long enough that she loses that small bit of a southern accent she once had. I hear it sometimes when she's been on the phone with Ali, her Mum or Dad, or we're working in Asheville on Cleremont. I've missed it."

Alex turned a bit red in her cheeks as she smiled at her husband fondly. "I'll try not to lose it again, then." Her color faded a bit. "I need to get some of your Scottie stationery. I'm nearly out. Our two dogs, Lady and Earl Grey, have become the production mascots of our company. We're here to finalize some contracts and set up a new corporation. We've been in with his Uncle Charles and the other founding partner all morning. I'd like you to make our company letterhead with the Scotties. Alison always gives me boxes of your note cards and half-sheets for Christmas every year when we come back east. They're perfect because we're all about Scottish terriers at our house."

"I'd be honored! Yes! Why don't we have dinner while you're here then and talk about the stationery you'll be needing? Lunch might work too, if you have time. We can celebrate with some bubbly, and perhaps I can talk you into giving me the recipe for the chocolate chip and almond mini-muffins you made at the tearoom."

"I'll have to pass on the bubbly, but I can write down the recipe for you. I made it so often it's permanently ingrained on my memory." Alex proudly put her hand across her abdomen. "We're expecting in May. Lunch sounds wonderful right now."

Parker laughed as they stepped into an elevator. "Always, hungry, this one. Let's go eat. I'm hungry too. She somehow managed to skip morning sickness completely, and I'm the one gaining weight magically. We're at The Surrey. Please give us a call." He handed Charlotte a card with both of their numbers. "Her new number is on the opposite side of the card from mine."

"Thanks. Congratulations to both of you." Charlotte was genuine with the sentiment even when someone she knew announced they were expecting, a pain over her own loss swept over her. The same day she lost Benjamin, she also lost their child.

The elevator descended, spilling them out on the ground floor, thrusting them into the throng of those entering and exiting the skyscraper. Charlotte's phone was ringing.

"I'm late! I'll call you, and we can meet up. Nice to finally meet you in person, Parker."

"You too." He waved as they walked away.

"See you all soon!"

God was kind to Charlotte's feet today, clad in short heels. Teresa Elliman, of Elliman Real Estate Group, was also running late.

The sun was hiding behind a gray cloud bank. Charlotte pulled up the collar on her pink coat, walking amidst the crowd. If there was ever a day to have worn slacks, this was the day, as a cold wind blew against her face and legs. She made it up the block with heels clicking against the worn cement. Charlotte was tempted to look up at the tall buildings surrounding her, but that would mark her as a tourist. The corner building's architecture identified it as being built in the twenties, by her best guess. The limestone and ornate carvings were beautiful, reminiscent of a Richard Morris Hunt design. The poor thing needed cleaning and attention. She tucked in against the vacant building, waiting on the Realtor, as a crowd came up from a subway exit nearby. Teresa was mixed in among them as many passed by Charlotte, staring at their phones and ignoring each other. Trash blew up at her feet from along the street.

"Hello, Charlotte?"

"Hi, Teresa!"

"I apologize for the mishap. I was waiting for a call back on the code to get inside. It's cold out here today. Let's go in." Teresa turned the key to raise the metal grate safeguarding the windows from would-be trespassers. The code for the entry system wasn't working. "I'm so very sorry. This doesn't seem to be working."

Charlotte looked at the system. It was a model she could quickly get around, part of a more extensive alarm system. It wasn't breaking and entering if you were with the listing agent, was it?

Click. The system succumbed to Charlotte's insistence.

"Seems like your code worked just fine, Teresa." Charlotte winked at her.

The south-facing windows were dirty and plastered with large FOR RENT signs. The east-facing windows had perforated vinyl graphics showing hanging clothes, and a special per pound price on laundry covered the glass front door. Between the dirt and intentional graphics, no one could see inside. Charlotte dug through her bag and pulled out a flashlight.

"I'm not sure if there's still power to the building." The Realtor's voice was breaking a bit.

"There's power, or the alarm and entry wouldn't be working. We just have to find the light panel." Charlotte was calm even though something about this place set off her "get out" instinct.

Teresa walked behind Charlotte as she shone her small, but extremely bright, LED beam around the room. The place smelled of solvents and detergents. Despite the smells, the front counters, floors, racks, and shelves were covered in a thick layer of dust. There were footprints in the dust leading to the back room. Charlotte found a panel and flipped on a few switches. The place seemed to suddenly buzz.

Both ladies squinted from the contrast between dimly lit to overwhelmingly bright.

"There we go." Charlotte took in the space around her as Teresa was spouting off figures regarding square footage, facts about the area, and the average rent on the block.

"How long has the place been unoccupied?"

"Fourteen months. I'm surprised nearly fifteen hundred square feet on this floor alone has been empty for this long."

"Are the other floors empty too?"

"Yes, ma'am. The whole building is for sale and unoccupied. There's office space upstairs, but it has its own entrance. I know this front entry seems tiny, but I'm sure it was only what they needed for pick-up and drop-off. There is so much room to grow behind this little area."

Charlotte looked around the small space. "There are several sets of footprints going back there."

When she walked around the thick front wall to a middle area, a rotating rack was suspended from the ceiling. Beneath the rack sat many large metal drums. Beyond them, another extremely rigid wall. Something back here was meant to be well hidden and guarded. There were racks with bottles of chemicals. She saw potassium permanganate, glycerin, sodium bicarbonate, peroxide, and curiously large bags of lime. This largest area at the back had more fifty-five gallon drums, stacked three high in the middle. There had to be at least thirty, maybe more. Several close to where Charlotte was standing were marked as sulfuric acid and smaller bottles of acetone. Some were empty, their lids sitting ready, off to the side on a rack. Even a car battery on a dolly was parked by a wall, complete with jumper cables. There were no commercial washing machines, dryers, clothes presses, hangers, or clothes bags—just a reinforced metal fire door. Yes, something was definitely off about this place. The smells emanating from all the chemicals coupled with the barrels, the car battery, and a hook in the ceiling holding a chain all spelled bad news to Charlotte.

"What is all this stuff?" Teresa looked puzzled, pointing to the rack of chemicals.

"Glycerin is used in detergents. Depending on the form, it can also be unstable and very volatile."

"It can?" Teresa recoiled.

"Don't worry. It's harmless unless it's mishandled and under pressure. You're fine. Potassium permanganate is a water conditioner. You'd need that for city water at a dry-cleaning operation, I suppose. You usually find it at pool supply stores. Baking soda is useful for oil-based stains, deodorizing, whitening. Peroxide can be used to clean biological stains and to whiten as well. It's more green than bleach."

"Oh, okay. How do you know all this stuff?"

Charlotte continued to puzzle over the large bags of lime and now sugar as they explored the depths of the space. "I'm an engineer. I spent a good deal of time in chemistry classes to get my degree. How much did you say the rent would be, again?" She looked up at a small camera in the corner. Someone was watching, and they needed to leave. This shop space was turning into a place of untold horrors. Some of these chemicals were common elements in bomb-making as well.

Teresa pulled up the listing on her phone. "That's odd. It says here the listing has expired. Let me call the owner."

Charlotte nodded affirmatively. "I only need to rent the building. I cannot afford to buy this place, I know."

"Hello. May I speak with Ashem? He's not. Alright. This is Teresa Elliman, of Elliman Real Estate Group. I'm showing his listing to someone now, and we have some questions. His partner? That would be fine." The receptionist put her on hold for a few minutes. "Mr. Darbandi, hello. I'm Teresa Elliman, of Elliman Real Estate Group. We had the listing on your building near Lexington Avenue. Yes, I'm quite sure it's your building. It's been listed with us for over a year now." Her face drew up in displeasure as she listened. "I don't mean to cause you distress, sir, but this is your building. I pulled the paperwork yesterday. The deed says Empire Accounting and Wealth Management. Yes, sir." Another pause. "I'll tell my client then. Thank you for your time."

Teresa drew a deep breath. "He says he didn't know he even owned the building. Then he says it's not for sale or even for rent."

"So I've wasted your time then. I'm sorry, Teresa." Charlotte seemed disappointed.

"No, it's me who should be apologizing. Weird! And rude! Come on. We'll keep looking. There's another place two blocks from here. The building doesn't have the same look about it, but I know they want to rent it at least. Then there's this other space, near Times Square…"

Charlotte shook her head. Oh, well! Teresa was resonating in the enclosed space. Her Staten Island accent was leading them right out the front door. They closed the grate and went on to the next listing nearby.

"So much for this limestone beauty." Charlotte was already lamenting the loss.

Dānā Darbandi left his office. His assistant wasn't at her desk. As he walked past the Empire Accounting and Wealth Management reception desk, genuine fear for his life began to take hold. Nothing was adding up. How could he own a building he knew nothing about? He had accidentally overhead a phone conversation two weeks ago that sent him digging through all the accounts that his partner had brought through the door with him to the firm. What he had heard and seen since rattled him so much that sleep didn't easily come at night. He wasn't eating much, which didn't hurt his rounded figure. He had quietly spoken to a Detective at the NYPD. He took the elevator to the observation deck on the hundred and second floor of the Empire State building. He often retreated to the deck to clear his head or resolve a problem. Lately, he'd been spending so much time here all the security guards waved him through, all the while chatting about their day and family life. They had become familiar. He had believed that Ashem Ahmadi was all he seemed. Ashem had become familiar over the last two years. A partnership agreement had been formed between them. Within another five years, he would buy out Dānā's half, as his son Bassem was living in Eygpt, uninterested in the family business.

Coming to America from Iran in the sixties had afforded him many opportunities to build a legacy. After college, his son had run after a woman whose family lived in Cairo. They were never married. Bassem had remained single and in Eygpt, working in accounting ironically. He wanted to build his own company, not stand in his father's shadow, were the words still fresh in Dānā's mind so many years later. Why couldn't he have been the one to partner with?

The New York City skyline never grew old to Dānā. He enjoyed watching the constant change of tearing down the old and building up the new. He had been here so long Iran was merely a faint childhood memory. He walked around the deck, looking into the distance where the twin towers of the World Trade Center once stood.

Now there was only a single tower. That day evil men with evil hearts forever altered the conscience of the United States and the world. That day planes were hi-jacked along with his religion. For many years he couldn't enter a business without getting stares and whispers. He had even been asked to leave at a restaurant a few days after it happened. Even though wrinkled and weathered, his face resembled the race that altered the world they all lived in. Thankfully, time had passed. Suspicions remained, and rightfully so, but were formed by caution more than prejudice. A new tower now stood as a reminder that hope can rise from the ashes of disaster, bringing a sense of normalcy to the island of Manhattan.

All that had changed with Ashem and Dānā wouldn't stand for it, especially not in his own house. It was time to pay a visit to Ethan Cooper, his long-time friend and counsel.

Racheal wondered what was happening with Charlotte. It had been three hours without a word from her. She picked up her cell phone to send a text when it started ringing. She smiled.

"Perfect timing. I was about to text you. How did it go?"

"Well, that was a bust. Found the perfect location not far from your office, no way I can get the space. Then off to see three more that were totally dumps, totally dirty, and totally wrong. Feel like lunch?"

"I'm kind of eating at my desk already, or I was. Get something and come back here. You can tell me all about it." Racheal glanced up to see Barbara standing in the doorway. "Hang on just a sec."

"Ethan would like to see you, no rush."

"Thanks, Barbara." Racheal laid the fork aside, staring down at her empty plate. "I'm a horrible friend. I've not spent any time with you since you came to town. Forgive me?"

"Of course. I know you're busy. You also know I have my own agenda while I'm here. I have to figure out if I'm going to be able to make this work and stay. You ate another piece of the sweet potato pie I made last night, didn't you?"

"Guilty. Barbara had one too. It's become our new favorite. Pumpkin Pie just lost the pedestal for best Fall pie."

Charlotte grinned, "I'm glad y'all like it that well. I'll wander over to The Boxwood and get something there. It's close. See you in a bit. Bye."

"Bye." No sooner than Racheal had put the phone down, it rang again. She smiled broadly, answering the phone in her most sexy voice. "Hello, honey."

"Hello, my lovely lady."

"You only call on Thursday when you're staying in Boston all weekend. Please tell me you're coming home tomorrow night." Did she really just whine?

"I'm coming home. I wanted to give you a heads-up. Mom and Dad finally caved about Thanksgiving in New York. They're coming for the parade and dinner. We've been asking them to come for years. Isn't this great?"

Racheal was happy about the news, then reality set in. "I truly am glad to know they're coming, finally, but what am I going to tell Charlotte? She's sleeping in the guest bedroom. We'll have to get them a hotel room. Or you'll have to buy me that new sofa I've had my eye on to replace our old one. Then she can sleep on that."

"We cannot get a pullout sofa ordered and delivered in time. You know that."

"What are we going to do then? I cannot tell her to get out just to house your parents. Let me figure this out. I'll call you back tonight. I have to go. Ethan's waiting for me to brief him on a deal. I love you."

"I love you, too. Tell Charlotte hello for me."

"Mwah! Bye!" Racheal put her phone down. "Oh, brother." The pie plate was staring at her from the corner of her desk, sealed up in plastic wrap. There were two pieces left. Perhaps she'd better take one to Ethan and give the other one to Lewis since he was also taken with the pie. She'd already eaten three pieces today. Lewis could eat a piece from the other pie in the fridge at home. Pie plate in hand, she headed to Ethan's office.

Racheal bounded up to Nancy's desk.

Nancy peered up over the glasses resting on her nose. "He's waiting for you. Go on in."

71

"I have a surprise for you, Nancy, a tasty surprise." She waved the pie plate in front of her.

Nancy stood up to properly view what Racheal's face was beaming over. "What do you have there, Ms. Maxwell?"

The words came out slowly. "Sweet potato pie. I know you and Ethan both like pumpkin, but this is like pumpkin pie on steroids. Go get a plate and two forks, and come on in." Racheal stood at the door to Ethan's office armed with the pie. "Knock, knock."

Ethan looked up, "What is that?"

"The best pie I think I've ever tasted. You have to try this. My friend Charlie made it last night. She made two, actually. I've offered the last two pieces of this one to you and Nancy. You know how picky Barbara is, and she ate every bite of her piece." She held the dish over his desk for him to inspect as she pulled off the plastic wrap.

He stood up and eyed the dish presented to him. "Oh, Racheal. Is that pumpkin?"

"No, it's sweet potato." She grinned at him. "Nancy's gone to get something so you can have a piece."

Nancy made it in the office in time to hear her name. "Someone say my name?" She smiled at them as she held out a plate to Ethan, two forks in her other hand. She surrendered both to him. "One of those pieces has my name on it."

Ethan chuckled before accepting the plate. Racheal placed the pie plate on the desk while he made quick work using the two forks to put a slice on the plate. He handed the plate and one fork back to

Nancy. They knew he'd eat the other piece right from the pie plate. Ethan might command two thousand dollars an hour and dress in hand-made suits, but they'd seen him do this before.

Racheal issued a laugh, watching him eat the piece with his left hand while continuing on with their business as though holding a pie plate was part of an ordinary day. The noise he let escape on bite two gave Nancy and Racheal pause to smile at each other, exchanging a sideways glance between them.

"I take it you like the pie then. Let me know if you need me. I'll be crooning over my own piece." Nancy took her prize with her to be eaten at her desk.

Ethan nodded, continuing to chew as he sat down. "Have a seat." Ethan put the pie plate and fork down on his desk, only long enough to flip open a large stack of papers. "The debt burden from the Napa end is enormous. I hadn't fully appreciated all the numbers until last night. Have Barbara call the bank and see if you can negotiate that down to pennies on the dollar-"

Racheal cut him off, "I've already called them myself. You've earmarked dozens of pages in that deal. Didn't you sleep last night?"

"Some, on my sofa." Ethan took another bite of pie. "I knew I'd be in with Charles and his family this morning. I wanted to go over this with you today. Nice work, by the way. Carter gets prime real estate for more world-class resorts, and Cassidy will save face for future business deals. I like the way you've presented the facts for the bankruptcy. Cassidy's not been very forthcoming on that. You did some number digging in that pile from the accountant. You're amazing with the numbers."

She blushed, "Thanks, Ethan. It's my forte. If I hadn't become an attorney, I'd probably have been an accountant."

"They're both useful vocations." He grinned at her. "How do you think we can get Cassidy to budge on the-" His cell phone began to ring. It was the Detective. He picked it up, said hello, then listened.

Racheal noticed the number. She recognized it from working in the District Attorney's office. Someone from the Police Commissioner's office at One Police Plaza was calling him.

"Yes, I will. Thank you." He hung up.

"Everything alright?"

"It will be." He inhaled sharply. "Detective Togo with the NYPD called me last night. I'm meeting him, and apparently my former father-in-law in fifteen minutes at The Boxwood. They're currently en route, according to the Commissioner's assistant. Togo has some new information about Stephanie's case."

"That's why you didn't sleep last night."

His face drew up as he finished the last bits of the pie. "You got it."

"I'll get back to this deal. Mr. Carter is in town as of this morning. Nancy informed me he wants to come by and speak with us while we're finishing this up. Let me know how the meeting goes with the Detective and Commissioner Fairchild."

"I will. You lost her too." He pushed the pie plate across the desk toward her, now empty.

Racheal picked it up and left in silence, leaving Ethan alone with his thoughts.

He waited a few minutes before grabbing his coat and heading downstairs. The ride down in the elevator made him bristle. They were playing Christmas music again.

The sky was a darker gray than earlier when he had arrived at work. He hadn't really paid attention to the weather, other than being glad he grabbed a scarf. The wind was whistling in his ears as he walked to The Boxwood. The dark Suburbans of the Police Commissioner's detail rolled around the block past Ethan, both finding parking on a side street. The Commissioner had the luxury of parking anywhere he wanted regardless. Ethan watched two of his security officers and Detective Togo egress from the vehicles. One officer in front, one behind, two remained with the cars.

Ethan walked in just behind them. "Hello. I have conference rooms at my office. We could have met there, Tom."

The Commissioner smiled, "I thought we'd meet here for old times sake. Stephanie always liked to come here when we'd all have lunch because it was near your office. She was proud of you. We all were, still are." He reached forward to shake Ethan's hand. "I'd say it was nice to see you, but I wish it were around more pleasant circumstances."

They all agreed.

Ethan caught the attention of Todd behind the bar. "Do you mind if we sit for a bit?"

"No, Mr. Cooper. Sit anywhere you'd like."

"Anyone want a drink or menu?" Ethan waited, "No? Todd, can I have my usual and a vegetable plate to go?" He redirected his attention to the group. "Gentlemen, let's sit over against the far wall. It's between shifts, and the place is usually devoid of crowds this time of day. We'll have until about four before people start trickling in." Ethan waived them to the large table he and Charlotte had been sitting at for the past few days. He suddenly wondered where she was today.

Detective Togo started speaking in a hushed fashion as soon as they sat down. He was across from Ethan, his back to the bar. "TARU overheard some chatter while working on a case with the gang unit out in the Bronx two days ago. El Carnicero is back from Mexico."

Ethan cringed, "You're sure?" He was distracted by the news and by the familiar pair of legs that belonged to the silhouette who entered the bar, Charlotte. She smiled at him, pausing to read his face and body language. He shook his head slightly, negatively, so she wouldn't approach. She remained at the bar. He kept looking at her over the Detective's right shoulder. Tom, who was seated beside Ethan, leaned into his right ear.

"Do we need to ask her to leave? You obviously know her."

Ethan shook his head negatively. "She's alright. Go on, Detective."

Charlotte was left to wonder about the almost clandestine feel of Ethan's meeting. No one could approach them. There were two men standing nearby, guarding their table. Instead, she'd focus on why she was really here. "Hi, Todd. Can I place a to-go order?"

"Sure thing. What you'll have?"

"Fried green tomato BLT and sweet potato fries, balsamic dip on the side, please."

"You got it." He entered her meal on a terminal beside them. "You're not joining them?"

"No, not today. It looks like they're having a meeting. Do you want to send Ethan a good bourbon on me today? I don't think I'll send one to the cop or the Commissioner sitting with him. They can buy their own."

"What? Who?"

"Oh, come on, Todd. I don't live here yet, and even I know that's the Police Commissioner for the City of New York. You have a rather important person in your restaurant this afternoon. He's all over the newspaper and the news." She pointed to the television behind him. "Case in point."

The anchors were talking about an officer-involved shooting and the response from One Police Plaza, or what they saw as a lack of response.

Todd looked up at the television and then over to the huddled group. "Yeah, you're right."

Charlotte smiled, "I'm going to step away from all of this to the other end of the bar. I have to make a phone call." She checked in with her dad, in Franklin, to see if a contract had come through from Washington.

Commissioner Fairchild pulled out a file from his briefcase. Pictures were carefully shown to Ethan before they were slipped back inside. "These were taken yesterday with his known associates in Club Thirteen. He's hiding in Harlem. Every time someone spots him and gets a photo, they lose him. He's here for a job or jobs. Dānā Darbandi is most likely at the top of El Carnicero's list. I know you affectionately call him the Persian Mafia because he handles so many accounts in this city. His firm has had you on retainer since you started with Charles. You're still his attorney of record, Ethan."

"I'm a lot of people's corporate attorney of record, Tom."

"Reach out to him. See if he will talk to you. We don't have enough for a warrant yet. If you want answers about Stephanie, like we all do, ask him. This could lead us to exactly what we're looking for." Tom's face drew into a frown. "We all want justice for Stephanie, her witness, and the two detectives we lost that day."

"What Dānā tells me is an attorney-client privilege and is protected. I want the rat too, but I'm not going to risk being disbarred to get him. Let me start the conversation and see what's offered. From what you've told me, he already suspects too much. I just need to ask.

"I get the feeling you don't ask a question you don't already know the answer to."

"I try not to. It's the first rule they teach you in law school."

"You know everything we do, so you won't be asking unaware. He trusts you. Reach out. Let me know. I'll keep the Commissioner apprised."

"We enjoyed seeing you at Easter this year at the church. We've asked you every year since Stephanie passed to have Thanksgiving with us. Please, come."

Ethan watched Charlotte depart. She left with a to-go bag. He still didn't have her number, and he'd missed the chance to get it again. "I appreciate the offer, Tom. I already have plans. Give my regards to Gayle." He stood up to leave. "Good day, gentlemen." He had left without his vegetables and bourbon too.

Catching Charlotte before she got away again was the plan. As he hit the street, he turned in every direction only to find her gone indeed. He exhaled deeply, seeing his breath form a cloud in front of him. The temperature was dropping in accordance with his mood. He pulled out his phone to call Dānā. Voicemail. He felt entirely off-kilter now.

The walk back to the office was a short one. Even in the coldness, he was starting to sweat. What was this? Fear? Every phone to Dānā yielded the same results, either his direct line at the office or his cell phone, voicemail. Where was he? Ethan waited for the elevator ride to be over. His breathing was faster than it should be as his heart was pounding in his ears. He didn't like being bombarded by

Christmas tunes while his mind relived the meeting with Detective Togo and Commissioner Fairchild. El Carnicero, the Butcher, had disappeared back to Mexico shortly after Stephanie and the others were killed. He hadn't returned until now. This was bringing back too many emotions.

He stepped off the elevator without speaking to anyone who was also getting off at his floor. Ethan pulled out his wallet to waive over the entry gate beside the reception desk. Momentum to get him to the safety of his corner office was increasing, taking him down the hallway, to the next, nearly colliding with Nancy as she passed through a door.

"You're back. Mr. Darbandi is waiting in your office." Nancy looked irritated. "I told him you were in a meeting. He wouldn't schedule a time to come back. He insisted he wait in your office and for me to tell no one he was here."

Ethan exhaled, letting the sudden panic that had gripped him pass. He inhaled and smiled at her, "It's alright, Nancy. I know why he's here. I'll take care of it. Hold my calls and funnel anyone that comes to see me over to Racheal. Oh, and see if you can get the Christmas music nixed. They're playing it again."

"Yes, sir. I'll see what I can do." Nancy could tell by the pallor of Ethan's face something was amiss. Even his posture was off.

"Dānā! You've not been answering your phone. Are you alright?"

The president of Empire Accounting and Wealth Management was sitting in front of Ethan's desk. His smile was missing along with the light from his eyes. The pair of bushy salt and pepper eyebrows were flat with no expression over his round glasses. Ethan knew that look; he had felt the same way coming up in the elevator. Dānā was scared.

"No, I'm far from being alright. I've been out of my office for several hours now. I'm not even sure I want to return to my office at all. I don't know who or what is waiting on me there. Ethan, my partner, Ashem, is involved in terrible things. I don't know where to start, who I can trust, or what to do." His accent, barely detectable after all these years of living as an American, was now more distinct as his emotions escalated. "I've spoken to Detective Togo. I told him very little. Mostly I asked questions about what would happen to me, to my firm. They are my family, all of them. Now Ashem Ahmadi has disgraced us all."

"Let me pour us a drink, and you can tell me everything from the beginning."

Dānā only nodded affirmatively. His hands were shaking so badly he could barely hold the glass of bourbon Ethan passed him. After several swallows, Dānā found liquid courage and began speaking louder with assurance. "Ashem left the office shortly after he arrived this morning. He told me he had business and would return tomorrow. When I started digging through his server yesterday, I couldn't stop. Discrepancies between what his accounts were billed for and what actually gets deposited took me some time to find. I stayed up all night. He's stealing money from them and putting it somewhere else. All those new bank accounts are in my name! The rat had his own clients when he came in. I never met these people. His billables were phenomenal. That's all I could see!" He stood, glass in hand, drinking more. "I never questioned it until I saw what I thought was a shady deal going down in the parking garage yesterday morning. I was still in my car. The windows are dark. They couldn't see me. Then I recognized the car from the white vinyl club sticker on the back window and who was in it, Club Thirteen. You don't mess with that gang. He's been laundering their money into thirty-two fraudulent dry-cleaning businesses all over the five boroughs. I received a notice from the IRS that they were being audited in the mail this morning. I drove by the buildings listed in their file that I found on my server, his server, and nothing is there. Some are vacant lots, but most of them are dilapidated eyesores. The corner shop, up the street from here, actually had a sign, and the windows are covered in advertisements. It looks like someone's actually been there. And I find out just a few hours ago that I own that building. I don't know what to do. You have to help me. I haven't gone back inside the building. I came here."

"Sit down. How much of this does Detective Togo know?"

"Hardly anything. He told me he could protect me. I don't believe him. I remember what happened to your lovely wife. She was protecting a witness with the police over this same gang. They will kill me like they killed the last accountant who came forward."

"We have to get everything copied from that server, just in case Ashem decides to wipe it or destroy it."

"I already thought of that." Dānā pulled a small drive from his coat and laid it on Ethan's desk. "It's all there. I couldn't copy the drive on his laptop. It was open and still on when he left. He has a password on it. I knew I had to be quick before the machine went to sleep, and it was locked again."

Ethan felt his jaw drop as he regarded the drive mere inches from his fingers, tightening around his glass of bourbon. "You're telling me it's all there?"

"All of it. Even his emails. They are in Farsi. They will not be of much use to anyone who does not know the language. The few I read let me know where the money is going. It's not good, Ethan, not good at all. And I must go back to the office like nothing is wrong."

"I agree. I appreciate you trusting me with all of this. Keep your head down and be safe. You need to call Detective Togo. He needs to know exactly what we're up against."

"I will. I am supposed to take a few days off over Thanksgiving along with all the firm. I'll stay in touch with you and the Detective."

"Don't worry about implication, Dānā. Racheal and I built a morality clause into the partnership agreement between you and Ashem. He's toast. You'll be fine. We will figure this out."

"I know. That's why I came to you. Have Racheal start with the shell corporations for the cleaners. The money trail begins there."

"I will. You still have that pistol in your desk at work?"

"Yes, with plenty of ammo. I need to go back to the office. I've been gone far too long. I'll wait to hear from you."

Ethan came around the desk with his own now empty bourbon glass to take Dānā's. "We'll talk soon."

Dānā surrendered the glass, then turned to leave. Ethan stood there with two empty glasses for a moment. He sat the glasses down on his desk and set his eyes on the silver hard drive. He needed to duplicate that drive as soon as possible. His left hand went to his forehead, dragging slowly down to rest over his mouth and chin. The drive looked innocuous enough. What it held meant life or death most likely. He turned to find Nancy.

She was sitting at her usual post, noting his color hadn't improved. His brow was deeply furrowed.

"Nancy, do we have any extra portable drives from past cases we're not using?"

"Yes, Ms. Maxwell has some extras in her office."

"Thanks." Ethan walked past the long conference room in-between them. He pulled his hand up to knock, but the door was open to Racheal's office. Someone else was sitting behind her computer too.

"You're here!" Ethan was hit with pure joy, welcomed after the last hour of horrific revelations. He came into the office toward her, stopping to stand beside one of Racheal's comfortable leather chairs.

Charlotte looked up over the monitor to see none other than Ethan Cooper coming into Racheal's office, wearing a shocked look on his face. "You're here."

"I own the place." He sat down in the chair on the left, to Charlotte's right as one would look across the desk.

"Oh good! You've met!" Racheal returned to find them chuckling.

Ethan raised his left eyebrow. "Yes, we've met. This is your sweet potato pie connection? That was very refreshing and welcomed in this season where pumpkin is the star."

Charlotte's cheeks colored a bit. "You're welcome. I prefer sweet potato over pumpkin. I didn't think Racheal would mind if I made that in lieu of pumpkin. How did you -"

"Oh, I let him have a piece. Did you get it fixed?" Racheal was utterly oblivious to the locked stare between Ethan and Charlotte. Her words finally broke the spell.

"I'm waiting on the driver to finish installing. That should take care of the problem. You need to clean up your drive, Rae. It's a mess." Charlotte pushed the chair back to get up. Racheal switched places with her.

"Thank you. If I called someone from tech, it still wouldn't be fixed come tomorrow. Charlie is your bourbon connection too."

"You're the one that picked out the bourbon she gave me for Christmas last year!"

"Guilty. She asked me to pick it up when I was in Kentucky on business."

"I should have known. Racheal doesn't drink bourbon, but you do."

Racheal stopped moving her mouse. "It's fixed! You're awesome, Charlie. Wait! You know she drinks bourbon?"

Ethan paused, licking the corner of his mouth. "Long story, Rae." He emphasized what Charlotte had called her for effect. "She fixes pens too and apparently computers."

"Sure she can. She's a genius." Racheal said it so emphatically because she genuinely believed it.

Charlotte shook her head from side to side in slight embarrassment. "If you don't have anything further for me to fix or supper demands, then I'm going back to your apartment. I do have some work to catch up on."

"Perhaps I can impose upon you both. I need one of those drives you keep for documents during cases for backup. Charlotte, can you plug up that drive to wipe it for me and copy another drive's contents to it for redundancy?"

"Sure. Happy to help." Charlotte's brilliant smile lit up her face.

Racheal went to one of her bookcases. There was a wooden box located on the top shelf which held wiped drives. She rifled through and found a cord to fit before handing both the drive and cable to Charlotte.

"Do you know anyone that speaks Farsi?" He was asking Racheal.

Racheal's brow furrowed, "You're kidding, right?" She pointed to Charlotte. "She's your woman."

Ethan scooted forward in the chair. "I wasn't expecting that. Farsi, really?"

Charlotte giggled. *Did she just let that out?* "And Arabic, Hebrew, Lebanese, a little Pashtu, just to name a few. My specialty is most middle eastern dialects. If you want romance languages, I'm not your woman. French puzzles me, so does Italian."

"That's refreshing. I'll stick to speaking English."

"Before I forget, I need to speak with both of you anyway. Gabriel's parents are coming to town for Thanksgiving. We've been asking them for years. The one year I have you here, Charlie, and they decide they're coming. Do you think Mr. Carter would be gracious enough to help her find a great place to stay until they leave? He does own three hotels here, and we're working on five more."

"I've only been here a few days, and I'm already being evicted? Geez, Louise! Did you not like my cooking after all?" Charlotte laughed, all in good nature. "I'll find a place. Don't worry about it."

Ethan's brain was already going. "No, the parade is next week, and people are going to be filling up the rooms. All of Carter's good suites will be taken. I have a better idea. Since I know I'll be monopolizing Charlotte's time with Farsi translation if she agrees, why doesn't she stay at the corporate suite? That will alleviate the problem and help everyone."

Racheal choked on some cold tea she had just sipped. "Wow! The corporate suite. Can I come too?"

Charlotte was standing at the end of Racheal's desk, looking back and forth between the two of them. She was puzzled by Racheal's comment. "Where's the corporate suite?"

"Not far from here, corner of sixty-sixth and Park Avenue. The views of Central Park are incredible, plus it comes with a great balcony."

Ethan wasn't going to divulge that it was the apartment next to his own home if Racheal didn't mention anything. "Shut the door, please, Charlotte. There's more to this."

She crossed the office, shutting the door, and returned to sit beside Ethan.

"We have a lot of work to do in a short amount of time. Charlotte, I know we've only just met, really, but I know Racheal. If Racheal trusts you to be in here on her computer and staying at her home, then I can trust you too. The pieces are fitting together about the friend she's mentioned for years named Charlie." He shifted his gaze between the two of them, focusing on Charlotte's face. "I have so much to tell you both. It's going to take us all working together. Are you agreeable to staying in the suite while the firm hires you to translate emails in Farsi?"

"Yes, of course."

Racheal chimed in, "And taking care of all new stationery for me and a dozen others here?"

Charlotte reached across the desk and squeezed Racheal's left hand. "I'll take care of it."

"Great. What I'm about to divulge to you doesn't leave this office. Understood?"

They both nodded in agreement. He was about to repeat Dānā's plight to a long-time friend who was also his business associate and a woman he barely knew, drawing them both into what was most certainly racketeering and mortal peril. The Butcher was back, and

Ethan would be guarding everyone he knew the only way he knew how to keep them informed and close.

4

Hi Neighbor

Lewis picked Charlotte up at the office and drove her across town to get her things. They had lingered several hours while Charlotte put three of Racheal's favorite meals into the freezer, soup for tonight along with a roasted chicken, and directions for how to re-heat everything left on the counter. If Gabriel was coming home, she wanted them both to have good food to enjoy. It was her way of saying thank you for letting her stay there. They were all going to have a meal together on Sunday.

Charlotte wrapped a towel around the remaining soup in the Le Creuset pot. It would travel with her to the corporate suite for dinner. There was plenty left to eat on for tonight and another day at least. One of the two roasted chickens would be traveling with her as well in a lidded pot. She would return the pots later. The other third of a french baguette was rolled into some foil and laid on top of the soup pot.

Lewis smirked, "Have dinner, will travel. Thanks for feeding me too. The car's all packed and ready to go when you are. Come on! Your new adventure here awaits."

She smiled at him with tired eyes and softly answered, "Thank you."

The doorman held the door open at sixty-sixth and Park, greeting her as she walked toward the building carrying one of the pots. Lewis was right behind her with both suitcases. The darkness didn't allow her to see the facade of the building very well. It looked to be limestone.

"Good evening, ma'am."

"Good evening, Mr. ?"

"Rodale, ma'am. May I help you with that?"

"I have it, thank you." She smiled at him. "I'm Charlotte Rose. This is Lewis. I have plenty. Are you hungry?"

"It smells delightful. Mrs. Nancy phoned earlier today. We've been expecting you. I trust she has already given you the entry codes for the building and apartment, but I'm here if you need anything else or have issues with the doors, Ms. Rose."

"Please call me Charlotte."

Her name passed through her lips, drawn out with a slight southern accent. He was intrigued. "Ms. Charlotte, I'm Adam. Pleased to meet you both." He turned toward the elevator bank. "I see you have a towel wrapped around the pot because it's hot. Are you sure

I cannot assist you in taking that upstairs? It would be my pleasure and will help you to easily get the door open because you'll have the use of both hands. I'm sure Lewis has more to attend to out front."

"Yes, Adam, please." She handed him the pot, looking around the lobby. It was covered in white marble, just like the entry of Grey Cooper. Ornate molding at the ceiling and floor covered the edges of the white marble walls. There was a tray ceiling with many recessed lights and a large chandelier hanging over a round table, topped with a grand fresh flower arrangement. There were two more arrangements on the front desk counter across from the elevator.

"Very good. One moment please, while I tell Donald, the other gentleman at the desk, where I'm going." He was gone for a split second. Donald waved to them. "We will be traveling to the top floor. Lewis, if you'll roll those in after I get her inside, I'll return to help you."

"See, doll, they're so much nicer here than in SoHo. I'll be up in a bit with the rest. You're obviously in good hands." The suitcases were placed in the equally ornate elevator car. He winked at her before returning outside.

"Donald will be at the desk all night until six tomorrow morning. I'll be here until eleven this evening." The elevator rose quickly to the top floor. "And here we are."

Her things had been put away into the tall, antique walnut dresser in the bedroom. Shoes were stowed underneath the hanging garments in the ample walk-in closet, part of the bath ensuite. She'd enjoy the rain head later, beckoning her from behind a glass enclosure for a well-deserved shower. There was no comparison between Racheal's apartment and this one. Each room was considerably larger here, with high ceilings, all painted the same pleasing creme color. Molding at the ceiling matched the details around door frames. Light bathed everything in the room, but a dimmer could tone it all down. Anything you could dream of needing, or wanting, was thought of in this space.

Charlotte had waited as long as possible before letting her inner child slip out. She leapt into the center of the king-size bed, adorned with a quilt, down-filled duvet, and more pillows than she thought were possible on a bed. Satisfaction reigned as she turned over on the bed to fully appreciate the room. There were shades of green, deep blues, and rich red in a Renoir print framed in thick gold molding. She had seen it before in Chicago at an art museum, Two Sisters on The Terrace. The decorator had pulled the colors used in the apartment directly out of this painting. The same soft pink flowers seen in the painting were in vases throughout the space. English cabbage roses were mixed with ranunculus, eucalyptus, and herbs that perfumed the air in each room.

She returned to the kitchen, just outside the bedroom door. The apartment was airy, not overly feminine or masculine, simply comforting and hospitable to anyone. This was classic architecture along with the decor. The kitchen was part of the living room in the open floor plan, along with a dining room table next to a bank of windows and two doors. The opposite wall from the kitchen had a double door, painted the same color as the walls, with inset carving and panels. Where did this set of doors lead? They were locked. She continued to sit and stare at the doors while eating the soup. Her imagination was getting the better of her, but her curiosity would not be dampened.

There was a knock. She rose and glanced at the clock on the wall next to the entry door, seven o'clock. Where had the day gone?

"Hi, neighbor." Ethan stood there, tie slightly askew, still in his wool overcoat and carrying a briefcase. "What's that smell?"

"Hi! It's pureed roasted vegetable soup or maybe the roasted chicken. I don't think the baguette has much odor." She grinned at him. He was the last person she expected to greet her this evening. "Are you hungry? Come on in."

"I'm starving. I'd try the nineteen ninety Burgundy from the rack with that."

"I didn't notice a wine rack."

She walked into the kitchen to look around. He followed after closing the door.

"That particular bottle is in my apartment, down the hall. I'm sorry. That sounded REALLY corny."

She snorted, "Ah. Hence the neighbor reference. I don't mind corny. I'm looking for corny."

"Good. When I'm tired, I tend to get very corny." He pulled out a skinny cabinet next to the built-in refrigerator. "This is New York

City. You have to be creative with storage in any apartment." It was loaded with wine bottles.

"I like that."

He pushed the creme-colored cabinet back in. "I'll be right back. I want some of all that, please." His circling finger referenced the soup pot, chicken, and baguette laying out on the island.

Ethan disappeared for only a few minutes. He returned with the aforementioned bottle of Burgundy, uncorked it, and used a gizmo in a drawer. She recognized it was a type of aerator. He deftly stuck it into the bottle to let the wine breathe a bit before pouring them two glasses. He moved around the kitchen with ease, knowing where everything was.

Charlotte was sitting at the table already. She had fixed Ethan a place next to her, his food hot and waiting thanks to the microwave. The bread was crusty and room temperature.

"You want some music on?" Ethan sat the wine glasses down, along with the bottle, onto the table. He crossed the room to the cabinets on the far wall, to the right of the locked double doors. He pulled a remote from a drawer, aiming it at a glass-front cabinet underneath the large television mounted on the wall. Music came on above Charlotte's head. He turned it down quickly as a jazz trumpet could now be heard over the rest of the instruments.

"There are speakers in the ceiling and walls. You can listen in here. There aren't any in the bedroom. Just don't turn it up too loudly, or Mrs. Holiday from downstairs will give you an earful."

He sat down finally, looking at her for a moment. He was grinning. "Hi."

She chuckled, "Hi." She paused for a moment as he continued to stare at her. "Do you want to ask grace over this so we can eat?"

"Oh, sure." He reached for her hand, then bowed his head. "Father, we're grateful for this food, which I'm sure will be amazing. We're grateful for this time of fellowship. Bless this food to the nourishment of our bodies and our bodies to your service. Bless the hands that prepared this food as well, in Jesus' name. Amen."

She gently pulled her left hand away from his right, placing a linen napkin into her lap. She was glad there were place settings on the table already.

"I know you like pink, so I had Nancy get the florist to use pink flowers in here for you."

"That's very thoughtful, Ethan. Thank you."

"Thank you for coming across town to stay here and help with this deranged assignment. I must have sounded like a mad man spilling all that today."

He finally ate a spoonful of the soup and a bite of the roasted chicken. The soup was velvety, flavorful, and possessed a hint of heat. The chicken wasn't tough at all. It fell apart under the touch of his fork. There was a familiar herb.

"This is wonderful. What is that little something at the end of the soup?"

"Green chiles. If you don't add them, it's too bland."

"I like it. What did you do to this chicken to make it so juicy?"

"Brined it. Kosher salt, sage, lemon, and a few other goodies."

"I knew I tasted sage." He took another bite.

She chewed her bite of chicken as he sipped his wine. The two sat in comfortable silence for several minutes, enjoying their meal. When she reached for her wine glass, she paused.

"I'm sorry to hear the man who killed Stephanie is back in town. That had to be a shock to hear. Now I know why you were completely ashen sitting there with them at The Boxwood. You didn't look much better when I saw you later at the office. That was a lot to process in such a short time."

"Certainly was. I used to think that people were good. After everything that's happened, I don't know what to believe anymore."

Charlotte swallowed some of her wine. The pinot was fabulous with their meal. "Nice choice, by the way." She put the glass down and didn't pick up her spoon right away for more soup. "I know it's hard to believe people when they say they know how you feel, but I can understand how you feel, truly. My life changed two years ago in a traumatic way as well when I lost Benjamin."

"That's what you told me."

"I know this isn't something you normally share over dinner with a new friend." She smiled at him warmly, "But hearing how that man hit the car, shot them all, then to add insult to injury slit their throats and cut out their tongues is heinous and barbaric. I know why they call him The Butcher."

"El Carnicero."

She drew a deep breath before shutting her eyes. When she finally opened them, she picked up her wine glass and hastily sipped until the glass was empty. She had to have enough wine in her to share this with him. "Benjamin…"

Ethan took the glass from her and refilled it. "You don't have to-"

"Yes, I do. After what you told me today, I do." She swallowed and cradled the glass once more, now full again. "His dad was sick. It was Hanukkah. Rivka, his mother, had called and told us to come and see him before it was too late. Benjamin was an only child, so off we went to Tel Aviv. We had been at the hospital all night with them. Just as the sun was coming up, his dad passed. We left to go to a nearby market and have breakfast with his mom. Benjamin sat us down at a table, and he got in line. I got up to tell him to get me some tea. I was pregnant and didn't want coffee. The next thing I knew, I came to, and I couldn't move. I couldn't breathe. I couldn't hear anything but this high-pitched hum, then nothing." Charlotte took another sip from her glass. She was staring into her soup bowl, almost empty now. She sat the glass down and picked up a piece of bread, tearing off a bit to sop up some soup in the bowl. The bite was chewed slowly. "The smell was something I never want to experience again. That smell of building dust and chemicals, mixed with burnt flesh."

The trumpet had changed to Miles Davis, *I Fall In Love Too Easily*.

Ethan had listened intently to her and the music. "I know that smell too. I was on Wall Street when the North Tower went down. I'll never forget that smell."

"Me either." She drew a shuddered breath. Charlotte wasn't crying, but she was close to it. "There was nothing left of the bomber and only a piece of Benjamin's foot. He was standing a few feet behind the man who detonated himself. Everyone in that cafe died except me. I lost the baby a few hours later in a hospital. I was so badly injured they had to take my spleen and my uterus too. No babies for me, ever again. So you see, I understand how you feel about losing Stephanie. If I can help you with the case and tie all this together to take the gang down and El Carnicero, I will. They're just another form of terrorism. I couldn't go after the men who changed my life. I had to leave that to the intelligence community and do my part to support them."

Ethan picked the bottle up and sat it down in front of Charlotte's plate. "You need this more than I do. I'm so sorry."

She picked up the bottle and poured more into the glass before refilling his. The bottle was nearly empty. "We all have our issues. That's why I try to be kind to people. You don't know what they're going through."

He leaned over and took the glass from her hand, sitting it down on the table. She quickly surrendered to the hug they both shared. Tears welled up in Ethan's eyes as he held her. He let her go after a few minutes, both comforted by the simple act of a hug.

"Let's clear this. We plowed through it quickly enough. All I had this afternoon was your pie and lots of bourbon."

She smiled through her own welled up tears. "You really must have been hungry then."

"I was. It doesn't hurt that the food was wonderful. I know why Racheal was loathed to lose you as a guest. Her loss is my gain tonight. Thank you for sharing all that with me, about you and Benjamin."

"You needed to know why I come with my own prejudices against anyone who propagates tyranny." Charlotte noticed Ethan didn't have a tie on anymore. "You won't have to be concerned over dipping your tie into dishwater tonight."

He smirked, "No, I decided I could forgo the tie for dinner since you're not in heels anymore."

She opened the dishwasher. "Did you know that Racheal keeps heels in her oven? I had to take them out before I could cook in her kitchen."

"That's Racheal. She doesn't cook, and space is more important when you're a Louboutin Queen."

They had cleaned up the dishes, discussing what they could eat tomorrow night.

"I'm buying dinner tomorrow night. I know you don't speak French, but allow me to introduce you to Daniel."

"Daniel who?" She waited.

"Daniel is the name of the Chef and his namesake restaurant."

"I know French enough to get myself into trouble when it comes to cooking. You may have to help with the menu. I don't have to eat a frog, do I?"

The way her nose curled up was adorable to him. He could fall in love too easily with her. "No, you don't have to eat a frog. The menu is in English mostly. I do think you'll like the mussels they serve there. They have a whole seafood section on their menu you'd appreciate. It's all served with lots of butter. I'll pick us out a great wine too."

"You had me at butter," she teased, batting her eyes at him playfully. She could be silly in front of him.

His playful mood suddenly faded as *Frosty The Snowman*, by Harry Connick, Junior, filled the room. Ethan's mouth drew up as though he were chewing a pickle.

"What? Not a Frosty fan?"

"I like Harry just fine. I don't want to hear Christmas music before Thanksgiving. No!"

He hurriedly walked to the table, seizing the remote in his left hand. The music was unceremoniously turned off, and the remote tossed onto the table as though it too had offended him.

"Thanks for dinner," he barked.

He stormed out the entry door without another word.

5

Weekend In Sight

Ethan woke up on his left side, his arm in an awkward position. He'd had a bottle of water before going to bed so that the red wine didn't give him a headache. As he rolled over, the feeling in his arm began to return with the familiar prickliness of circulation. The heaviness in his arm was subsiding, but the heaviness in his conscience was still present.

His leave of Charlotte was in poor taste. He needed to apologize. The wine hadn't helped his behavior. The closeness of the meal, what she had shared, the vulnerability presented, and a thoughtful hug between friends had all been shoved aside by out-of-season music. *Why did he behave in such a manner?*

What triggered his disdain for Christmas music in general?

He lay there on his back pondering, and the feeling he might have caused Charlotte to question helping him at all now. It was a very Jekyll and Hyde moment. Christmas music was associated with Stephanie. She'd listen to it whether it was Christmas or not. She was killed during the holiday season. He had no closure over her senseless death either. That was all stirred up again yesterday. Frosty never stood a chance after the day he had.

He exhaled into the open room, threw the cover back, and rose for the day. He put on a pair of glasses he kept by the bed and headed for the bathroom in his grey boxers. As he leaned over the sink, contact solution in hand, the decision to get dressed and apologize for his actions before they headed to the office was made. His car would be there to get them at seven-thirty. He had forty-five minutes to shower, dress and visit with her.

After speeding through his morning routine, he gathered his coat, a scarf, gloves, and briefcase. He reached for the doorknob to walk out into the hall at ten minutes after seven.

Charlotte heard a knock on the entry door. According to Nancy's instructions yesterday, she was to be ready by fifteen after seven. Their car would pick them up by seven-thirty. Ethan would have the driver stop on the way to pick up anything she wanted for breakfast and have them to 601 Lexington Avenue before eight. He was five minutes early.

She opened the door smiling and stood there. "Good morning."

"Good morning. I trust you slept well." Ethan's face gave nothing away. He'd perfected a poker face after all these years. Oh, who was he kidding? His heart fluttered every time he was around this woman. *Apologize, you numb skull!* "I hope you'll forgive me for my outburst last evening. I drank too much wine after a tiring day and behaved badly." His eyes dropped along with his head slightly.

She pushed the door open and allowed him entry. "I said a prayer for you last night for closure and healing. Frosty was only a trigger. I don't hold that against you, Ethan. A person is more than the last conversation you had with them. There are too many mitigating factors from yesterday to count. Don't worry. Apology accepted." She placed her pink wool coat on the back of the sofa and stepped into her heels, waiting by the kitchen island. "Oh, lipstick. I almost forgot."

She pulled out a tube from her laptop bag, lying open on the kitchen island, applying the nude shade without looking in a mirror. Ethan watched her every move as he stood there by the island. The application was quite seductive and made him feel like a voyeur. He noticed the tube was Chanel. "You possess a sartorial elegance about you."

Charlotte grinned and returned the lipstick to her bag. "Thank you, Mr. Cooper, as do you." She stood up fully in her heels. "You're staring. Do I look okay?"

"Lovely. I like the pink blouse. The buttons are pearls, correct?"

"Yes, they are. Benjamin gave me this just before I lost him." Her right hand came up, smoothing the front of the blouse, coming to rest on her right hip. "Would you ask your driver to stop on the way in, please?"

"Certainly. Where would you like to go?"

"I'd like eggs and a pastry for breakfast. I've already texted Racheal. She went in early and didn't have Lewis stop for coffee.

Some sort of trouble printing the latest revision of the deal you're finishing up for today."

"We'll drive past half a dozen Starbucks on the way in. I think we can manage that. I can get Nancy a hot chocolate. She's quite fond of them. I have an app. Let's just place the order now and stop on the way down Lexington."

"I heard LaDuree, up the street on Madison, has the best hot chocolate and macarons around."

"Oh, did you?" He smiled at her. "Another day then." Ethan held her coat out for her and waited as she slipped into the warm garment. Out the door and down the hall, they were still adding to the order as the elevator came to rest on the bottom floor. Marcus was parked out front. "What should we get for Barbara?"

Charlotte answered quickly as she stepped through an open door, greeting another doorman. "Good morning! Venti, dirty chai, and Racheal wants a-"

"Venti, quad-shot caramel macchiato." A smirk rested on his face. "I've known her a long time too. She and Stephanie used to..." He stopped before finishing.

She reached for his free hand and squeezed it before letting go.

"Morning, Marcus."

"Morning, Mr. Cooper."

"Marcus, this is Ms. Charlotte Rose. She'll be staying here at the suite for a while. Take her anywhere she wants to go. She has your number." They slid into the black leather-covered backseat of a black Mercedes Benz, S Class. It was warm inside, a contrast to the cold morning. Ethan waited on Marcus to get in himself. "We'll be stopping at the Starbucks on Lexington, one block from the building. Anything we can get you?"

"Sure. I'd like a grande mocha. Thanks, Mr. Cooper."

"Absolutely." Ethan finished up the order and put the phone away in his coat.

Charlotte stared out the window up at the building as they pulled away. The building was as beautiful as she had expected; another limestone masterpiece, complete with ornate carvings and copper trim. Her gaze turned away from the mystery of New York architecture, back to Ethan beside her.

"What were you going to say about Racheal and Stephanie before we got into the car?"

Ethan swallowed, "They used to have me bring them coffee if I wasn't busy. They were so swamped at the DA's office usually, leaving for too long to get coffee wasn't a luxury they enjoyed. I had more time on my hands. I made a coffee run to spend time with them at least three times a week, always about ten-thirty. Marcus was driving me even then. He's been with me for years. Stephanie knew Racheal needed a change. We discussed it. Stephanie knew how talented she was with numbers. That was wasted in the DA's office, but she had to get started out of law school. The DA's office is where most of the city's attorney's begin their careers. I hired her with Charles' blessing. We usually only hire out of Yale, Stanford, Harvard, Northwestern, Columbia, NYU, or Penn, and since Racheal was from Vanderbilt, it took some convincing."

"Vanderbilt is the Harvard of the south. That's where I met her."

"I have to translate everything I've heard her say about Charlie in my head now that I know that's you. Stephanie and I spent a lot of time with Racheal. Gabriel wasn't around for periods at a time. We watched out for her. Racheal was Stephanie's best friend. I've bought a lot of coffee for Racheal over the years. She's a terrific attorney. No other partner commands the associates pool so well. Even the other partners look to her. They really respond to her. It doesn't hurt that she's pretty and smart, just like her other best friend."

Charlotte blushed to match her pink shirt and coat but said nothing for a moment. "Thank you, and thank you for sharing that with me about Stephanie."

"Thanks for letting me."

"I'll buzz us through reception. Hang on." Ethan handed a bag to Charlotte for a moment while he fumbled his way through the entry gate with her. There wasn't anyone sitting there yet to help them. "Here. I'll take that again."

"We're loaded for bear. Thank you for breakfast and my coffee." Charlotte had two large Starbucks bags to match Ethan's two.

"You're welcome. I have to keep you happy while you're working on projects and this case for us." He winked at her as they walked down the hall.

The firm was just starting to come to life for the day, with people trickling in. Racheal had come in very early. Lewis was asleep in one of her chairs, snoring lightly. Ethan waived through the glass to her, motioning to come out. He walked into the conference room, between their two offices, with Charlotte, placing their bags on the long walnut table.

"Good morning! We have goodies for everyone." Ethan started unpacking bags.

"Good morning." Racheal looked like she was still half asleep. "Please tell me there's a very large caramel macchiato in there for me." She waited patiently.

Charlotte pulled out the first tray from a bag. "Here, Rae, this one's yours." She pulled it out of the drink tray and gently gave it to the eager owner.

Racheal pulled out the green plastic cap stopper and licked the foam off. "Oh, thank you." She threw the cap stopper into the trash can near the door.

"Go sit this grande, black, Pike Place in front of Lewis. Maybe he'll absorb it by osmosis." Charlotte laughed and handed the cup to Racheal. "How early did you come in?"

"I've been here since six. I couldn't sleep. I thought I'd get this wrapped up and printed before you two came in; no such luck. The document hub in the associate's area won't print. I'll have to send it to the Partner Suite on the other side of the building. I had to wait until you came in because I don't have keys to that side yet."

Ethan pulled his coffee out of another tray. "We will remedy that today. It won't print?"

"No. Everything was fine for me after you fixed the driver yesterday." Racheal motioned to Charlotte. "I went home last night and left the associates to finish up the underwriting. I guess it quit sometime before nine. Zach, one of the first-year associates, texted me around then. I told him we'd worry about it in the morning and to send an email to tech before he went home."

Ethan's brow raised. "I'll make a phone call when someone gets into the office downstairs in Tech Support around nine. Everybody on this side of the building uses that document hub. The senior partners aren't going to appreciate having the associates waltz through their neck of the woods all day, flirting with their paralegals."

Charlotte pulled out a bag with egg bites in it, sitting down to eat them. "Tell me about this copier I installed the driver for yesterday. I walked back to get the model number before I pulled the new driver offline. Why such a big machine?" She took a long sip from her black coffee.

"Let me sit this cup in front of Lewis in case he wakes up. Be right back. I want to try one of those." Racheal returned quickly. "We call it the beast." She tasted the bite given to her from one of Charlotte's egg bites. "That's good." She picked up a bag, checking the contents, a chocolate croissant. "It's a fast machine. I printed a thousand-page brief in no time."

Ethan tore a piece off his chocolate croissant and followed it with a sip from his black coffee. "I had it replaced two months ago with a larger unit. We were cranking out too many pages for the other one. This one will go through ten to twelve thousand pages easily on a light day. That's what they told me."

"That's a lot of paper." Charlotte kept eating.

"Twenty-two associates use that machine, plus the assistants down this side, paralegals, me, and Ethan. There's another machine just like it on the other side of the building in the partner suite. They don't use as much paper, but their paralegals and assistants put it through its paces. There's another document hub in the library downstairs, a smaller one in tech support, and another large one on the file floor and storage area."

"Three floors. Big firm." Charlotte was almost finished with her small egg bites.

"Not really, just efficient as possible." Racheal swallowed the last of her pastry. "Did I eat yours?"

Charlotte smiled, "No, I knew you'd eat one. Ethan bought extras."

"I know your eating habits too, Racheal." He smiled.

Nancy noticed the three of them sitting in the conference room. "Good morning. What are you three plotting today?"

They all returned her greeting.

Ethan stood up, "How to take over the world, Nancy. Any pointers?" He grinned and handed her a cup. "It's hot chocolate, your favorite. And there's a slice of banana nut bread in here for you if you want it."

"You spoil me. Of course, I want it!" Nancy took a sip from her hot chocolate. "Just the perfect temperature for drinking. Thank you."

"You're most welcome. Have to take care of the lady who takes care of me."

"I've been taking care of things for you for the last eighteen years. It's what I do."

"I know, and I appreciate that." Ethan picked up his cup. "Ladies, shall we go check on the beast?"

"Oh, no. What's wrong with it today? I couldn't print yesterday afternoon before I went home." Nancy walked out toward her desk nearby.

They all followed her out.

"We're going to walk down and take a look." Ethan followed Charlotte and Racheal to the document hub in the associate's area. It was early, and the place was quiet.

"This end still feels more like home to me than my office. I've spent so much time in this area of the firm." Racheal looked around the associates pool.

"You earned your office and the title of partner." Ethan looked at the front LED panel along with Charlotte and Racheal. "Just says paper jam. That's easy to fix, right?"

Charlotte opened one end. "This is the side where the rollers pull the paper up. According to the screen, there's a jam on this side, one in the middle, and one on the sorting end." She cleared a piece caught near the fuser and closed the door. One area of the screen went back to normal. The rollers that pulled the paper along looked to be in pristine shape.

Ethan lifted the center section and pulled out a sheet. Racheal removed a piece caught in the sorter.

Charlotte felt the paper in between her fingers. "This is heavy. It's card stock."

Ethan put the crumpled jammed pages into a secure recycling bin nearby. "We use card stock for covers on certain document packages to give to clients."

Charlotte knew having this much cardstock piled up was wrong. "But it's not what you normally feed through all the time, correct?"

Ethan looked at Racheal. "No. It's usually just plain paper."

"Depending on what the documents are for, sometimes we use a higher grade than just regular copy paper." Racheal pointed to a shelf nearby with paper boxes. They were also stacked up on the floor.

Charlotte looked at the end of the boxes quickly. Twenty-four pound took up the most room on the floor in ten ream boxes, and there were reams of thirty-two pound, along with card stock, legal reams, and eleven by seventeen. She came back over to the document hub and pulled out the first tray, legal size. The second was empty, but according to the guides in the drawer, it was standard letter, thirty-two-pound premium, turned horizontally. The third was ledger, and the fourth was full of card stock. Next to the unit was a large capacity drawer that looked like it would hold an entire case of paper and then some. She lifted the lid.

"Someone was half asleep when they loaded the paper then. The large capacity tray, where the bulk of your normal paper should be, is full of card stock. The rollers in here aren't up to pulling all that through. It's set for regular weight paper. Do you have someone new here that maybe doesn't know how to use this yet?"

"We have three new associates. Zach's the newest. I think he's who loaded the paper in here."

"Let's pull this card stock out and see if that helps the matter. Ethan grabbed a ten-ream case of regular paper on the floor. We can switch this out."

With teamwork, the card stock was removed and placed back on the paper rack. The regular copy paper was once again loaded and ready to go. Charlotte cycled the power, but there was a new error code now on the screen. She grimaced.

"Rae, go grab my laptop bag, please." She crouched down on her knees, pulling the sorting door open. "Can you pull the cord out of the wall please, Ethan?"

"Sure." Ethan also took off his suit jacket and put it down on the hard, cold floor to protect her knees a little. "It's better than just the floor under your knees."

Racheal returned with her bag. Charlotte dug into a zippered pocket and produced a Swiss Army Knife with every gadget available on the tool. Her bright LED flashlight came out too. She inspected the sorter where the folding occurred. After several moments, she pulled out the equivalent of a hairball made of paper using tweezers from the knife. "Do you have any canned air?"

Ethan chimed in, watching her in total amazement. "Nancy keeps some in her desk. I'll be right back."

She used the canned air to blow built-up paper dust out of the sorter, the bypass tray, and the exit from the top tray above the sorter, which was utilized the most. She handed Ethan his jacket from the floor. "Thanks for the loan. Plug it back up."

Another error cleared, and another message took its place.

Charlotte smiled, "This one is easy. I need to replace the waste toner box."

"I know where they keep the supplies in the tech support area, downstairs. I don't know what I'm looking for, though." Ethan waited.

"I'll go with you. We'll figure it out." Charlotte waited to be taken along.

Racheal was still trying to stuff all the open card stock, laying in the wrong slots for now, back onto the burdened correct shelves. "Take him for sure. My keys will get me in, but if they still keep the toners and stuff where they used to, I'm too short to reach them, and so are you, even in heels."

There was no pretty marble in the tech support area on the lower floor. It was fluorescent lights, racks of servers behind air-conditioned glass walls, telephony boxes, monitors, and a group of desks in the middle of a large open room. Work and testing tables, with soldering irons and Fluke meters, stood at the ready nearby in case of a down machine. Cables were neatly tucked under grated-top chases in the floor. Charlotte was careful to step over them in her heels. There was an area of shelves at the back of the room.

"This place is a ghost town." She could hear the hum of the server room.

"Oh yeah, always, until about nine or so. Most of the tech support staff has another life outside of here. They game, have tournaments; it's a totally different mentality than upstairs. Brilliant still, but different. I admire their knowledge but don't understand what they do totally. I just try to pay them well, so they'll stick around."

On the last shelf, in the very back, Charlotte spotted her quarry. True to Racheal's word, even in heels, she was too short, and she was five-ten with them on her long feet. Ethan's six-one height and even longer reach would be helpful here.

He seemed to sense her dilemma. "Is that it? I'll get it down. Which box is it?"

Ethan stood so close behind her all the hairs on her body were now at attention. His energy crashed into hers, sending a tidal wave reaction down to her toes. Her breath hitched for a moment. She regained the power of speech and reached up as well to just touch the end of the box. Their hands met for a moment.

He held his breath as he slowly slid the box forward, careful not to pull it down on her head. Her scent was heavy in his nostrils; she was so close to him. The box had to be moved quickly so he could step away from her body. He pulled the box down a little too zealously and lurched forward to keep another box from falling on them. He had pushed himself into her, trapping her next to him. She was so warm and soft, even through his suit. He grabbed the correct box and stepped backward.

"Excuse me." He could feel his face coloring.

The electricity faded as he moved away from her. She turned around. "No problem. At least we have our solution in hand, well, your hand."

Ethan held the box up in front of himself like a shield to maintain a sufficient distance from her. He tried not to focus on her lips, squinting his eyes as he turned back toward their entry path. If he didn't keep walking, he was going to turn around and kiss her, right here, right now. *Keep walking!*

Charlotte lifted her hand and ran it through her loose, wavy blonde locks. *Oh, Mylanta! Keep it together, sister. He smells so good.*

Racheal was waiting for them when they returned. Zach was standing beside the document hub wearing a guilty expression on his face.

"He knows now which paper to load in what tray." Racheal grinned, "Don't worry, Zach. Nobody died, except the copier, but I think Charlotte's about to remedy that as well."

"I'm sorry. It won't happen again." Zach's shoulders crumpled as he disappeared to his cubicle. Eager to get away from Ethan Cooper. He was the boss, and Zach had halted progress in the firm.

Ethan handed Charlotte the box. They hadn't said a word to each other since getting into the elevator and coming back upstairs. She used the knife again to slit the tape open on the cardboard and remove a black bag along with a new waste toner box. Another panel was opened, the old waste toner box removed, then slid inside the black plastic bag provided in the new part box. As the old went inside, a gray cloud of excess toner erupted from the bag, covering Charlotte's hands and sleeves.

"Oh no! Yuck!" Racheal stepped away so she wouldn't have the cloud settle on her too.

Ethan took the bag from Charlotte, putting it into the cardboard box, and closing the flaps around it. "I'll deal with this." He walked away with the box.

Charlotte could only press on and finish what she had started. Ethan returned with some damp towels for her hands. She had replaced the part and was about to close the door. Racheal put her tools away so they wouldn't be covered in the waste toner as well. As the lid closed, the machine hummed to life with no errors on the panel.

"You did it!" Racheal smiled, "I'll take your bag back to my office. You need to go clean up. I'd give you my extra shirt, but your arms are too long for the sleeves."

"I'll live. Go print your documents for the Carter closing. I want to make sure it's fixed before I leave to change my clothes. Make sure you open the print queue and clear it first." Charlotte wandered to a ladies' room to wash up. She returned to Ethan still standing there, watching.

Racheal was calling Ethan's cell phone. "Yes, send it." He waited.

The machine started printing, collating sets for the deal.

"Success!" Charlotte waded up the paper towels in her hand, tossing them into a trash can nearby.

"It's working, Racheal. Okay, bye." Ethan stared down at Charlotte's gray sleeves. "I called Marcus while you were washing up. He's waiting downstairs to take you back to change clothes and soak that shirt. I don't want my mess that you so easily remedied to cost you a shirt Benjamin gave you. I'll text you the code for opening my door. Racheal can give me your number. You don't have a laundry area, but I do. It's off the kitchen. For what it's worth, thank you, Ms. Fix-it."

She chuckled, "I'll be back soon."

Ethan walked back down the hall, papers in hand for Racheal. "Here's the first copy. That's a lot of pages. When the rest comes out, bring me one. We can run through it together."

Racheal nodded, "I will. Thanks."

Ethan handed her his cell phone. "Will you put her number in, please? I need to text her the code for my door."

Racheal took the phone, her thumbs flying as she entered Charlotte's contact information, including her email address.

He waited patiently, watching. "She made it look so easy to fix that. I feel bad that she left covered in toner, but I admire anyone who's not afraid to get their hands dirty. Where did she learn those skills?"

"Charlie is a Master of Electrical Engineering with a minor in chemistry. She runs one of the largest civilian repair operations for the military in the world, taking care of legacy aircraft. Part of her job is training covert operatives with entry systems, attack radar, and the latest high-tech defense gizmos that her company designs and repairs. A misbehaving copier is a breeze. Look her up, Rose Aerospace and Defense, Franklin, North Carolina. Engineering is her job. Paper is her passion."

Ethan was speechless. He walked back into his office and began digging, starting with the company website. There was a picture on her public profile standing next to a military jet, with glasses on, looking at the circuit board that had been pulled out of the aircraft. He scrolled to more photos of her teaching small groups dressed in military fatigues, obviously near the front lines. Then pictures of her with high-ranking military officials, a view of the Navy Yard, in Washington, D.C., behind them according to the caption. One of the paragraphs referenced guest lecturing at MIT. Then there was the token business portrait, dressed to impress, just like she had been each time he'd seen her here. Being a corporate law specialist, he knew how to find the goods on big business. After still more digging, financials, and contract research, boy did he find them! *This is a multi-billion dollar company, and she's here to open a stationery store?*

Charlotte touched the numbers on the keypad then heard the deadbolt move. Double doors greeted her near the entry inside. Her suite was a part of his that had been cordoned off through construction. The hardwood floors were the same as on her side of the wall too. Now the destination was known to her. She took a few more steps in, holding her dirty blouse in hand. She had changed into another before entering his dwelling.

The decor was also similar, classic, tasteful, same neutral wall color, but the kitchen was much grander. Charlotte had a small area to reheat items with the tiniest refrigerator and range she'd ever seen. Ethan's kitchen was for someone who cooked. Professional stainless steel fume hood, Wolf eight burner range with a griddle insert in the middle over an oven on each side of the four burners, oversized sink, Cove dishwasher, and the largest built-in Sub Zero refrigerator combination she'd ever seen. There was a full-sized thirty-six-inch stainless steel door, she was guessing, on either side of a wine cooler, the same height as the two other doors. Each door was six feet tall. She walked forward and peered inside the glass door of the wine cooler. It was dark until she opened the door.

The racks were deep enough to hold two bottles. With all the shelves loaded down, there had to be at least a hundred bottles, if not more. She closed that door and opened the door to the right. Refrigerator side. That would mean on the other side of the wine cooler was the freezer. She closed it up after investigating that side, reminding herself she was there for the laundry, not snooping in Ethan's kitchen.

More steps past the refrigeration bank, and there was a small room behind the kitchen that held a pantry. She walked through shelves of dry goods, utensils, plates, pots and pans, bakeware, and more. At the end was the laundry, delineated by a pocket door, already open. There sat stacked, front-loading charcoal gray units. She smiled, more gray. There was a small sink, a bottle of Woolite, stain removers, detergents, a drop-down ironing board from the wall, a laundry basket on the floor, and a collapsible drying rack. She went to work soaking the shirt and using Woolite. The toner was released immediately. After washing and rinsing the garment, she pulled the drying rack from the wall and left it to drip dry over the sink.

She phoned Marcus, who stated he'd be back in thirty minutes. She still had some time. Charlotte returned to the open area of the kitchen and living room. You could see Central Park if you were working behind the quartz-topped counter of the large kitchen island or sitting on the leather sectional sofa. The light was everywhere from the bank of windows. It was cold outside, or she might be tempted to step onto the ample balcony. The view of the park was spectacular, either way.

Charlotte began thinking of the gray in the laundry room and wondering if Ethan had more than just gray suits hanging in his closet. It would be improper to invade the privacy of his bedroom and closet. Her mind would just have to wonder indeed. The buttery soft, deep leather sectional would be her resting spot while she waited on Marcus. Her eyes made their way around the room over art, several full bookshelves containing familiar cookbook spines and classic literature, coming to rest finally on a bar area. The slab top was equally as thick as the kitchen island, probably the same coloring by the looks of the visible edge, with three shelves full of amber bottles above it. Ethan had a considerable bourbon collection.

The tufted gray ottoman in front of her had a slight depression on one end. Beside that depression, obviously left where Ethan put his feet up, sat a journal and a leather-bound Holman Christian

Standard Bible. The black cover was worn from considerable use. Beside this was another Parker Jotter pen.

Charlotte smiled as she pondered him sitting here, deep in Bible study or sitting quietly while the Holy Spirit had His way. Smart men knew where to find wisdom, and it did not lie with men but in every word from God. Ethan was a smart man, one she could envision herself sharing time with.

Did I just think of another man that way?

Benjamin's face came into her mind. She could see him smiling. Even though two years had passed, the mere thought of Ethan felt like a betrayal. Her hands rose to her neck, finding the snowflake charm and holding it between her thumb and forefinger. She closed her eyes as her breath hitched.

"I miss you."

There was no one in the room with her, but Benjamin's voice came clearly to her. "I miss you too. Ethan's a good man. It's time to let me go and be happy again."

Her eyes sprang open, darting around the room. That was Benjamin's voice. She jumped up from the sofa and left the apartment. Waiting down in the lobby seemed like a better place to be.

Nancy was waiting for her as she came off the elevator, handing her an official badge. "You're back! Did the blouse survive?"

Charlotte chuckled, "Of course. It's taking a moment to drip-dry over Ethan's laundry sink. What's this badge for?"

"That will get you through the reception gate, into the offices, library, tech area, and open the conference room between Mr. Cooper's office and Ms. Maxwell's. She had me add her office, and he wanted you to have access to his as well. Offices are locked manually. The conference room is locked after business hours only. If you need to access any other areas, just ask me."

"Thank you, Nancy."

"You're welcome. Use whatever area to work in that you feel comfortable. Ms. Maxwell and Mr. Cooper are in conference with a client. Let me know if you need anything before they're free. I will say the sofa in Mr. Cooper's office is more comfortable than Ms. Maxwell's chairs, my opinion."

"I'll take that under advisement." She smiled at Nancy as they came upon the secretarial pool area.

"Mr. Cooper has taken the liberty to move your things into his office." She winked at Charlotte. "Let me know soon if you'd like me to order lunch, Ms. Rose."

"Yes, ma'am."

"It's Nancy."

"Yes, Mrs. Nancy. Please call me Charlotte."

"I'll take that under advisement." Nancy grinned, then disappeared down the hall toward the partner suites on the other side of the building.

Charlotte stepped into Ethan's office, walking forward to admire the view. Her work could wait for a moment. She pulled out her laptop finally and sat on the sofa to work. Nancy had given her the network password. Stationery designs were created, emails answered, and the portable drive plugged in after being retrieved from a safe. She was working from a copy. Ethan had instructed Nancy to give her the copy when needed. By one-thirty, a break was in order. The view from the windows was calling once more. She was lost in thought regarding hearing Benjamin's voice when another garnered her attention carrying a somewhat softened Boston accent.

"That view never gets old, eh?"

She turned around. "No, it doesn't."

"I'm Jared Carter." He moved forward to shake her hand.

"Charlotte Rose." *Firm handshake. Nice.*

"I thought I'd find my old Harvard buddy Ethan in here, but I'm pleasantly surprised to find you instead."

"I'll get Nancy if you need Ethan."

"It's alright. I know where he's hiding. I'm waiting for him to tell me it's a done deal. I gawked at a car on the street long enough to buy him some time with finishing the paperwork." The man sat a wrapped gift down on the vintage French glass-topped brass bar cart near her.

"The Packard?"

"Yeah, the Packard. You saw'er it?"

Charlotte thought she heard a slight Boston accent on his words. His use of the chopped-up word "saw'er" cinched it. "On my way in earlier. Someone's using it as a chauffeured car. I've seen it around for the last few days. It's a beautifully restored piece of history. Most modern cars don't possess the lines that cars from the thirties and forties carried. They're moving art." She guessed the gift was a bottle of bourbon from the size and where it was placed.

"That's a great way to say it. I like the way you think. My grandfather had one, a nineteen thirty-seven Packard, in Regatta Blue. He called her Lovely. He raised me. I have fond memories of that car. I'm hoping one day I can find it, buy it back."

Charlotte sized Carter up. He was about five-nine, brown hair, hazel eyes, clean-shaven, wearing dark wash jeans, a green cashmere sweater with a white t-shirt underneath, tweed sports coat, and Italian loafers. *Casual, clean-cut, doesn't take himself too seriously, bit of a flirt.*

"I have a friend where I'm from who chases classic cars for other people. You should give her a call. I know she could find the car for you. It won't be an overnight find, but you could start the process." Charlotte crossed to Ethan's desk, pulled a piece of paper from a notepad, and scribbled down the information. "Her name is Lauren Coleman."

Jared put the note into his jacket pocket. "I will. I appreciate this, thank you." He sat down on Ethan's leather sofa, grinning broadly at her. "So, are you new here cause I don't recall ever seeing you before?"

"I'm a consultant."

His eyebrows raised as he tilted his head toward her. "I see. What exactly are you consulting him on?"

"The united brotherhood of none of your business, Carter." Ethan came barreling into the room to stand behind his desk, dropping papers on top. "It's done. Racheal worked her numbers magic. He's signing the last copies now. You're the proud owner of more prime Manhattan real estate for pennies on the dollar and now Napa Valley as well. Congratulations!"

Carter stood up to shake Ethan's outstretched hand over the desk. "Thank you. I came by to drop off a gift I picked up while I was in Lexington last week, checking on one of my hotels. Enjoy Kentucky's finest, on me." He stepped toward Charlotte. "I'd like to hear more about this friend of yours, Ms. Rose. Have you had lunch yet, or can I have the honor?"

Charlotte turned as pink as her cashmere cardigan. "You are direct, aren't you?"

"We're going to The Boxwood if you want to join *us*, Carter." Ethan came around the desk to stand in between Charlotte and Carter, silently giving him a look that said everything.

The body language and the stare weren't lost on Carter either. "How about dinner some time, Racheal too, on me? It's the least I can do to say thank you for taking care of me all these years. We haven't been out to see a game in a while either. You won't let me leave the Knicks tickets for you."

"Perhaps another time, Mr. Carter." Charlotte moved to stand beside Ethan, closer than she intended.

Ethan felt the back of her hand brush his.

Carter patted his jacket pocket. "Yes, another time. Thanks again for the number, Ms. Rose."

The closeness said everything to him. Ethan and Charlotte were an item, whether they knew it or not. He was happy that his friend was finally moving on.

"Give you a call later on the final numbers?"

Ethan nodded affirmatively. "You bet. You're still coming to the gala, right?"

"I never miss it. See you later." Carter smiled at them. "Nice to meet you, Ms. Rose. Keep this guy on his toes. He's a good man."

Charlotte turned her head to look at Ethan. "Yes, he is."

Several moments passed as they stood there, Ethan's face reflecting in her eyes.

"That was very presumptuous of me, speaking for you. Shall we head over to The Boxwood and get some lunch?"

She smiled, "Of course. Todd won't know what to think with us showing up before three. Lunch at lunchtime. What a novel thought!

6

Downtime

What started as an early day had passed smoothly and incredibly quickly. Racheal approached the open door of Ethan's office. "Knock, knock."

Two heads looked up at her.

"You heading out?" Ethan checked his watch, six-thirty.

"Gabriel just called. He's waiting on me. I'm going to take off. See you both on Sunday for brunch?"

Charlotte slipped her heels back on and stood up. "You bet. I'm looking forward to it. Tell him hello for me."

"I will. Goodnight." Racheal turned down the hall to leave.

Ethan looked up across his desk at her. "Are you ready to go as well?"

She grinned, "Yes."

His own smile grew. "Me too. Let's get out of here."

Their table for dinner wouldn't be ready until seven forty-five.

Daniel, the restaurant, was near Ethan's apartment. The lighting in the bar fit the mood of understated elegance with contrasting dark hues in wood and high, white arches behind the liquor selections. The view into the dining room revealed a soaring coffered ceiling with neoclassical architecture, reflecting a bright white sea of contrasting refuge from the pace of city life.

Ethan drank from the large wine glass. "What a day! If I didn't get away from those emails you've been translating, my brain was going to turn into mush. All that talk about cousin so-and-so and being honorable with their resistance was getting to me. Dānā was right. Who is this guy? I feel bad because the investigation we ran when he brought the guy on for a partnership didn't turn all this up. He's a radical extremist alright, but in this for profit according to your translations."

"If this hadn't all come about, you wouldn't be pursuing justice for Stephanie either. Convergence might have happened unexpectedly, but it has happened."

He stared into his wine glass. "True." He reached for the open bottle of Burgundy sitting between them on the bar, refilling their glasses as they waited for their table.

"I took the liberty of calling a trusted friend in the Navy intelligence community to see what she could turn up for me on a deeper dive than what you could have possibly uncovered. I should hear back from her on Monday." Charlotte's face scrunched up. The noise of the crowd around them was wreaking havoc on her hearing aids. She pulled her long, blonde locks aside to expose her right ear, then her left. Ethan looked on in astonishment as she adjusted the level on the devices hidden by her hair.

"Is everything okay?" He was concerned.

"It's just deafening in here, and it makes it difficult to hear you over all this magnified noise in my ears. Plus, this crowd makes me nervous. I still have trouble with dreams at night. Being out in crowds or sudden loud noises gets to me in lots of ways."

"PTSD?" He could only imagine her dreams.

"Yes."

His heart wrenched in his chest. The thought of enduring such a tragedy as hers made him feel incredibly blessed, even though he had suffered his own horrendous loss.

"Are the hearing aids because of the blast?"

She nodded affirmatively. "I have a love-hate relationship with them. I recharge them at night. When I forget, I feel their loss. They are Bluetooth, but it's usually easier to adjust them with my finger than drag out my phone and play with the levels. When I answer my phone or walk near certain electronics, the screech I hear makes me want to throw them across the room. That blast altered my life in many ways."

The Maitre D' approached them. "Your table is ready."

As they moved to the more quiet dining area, overhead noise brought a new focus, Christmas music. The open bottle and glasses came with them.

"Your waiter will be with you shortly." He sat the menus on the table. "Enjoy your evening, Mr. Cooper."

Charlotte waited for Ethan to comment on the music. As they looked over the menu, he only scowled.

"Do they not realize it's almost a week until Thanksgiving?"

And there it was.

"Why does Christmas music offend you so?" She put the menu down and looked at him.

"It's a reminder of Stephanie. She listened to it all year long. It made her happy. She didn't care if it was the middle of July. She'd watch Hallmark Christmas movies too. It's the holidays in general. Christmas was a sore spot in my family too. Mother would have the house decorated, so it looked good for the tour of homes, but she didn't want any decorations Jane or I had made to be seen in the house. Jane had this little tree we kept in her room. We'd put the ornaments we made with Mrs. Icey on that one because no one saw our rooms. Once upon a time, I promise you, I really did like Christmas. I don't mean to be such a Scrooge about it. I think the music causes me to mourn what could have been with Stephanie and my family. Wow, years of therapy don't usually bring this much clarity!"

The waiter appeared, discussing tonight's Chef selections along with suggestions before leaving them to talk once more.

"You have family coming soon, right?" She waited on his answer.

"Yes, Jane and the boys."

"Why not make this a holiday season to remember in a good way then? Blast Stephanie's favorite Christmas music if you want. We'll invite Mrs. Holiday up to listen so she won't mind. Then put up a tree and decorate your place with Jane and the boys before they leave. Make new memories. Honor Stephanie's memory, not the pain, with enjoying the music and the season. If you don't, that's just letting the enemy steal your joy and peace that Jesus died to give you."

Tears were welling up in Ethan's eyes.

She continued, "I have the same reservations about this time of the year. I dread it. I've resolved this year is going to be different. I'm going to use this time to celebrate the person I lost and enjoy the people I'm still blessed to be around. I came here because I knew I had to make some changes in my life. I'm determined to make the best of this life. Benjamin would have wanted that for me just like Stephanie would have wanted that for you."

Soon the tears abated, and his smile returned. "People have been telling me to get on with my life, but I don't think anyone has put it quite so well as that." He reached for her hand across the table. "Thank you."

She smiled at him as he squeezed her hand. "Racheal misses her too. I saw the photo on your desk of you and Stephanie out in the snow. I adore snow. So did Benjamin. Did she like winter?"

"Oh yes, even when it fell in late April, and everyone else was sick of it."

"Benjamin had never seen snow until he moved to the States from Israel. He told me the first time it snowed, his roommate at MIT called campus police because he was afraid Benjamin would freeze to death. He stayed outside, walking in it as it fell. Campus police found him playing in the snow and took him back to his dorm to get warm. Snowflakes fascinated him as much as they do me. We talked about fractals and the unique shapes of flakes." She paused, then laughed, "Okay, we were nerds. My favorite shape is a snowflake. Benjamin gave me a dendrite for our first anniversary." She pulled out the charm from underneath her pink sweater for him to see. "We don't have much snow where I'm from anymore. Every time it snows, I get excited like I did when I was a little girl."

"It's fair to say you like snow then?" An impish grin appeared on his face.

"Definitely. I hope it snows while I'm here."

"You're going to need warmer clothes then." He laughed and drank from his glass. "When it snows here, it piles up fast. You won't be able to walk in those heels."

"I travel during the winter. I did bring snow boots and heavier clothes. At least they're colorful. My boots are pink."

He chuckled, "Pink, of course! Is that a poke at me for all the gray I wear?"

"I was tempted to visit your closet today and see for myself if you possessed other colors in your wardrobe. I refrained."

"Well, thank you. I do have other suits and clothes in my wardrobe that aren't gray."

"Prove it." She smirked.

He laughed again. "You do enjoy provoking me, don't you?"

Their conversation continued over an excellent multi-course meal. Marcus was waiting outside for them a few minutes after ten. Ethan plucked up the courage to hold her hand as they left.

"Thanks for the late run, Marcus. How was your evening?"

"It's been great, Mr. Cooper. Thanks. Will you be needing my services tomorrow?" Marcus opened the rear passenger door for them.

Charlotte shook her head negatively. Ethan agreed.

"I don't believe we will. We won't need you again until Monday, for work. Do you mind taking us on a long trip home? Most of the Christmas lights are up, and Ms. Rose is new to town."

"Very good, then. I know just the places for great lights."

Traffic passed them by with one car backfiring as it accelerated away. Charlotte's hand gripped his, the other rising to cover her speeding heart. The noise had set off a panic attack. Ethan quickly put her in the car.

Once inside, Marcus shut the door.

Charlotte reached for his hand in the darkness of the rear seat. He didn't bother to buckle his seatbelt, instead sliding over to pull her to him. She buried her face in his jacket.

"Focus on your breathing. You're okay. I've got you. It was a car backfiring." He continued to whisper, knowing her hearing aids could pick up his voice. "Repeat after me, five, seven, twenty-one, three, eight."

She complied. He issued a second set of random numbers, then another. After the third set, her breathing had normalized along with her heart rate.

"How...how did you do that?" She raised her head to look at him.

"My sister used to have panic attacks when we were younger. Mild, but still debilitating. I learned that trick with her. The attack cannot escalate when your brain is forced to concentrate. Counting numbers out of order takes concentration."

"That's incredible. Thank you."

"You're welcome."

Neither moved from the embrace as the car passed by elegant windows and trees wrapped in twinkling lights. Marcus enjoyed the drive as much as they did, taking them back at nearly midnight.

Ethan stopped with her at the door to the corporate suite. "Make sure you drink enough water before you go to sleep. We both killed a bottle of red wine, and I don't want either one of us having a headache in the morning."

"Yes, sir." She grinned and stood with her back to the door. "Thank you for a wonderful dinner. That reservation couldn't have been easy to get on such short notice."

"The Maitre D' is a friend; Nancy helped."

"Remind me to thank her on Monday then." Charlotte took a deep breath and spoke slowly. "What you did...in the car."

He winked at her. "Did what?" A smile erupted as he tilted his head slightly, telling her silently to think nothing of it. "Good night." Ethan leaned forward and kissed her left cheek. "I enjoyed the lights. Let's do that again. Sleep well."

"You too."

She stepped inside and touched her cheek, where he had just kissed. A smile appeared on her lips that remained in place as she sipped a bottle of water and readied for bed. The panic attack had been stopped dead in its tracks by one Ethan Cooper. He certainly was a good man and an unexpected blessing.

The gray light of late Fall was coming in through the large windows of the corporate suite. Charlotte walked into the kitchen area a few minutes after seven, clad in warm pink flannel pajamas and a soft dove gray robe. Her slippers made no sound on the floor as she rummaged through cabinets in hopes of getting some coffee started. As she bent over to look into a lower cabinet, she heard something slide under the door. She glanced to her right to see a piece of paper on the floor.

She retrieved a note and read the hastily scribbled words on the bright white scrap of cotton paper.

Morning! I have coffee and breakfast if you're interested. Pajamas required. My door is open. Ethan

A smile graced her face. *True hospitality from a southern gentleman. He thinks of everything.*

Moments later, Charlotte was knocking lightly on Ethan's door before turning the handle to step inside.

"Hello?"

"Come on in, Ms. Rose." He spun around to grab a coffee cup already waiting on the counter for her. He was sporting solid gray pajamas and a gray robe. "I figured you might like some coffee." Ethan poured the white mug full of hot coffee from the French press resting on the kitchen island beside his cup. He looked up to see a sleepy-eyed blonde padding toward him. Her hair was up in a messy bun, wearing black-framed glasses. From the looks of it, she had not been awake long. This was the first time he'd seen her with her hair up. He could see both hearing aids. She looked a bit vulnerable, touching her ears where he could plainly see the devices. "Did you sleep well?"

She reached across the island, taking the mug from his left hand. "Thank you." After a few sips, she replied. "I did. Did you?"

"I did." Ethan also had glasses on, preferring to let his eyes breathe on the weekends from the daily wear of contacts. The square black frames were still a bit foggy from taking a sip of the hot coffee.

He came around the island and sat on one of the stools, inviting her to do the same. There were two place settings with the same pattern of silverware and plates from the corporate suite.

"Are you hungry? I made French Toast from Challah bread. It's in the oven so it would stay warm. I wasn't sure how long you'd sleep. I have maple syrup for it and fried out some crispy bacon."

"How long have you been up?" Charlotte grinned at him over her coffee.

"I woke up about six. I had a loaf of Challah in the freezer. I like it for French Toast. I figured you'd enjoy the bread and the bacon." He smiled broadly. "Did you and Benjamin eat Challah?"

"That was very thoughtful of you, Ethan. Thank you." She paused, "We did eat Challah. I can't remember the last time he cooked breakfast for me, though. This is such a treat!"

"I'm hungry. Let's eat!" Ethan wasn't sure if mentioning Benjamin would upset her. He hadn't noticed an adverse reaction. He rose from his seat to serve them both, leaving the syrup between them within easy reach of both.

They ate in silence until Charlotte made an interesting noise that had his complete attention.

"I take it you approve?" He waited.

She swallowed, "Oh, I approve. You can cook for me anytime, Mr. Cooper. I appreciate a man who knows his way around a kitchen." Another bite of bacon was chewed, issuing a crunch as it met her teeth. She had forgotten about the hearing aids being exposed to him.

Ethan caught a glimpse of her face out of the corner of his eye. She was eating her second slice of bacon. He reached across the island with his long arm grabbing another piece with tongs before placing it on her plate. The gesture was repeated for himself.

"This is delicious, thank you."

"You're welcome. I don't often have occasion to cook for anyone but myself. Racheal and Gabriel are over occasionally when he's in town. It wouldn't be proper for Racheal to be here unless he was with her. You're the first person in a while I've been alone with." Ethan said the last words slowly.

"I'm the first woman that's been here since Stephanie."

He nodded affirmatively. "Everyone kept setting me up on dinner dates. I never brought anyone back here. I just couldn't. For the longest time, I couldn't even stay in the closet for too long, having empty space where her things would have been. We were in the process of moving here when she was killed. Stephanie would have liked this place. She would have spent every moment she could on the balcony, even if it was ten below. She liked being outside, and I liked the kitchen; she didn't even cook." Ethan blew out a breath and paused; tears were welling up in his eyes. He pulled off his glasses and set them on the island. "I'm finally at a point where I feel like I can put this behind me if we can nail this bunch and put El Carnicero behind bars. For the first time in five years, I have hope for a future I couldn't see anymore."

Charlotte laid her fork down, listening to him. He lost it finally, and the tears came like a flood. She knew exactly how he felt. Her own glasses were laid aside, and she embraced him. They both let their tears flow, releasing emotions both had long held inside. After the worst of their sobbing had passed, she pulled away from him. They parted to sort themselves out. She was pointed toward the guest bathroom.

Both returned to the kitchen island to finish their breakfast, although still sniffling a little.

Ethan pulled the French Press over, sliding the hot pad across the shiny quartz counter. He refilled their mugs from the insulated press.

"I think we both needed that." She took a good long drink of the refreshed liquid. The last few bites of the second slice of French Toast were enjoyed in silence. She pushed the plate away and placed her napkin back on the quartz. The warm mug was now gripped in her hands. "A few days before I came here…I finally packed up Ben's clothes from our closet. I kept putting it off and putting it off. My brother and his family are buying my house from me and moving back. After Thanksgiving, I'll most likely be homeless. I knew I had to deal with purging the house before I came here, or I wasn't going to do it at all. I packed up most of what I own and put it into storage the day before I flew up here. I keep waiting for the phone call from William telling me that his house has sold and I'm officially homeless." She laughed, "I have no apartment here and no building yet for my business. I didn't expect to be using language skills on a case to help you and Racheal, but I'm glad I can help. A friend of mine helped me know what happened to the particular group who took credit for the bombing that changed my life forever. That helped with some closure that I needed. I want that for you too."

He only nodded his head repeatedly, unsure what to say for a moment. "I didn't mean to dredge this up over French Toast on a Saturday but thank you. Thanks for listening to me. Thanks for knowing exactly how I feel and letting me talk about it, not cutting me off and telling me just to move on."

She sat the coffee mug down and took his right hand in her left. "You're welcome; right back at you."

"And for the record, you're not homeless. Stay here as long as you like."

She smiled at him. "You keep cooking like this, and I may never leave."

He chuckled, throwing his head back.

"Now, about your closet..." Charlotte had a childish grin on her face.

Ethan kept laughing. He pulled their intertwined hands along, taking her through his immaculate bedroom and into a walk-in closet where he let go of her hand. "I do possess other attire. It's not all gray."

"Just most of it!" She thumbed through suit after suit in varying shades of gray, all handmade. At the back of the top rack, almost hidden, were four different colored suits and one black tuxedo inside of a clear dust bag tagged as his backup. One medium blue suit, a dark navy, a black, and a beige of lightweight fabric hung before her. She pulled the medium blue down, holding it in front of him. "Why don't you wear the others?"

"I had two gray suits when Stephanie passed. My whole world became shades of gray, I suppose, and my wardrobe followed." He grimaced at her, taking the hanger and putting it on a hook in the wall rather than rehanging the garment. When he said it out loud, the full realization hit him. His world truly had turned gray.

Charlotte was busy thumbing through another section. There were collared shirts in varying colors, sport coats, sweaters, khaki pants, golf shorts, and even jeans. Past the jeans was a hard black case propped against the wall. The case wasn't touched or moved often due to the thick layer of dust covering the surface.

Ethan knew it was pointless to stop her. She was going to pull it out.

"Is this a cello?"

"Yes." He kept his eyes fixed on hers. "I haven't played it since…"

"You are a man of many talents, are you?"

He took her hand once more, leading her to the guest bedroom. The door had always been shut before. Inside the smaller guest closet, there were more cases.

"What are all these?"

"Three guitars, a violin, trumpet, keyboard, some stands." His throat felt dry. Had he really resigned all these for so long to a forgotten closet? His face felt hot with shame. Stephanie would sit for hours, working on her cases, while he played in the background to relieve stress. "I put them all away in the move, and after…never got them out again. I haven't painted in years either." He pointed to a covered easel in the corner. Next to it were standing canvases, at least a dozen of various sizes, wrapped in cloth.

"How many instruments can you play?"

"Anything you put in my hand. Music and painting were my escapes when I was younger. I'd sneak off at night and go listen to jazz being played at a nearby club. Jane went with me sometimes. The owner was our housekeeper's brother, Leon. He always kept an eye on me, so Ms. Icey didn't worry. Jane had proper piano lessons. I took lessons from the musicians on everything I could. As I got older, I would sit in with them on some nights. My mother felt it was shameful to do so, and I didn't pursue music, obviously, or painting. In her eyes, they were fine things to do but only at home and not for income. 'If we didn't have money, you'd starve,' that's what she'd say."

"What was Stephanie's favorite instrument?"

Ethan felt lighter just talking about Stephanie today with Charlotte. "The cello. I always liked playing the trumpet best. It's loud, and she couldn't concentrate on her work if I played in the background with the trumpet. She preferred strings, like the violin or the cello."

"Did Stephanie paint too?"

"No, that was only me as well. I'd started an abstract winter painting before she died. I have never finished it. I painted what's hanging in your suite and mine."

"Even the Renoir's?"

"Guilty. I can paint reproductions better than I can my own. I've had trouble getting inspired. But since you came to town…something is different. I've not talked this much about her or music with anyone. I usually shut Racheal and Nancy down too. You're just…"

"Full of questions?" She waited.

"Special." His left hand rose to cup her right cheek, staring into her brown eyes. The urge to kiss her was overwhelming, and he'd not kissed anyone since his wife had passed.

The poignant moment was interrupted by her phone ringing from the kitchen island.

They shared a smile before leaving the closet to return to the kitchen.

The phone was answered in a throaty foreign language. Ethan listened to her speak for several minutes, not understanding a word. She wore a sheepish grin after laying the phone down on the island and moving her plate over to the sink. He had been cleaning up during her call.

"King of Saudi Arabia, again?" He was joking with her in a playful tone. "I thought I told him never to interrupt breakfast."

"Assistant Director of Training for Mossad, in Israel, confirming who will be updating the teams on new entry protocols for wireless devices installed on their bases by Rose Aerospace and Defense. They have a training exercise with American troops in January. Ordinarily, it would be me, but William will have to field this one, even though I built their training modules."

"That was Hebrew?"

"Yes, it was."

"That amazes me to hear you speak like that." Ethan smiled at her, holding her gaze so long the dish he was holding slipped from his wet fingers back into the sink with a thud.

"William isn't as comfortable with them. I feel guilty leaving him with all this to do."

"Have you been transitioning for this?"

"William and I have been planning for this. My parents don't know I'm leaving yet."

"Ouch!"

"Dad still thinks he's going to retire, and I'm going to keep on running the show. If I can't get all this figured out, I may not get my stationery shop after all."

"A dream is still a dream, even if it's postponed a little. Don't give up." He winked at her.

"Right back at you, Mr. Musical Painter. How did you wind up as an attorney with all of this creativity?"

He grew pensive, considering his answer. "I had to make a difference, and I had to get as far away from my mother as possible. Vanderbilt wasn't in the running because it wasn't far enough, but when Harvard accepted me, I never looked back. I met Carter there. He's younger than me by about three years. We were in the same fraternity. That reminds me. I received a text late last night from him. Would you like to have dinner with him tonight?"

"I'll leave that up to you. You seemed determined to have him leave the room yesterday."

"Don't laugh, but something strange happened when I came in and found you two in my office. Jealously overcame me for a moment."

"Oh! He strikes me as a harmless flirt." Charlotte grabbed a towel and began drying dishes.

"He is. Carter was a gentleman when we were in college. I never saw him mistreat or speak ill of anyone. He's generous and kind, just like you."

She blushed, "Thank you."

"Racheal tells me you've not been out to see the city since you arrived. What do you say to acting like a tourist today?"

"Just the lights last night. I thought you'd want to dive into the drive for Dānā." She was puzzled by his suggestion.

"That's not going anywhere. Dānā knows this is going to take time. I'm still waiting for the NYPD to get back to me on how far I can take this on our side before we have to turn it all over to them. I have your help and Racheal's. I trust you both. Today, let's get out and have some fun."

"Fun? Two workaholics can have fun?" She laughed at the words.

He rolled his eyes and changed to a higher pitch with his voice. "I know it's a stretch, but humor me."

Ready in less than thirty minutes, they bounded out the front of the building by nearly nine in the morning. Their first stop was across the street to walk in Central Park.

The wind wasn't blowing much, and the sun warmed them as rays peeked through the clouds. Ethan didn't want to forget any moments of today. The prison of grief and uncertainty that had held him captive for the last five years gave him a reprieve. He pulled his cell phone out.

"Turn around, Charlotte."

She turned to see The Plaza Hotel south of them, with a lovely bridge in between. Her phone was held up to take a photo of the view.

"Give me your phone, and I'll take a picture of you."

"I have a better idea. Let's make some new memories today." She smiled and pulled him toward her, turning around to face North with him. She switched to the front camera before putting her arm around his waist to get closer for the photo. "Smile, Mr. Cooper." She held the phone out as far as possible from them and snapped a picture.

He loathed the thought of letting her go after the picture, but she soon slipped away after several were taken.

They repeated the pose with more photos trading off phones in Times Square, Herald Square, with hot coffee and pastries outside Tiffany's, on the Statue of Liberty tour, the bull near Wall Street which drew much laughter from both, then back uptown to the Empire State Building. They stood gazing off the observation deck with him pointing out landmarks all over the city to her. The day had been well spent with breaks to nibble something while they enjoyed people watching from benches.

Ethan's brow raised in thought. "I have an idea for dinner. Let's meet Carter where we can have a view of this beautiful building that Dānā works in every day. There's a great place here in the financial district called Manhatta Restaurant." He pointed to a skyscraper nearby. We can eat and see the building here all lit up."

"That sounds wonderful. Won't we need a reservation and better attire?"

"Let me handle that." His smile showed up again with an all-knowing gleam in his eyes.

The restaurant's bar was busy, full of suits and heels, pressing into their conversations and ignoring others who wandered in to dine for the evening. They had made it by seven.

Ethan pulled her toward the bar to order a drink. "We're not late. I promise. Bourbon?"

She nodded to him affirmatively, looking around the room at all the people surrounding them. He watched her fingers go to her ears to adjust the levels on the hearing aids.

"Are you alright?" He was genuinely concerned. She seemed tense.

Charlotte paused before answering, looking straight into his eyes as they waited on their drinks. She stepped even closer to him to hear him more clearly in the din of noise. "I'm okay. I'm just a little tired from the walking today. All the noise and people wear on me at times. It's the uncertainty of crowds."

"I can understand that." He liked having her so close to him, although he knew she had done so because of the noise level. "There's a lot of people here. If it bothers you, don't let it escalate into a full-blown attack, okay? We can leave. I'll call Carter and tell him some other time. He won't be here for a bit anyway."

She shook her head. "No. I'll be alright. I have to get used to this if I'm going to live here. I can't live my life waiting on something bad to happen in the crowd I'm standing in."

Their drinks were slid onto the bar, and Ethan handed the bartender his card.

Charlotte took a sip. "I thought you told him six-thirty?"

His eyebrows rose. "I did. Carter is late for everything. If I tell him six-thirty, he'll be here by seven-ish."

The crowd thinned considerably as a large party was seated for dinner, then another. As they departed the bar, the noise level dropped enough to hear Ella Fitzgerald and Louis Armstrong's trumpet drifting down to their ears. People were dancing. Charlotte moved away from him now that she no longer needed to be so close to hear his voice. The loss of her warmth was felt immediately. He reached out to pull her back gently.

"Where do you think you're going?" He looked so serious for a moment, but the growing smile betrayed him.

She was close enough again that he could feel the vibration of her laughter.

"Fine then. If I'm to remain, then you, sir, must dance with me."

"Gladly."

He spun her around, leaving their glasses on the bar. The two were enjoying *The Nearness of You* so much that they began softly singing the parts amidst laughter while dancing. The trumpet's solo was echoed by Ethan humming the part. Charlotte noticed the practiced ease with which he led her as they slowly danced. The song lyrics passed through their lips, singing the part to the other as if they were the only two people in the room. As the song reached the end, the dancing had all but ceased leaving them to stand nestled in each other's arms staring at one another. The magic moment ended with Carter's appearance.

"Don't you two look cozy." He waited a moment before coming any closer. "Our table is ready."

Their table position enabled a perfect view west at the Empire State Building, the top already sporting a Christmas light show. They had placed their order off of another French-inspired menu, Charlotte deferring to Ethan's recommendation. Half an hour had already passed quickly as the trio talked.

"I ran Racheal's numbers on the buyout by Jason, and he agreed with her. I did get a great deal. Here's to the help of old friends." Carter smiled at Charlotte, seated next to Ethan, across from him. "To new friends as well, and finding happiness for us all. Cheers!"

They clinked their bourbon glasses together.

Ethan leaned in slightly toward her. "Jason is Carter's accountant in Atlanta. He's also another fraternity brother from Harvard."

She nodded her understanding as he pulled away. "You and Jason should visit Lauren together. He's not very far away from her. Have you called her yet?"

"Not yet. I don't have the time in my schedule right now to get the ball rolling on the car. I'll get to it next year. I have two properties I'm spending time at after Christmas and the first part of next year. Then it's on to Denver, Scottsdale, Cali." Carter fixed his focus on Ethan. "How did you manage to convince this lovely lady to have dinner with us?"

A chuckle burst from Ethan's lips. "She's my bodyguard, goes everywhere with me." His comment in jest could very well be valid.

Carter laughed at his joke. "No, seriously."

Ethan figured she could very well be his bodyguard, judging from the photo he saw online of Charlotte shooting a pistol at a military range. To the eye that didn't know any better, she was simply a well-dressed lady. Dig deeper, and she was a not-to-be-messed-with woman. "We didn't feel like cooking tonight, and I wanted to catch you before you left town. It wasn't my intention to be so bold with you in my office yesterday. Forgive me, but you do have a penchant for stealing women. That reputation was well earned in our frat house."

"I don't know why everyone thought that. I would sit and talk to girls. I listened well. It never went past that. Yeah, okay, they did wind up in my room at times."

"A lot!" Ethan tilted his head and gave Carter a knowing look.

"Okay, a lot!" Carter rolled his eyes with the admission that made the entire table laugh. "But it was very obvious to me when I arrived tonight there's more here than just a business relationship brewing."

Charlotte reached under the table for Ethan's hand. "We understand each other's losses all too well."

Ethan squeezed her hand. "That loss may lead us to build our friendship on more than bourbon and bacon." He smiled at her then looked over at Carter. "That's how we met, actually, bourbon and bacon."

She chuckled, "Crispy bacon."

Carter rested the tip of his tongue on the back of his teeth for a moment in thought. "You have this Jewish boy's attention. I'm up for any tale involving bourbon and bacon."

The welcome bitterness of black coffee was savored with every sip this cold November morning. Ethan stood at the bedroom window, watching the sunrise, wondering how Sunday could possibly top yesterday. He felt alive again, hopeful. He took the coffee cup with him and stood in his closet. Yesterday was a dressed-down version of his work attire, in primarily gray. Today would be more of a departure from usual. His eyes ran over the section of pants. With a grin and a plan in mind, he retreated to the shower after leaving his mug on the sink.

Intent on having a simple breakfast for them before she woke up, he pulled out a pair of jeans that hadn't left the hanger in years. The cut was classic Levi's, slightly faded in the knees but soft, worn, and comfortable. A winter white cashmere sweater was layered over a t-shirt and light pink button-up shirt. No tie today. He unbuttoned the top buttons on the shirt and left it open. A scarf, gloves, and trench coat were donned on the way out the door. He was headed to Starbucks down sixty-sixth on third avenue to grab a few pastries and some egg bites. The cold air on his freshly shaven face was invigorating.

Upon returning to the building, he walked inside toward the elevator and out-stepped one of his neighbors. "Good morning, Mrs. Holiday." Ethan paused and looked down at the white Shih-Tzu. The timbre of his voice changed. "Good morning, Sugar."

Mrs. Holiday froze, eyes wide with surprise. Even her fur coat seemed to echo the shock, ceasing to sway around her. She couldn't recall the last time Ethan wore a smile like today, nor had she ever seen him in jeans. *How pleasant! He even remembered Sugar's name.* "Good morning, Mr. Cooper."

Up the elevator, he went. He had asked for the warm food to be double bagged and had used his scarf to wrap the outside for extra insulation. As he pulled the egg bites out of the bag, the remaining warmth was fading fast. He went to listen at the locked double doors separating their spaces. She was up.

He walked to his entry door and the few steps to hers, choosing not to push familiarity by opening the center doors yet.

Charlotte heard a light knock on her door. She opened it to find him dressed in…jeans? "Morning. Did I wake up in an alternate reality?"

A loud chuckle came from his belly. "You did." He kept laughing. "If you'll follow me, I procured some breakfast for us. We can watch an early service on television before we meet Racheal and Gabriel at eleven-thirty."

"You've already been out?" She still looked sleepy even though she was dressed in winter white trousers and a warm pink sweater.

"Yes. I didn't feel like cooking. And I have fresh coffee too."

She followed him to find breakfast laid out on the kitchen island. "Thank you. Racheal sent me a text about half an hour ago with the menu for Upland."

"I'm surprised they're up and at'em this early on a Sunday."

Charlotte smirked, "Me too."

"We made it through traffic in that cab faster than I thought. It's only ten minutes to eleven." Ethan let his right arm settle from viewing his watch. He spotted a place he used to visit often and get lost in. He grabbed Charlotte's hand and pulled her to the crosswalk. "I know the perfect place to kill some time while we wait."

She squeezed his hand. "Where are you taking me?"

"Callahan's Vintage Market is four stories of treasures. It's been open since 1918 and still belongs to the original family. They're open, and it's cold out here. Come on."

They stepped into the old building together and were immediately met by a short blonde shopkeeper's greeting instructing them to browse while the staff decorated. She was directing other employees to take boxes to specific areas for lights to be strung up. The place was empty of customers, it seemed.

"This is perfect!" Charlotte was smiling widely at gilded mirrors, a pink velvet chaise lounge, and a Christmas tree full of vintage pastel glass ornaments amidst white twinkle lights on the ten-foot plus tree in front of her as they walked farther inside. "I like their style."

He had to laugh. "I'm not even going to grumble about it being out early or the fact that they're playing Christmas music."

She pulled a snowflake from the tree composed of pearls. "Good, because I like Rat Pack Christmas music." There was no tag on the ornament. "I'm going to ask the price on these. They're lovely."

"I'm going to go find where they've moved the vintage clothing. You'll get a kick out of what they have here."

"I'll catch up in a minute." She had the clerk hold a dozen of the snowflakes at the counter while she shopped. Then she walked through the first floor of home decor, furniture, and three more Christmas trees; all lit up by hanging chandeliers of varying shapes and sizes.

When she caught up to Ethan on the second floor, he was playfully rolling a dark gray fedora down his arm, an elegant trick. Upon reaching his left hand, he popped the hat up and placed it on his head before catching a glimpse of her in the mirror he faced.

"Clad in true style, Mr. Cooper. On the plus side, it also keeps your head warm. You should buy it."

His face scrunched up. "I'll think about it." He removed the hat. "Look at this! The original tag is still hanging inside." Daché Milliner's yellowed tag was still attached, along with a hand-sewn label bearing their name as well. "Daché had their own building here during the depression. The tag is dated 1931, the same year the Empire State Building was completed."

She came closer, peering inside with him. "Does that say eight dollars?"

"It does!" He laughed then sobered. "But today's price for buying is considerably more. I used to come here quite often and wander. We liked to go antiquing. It wasn't as much fun without..."

"Her." Charlotte patted his back. "We didn't call it antiquing. I liked going 'junkin' with Benjamin too. That's what we called it. We used architectural salvage in our house. Molding, vintage lighting, doors, furniture."

"My sister bought most of what's in the apartment here. She wanted period pieces from the nineteen twenties, correct for the building. She found lighting here too."

"So Jane decorated for you?" She smiled.

"She did. I painted reproductions for clients in the Charleston area for years. She owed me one. She visited here a few times and helped decorate the place. She took care of my office building too. You'll meet her and the boys while they're here. I think you'll like her."

"I'm sure I will. She did a great job, a beautifully furnished apartment in an architecturally striking building."

They lost themselves in hats, scarves, jewelry, and coats. Laughs were had as pieces were tried on, each assuming the persona of the article in question. Flappers, gangsters, socialites, the items were in like-new condition from each period. They were singing with Frank Sinatra and Dean Martin as Christmas songs played overhead, unaware that time was flying by.

Charlotte spotted a rack of dresses nearby. There was one, in particular, hanging on the end of the rack that caught her eye. It was made for a ball or a special event. She pulled the dress down a moment later. It was soft pink blush in color with a floor-length skirt that flowed away from the top bodice, covered in thousands of sewed-on seed pearls: the lines, the color, the size, all perfect for her. The blush color would be flattering on anyone.

Ethan was swept up in the moment, staring at her, twirling around in the mirror, holding the dress against herself. "You should buy it. That dress was meant for you."

She exhaled, "Christmas is coming. I have others to think about. I don't have an occasion planned for such an elegant dress."

Charlotte was thinking of others. Ethan had witnessed her care of others, one of her many good traits. Why couldn't he ask her to the gala? What would his mother say? He paused for a moment before letting the butterflies in his stomach settle. "My family has a charity gala here every year, the second Saturday of December, to raise money for the arts in local schools. It's the only thing I've ever done that my mother approves of enough to help me with the cause. Come with me and wear the dress." *There! He had asked. Mother would just have to stuff her 'no ring-no bring' family policy.*

Her mouth hung open for a moment before answering. "If I'm still here, yes. I'd like that. I'm just not sure I should wear this. Isn't that kind of gala a black-tie affair?"

"Yes. I could never see you attending in anything but pink, this pink." He gazed deeply into her brown eyes, noticing flecks of gold in the irises. She was enchanting.

Charlotte's phone was ringing in her clutch. She answered after hanging the dress back up. "Hello, Rae."

Once again, a ringing phone had broken the spell of the moment.

"Charlie! Where are you guys? Do you want us to order?" Racheal looked around the restaurant for them.

Charlotte's brow furrowed. They'd lost track of time. "Sure! We sent you an email with what we wanted in case you beat us there. We looked over the menu earlier. We're down the block. Give us a few minutes to get there."

"Okay, bye."

They left the building with a bag of snowflake pearl ornaments. Ethan was wearing his new-old hat.

Gabriel shook hands with Ethan across the table. "It's been too long." He had already hugged Charlotte, whom he also referred to as Charlie. "Sit down. Your coffee is getting cold. The food should be up soon."

Racheal looked like she was about to burst.

"I'm sorry, we're late. Spill it, Rae." Charlotte stuffed the shopping bag under the table.

She grinned at Charlotte. "First of all, who is this guy with you in jeans? Did you find him on the street?"

"Alright, alright. Don't pick on me." Ethan was stifling his laughter.

"I can't help it. I don't think I've ever seen you in jeans, not even when you helped us move. I like it." Racheal was smiling broadly at Charlotte, who had obviously influenced this new turn in Ethan's behavior. He was acting like his old self again. She grabbed her husband's hand on top of the table before continuing. "Gabriel is leaving his Boston firm and will be a permanent resident with his wife as soon as his new job starts."

Charlotte and Ethan both lit up with smiles and simultaneous congratulations.

The half Puerto Rican wealth management banker was just as eager to share the news. "After Thanksgiving, my family will go back to Boston, and I'll stay here."

Racheal's Spaniard lineage kicked in with a slight accent. "Gabriel Micheal Rodriguez! You told me it wouldn't be until Christmas!" She playfully smacked his shoulder, which seemed to entice him. He leaned over and kissed her cheek before whispering something into her ear. Her face turned red for a moment as they spoke suggestively to each other with their chocolate brown eyes. "We can try that later."

Ethan smirked, "Okay. I don't want to know."

Racheal cozied up to her husband in the comfortable booth. "We're being rude, Gabriel."

Charlotte turned to Ethan. "A Spaniard and a Puerto Rican. I'm surprised she's not broken out the Spanish yet to scold him or maybe rile him up. I can never tell."

Ethan put his arm around her without thinking, mirroring Gabriel with Racheal. "Neither can I, but they do seem happy."

Racheal and Gabriel noticed the move but said nothing. Charlotte seemed comfortable with Ethan, which they were both pleased about.

Gabriel wanted to celebrate. "How about some Mimosa's?"

"Absolutely." Racheal smiled approvingly at him. "We have many things to be grateful for."

Ethan squeezed Charlotte to him as he turned his head to look at her. "Yes, we do."

7

The Call

H ello?" Charlotte could barely see the phone to answer the call in the early morning darkness. It was Captain Caroline Blaine.

"I would apologize for the wake-up call, but I knew you'd want this as soon as I read it. You were correct to reach out to me. Ashem Amadhi's not triggered red flags in the States yet, but he should have. This guy really is bad news and we're just scratching the surface on a deep dive."

"When you say that it sounds even worse." Charlotte was reaching around on the nightstand to find her glasses. No luck. She turned on a light and finally located them, recoiling from the brightness. The nearby clock read five thirty-two in the morning.

Blaine's face drew up in a scowl. "Where did you uncover this man?"

"I was asked to translate documents and just had a horrible suspicion about him. He's partner in a top accounting and wealth management firm here, intending to buy the owner out. I gathered from everything I'm reading so far that he's truly an extremist. I'm still digging through the material and need more time. There are files missing that I don't have access to yet."

A sharp breath intake could be heard. "Get to those files. This man's tied to terrorists in three countries so far. Keep your six covered, Pink. I'll call when I have more. You make sure you do the same."

"I will. Thanks for letting me know."

"Anytime. Bye.

"Bye." Charlotte was wide awake now. She swung her legs over the side, feet dangling from the height of the tall bed. The warmth of the wonderful weekend with Ethan was still fresh on her mind. That feeling was the only thing keeping the chill due to Captain Blaine's phone call from setting off a panic attack. Terrorists in New York City? What had she gotten herself involved in with translating documents?

"Mr. Cooper, it's Detective Togo. Four more people were found half an hour ago in Harlem, other drug dealers fairly high up on the chain of command with their gang. Our people sitting in that area monitoring El Carnicero lost him just after midnight. They thought he was in one place, but he got past the sitters and wound up somewhere else. He made it back into the house, along with other gang members in East Harlem a few minutes ago. I want to meet with

Dānā, today. This cannot wait any longer. I want to figure out the ties and go after these guys."

Ethan was struggling to wrap his head around this early phone call. More people were now dead at the hands of this killer. "I'll call Dānā when I go to work. Have your team come to the office this time. I'll call you back with when. It's up to him though."

"I know, but he trusts you. If you can convince him to do this we can take a lot of bad people down all at once. He's the cog to make the rest of the pieces fit, but he has to be willing to let us into everything."

"I'm aware." Ethan wasn't about to admit he already had access to most of what they needed. "Did the commissioner agree to release all the files to my team so we can be up to speed on this from your side?"

"Not yet."

Ethan held his breath for a moment. "I was hoping to avoid playing this card, but he's leaving me no choice." He sat up and ran his hand over his face.

"What are you talking about?"

"Have him and his detail there today too."

"I don't know what his schedule -"

"I don't care. Call his handler. We all want the same thing. I expect some cooperation from the NYPD. I'm extending my firm and resources as a courtesy, the least he could do is the same."

"I'll do what I can and wait to hear from you."

"Alright. Thanks, Detective."

"Mmm. Bye."

"Bye." He threw the covers back, grabbed his glasses, and got up. It wasn't even six yet. *Happy Monday*, he thought.

The apartment was freezing. Having the temperature low was better for sleeping, even Charlotte felt the same as they had discovered while talking late into the evening over a glass of wine. This morning's chill meant the outside temperature had taken a nosedive overnight. He took the phone into the bathroom and hurriedly used an app to turn the heat on and avoid walking all the way out to beside the entry door. In a few minutes the place was toasty warm making it comfortable once he stepped out of the shower. Once his contacts were in he could get dressed.

Today was going to be one of those days. He pulled the first suit his fingers came across, Tom Ford, wool, gray of course, but when he reviewed his ties one in particular caught his attention. The tie in question was soft pink, hanging at the back of the rack. With his pants and shirt now on, cuff links in, the long mirror in the closet was used to tie the surprise more efficiently into a full Windsor knot. The jacket, with peak lapels and five button cuffs, was left on the hanger along with the vest for now. There was a light knock on his door. He glanced at the clock on his nightstand while passing through the bedroom, it wasn't quite six-thirty. The best thing to happen so far today, Charlotte was standing there when he opened the door, again in winter white trousers and yet another pink sweater.

"Good morning, Mr. Cooper. I apologize for the intrusion." She stepped inside behind him, shutting the door.

"No, no, come on in. I was just about to make some coffee." He walked around the island to grab the kettle.

"I appreciate that. I received an early morning phone call and I'd really like some." She truly looked at him for the first time since entering. He was wearing a pink tie.

"Everything alright?" He was filling the kettle up.

"No, but let's have some coffee first and I'll tell you. By the way, I like the tie."

He chuckled, "I thought you might approve." He sat the kettle down. "Do you mind making this? I need to finish dressing. I have news too."

"Of course. Go." She shooed him toward his bedroom then pulled out the French Press and coffee beans from the canister to grind.

Ethan was back before she could grind them, already wearing his knee length wool overcoat. "On second thought, turn the kettle off and leave that. We can walk down the block to Starbucks and Marcus can meet us there. Do you mind?"

"Not at all. I'm eager to get to the office this morning. Let's go."

"So am I." He stopped in his tracks as he approached the door with her. "I don't want you to feel like you have to wait on me in the mornings. I have coffee and some food over here if you're up before me. Please come over and help yourself. And if we don't have what you want to eat or drink, we can stop on the way in and pick it up."

He had never offered his home to someone residing in the corporate suite before.

"I appreciate that, but I feel like I would be intruding upon you."

"Nonsense." He took a few steps from her and turned the lock on the double doors that separated their spaces. "Shall we get your things and go?"

She smiled, "Sure."

Moments later they headed out the front entrance of the building to be met by a stiff wind and brutal temperatures drawing both of them closer together. Charlotte carried a large laptop bag and Ethan his briefcase. Even with her long legs, she struggled to match his driving pace in heels. Noticing her effort, he adjusted his pace and offered her his arm.

She was comforted by the gesture as they passed people on the sidewalk. "My intelligence contact called about five-thirty this morning. Dānā had every reason to be alarmed. Ashem's a very dangerous man. We need to find out more than just what's on those emails I've read so far. I'm missing files that are linked and referenced, but missing from the drive. I'm guessing they're on a virtual drive, linked to the server at Empire. I'd need to be in the building and preferably with Ashem's laptop to get to them. Cell phone hack for his phone wouldn't hurt either, but that's not possible without a warrant."

Ethan opened the door for her a moment later at Starbucks. "Listen to you! Speak legal to me!"

Charlotte's whole body shook with laughter as she stepped inside. "You don't spend years on the phone with Racheal or in the business I'm in and not pick up a thing or two."

The grin that enveloped his face still hadn't faded. "I think I know someone who can help with that. He should be coming to the office this morning."

Dānā Darbandi sat across the desk from Ethan. His forehead was covered in a sheen of sweat despite the cool weather and temperate office. The tie around his neck seemed to tighten it's silk grip through his tailored shirt. Shaky hands rose to loosen the offending garment along with opening the top button. The longer he sat there, the drier his throat felt. Was the air in the room being sucked from his lungs?

"I need to find a way out. I fear for my life, my family, and this city."

"Stop, Dānā. Have you spoken to Detective Togo again?"

"No. I simply came to you."

"You're my friend and a longtime client of my firm. I want you to know that the Detective has approached me with the carrot you dangled. Due to attorney client privilege, I could not discuss things you've said to me. Do you agree to full disclosure of the facts to all of us on my team, including Detective Togo, the ADA, and the NYPD?

"Yes."

Nancy knocked on the glass door. "They're here, Mr. Cooper," coming through reception right now. And I like the tie."

"Ten o'clock. Right on time. Thank you. Put them in the conference room, please." Ethan pushed back away from his desk. "I'm going to get my team and then we will join them. Sit tight, Dānā. Nancy, don't go anywhere. Stay near your desk after you get them situated, please. I'll need you in the conference room too. Bring Dānā in with you."

Ethan walked out the door into the secretarial pool area. He looked around, forming a plan in his head. *We're going up against the NYPD, the Police Commissioner, and the ADA is with them. I need a show of force and fast or they're going to take this away from us.* He walked past Barbara, then took a step back. "Are you busy, currently?"

Her eyebrows shot up in surprise. "No, sir. Can I help you?"

"Wait for me to come back through, then follow us into the conference room."

"Yes, sir." Barbara's eyes searched nearby for Nancy. She used her finger and motioned for Nancy to come over. "Do you know what's going on?"

Nancy only shook her head negatively. She had learned long ago to trust Ethan first and ask questions later. He had been using please more lately and wasn't as short with people.

Lewis was sitting beside Charlotte in front of Racheal's desk, drinking coffee and chatting, always the impeccably dressed driver just like Marcus. Ethan's presence came into the room before he stepped inside Racheal's office. Charlotte felt the surge, his energy becoming familiar to her over the last few days. Her head turned to see him enter.

"Racheal, call Zach, tell him to get down here, now. Make sure he's wearing his suit jacket and his tie is on straight. Lewis, I need a favor. Do you know if Marcus is still in the building after dropping Dānā off?"

"He's in the lavatory. We were about to go run the cars through a wash."

"Go get Marcus, please. I need him. We're all going into the conference room. I don't have time to explain. Just leave your overcoats in here, then follow my lead and don't say a word. Charlotte, I need you to be ready when we're asked about Ashem, since you know what you've read so far. You know how dangerous he is and what's going on. They don't yet. Don't over share with them unless they go quid pro quo. The NYPD's going to want to take this over and give it to the DA's office. I'll work with someone in the DA's office, but I want us to run point on this until we're ready to hand this over to them wrapped in a bow. We're two steps ahead and I want to keep that way if I possibly can."

Two minutes passed in silence as Ethan waited on the improvised crew to assemble. Lewis returned with Marcus, Barbara stood waiting outside the office door, Racheal met Zach as he neared the door and Charlotte caught Ethan's stare.

"Looks like your team's all here." Charlotte's chin dipped slightly as her eyes silently reassured him, she had his back. They all did.

169

The look wasn't lost on him. He understood perfectly and was grateful. His fists clenched for a moment. His posture was ram-rod straight. "Let's go."

Nine people representing Grey Cooper filed into the conference room, dressed to impress in their corporate armor, to sit opposite from four individuals: Detective Togo, Commissioner Fairchild, one protective officer, and Assistant District Attorney Jennifer Brown. She had worked with Stephanie and Racheal. The Commissioner excused his security officer to wait outside, shutting the door upon exit.

Nine now stared down three. Ethan liked these numbers.

Ethan began, "Gentleman, ADA Brown, thank you all for coming here on such short notice." He introduced everyone in the room sitting on his side of the table from the firm, only names, no titles. "Forgive me for repeating myself, Mr. Darbandi, but I have to ask you some questions again with all parties now present. Do you want my firm, a team I've assembled carefully, to help you through this matter even if it means facts found in discovery could lead to arrests that may not be in your favor as I'm bound to surrender these to ADA Brown?

"Yes."

"Are you here willingly to discuss matters regarding your firm including what you've previously discussed with Detective Togo and me?"

"Yes."

The Detective continued staring at Dānā. He hadn't taken his eyes off of him from the moment they had all entered the room. Charlotte regarded the effect on Dānā. He repeatedly cleared his throat as though the scrutiny was robbing him of speech. Perhaps it wasn't the scrutiny, but the dry, hot air circling the room from air vents. She too felt her throat go dry. Her eyes circled the room to the beverage cart that held bottles of water.

The ADA pulled out a file from her briefcase and began scribbling notes. "My office was informed just this morning of new developments in Stephanie's case. I don't understand how Mr. Darbandi's predicament relates to this matter."

"We'll get there, Jennifer, I promise." Ethan watched Charlotte get up and go to the beverage cart. She picked up two bottles, then walked to Dānā. She swallowed, then spoke in Farsi. "If you need water, please help yourself." Everyone in the room heard Charlotte's command of language when she offered Dānā a bottle of water.

His posture relaxed, comforted by the gesture, accepting her hospitality. Her face was new to him. The air in the room was finally making it into his lungs. He drank deeply from the water, finally sitting the bottle down on the long, walnut conference table. "Perhaps I can shed light on all of this for you. Mrs. Brown, is it?"

Dānā continued on with what he knew and had passed on to Ethan, leaving out the hard drive details. He spoke for almost twenty minutes, fully explaining the predicament he was in because of Ashem's actions and dubious dealings. Charlotte smiled at him, lending her support by keeping great eye contact while listening with the group. When the last words left his lips a sense of relief washed over him. He couldn't totally find peace until Ashem was behind bars and out of his life, but he'd take this for now.

"We'll need full access to your business, all of your records, telephones, cell phones, security cameras, servers, everything. ADA Brown will help us get warrants secured for what we need to keep the case airtight, but you'll need to give us permission to enter and start." Detective Togo drummed his fingers on the table, his impatience was simmering beneath a calm demeanor. He wanted to get moving on this case.

"You have that along with probable cause. You'll need help. Most of Ashem's business is in Arabic or Farsi. Only the local dealings are in English. It's going to take time unless you have someone who understands the languages well." Dana wondered if this woman, who obviously spoke Farsi, was a part of Ethan's plan.

Charlotte sat forward in her chair, speaking in Farsi once more. "I'm willing to help in any way I can." She repeated herself in English for everyone else.

"No offense, but the NYPD has it's own investigators. Our techs in the Technical Assistance Response Unit, TARU, can handle this." Detective Togo leveled Charlotte with his gaze.

She didn't want to let them know they had almost everything from the servers and office computers already. She needed extraneous files Ashem had buried on another machine, most likely a server Dānā didn't know about or a cloud based site. "With all due respect, Detective, this is bigger than the NYPD. This is matter of national security from what Mr. Darbandi's told us. That's why I am involved. I'm already familiar and up to speed on this matter. Once I pull what we need from the servers and from Ashem's personal machine, I can get through the information faster than your team. Involving too many people from your side is only going to cause delays."

"I don't want that, but going in to this office could get dicey pretty quick, lady." Togo fired back, his old fashioned boys club attitude came to the forefront. *Who was she to say the NYPD couldn't handle this?* "This is no place for a skirt."

"It's Ms. Rose, and I'm not a lawyer. I'm a Defense and Aerospace Engineer." Charlotte's lips tightened at the demeaning inference that she was merely a pretty face. "I have top security clearance from the U.S. Government. I've worked in the defense industry my entire life. I was trained in close quarters combat if I need it when I'm out on the job. I know how to handle myself. I've served my country in many ways with covert operatives over the years. If the military can trust me with their secrets and missions, I believe you can too."

Togo's lips tightened with the decision. She had a point. "We'll go in with a small number of people so we don't draw attention. Can you follow orders and shoot a gun if we meet resistance in that office?"

"I can. I prefer to use other weapons though. Guns can you make you over confident. You need to be able to think your way out of problems and use what's at hand. My job has taught me that."

Togo smirked at her confidence. *She's got fight, for sure.* "Alright then, Ms. Rose. I'll pull an extra pistol out of firearms, but you'll only use it if someone is firing at you." He decided to test her. "Do you have a preference for manufacturer and caliber?"

"Glock 23 if you have it. I prefer the larger forty caliber with a full size grip. We're going in an office building, with thin walls, so hollow point ammunition, Gold Dot if you have it and I'll need an extra clip. Otherwise I'll take a nine millimeter Glock. And I have my own vest. I'd have brought my own firearm, but New York isn't concealed carry friendly to my permit."

Commissioner Fairchild shared a glance with Togo, impressed with her straight-forward declarations. "You sound well versed in weaponry. Our population density and the general public's ignorance of proper training for firearms presents a danger with concealed carry here. If someone started shooting on the subway, even in self-defense, the results would be catastrophic."

"I understand, Commissioner. I just don't agree with your city's stance on the matter when individuals are properly trained and use the correct application for defense. I feel it's in direct conflict with my second ammendment rights." She replied calmly, but firmly.

"Not everyone who would apply for a concealed carry permit would take the time, as you have, to become as well trained. If they were all like you, concealed carry wouldn't be so contentious. Now, back to the matter at hand." He smiled at her as he redirected, then to Ethan and the rest of the room.

Ethan shook his head slightly, hiding a smile, amused by the exchange between Charlotte and his former father-in-law. She didn't back down from the Police Commissioner of New York City or a seasoned old-school Detective. He had a new respect for her, above what he had already developed. She was tough as nails. She'd have to hold her own working with the top brass in the military, all heavily decorated, top ranking, and mostly men. He'd asked her about the vest later. He didn't like the idea of her suiting up and carrying a firearm, but there would be no dissuading her. Of that he was certain. "Now for what I want. I'm extending my firm in help. I want the complete files of what you have on El Carnicero and these gangs you suspect are tied to Ashem."

The Commissioner's brow furrowed. "I don't think that's necessary."

"Oh, but it is." Ethan was going to have to bring up something he'd rather not, but the Commissioner was forcing his hand. "You cannot expect me to not want to read the final reports of what's really happened since she died, Tom."

"Don't make this about her, Ethan."

"It's already about her. It never stopped being about her. All I know is what I was told happened. You railroaded me, shut me out, lied to me to keep me at a distance so your people could cover their butt. I want all the reports that led up to her execution and what you uncovered beyond that and your trail back to my office or we walk out of here, right now, all of us." Ethan's nostrils flared out. He was desperately praying his bluff with having the table full on his side would help his plea. He needed answers.

Detective Togo cleared his throat. He answered for the Commissioner. He wasn't about to lose this. "I'll get them to you, this afternoon. I'll inform TARU after we leave here so they're on board. I'll need to take Ms. Rose with us as well. TARU can hit the telephones, the security footage, and the offices so we can have eyes and ears on the place. We will have to wait on cover for the warrants. When's the best time to make that happen, Mr. Darbandi?"

"Wednesday. There will be limited personnel through tomorrow. Everyone should be gone by three, but Wednesday would be best. No one should be there, really, all day. I wanted to let everyone have time for the Thanksgiving holiday."

"Great. Ms. Rose, you get what you need from the computers and then you're out of there, understand?"

"Yes, sir." Charlotte wouldn't need long with the machines, just the opportunity to find the files they were missing. Charlotte gathered her things upon leaving the conference room, disappearing with the Commissioner and Detective Togo. She left Ethan standing at the head of the conference room table, his place, with a smile and a nod.

8

Kevlar and Coffee

Charlotte spent the rest of the afternoon on Monday and most of Tuesday at One Police Plaza, meeting with the TARU unit, the Commissioner, and Detective Togo. When she finally made it back to the corporate suite just before nine o'clock, Tuesday was nearly a memory. She checked her watch upon opening the door.

Ethan sprang up from his side of the double doors when he heard her return. He'd not had five minutes with her since leaving the conference room yesterday, but had poured over case files from the NYPD. He needed a little life to lift his spirits from all the reading. Right now, he didn't want to discuss the horror of Stephanie's death with her. He carefully knocked on the doors separating their spaces while holding two glasses of hastily poured bourbon. She didn't immediately come to the doors. Had he been too zealous by using the interior doors, overlooking the proper use of the corporate suite's entry door. He continued to stand there. Three minutes passed. He turned to walk away when the door suddenly opened from the other side.

She was breathless, taking a glass from him and smiling not missing a beat. "My apologies. I couldn't get out of those heels fast enough and into my pajamas. Thanks for the bourbon. I need it."

His nervousness regarding the center doors abated with her smile and admission. Why was he worried again? "I wasn't sure if you heard me knock or you just didn't want to see me."

"Fat chance of that." She grinned.

Without a mention of coming over into his side, they both started moving toward the sofa in his apartment. She took the middle and he sat on the end near the ottoman, putting his feet up. Her legs were folded up under her as she casually sipped the bourbon.

"We secured the warrant for Ashem's cell phone. We'll get one for his apartment later if we don't get all we need from the office. ADA Brown had a judge sign off on a few more blanketing our entry even though Dānā gave us permission. I asked her to call you and tell you. I wasn't allowed to use my phone today while I was at One PP. The room we were in blocked cell transmission. Did she call you?"

"She did, about two-thirty today." His head tilted back and rested on the cushion. "Did you play nicely with the NYPD?"

"I did. I actually like Detective Togo and the Commissioner, once I got past their prickly persona. They're nice guys."

"It's their job to be tough on the outside, command presence they call it."

"Makes me think of something Benjamin used to say about me sometimes, sabra. In Israel there is a desert flower called sabra that is pretty, but prickly on the outside, soft on the inside."

"Sabra?" He raised his head away from the cushion to take a sip of bourbon from the glass on the end table. His eyes were locked on her, amused and happy that she was sharing something with him. "Isn't that also a hummus?"

They laughed. He replaced the glass on the end table.

"It is, actually, now that I think of it." She sipped from her glass again, still cradled in her palms. "Did you and Racheal find anything more in the accounting we can use to hang this guy out to dry with?"

"Racheal did. I went over it with her. We're compiling all the RICO violations, money trails, the list is long and very distinguished. I just want to say thank you, again, for taking this on like it's personal to you."

"It is personal to me. National security should be personal to everyone. Nailing this gang and the hitman is just the cherry on top for Stephanie. It's long overdue."

He nodded, affirmatively. "Yes, it is. I appreciate the effort. Dānā spoke with his son, in Egypt about returning to the States. Once he's out of the partnership with Ashem, he's going to need a new partner to take on the business. He's ready to hand it off and wanted to offer it first to his son. I thought about Gabriel. I'll have to mention that to Dānā. I just have this feeling that the new job Gabriel's starting isn't going to work out."

"That's brilliant!"

"We'll see." He sucked a breath in through his nose and allowed his head to sink back into the cushion. "I liked watching you hold your ground in the conference room on Monday. Those two aren't used to someone being so forceful with them. Most people concede to whatever the NYPD or the Commissioner wants. I was never good at telling him to buzz off when I was married to Stephanie. She wasn't either. I had the same issue with my mother." He laughed, "I still do. She has the ability to frustrate and belittle me like no one else. I love her, but I cannot stand to be in the same room with her for any length of time."

"That bad, huh?" Charlotte drained the glass, stretching over him to sit it on the end table next to the lamp. The bourbon and the day had her feeling a bit odd. She settled next to him on the sofa, laying her head against him. Only a moment later his arm came down around her, pulling her closer.

"My mother is a bully, a perfectionist, and a snob. My sister, on the other hand, Jane, is charming. She's the refreshing antidote to the vacuum my mother creates in any room. We're going to watch the parade together. Why don't you ask Racheal and Gabriel to join us all for the parade? And you can spend the rest of the day here and have dinner with us."

"I think having everyone together for the parade will be fun. I'm looking forward to meeting Jane and the boys. Dinner is a family thing. I feel like I'd be intruding on your holiday."

He inhaled fully before answering in a low voice. He knew she could hear him because she had not removed her hearing aids for the night. "I want you there. Please. Besides, I'll need help cooking for everyone."

Her head tilted back in laughter against him. "I knew there was an ulterior motive." She burrowed in against him even more.

Ethan liked having her so close. It was unexpected and very welcome, but would be short lived.

"I can't get too comfortable or I'll fall asleep on you."

He let his head roll forward and rest on top of hers. "I don't mind if you do."

She felt the gentle rumble of laughter in his chest. "I do. Both of us will wake up contorted and sore. I have to go to bed soon. I'm supposed to be picked up at six-thirty and taken to Midtown Precinct South. Detective Togo is using it as the base of operations. The thirteenth precinct is backing us up. There'll be several unmarked vehicles near the Empire State Building. Everybody going in will be plainclothes. Color of the day is blue so I picked up a blue sweater today."

"Because I have yet to see you in anything blue, that's for sure. It's pink, pink and pink." The chuckle he issued shook his chest as she felt the laughter move through her as well. "I happen to like the fact that you mix up the pink with winter white, gray, black, and beige. You wear it well."

A yawn came out before she could stop it. "Thank you. I like you in gray, but I'm happy to see you wearing more color in your wardrobe. I'm sure all the women in the office have noticed, even if they haven't said anything yet."

"Nancy noticed, for sure."

"Nancy notices everything." Charlotte was certain of that.

He raised his head. "Yes, she does."

They sat in companionable silence for a while, just enjoying each other's close presence. He had missed her the last day and a half. He only hoped she had missed him too. Ethan coughed at ten minutes until ten o'clock, rousting them both.

"Sorry for startling you." He felt her pull away to sit up.

"I was almost asleep." She stood and held her hand out to him.

He grasped it and also stood up. "Me too. I'll get up with you in the morning and make some coffee."

They stood there, looking at each other, with Ethan still holding her hand.

"I'd like that, if you don't mind."

"Why would I mind? I'm worried actually. What time are you getting up?"

"Five-thirty. It'll take me half an hour to get ready. Don't get up until six. And don't worry. I'll be fine. For all this posturing and planning, we'll be in and out in no time. Everyone is being very cautious. That's all."

"As well they should be. You're precious cargo, taking a big risk going in there to stay ahead of this. Don't think I don't appreciate what you're doing for a minute."

He leaned forward and kissed her cheek.

"I'm glad I can help. I'll be fine." She blushed and pulled her hand away. As she reached the interior double doors she paused, looking back into his eyes." Good night, Mr. Cooper."

"Good night, Ms. Rose." He picked up their bourbon glasses and sat them in the sink. He'd wash them in the morning.

Morning had come all too quickly. Ethan rolled over and turned off the alarm on his phone. Ten minutes to six; time to make some coffee. He donned his glasses and fumbled around for the robe on the foot of the bed upon getting up.

Charlotte knocked gently on the doors a few moments later. He was standing in his robe at the kitchen island, sipping coffee and reading the paper.

"Come on in, Charlotte."

The handle turned and in she came, wearing beige slacks and a navy blue cashmere sweater with a pink and blue striped collared shirt underneath. Perhaps it was the layer beneath the sweater that didn't flex the same, but something was off. He poured her a cup full of coffee from the French press and sat it near his, hoping she'd come close to him this morning. The ploy worked.

She walked right up to him to get the cup. "Good morning! Thank you for making coffee and getting up with me."

He turned toward her grasping his own cup, continuing to study her. She was very close to him indeed. Her scent and proximity were doing a number on him. *Get your mind back where it should be, Cooper.* "Good morning. I like the blue. It's different. Off course you managed to get some pink in there with the collared shirt. Nice. I like the cuffs peeking out at the wrists too. Something is odd though. Forgive me for asking this, but what do you have underneath that makes you seem...stiff?"

Charlotte snorted into her coffee trying her best not to spill the hot beverage on herself or the floor. She sat the coffee cup down. Holding his gaze, the collar was pulled apart and down slightly, baring the top of something black. He rose up on the balls of his feet and forward a few inches toward her to see better. Beside her right collar bone was a strap. She raised an eyebrow at him as he dropped back down on his heels, away from her. He obviously didn't know what he was looking at.

"Forget diamonds. Kevlar is a girl's best friend. The Navy's best covert operative taught me that."

"Kevlar, huh?" He swallowed as worry ratcheted up even more. If she carried Kevlar in her suitcase, and usually a concealed pistol, what exactly did her job entail? "Promise me you'll take every precaution. I couldn't bear the thought of something happening to you." He stepped even closer, taking her face into his hands. "Please, Charlotte."

Her mouth opened to answer, instead it just hung open. He obviously felt something very deep for her. She was falling for him too, but his hands on her face and the pleading in his voice made her heart skip a beat. Her voice broke as she answered finally. "I promise. I'll get this wrapped up and meet you at the office for a late breakfast."

"I'm holding you to that because I'm going to be a nervous wreck until then. Please be careful." Abject honesty. Acting like this was probably going to send her running back to North Carolina. *Too clingy, too fast.*

She put her hands on top of his, pulling them from her face. "I'll be fine. I'm just visiting an office building. That's all. We need those files." *Should I hug him right now? Will he think that's weird? Who cares!* Charlotte let his hands go and wrapped her arms around his torso, burying her face into his robe. It was soft against her cheek and smelled of him. She could stay here all day.

The video monitor portion of the phone sitting on the kitchen island buzzed and came to life. It was Adam from the front desk of the building. The NYPD was early. "Mr. Cooper? I'm sorry to disturb you, but a car from the NYPD is here for Ms. Rose. I couldn't raise her on the intercom phone in her suite."

They broke apart.

"It's fine, Adam. I'll send her down. Thank you." He walked her to the door and waited. She had to put on her coat, hat, and gloves. It was blowing snow outside. "Call me, as soon as you're finished, okay?"

"I will. See you in a few hours."

Togo cleared his throat and spoke into the com link. "It's ten minutes to eight. Dānā is in the building. Let's roll. Everybody stay on alert, keep us informed if we have any un-friendlies approaching."

Detective Togo, two male TARU techs in their early thirties, and Charlotte exited a black SUV to approach the Empire State Building for entry. So that no one would be flashing badges, security on the ground floor were already expecting them under alias names, cleared for entry to the accounting and wealth management firm. The techs carried laptop bags, but neither contained a laptop. Each held small cameras, tiny listening devices, and hardware necessary to infiltrate video feeds and tap into the phone system. All of these items would piggy back off of wifi to give them access to daily operations at the firm. Charlotte was tasked to get hands-on with the servers and Ashem's laptop, which Dānā had confirmed half an hour ago was in the building. The keystroke logger TARU had set Dānā up with on Monday afternoon had been doing it's job. Since plugged in, passwords had been gathered and sent back for Charlotte to use in the search for missing files.

The elevator ride up was the worst part, so far, for Charlotte. She could hear her heart beating in her ears. One of her hearing aids was missing, replaced with an earwig to keep her in-touch with the team. Now wasn't the time for a panic attack. *Deep breathing, yeah. That's it*, she thought. Sweat was starting to form on her upper lip. *Was the elevator car getting smaller?* She hadn't been on a covert op since Benjamin died. The anxiety and post-traumatic stress hadn't allowed her to function in that capacity. Captain Blaine had insisted she let some time pass before they reevaluate her for ops. Why had she agreed to this? Ethan. Ethan and finding out exactly what Ashem was doing in her country. She had to stop Ashem. Men like him were the reason she'd lost Benjamin. Flashes of his smile were coming at her mixed with Ethan's face. The motion of the two in her mind was causing nausea.

Togo could hear a pin drop when the doors opened. The place was completely devoid of noise or activity, but brightly lit. He turned to see Charlotte pale as a ghost. "You don't look so hot. What's going on?"

The techs made eye contact with her her and Togo, pausing at the front desk to the entry of the firm. Dānā was coming out to meet them, hearing the elevator close behind them.

Charlotte could feel herself sway on her heels. She wasn't feeling so great. "I think I should have eaten something before we came here." Laughter began to reverberate in her chest.

All four shared a strained chuckle.

She could do this. She had to. People were counting on her. Dānā made eye contact with her. Just as Charlotte had eased his panic on Monday, his touch on her hand suddenly snapped her back to the task at hand. He greeted her in Farsi. The foreign language to other's ears was soothing to her own. The nausea abated and the myopic squeeze on her vision cleared. For a moment she saw Benjamin's face in her mind, again. His voice was there also. What was he saying? Or was that Dānā?

"Such strength wrapped in a kind smile." Dānā held her hand for a moment. "You look like you could use some water."

"I think I could. Thank you." Charlotte walked forward with him, the rest of the team following behind her. "Let's get started."

"This way. I'll bring you something while you're working."

Dānā left Charlotte sitting behind Ashem's desk, fingers flying inside gloves, urgently using the seized passwords to navigate file trees on the servers. *What was that? Cloud storage! Bingo!* She sipped some water and nibbled a bagel with salmon Dānā had shared with her. It was from Russ and Daughters, a New York institution. The panic that had consumed her earlier was no where to be found now. The files had been located and were being copied via the internet to her own encrypted cloud storage and an external micro drive. The task was nearly complete.

Togo paced the hall between Dānā's office and Ashem's, on opposite ends of the hall from each other. Ashem's was closest to the lavatory. Suddenly his coffee overtook his nervousness. The tech's were finished doing their jobs, waiting in the lobby chairs. Charlotte was set, but still working. He walked away to relieve himself.

That's when a team voice came over the coms. "Head's up. Amadhi's car is heading south on Fifth, approaching Thirty-Fifth Street now."

That had Charlotte's attention, along with everyone else on the floor. The files were almost finished copying onto her drive. She couldn't pull the plug now. "I'm almost finished. I'm at ninety-two percent."

Togo exited the lavatory. "Finish it up, Ms. Rose." He stormed down the hall toward Dānā's office to inform him.

"I can't make it copy any faster, Detective. I'm not leaving it yet. No offense, but you look like a cop even in plainclothes. Take the techs and get out of here. I'll give this a few more minutes and head for Dānā's office. I'll leave with him." *Did she really just say that?*

"I can't just walk out of here and leave two civilians."

"Yes, you can. I'm at ninety-five percent. Go. We'll be fine." Her eyes watched the spinning icon on the upload link.

"This is against my better judgement."

"It's the best bad-idea we have right now. We'll be right behind you."

"Mr. Darbandi, be ready to go the minute she comes down that hall."

"I will." Dānā was trying to remain calm. Ashem wasn't supposed to come in today, then again, neither was he.

Another team member on the street spoke up. "Amadhi's exiting the car now and on foot. He's approaching the south entrance."

Togo was already sweating. "Let's go, now!"

"I'm almost there." Charlotte watched as the progress ticked closer, ninety-eight percent.

The techs stood by the recalled elevator waiting on Togo to join them.

"We're going up, Ms. Rose, to the observation deck. Get yourself and Darbandi on this elevator and meet us there. It'll be faster for us to come back down a few floors than up from the ground if there's a problem."

The elevator doors shut behind them and suddenly the office was quiet again.

"Yes, sir." Charlotte didn't like wearing latex gloves while working on a computer, but Amadhi could pull prints from the surface of the desk or the computer if he were to grow suspicious. TARU was going to wipe the video footage of their presence as well. *Oh come on, computer! Copy!*

The last one percent was taking it's dear sweet time to finish. Her heart skipped a beat when the elevator chimed. Ashem was about to step out of the doors. There she sat at his desk.

"What's your status, Ms. Rose?"

She began to whisper. "He's here. I'm about to shut the computer down. I can hear him down the hall speaking with Dānā in Farsi. Ashem's not surprised to see him. They're saying they're both workaholics. Dānā's telling him about a quick meeting with a potential new client, then he's leaving. Darbandi's doing fine. See you in a minute."

The files were finally copied. *WHEW!*

Counter intelligence jobs were something she relished along with the science in her arsenal, before the bomb when she lost Benjamin and their baby. She'd helped Captain Blaine and her Navy Intelligence team, ARES, out many times. Adrenaline was flowing readily. Yep, the old Charlotte was alive and well again. The panic attacks could take a back seat and never show their ugly presence again. Deep breaths came with perfect clarity of mind, her heartbeat was slowing down to normal. *Now to get Dānā and walk right out of here, no sweat. Yeah right!*

"You need to leave that office, now!" Togo's voice screeched loudly in her ear.

Charlotte shutdown the computer and closed the lid. She pulled off her heels and walked softly to the women's lavatory. They were still talking about business in Dānā's office. She put her heels back on while standing in front of the door. If Amadhi stepped into the hall she would appear to be coming from the lavatory and not his office. Pausing for a moment more, she pushed the door in, causing it to squeak. Her heels announced her presence, coming down the hall on the hard surface of the floor.

Ashem Amadhi made eye contact with her as she rounded the door frame. She patted her lower abdomen and exhaled. "Thank you for allowing me the use of your ladies room, Mr. Darbandi. I've had a bit too much coffee already. You must be Mr. Amadhi." Charlotte stepped forward toward a leather chair in front of Dānā's desk, closer to Amadhi. She'd placed her coat, scarf, gloves, and laptop bag there when she arrived. Doing so then had lended their plot credence now.

"I am." He was sizing her up as she stood before him. She was an impeccably dressed beautiful blonde, very tall, like himself. With her heels, she stood eye level with him.

Charlotte noted the hand stitching on his suit lapels when he removed his long wool overcoat and scarf. He dropped them over his left arm, and stretched out his other to shake hers.

"I'm Charlotte Cooper." The last name came out without thought. *Where on earth did that come from?* She'd hand Ethan a good laugh later when she relayed the tale. *Should I really admit that?*

The hand stitched, tailored wool suit, shiny Italian shoes, slicked-back dark hair, Rolex, pocket square, cuff links, and tie pin screamed money. He had to be appealing as a salesman for wealth management. She'd seen men like him all her life in sales. Ashem had sharp looks, but would leave a slime trail behind him if he didn't have two legs. The fancy dressing might help with some, but Charlotte could see the evil in his dark eyes, staring back at her. The measure of God in her was causing the demons in him to be very uncomfortable.

Ashem held her gaze. After a moment more, his eyes squinted slightly. He took a step back from her. "Nice to meet you, Ms. Cooper. I look forward to helping with your financial needs if we can be of service. What business are you engaged in?"

"Stationery. My printers are nearby and I'm checking in on several orders. I'm also looking for retail space for a new boutique. This trip certainly is all about business." She tipped her head. "Mr. Amadhi, Mr. Darbandi, thank you for fitting me in on such short notice. I apologize for imposing on you during the holiday."

Charlotte picked up her belongings and began to dress. "Gentleman, Happy Thanksgiving. I can see myself out."

"I'm always happy to accommodate you. I'm leaving myself. I'll walk you out. My wife won't be pleased with me if I linger after I've already promised her my time today. I'll see you next week, Ashem. Happy Thanksgiving."

Ashem returned their holiday greeting and walked down the hall to his office.

Dānā and Charlotte waited on the elevator.

"Are you doing anything special for Thanksgiving this year?" Charlotte wanted to keep the small talk going as long as Ashem could be listening.

"I think it will be a quiet meal for us as my son is still out of the country."

They stepped into the elevator car. As the doors closed in front of them a loud exhale came forth.

Charlotte triggered the com link. "We're on our way to the ground floor. We each told Amadhi we were leaving. See you in a few minutes at the car."

They had pulled it off.

Dānā grabbed her hand. "I feel like the elephant on my chest finally moved!"

She smiled so sweetly at him. "I know exactly how you feel."

"I like the new last name." He chuckled. He wondered exactly how close she was to Ethan.

Her eyes rolled. "Oh, please don't tell him! It just came out."

"Perhaps your heart knows something your head does not, yet." Dānā patted her hand before releasing it. "Love comes when we're not looking for it sometimes. Enjoy your holiday, Ms. Rose."

They stepped off the elevator, walked through the lobby area and parted ways into the crowded street a few moments later. Charlotte met up with Detective Togo at the parked SUV down the block. The techs departed in another SUV, passing them on the street as they hopped inside.

"You're remarkably calm for what just happened." Detective Togo observed her behavior.

"I'm sure it'll hit me later." She looked around the street. "Do you mind if we stop at a deli? I need something else to eat. When the adrenaline wears off I'll be starving. I'll buy you a bagel and a smear too if you want one."

He watched her fumble around in the laptop bag. She pulled out the ear wig and laid it on the console. "I hear much better with both ears." Charlotte smirked at him and inserted her other hearing aid from a hard case pulled out of the bag.

"Aren't you a little young to need that?"

"I have them for both ears. I lost most of my hearing range after a bomb exploded near me in Israel a couple of years ago."

"You really have seen some action then. You weren't lying to me." Togo wondered exactly how much she truly had seen.

"I'll save the rest of the story for another time, Detective."

9

Meet The Family

As the day wore on, the office became more quiet. Ethan had been walking around the firm telling everyone to enjoy their holiday and to go home. Perhaps the most surprised person was Nancy.

"And are you going to take your own advice, Mr. Cooper?"

"I am, indeed. Jane and the boys are here. I'm getting Charlotte, and we are leaving. See you Monday, Nancy. Enjoy your holiday. Oh, and be thinking about our Christmas list this year. I want to do something different for everyone at the firm. Have you thought of anything special you'd like?"

"If I can't drink it, eat it, or smoke it, don't give it to me. I don't want to dust it."

He chuckled, "That's the same thing you tell me every year. Although the only thing I've ever seen you smoke is a cigar over some brandy and that was years ago. Happy Thanksgiving, Nancy. Enjoy the time with Jimmy while he's visiting from San Francisco."

"I will. We stayed up last night, very late, talking. I've never seen a son so adamant about moving his widowed mother in with him. I keep telling him if his mother lives with him he's never going to get married. I gave up on grandchildren a long time ago. I don't think he'll ever marry. He's already married to being a surgeon."

"Are you leaving me for San Francisco, Nancy?"

"I was born on Long Island. I've lived my entire life here. Frank and I met on Brighton Beach. We had Jimmy here. I lost Frank here after fifty-two years of being married. This is home, harsh winters or not. New York is in my blood. I can't imagine living anywhere else."

"You know what's best for you. You've had my back for eighteen years. You're my girl Friday."

She smiled at him over her glasses, always perched on her nose. "I'll always be your girl, Mr. Cooper, even if I'm seventy-two. You take care of me like I'm your mother."

"And I always will. Now let's get the heck out of here."

Ethan observed Charlotte's work ethic, already back into the files she'd garnered. "Come back to the apartment with me. I want you to meet my sister and nephews, they just arrived."

"Alright. I'm just anxious to continue on these files and more of the emails that match them."

"They'll still be there after Thanksgiving, I promise. Step away from the laptop or I'll have Togo arrest you for obstruction of a holiday." He practically cackled with laughter.

"Okay." She reluctantly pushed the laptop away and closed the lid. The laptop bag was pulled up on the sofa to stow the machine away for transport.

Ethan stepped toward her, pulling her up from the comfortable perch. "And you'll go to dinner with us?"

She met his gaze, unsure of her place. "That's a family thing. I don't want to intrude on that."

"Nonsense. Please? They do need to meet Mrs. Cooper."

Yep, he was going to play that card.

"You're never going to let me live that down, are you? I told you, it just slipped out. I couldn't give Ashem my real name." She only considered his plea for a moment before conceding, feeling guilty about using his last name like that. His pleading eyes didn't help. Now he was adding a pouty lip to the mix. "I'll go. I'll need to change before dinner though."

"No, ma'am. Leave the sweater combo on. I like it. I'll need to change out of this suit, actually. I'm glad you ditched the Kevlar when you came back here to the office. You wearing that drove the point home just how much danger you put yourself in for me today. I won't forget that, ever. Let's get out of here, shall we?"

Jane and boys were settling in to the apartment. To their surprise, Ethan came strolling through the door before three in the afternoon accompanied by a tall, blonde woman, sitting grocery bags on the floor at their feet. Jane's eyes nearly popped out of her head.

197

"When you said you'd be here soon you really did mean that! Wow!" She hugged Ethan, then stepped back, trying not to trip on the bags.

Ethan grinned, "Jane, I'd like you to meet Charlotte Rose. Charlotte this is my sister, Jane. Where's what's his face?"

"Colin? Who knows where my wayward husband is! Boys? Come over here, please. Put the tablets down. You can play games later." She shook her head and grinned. "It's lovely to meet you, Charlotte."

"You as well."

The two boys bombarded their uncle with bear hugs. Then Charlotte and Ethan removed their coats and winter weather accessories.

Jane put her hands on the shoulders of the shorter child, after pulling them both out of the way, toward her. The boys resembled Ethan and Jane in coloring, blue eyes with light brown hair, and fair skin. "This is Nic." She moved her left hand higher to rest on the shoulder of the taller child. "This is Andy. We're celebrating his birthday tonight. He'll be thirteen on Friday, but we will be flying home that day."

"Nice to meet you both. Happy birthday, Andy. And how old are you, Nic?"

He smiled at her and bit his lip, acting a bit shy. "I'm eleven."

"I have two nephews just a bit older than you both. I'll bet you like video games as much as they do, right?"

They both nodded affirmatively and excitedly.

"So tell me what your favorite games are while we carry these bags to the kitchen, please."

As soon as the bags were plopped down, Ethan waved her over to the sofa with the boys. They were sharing their tablets with her the moment they sat down. Chatter began about the latest and greatest games they were playing. Jane listened, surprised that Charlotte knew exactly what they were talking about.

Ethan and Jane walked to the kitchen island. He grabbed the electric kettle and began filling it up.

Jane came around the island. "Making tea? I didn't bring any hot chocolate for the boys."

"I picked some up today. It's in one of those four bags. I made reservations for us to have dinner at the Napkin place earlier in the week."

Jane watched Charlotte's easy way with the boys as she put the groceries away. They were both engrossed in the game they were playing against each other. She was giving them advice on how to maneuver a helicopter for the win to Nic. "You mean Nancy made us reservations, right?"

Charlotte turned her head at Jane's question. "No, Ethan did. I overheard him calling myself."

Jane laughed, "Well wonders never cease! Charlotte, I hope you like burgers. The boys just loved Napkin the last time we were here and they wanted to go back."

Charlotte looked down at her outfit. "That's fine with me. I won't have to worry about what I'm wearing." She turned back around. "Don't let him get away, Nic. You've got the high ground with the helicopter. Get him!"

Jane smiled at Ethan. "Listen to her! I think the boys have a new friend."

The fresh turkey had been picked up, along with all the ingredients they'd need for the brine, along with raw ingredients for sides. All this was now stowed away and Ethan was pulling the top off the can of Redi-Whip. "Fix us some too, Janie."

"Are you feeling like a kid today? You're certainly smiling like one. And calling me Janie?" Jane spooned out gourmet hot chocolate mix into five mugs.

Something was blown up by the sound of victory coming from one tablet. Nic was delighted to have the win over his older brother. "Yes! That was so cool! How did you know that would work?"

Charlotte high-fived Nic. "I told you, I play games too with my nephews. Andy, you're going to have to improve your concealment or he's going to keep finding you." She looked over Andy's shoulder. "This isn't just a hide-and-blow them up game. Look right there. You've got sulfuric acid in that tank. Over on that shelf is sugar. Collect them both. You can use it later to your advantage."

"Don't tell me they can actually learn something from that game?" Jane let out a snort as she put the hot chocolate away into the pantry.

Both boys put their tablets down and exchanged sideways glances with each other as Charlotte sat between them on the sofa.

Andy looked confused. "I know what acids can do from science class. But I don't understand the sugar."

Charlotte licked her lips, jaw jutting out sideways. Maybe she shouldn't have said that. "You can use both together to create a reaction. If you're trapped inside of confined space, like that sewer you just hid inside of Andy, and needed to get out, the exothermic reaction could help push a heavy manhole cover off if you have enough of the ingredients. Keep collecting those items."

Jane sucked in a worried breath. Charlotte knew her games alright. Now she was telling her boys how to blow things up.

"Just don't use either of those ingredients together, for real, unless you have your mom or a teacher to help you. Deal?"

Both boys agreed. "Yes, ma'am."

Charlotte turned to see Jane and Ethan's slightly concerned faces. "I have two nephews. I know how boys are."

Andy put his tablet down on the ottoman in front of them. "Can we try that, for real?"

Charlotte stood up, turned around, and looked down at the expectant, eager faces before her. She saw the kettle just beginning to send steam up, not quite boiling yet. A change of subject was in order. "That depends. How about some hot chocolate first?"

"Alright!" Nic hopped right up, putting his tablet beside the other.

Charlotte was wearing a whipped cream mustache at the kitchen island ten minutes later, sitting on a stool between the boys, laughing and joking with them, whipped cream on their noses each time one would take a sip. It had become a game. The beverage was sipped slowly because of the temperature. Given the seriousness of the morning, the laughter shared with the boys was welcomed levity. Ethan had changed out of his suit and into different slacks, a button up shirt, and a sweater.

"Ms. Charlotte? Can you explain how the acid and the sugar work, please?" Andy was still thinking about the reaction.

She smirked at them and sat her mug down for a moment. After swallowing and licking the whipped cream off, again, she spoke. "Do you know the chemical composition of a sugar molecule, Andy?"

"We just started chemical reactions in science class."

"Nic, I realize Andy is at a different grade level than you, but this is really cool stuff that you'll use later."

"Science is cool." Nic's head bobbed a little with his answer. He was hugging the hot mug in his hands.

Charlotte reached for the notepad on the counter. "Can you hand me that pen, please, Ethan?" She drew a carbon chain of six atoms, complete with the bonds between the twelve hydrogen atoms, and six oxygen. "I'll bet you know the formula of water."

Nic exclaimed, "H 2 0!"

"That's correct. Very good, Nic." She continued to sketch, this time a molecule of sulfuric acid, pointing the pen toward the hydrogen and oxygen surrounding the carbon chain in the sugar. "Sulfuric acid has two hydrogen atoms, one sulfur, and four oxygen. These bonds on the outside of the carbon are holding...what did you just say, Nic?"

"Water!"

"Right. So when you combine sulfuric acid with the sugar, the acid pulls off the water on the sugar, or sucrose, and dehydrates the molecule. What is that called, Andy?" Charlotte waited for the his response.

"A chemical reaction."

"You're good!" Charlotte shared a smile with both boys. "You get heat, steam from the water being released, and sulfur oxide fumes. It looks like a black log that puffs up and comes shooting out of whatever container the sugar and acid are mixed in. It smells like caramel and a little like rotten eggs."

"Eww!" Nic recoiled.

"Yeah, eww." Her face scrunched up before she smiled at Jane.

"Can we try it, Uncle Ethan?" Andy practically whined.

Ethan looked apprehensive. "No whining."

"Please! We're celebrating my birthday." Andy waited for an answer.

Charlotte mouthed the words 'sorry' as she kept eye contact with Ethan for a moment.

"You're not going blow up my kitchen are you, Charlotte?"

"No, I promise. This'll be fun. We can all participate. We just need to turn on the fume hood and gather a few things."

Jane was assigned getting the drain cleaner from underneath the sink and told to find the rubber dish gloves. Ethan found a large glass marinara sauce jar he didn't mind parting with from the recycling bin in the pantry and a sheet pan that needed to be tossed anyway from years of use. He laid it in the middle of the large Wolf range, protecting the burners and directly underneath the running fume hood. The boys measured out a precise amount of sugar, with Charlotte's help, awaiting their next instructions which were to dampen the sugar with a bit of water, making it look like wet sand inside the jar.

"I'll be right back. I have to take out my contacts and get my glasses to protect my eyes." Charlotte took the gloves and drain cleaner from Jane upon returning, then wrapped the thick kitchen apron around herself. "Once Uncle Ethan puts the jar on top of the stove, I need everyone to back away from the range."

Ethan stood behind Nic, Jane behind Andy, their hands on the boy's shoulders keeping them at a safe distance to watch and prevent the boys from creeping too close.

"Here we go!" Charlotte used a long set of kitchen tongs to hold the drain cleaner over the jar. She poured the amount of liquid needed and stood back.

A large, black carbon snake erupted from the wide mouth jar, steam escaping with a hiss into the air, filling the kitchen area with a sweet smell and slight rotten egg odor for a moment until the fume hood could pull the vapors away.

"We're left with what's called elemental carbon in a type of elimination reaction."

Andy repeated the term out loud, "Elimination reaction. Science class is never like this!"

"That's sic!" Nic tilted his head sideways to look at the carbon snake, perfectly curved out of the jar and onto the sheet pan.

They cleaned up and were off to dinner a short time later.

"I don't remember the last time I've seen the boys so exuberant about learning something, unless it's music or a new game." Jane propped her feet up on the coffee table in the corporate suite. The boys were tucked in on the pullout sofa, but still chatting, before falling asleep, in Ethan's apartment. The chance to put her feet up, sip some excellent bourbon, spend time with her brother, and relax was welcomed. This new woman in his life was having a profound effect on Ethan. Jane noticed him smiling all throughout dinner at Charlotte. Ethan never came home before three in the afternoon, not even on a holiday. He was more relaxed. Jane liked seeing him enjoy himself again. He conversed actively with the boys more than their father did at a meal. They usually called Uncle Ethan when they had an issue, rather than wait to see if Colin might come home that night. When was the last time they'd all had a meal together with their father?

Jane exhaled loudly and looked at Ethan on the other end of the sofa. Charlotte sat in a chair, facing them. All had their hands on a night cap of bourbon.

"Did you hear Nic, during dinner? He said he wanted to be a scientist three times." Ethan sipped from his glass. "I'm sorry they kept asking you questions, Charlotte, while we were eating. You're officially the coolest person they know." Both boys obviously liked having Charlotte around as much he did.

"I didn't mind in the slightest, Ethan. I cannot recall the last time I enjoyed eating a burger that much. Seeing their faces when we were in the kitchen earlier was positively priceless. Listening to them relive that experience again and again while taking bites and talking is precious to me." A look of melancholy came over her face for just a moment. She sighed.

Jane noticed, but wasn't about to ask if the answer wasn't offered.

"I can't have children, so it's the next best thing." Charlotte wouldn't sour the evening with the pain of her history. She'd made peace with it. Tonight there was delight in sharing her talents with Nic and Andy. Her face brightened again, she could see in her mind the joy in their faces when the carbon snake had come shooting out of the glass jar. "That moment when science becomes real to a child ignites their imagination and the possibilities become endless."

"My boys don't take up with anyone so quickly. They didn't leave your side, after dinner, when we walked along the parade route looking at the balloons being unrolled for tomorrow. I wasn't sure what to think when I met you this afternoon. Half an hour after making your acquaintance, I felt like like a mad scientist. You're great with my boys. Thank you, so much, for talking to them and listening to them. You made them feel very special, Charlotte." Jane had tears welling up in her eyes. No, she wasn't going to cry over the fact that Colin ignored his children. Being Mom and Dad was tough. Having Ethan around them more would be terrific, and Charlotte, too. *What were the odds of that happening if she wasn't willing to move to NYC? Fat chance.*

Charlotte swallowed her bourbon. "I didn't do anything that out of the ordinary, but you're welcome. They're great boys. They're very intelligent. Being around them is easy, just like spending time with my nephews is, every summer, when they stay with me."

"How old are they?" Jane shifted on the sofa, her feet were starting to tingle.

"Tyler is fifteen and Lee is seventeen. Their Dad is my younger brother, William. The whole family is moving back east, from Kitsap, near Seattle. He's taking the lead in our family's defense business back at our headquarters, in Franklin, North Carolina. William's been handling operations at Naval Base Kitsap since two thousand four."

"What does he do for the Navy in Seattle?" Jane was curious now about Charlotte and her brother.

"William keeps in close contact with the Navy brass on base for any needs they anticipate. If the Navy doesn't have the time to handle a repair themselves, or doesn't want to, William calls me in, if I'm available, or another engineer is flown in to help. Kitsap is the

Navy's largest fuel depot and the only dry dock capable of accommodating a Nimitz class aircraft carrier on that side of the Pacific for repairs. If a nuclear sub or an aircraft carrier needs help, and they call, we go. We serve all branches of the military, but the Navy is our largest client and top priority."

Jane and Ethan's mouths were relaxed and slightly open. Ethan had a fairly good idea of what Charlotte could do from reading her bio on the website. There was nothing like watching her the last couple of weeks, in action, and listening to her own words. Jane shared the same look with her brother, one of awe, complete with raised eyebrows.

"Not that my brother isn't brilliant, sorry Ethan, but what are you doing hanging around with him?"

"Oh, gee, thanks, Jane." A chuckle left his lips, but Jane was correct. Ethan's Harvard education prepared him for many things, but not Charlotte Rose. Put him up against a corporate tycoon and he could back them into a corner. But Charlotte, she was a different kind of genius, a working class (occasionally riddled with anxiety) hero in heels, armed with brains. And he found that sexy as hell.

"I was here visiting Ethan's partner, Racheal Maxwell-Rodriguez. She uses her maiden name though professionally. We met at Vanderbilt. She wanted to catch up before the holidays and get me to design new stationery for her at the firm. While I've been here, some thing occurred that garnered my attention for further scrutiny instead. Ethan brought me on as a consultant and here I am, until further notice." Charlotte smiled at Ethan, holding his gaze a little too long.

Jane returned her smile. She had seen the long glances between them all evening, how they stood near each other (when the boys were commanding Charlotte's attention), and the way Ethan took her coat at the restaurant and again when they returned home. The question was, did they know they were completely smitten with each other yet?

Ethan stood up from his end of the sofa with an empty glass. "I'm going to get just a tad more of this. Anyone else?"

"I'll take a little more." Jane held her glass up.

Charlotte yawned, covering her mouth with her hand. It was barely nine o'clock and she was exhausted from the day. "No, I think I'm going to turn in. See you both, bright and early, so we can walk to Central Park West before six thirty for the parade. Good night."

"Leave the glass, Charlotte. I'll pick it up when we turn in. Sleep well." He smiled warmly at her. When he returned a moment later with refilled glasses, the questions began as expected.

Jane lowered her voice to barely a whisper and scooted down the sofa toward her brother. "Who exactly is that woman? Stationery? Really? Is that code for something else?"

Ethan's body shook with stifled laughter. "Don't hold back on my part. You can speak normally, Jane."

"She's right through that door and I know she's not asleep yet." She continued to whisper.

"Charlotte can't hear you. Once she takes her hearing aids out for the night, unless you're speaking directly in her ear, loudly, she can't hear you."

Jane sat up straight with a look of curiosity on her face. "Okay, Ethan. Spill it. All of it, because I know she's not staying here, in your suite, with the doors wide open between, over stationery."

Her gaze leveled him. Ethan had a lot of explaining to do. His forty year old baby sister did have two boys and she could grill someone like a seasoned interrogator.

"Let me back up. I've known Racheal just about as long as I knew Stephanie. Rae always referred to her college friend Charlie. Well turns out, Charlie is Charlotte. She's responsible for the bourbon in your hand from last Christmas. Racheal had her pick it up as my gift. When Charlotte arrived, I had no idea who she was. I met her across from the building on a break at The Boxwood."

"But how did she end up here?" Jane just didn't understand.

"Have patience, Jane. I'll get to that, after I tell you a funny story about bacon. Because of Charlotte, the NYPD is closer to catching Stephanie's killer. That's why she's staying here."

Jane gripped the glass a little tighter, eyes now bulging with surprise, listening with rapt attention. Her lips drew up in silence.

Ethan could see this was going to take some time to explain it all and he didn't have all night if he wanted some sleep.

10

Of Parades and Turkeys

The boys were quiet in the elevator, barely awake at six thirty in the morning on Thanksgiving Day, despite their excitement over the parade. Who were they kidding? Jane, Ethan, and Charlotte were barely awake themselves. The elevator only dropped one floor when the doors opened to Ethan's neighbor, Mrs. Holiday and her dog, Sugar, waiting.

Nic immediately knelt down. Sugar, so excited by the prospect of attention from the boy, pulled the leash out of Mrs. Holiday's hand. The dog rushed forward with his new freedom, standing on his hind legs while receiving affection. The creamy white bundle of energy was enjoying this.

"Sugar!" Mrs. Holiday tried to recall her dog. He hadn't behaved this way since he was a puppy. That was five years ago, when Ethan and his then wife were moving into the building.

Ethan put his hand up and caught the doors as they began to close. "Come on down with us, Mrs. Holiday."

Uncertain, she cleared her throat. *Well, why not ride down with them?* Sugar was an excellent judge of character, giving her the cues she needed of whether to pass by or steer clear when they were walking. Sugar seemed to approve of this lot wholeheartedly. "Alright, if you don't mind." She stepped in, everyone shifting to make room. "He's usually very well behaved and doesn't pull away from me."

The doors closed.

"Sugar couldn't resist the thought of not being petted by my nephew, Nic." Ethan gathered the looped end of the leather leash and handed it back to her. "It's been a while, but you remember my sister, Jane, and her boys, Nic and Andy?"

Jane held out her hand to gently shake the hand of the woman sporting the fanciest fur coat she'd ever seen, complete with a hat. "Nice to see you again, Mrs. Holiday. Your coat and hat are quite lovely, and very warm, I'm certain."

"Thank you. They are indeed. My late husband, Harold, gave them to me for an anniversary gift many years ago." The two boys had grown considerably since the last time she'd seen them. A look of sadness came over her face when mentioning Harold. Her eyes dropped.

Ethan and Charlotte didn't miss the look. They knew it well, loss. Ethan took Charlotte's hand and squeezed it through their gloves.

"Boys, say hello." Jane turned to Andy, also busy on his knees with Sugar, scratching behind one ear while Nic scratched his belly, as the dog had rolled onto his back.

"Hello!" Andy stood, along with Nic. Sugar immediately began to whine from the loss of attention.

Mrs. Holiday gave Sugar a pointed look. He ceased whining.

"Good morning. I'm Charlotte. We met on Tuesday, as you were coming in from an early walk. I was leaving."

She smiled, "Yes, you had on a beautiful wool beret." Mrs. Holiday was curious. "Where are you all headed, bundled up, this time of the day?"

Jane answered, "We're walking over to Central Park West, to watch the parade from the Olmsted Hotel."

"I see." Mrs. Holiday looked at the happy smiles on Nic and Andy's sleepy faces. "Enjoy the parade. It's been years since I've watched from the sidewalk. My granddaughter, Sterling, was nearly a teenager." She chuckled, "I'm dating myself."

The adults shared a laugh. The elevator doors opened to the lobby, the group spilling out of the car and onto the marble floor, all moving toward the front entrance.

Nic patted Sugar's head one last time before they parted, outside. They were headed one way, Mrs. Holiday the other. "Happy Thanksgiving, Mrs. Holiday."

"Thank you. And to you, Nic." She pulled the leash slightly. The tug on the leash didn't faze the dog. He wanted to go to with Nic. "Come along, Sugar."

"Why don't you come and watch with us? We're getting break-fast along the way and my Uncle's friend, Jared, owns the hotel. They allow dogs."

Mrs. Holiday smiled at him. "Yes, they do, and I appreciate the gesture. Sugar and I need to take our walk and get back inside. Enjoy the parade." She hesitated to voice what she was now think-ing. "When you come back, if your mother agrees, come and see Sugar for a visit."

Nic would have to settle for that. "Yes, ma'am."

Manners. How unusual nowadays, but refreshing, she thought. *Then again, they are southern.*

The group turned to part ways. They were almost to the cross-walk when Sugar came crashing into Nic's feet. They turned to see a horrified Mrs. Holiday walking as fast as she could toward them, her coat swaying with each step.

"SUGAR! STOP!" *What would I do if Sugar ran out into traffic?* Her heart settled when he came to a halt beside Nic. She put her glove covered right hand to her chest. Her eighty-two year old body didn't need this excitement so early. It wasn't even daylight yet. She might have her notion as to how the day would proceed, but clearly Sugar had another.

Nic picked him up and handed him back to his owner. "I'm sorry he pulled away from you, Mrs. Holiday."

"I'm just happy he ran toward you and not out into traffic. I don't know what's gotten into him this morning." She looked down at Sugar's happy face in her arms. "You can't go with them. You need your walk."

Ethan found the end of the leash again, lying on the sidewalk. He secured it in her hand once more. "We'll go back inside for a few minutes so you can make a clean getaway with him this time. Once you're down the sidewalk, we can come back out."

"Thank you. I'm sorry for the trouble." Mrs. Holiday was grateful.

"No trouble. And if you're free, about six tonight, come upstairs for dinner with us."

She froze for a moment, staring at him. Her mouth opened to politely decline the invitation, but the words came out before she could rescind them. "Only if I can bring something." *Did she just agree to dinner with strangers? Well, they weren't totally strangers.* It would be wonderful to spend the holiday with someone, even if she barely knew them. She missed Harold terribly, and Sterling hadn't been home for Thanksgiving in years, much less Christmas.

Ethan was pleasantly surprised at the immediate response. "Alright. That would be wonderful." He caught the big smile gracing Charlotte's face as Mrs. Holiday conceded, even offering to contribute.

"Harold used to love my sweet potato casserole. I use chopped pecans on top, not marshmallows."

"That sounds delicious! I'm sure I'll want the recipe." Jane piped up. She was getting hungry just thinking about that.

"See you at six then?" Charlotte smiled at Mrs. Holiday.

"Yes, see you all then." Mrs. Holiday wouldn't be alone this year after all.

At nearly five-thirty, the scent of the cooking turkey was enveloping the entire apartment, swirling about mixed with the heavy aroma of sage, thyme, and rosemary, hanging in the air. The boys were discussing their upcoming music recitals as silverware was correctly placed on the dining table for each setting, complete with a linen napkin. Jane, sporting a Thanksgiving themed Williams-Sonoma apron, was overseeing their tasks from her perch behind the sink as head dishwasher for the day. She left the cooking to the pros, her brother and his tall, very elegant girlfriend. And she was his girlfriend, Jane didn't care whether he'd admit it to her or not. Charlotte's height matched Ethan's perfectly. Jane felt short at only five-four standing anywhere near the woman. Jane hadn't inherited the tall gene, as her brother and boys had. Nic and Andy were already taller than she was.

Charlotte used a basting brush to deftly grace the tops of risen yeast rolls, bathing them in golden melted butter. Ethan pulled the cornbread dressing from the oven, walking to the table with the hot casserole dish between his oven-mitts to leave it on a waiting trivet. He reminded the boys not to touch the hot dish as they decorated the table with little pumpkins, purchased on the way back from the parade, tucking them in between varying sizes of low cream-colored pillar candles, cranberries and nuts, all scattered down the center of a linen runner. Jane's hand could be seen quite easily in the beautiful table decorations, now set for their meal. Nic and Andy had spent part of the afternoon with Mrs. Holiday, entertaining Sugar and unbeknownst to their mother, listening to Mrs. Holiday speak about her late husband's music. As Charlotte finished buttering the rolls, Ethan pulled the sheet pan from the island and quickly opened the right half of the oven doors. He peeked into the left side, impatiently waiting. The bird was golden brown, and now the probe was registering the correct temperature. The thermometer attached to the probe, timing the whole process, began to buzz. He slid the switch over, turning it off.

"Stand back!" Ethan threw the door completely open, dry heat flooding the immediate area around the oven. The twelve-pound bird's All Clad roasting pan was placed on a cork trivet, beside the range, then covered with aluminum foil, where it would rest until carving time.

Jane's nose turned up into the air as a fresh wave of the turkey's aroma now encapsulated her. "Good grief, that smells wonderful! So does the dressing. If she's not early, we may just have to eat without her."

A low chuckle left Ethan's lips. "You're as bad the boys, Jane! Mrs. Holiday will be here, I think."

"She sure was surprised you invited her." Jane smiled at him as she licked the spoon from transferring Israeli salad into a serving bowl before plunging the utensil into the hot dishwater. Ethan chuckled at her antics. "What? I'm hungry."

Ethan sighed, "We've had minimal interaction since I moved in here." The next words came out without thought. "I work too much to get to know anyone really and I'm never at home." He grew quiet as the full weight of that statement settled over him. His left hand came up, covering his mouth. He couldn't take the words back. As much as they were true, hearing them made it so much worse to process. Life had been passing him by for the last five years, actually longer than that.

Charlotte stepped toward him, letting her right hand rest on his right forearm. She gently squeezed his arm and let go, acknowledging his admittance and silently supporting him. Her eyes met his before she turned to pick up the bowl of Israeli salad Jane had just finished filling over to the table.

Ethan let his hand fall away from his face, and turned to pull a pitcher of sweet iced tea from the fridge. Jane had made it earlier while the boys were gone, after they had all taken a little nap to recover from the early morning. She couldn't cook a decent turkey to save her life, but sweet tea she could handle.

Jane noticed the interaction between them. "You seem to be finding some balance, Ethan. The boys and I haven't had this much uninterrupted quality time with you in a long time. Since before..." Her voice trailed off. Everyone knew what she meant, since before Stephanie was killed.

The lighthearted day had suddenly turned very serious.

Nic and Andy had grown quiet, both listening to the adult conversation. They both stepped over into the kitchen area. Andy grabbed a towel and a bowl from the drying rack, wiping it down to put away. Nic took the pitcher from his Uncle's hands and sat it down on the island.

"I'm glad we're spending Thanksgiving with you, Uncle Ethan." He hugged him tightly as Ethan embraced him as well. The emotion of the moment quickly changed. "We finally get to eat a really good Thanksgiving meal again!"

Everyone shared a good laugh. It was levity they all needed in that moment. The door chime rang.

Nic let go of his Uncle and sprinted for the door. "I'll get it!"

Mrs. Holiday was followed in by the evening watch, Adam, carrying a covered casserole dish. They greeted everyone upon entry. She found herself looking at all the food, some on the table, some on the kitchen island resting on trivets.

Charlotte showed Adam where to sit the hot dish, wrapped snuggly in a quilted, handled carrying case. "Nice to see you again, Adam. Happy Thanksgiving! Tell me what you like to eat and I'll bring you down a plate."

"Oh, you don't have to do that, ma'am." He removed the case and handed it to her.

"I know I don't, but tell me anyway." She smiled at him.

"I never met a food I didn't like and this all looks wonderful." He was eyeing the cornbread dressing.

"One of everything then. Got it!" The scent of browning rolls in the oven caught her attention. "I think it's time to pull the rolls out. Excuse me." She walked back into the kitchen. "Boys, would you like to help me make the gravy? Wash your hands, please."

Nic and Andy picked the meat off the turkey neck earlier. It sat in a bowl, covered with a damp towel along with the turkey liver she'd chopped up and added. A large liquid measuring cup sat nearby with chicken broth, and half and half was taken out of the refrigerator along with butter. Ethan pulled the roasting rack out the pan and placed the turkey on a platter. The pan had broth left in the bottom. Charlotte had Andy turn the pan on end, pouring the contents through a strainer she held and into the liquid measuring cup, now completely full. Nic was assigned getting four tablespoons of all purpose flour into a small bowl. Salt and pepper were already beside the range. Giblet gravy was on the way.

Jane tied a towel around the iced tea pitcher before sitting it on the table. She was amazed at all the ways Charlotte included the boys. Ethan was placing the rolls into a towel lined basket, near Mrs. Holiday at the kitchen island. The potatoes had just been mashed, peeled earlier by Andy, Nic and Charlotte. Jane realized Andy could be trusted with a pairing knife because he already knew how to use one. Nic was now a pro at wielding a vegetable peeler. The entertainment was now at the range as Nic and Andy framed Charlotte around the roasting pan, and everybody was watching.

"Cooking is simply delicious science. Gravy is about ratios. You need the same ratio of fat as you do flour." She cut off four tablespoons of butter into the roasting pan, then grabbing a whisk out of the utensil caddy beside them, handed it to Andy. "Use the whisk to move the butter around and help it melt. Alright, Nic. It's melted, add the flour." He turned the bowl into the pan, dashed to the sink behind them with the bowl, returning, eager to continue. Charlotte placed her hand over his right and took a good pinch of salt from the olive wood vault, adding that to the pan, then pepper. "Keep stirring, Andy. We want to cook out that flour taste. Do you see how the flour is absorbing all that butter?" Both boys nodded. "We want it to get a little brown. We don't want the flour to get too dark, but we don't want gravy that tastes like flour." She reached for the half-and-half, unscrewing the lid, and handed that to Nic. "Keep stirring, Andy. Here we go with the liquid, Nic." Charlotte picked up the large liquid measure, carefully pouring in the amber broth. "Liquid gold into our gravy. Stir, stir, stir, Andy! Get up all those good brown bits in the bottom of the roasting pan. They're called fond." Both repeated the word back to her as she poured in more liquid. "Okay, Nic. Pour in yours." Charlotte figured from the weight of the carton there was about a cup or so left after mashing the potatoes. Perfect for their gravy. "Keep stirring. Is your arm getting tired?"

"No, I'm fine." Andy's grin matched Nic's.

Charlotte was waiting for the moment when the gravy began to thicken. "It's time to add the giblets, Nic." He dumped the giblets into the pan, then placed the bowl in the sink.

"I want to stir!" Nic was watching all the giblets mix in as his brother switched hands, continuing.

"Let Andy keep going. You can get three tasting spoons and we'll check our seasoning." Charlotte kept an eye on the pan.

Nic grabbed spoons from the utensil drawer and was right beside her again.

The gravy was getting to the correct consistency. "Let's pull the pan from the heat. It will continue to thicken as it cools." She hefted the pan over onto the nearby cool burners, then pulled a spoon through for each of them. "Hold your hand under and step back from the range. Blow on it! It's hot." She watched them, cooled her own spoonful, and tasted it. "Needs more pepper? What do you think?"

They agreed, depositing their spoons in the sink. She used the whisk, resting in the corner where Andy had left it, to stir in a pinch more. After a clean spoon made it in for another taste, Nic pronounced it ready. Jane handed him the gravy boat from where it rested on the island. She mouthed the words 'thank you' to Charlotte who winked at Jane in return. Nic sat the dish beside the roasting pan. Andy had pulled a ladle out of the utensil caddy, then carefully ladled gravy into the boat. He even let Nic have a turn, reminding him to be slow because the gravy was very hot.

At five fifty-five, they all sat down around the table, holding hands. Ethan asked a special blessing over the bountiful table and their guest.

"I'll have to admit, I was expecting a catered meal not a freshly cooked feast. That was marvelous! Thank you for inviting me." Mrs. Holiday was on her third glass of tea, the second, post meal.

No one was in a hurry to do anything, lethargically full from the meal.

Ethan relaxed in his dining chair allowing his elbows onto the table. "You're welcome. I'm happy you joined us. That casserole was my dessert. I'm sorry, Charlotte, your pie will have to wait."

Charlotte smiled at him, echoing his relaxed posture. Their elbows were touching, arms folded, allowing her right fingers to barely touch his. "I know how you feel. I'm stuffed, too."

"I'd like the recipe for your stuffing or dressing, whatever you call it." Mrs. Holiday was still lingering over a few bites of her casserole.

Ethan looked across the table to Jane, to share a memory. "The housekeeper that raised us, in Charleston, Ms. Icey, always said if you put it in a bird it was stuffing. If you had it in a casserole dish, it was dressing. She never put it in a bird because she thought it harbored bacteria and didn't cook properly. So we always had dressing."

"I never really learned to cook from her like Ethan did. I was always happy to eat and then help with the dishes." Jane laughed quietly. "I've watched my brother and Charlotte today. Neither one of them uses a recipe. And I'll have to say, I can't argue with the results. It was delicious!"

"Practice." Ethan and Charlotte said the word at the same time, smiling at each other.

"I've never seen that cucumber salad on a Thanksgiving table before. It was a wonderful departure." Mrs. Holiday liked the crunch of the vegetables and the bright seasoning.

Charlotte's smile softened. She looked at the nearby empty bowl near her. "It's called Israeli salad. That taste comes from lemon juice and a spice blend called za'atar. The sumac gives it a hard to define brightness. Before I lost Benjamin, we ate that salad at every meal practically. I made it today so I'd have a little bit of him with me. I've gradually been making less and less typical Israeli food since he died." She exhaled. She was getting teary over salad and the memory of Benjamin eating it constantly.

Ethan's fingers blatantly intertwined with hers, with everyone at the table able to see. He didn't care. "And you're eating bacon again." He tried to make her smile.

"Yes, I am." She did smile at him. "I'm sorry. The holidays are difficult for me."

"No apologies at this table over lost spouses." He squeezed her fingers. "Stephanie liked cornbread dressing. That's why I fix it. I grew up with just plain bread and saltines in ours. But she preferred cornbread because it's what she grew up with. I think of her every time I make it." Ethan turned his head toward their guest. "Just like Mrs. Holiday thinks of her husband when she makes sweet potato casserole. It's only been two years, Charlotte. Give yourself some grace. Grieving over a spouse changes us. You eat differently. Your circle of friends changes. Your work habits change. Your sleep patterns, your hobbies, interests, wardrobe. You get handed a life you didn't ask for and make the best of it, one day at a time. You have to figure out how to be just you again, without them."

Jane stared down the table at Mrs. Holiday.

"I know that look, Jane. Divorce is another kind of death, only the survivors have to walk amongst the living." Mrs. Holiday waited on her to say something.

"You're right. I just haven't figured out how I'm going to untangle myself and them."

Andy put his fork down. "You don't have to worry about us, Mama. We just want you to be happy again."

Nic nodded, chewing a bite of casserole. He swallowed, "Dad is never around anyway. And when he is, he's always angry. I don't like that. It upsets you. So I say we move up here. You've been happy here. I like it here."

Jane reached over and took her youngest son's hand. "Oh, honey. If it were only that simple."

"I don't understand why it can't be." Andy got up from the table and disappeared into the guest room, where his mother was staying while there.

Jane got up to go after him.

"Stay. I've got this one." Ethan stood, taking his time to check on Andy.

"Andy?" Ethan waited at the open door, looking at his nephew, sitting on the floor at the foot of the bed.

He looked up at his uncle and motioned him over. "Shut the door please." He waited for Ethan to sit beside him. "I don't want Dad to come back. The last time he was home I heard them fighting. It was really late. I only heard them because my room's closer than Nic's. They kept getting louder and louder. I heard him hit her, more than once. I'm pretty sure the thud I heard was Mom hitting the floor finally. Then it...got quiet. Dad left. I knocked on the door of their bedroom, Mom opened it. Her lip was cut and puffed up. We didn't go to church that week. She wore big dark glasses for days to hide the bruise on her cheek."

Ethan sucked in a breath, trying desperately to maintain his composure and not let the anger he was feeling overtake him. The attorney in him hoped he was pulling off his best poker face. "Has this happened before?"

Andy quickly nodded affirmatively.

Nic opened the door and came in, standing near them. "You told him, didn't you?"

"I had to, Nic." Andy wore a look of fear.

"But Mama asked us not to say anything." Nic sat down in front of his brother. "She said to let her handle it."

"But she's not handling it and I don't want Dad coming back to hurt her again. You have to talk to her, Uncle E. We could move here and get away from him." Andy looked hopeful at that statement.

"You have too many music lessons and recitals that you're committed to. Your teachers are there, you're both in a great music school there, your friends are there. You don't want to live here and sleep on my sofa." He smiled at them both. "I know it's not THAT comfortable." Both the boys had legitimate concern for their mother's safety. "I'll talk to your mom, after Mrs. Holiday leaves. And Andy, thank you for telling me. I know that took a lot of guts to admit that."

Andy only nodded his head again, agreeing.

Ethan had to do something to get them back out into the main room and their minds off of the present conversation. "Speaking of music. Don't you have a big Christmas recital coming up soon at your school?"

Nic smiled, his eyes growing wide. "Yes, we do. I'm playing a piece with Andy. We usually never play anything together, except at Christmas."

"What did you pick?" Ethan's voice rose echoing Nic's excitement.

Andy answered for them. "We chose Hallelujah. It's the same arrangement Chris Botti has on his December album. It's the one piece we could both agree on. Hey, did you know that Mrs. Holiday's husband was Harry Holiday, the jazz guitar player?"

Ethan wore a look of shock for a moment. "No, I didn't. I guess she shared that with you today, huh? She comes marching up here every time I play music too loudly, usually jazz, come to think of it."

Nic was getting fidgety just sitting still. "Maybe it reminds her of him and makes her sad."

"You might be right, Nic. What do you say we ask everybody if they'd like to hear some music tonight?"

"Yeah!" Nic stood up.

"But Mom didn't let us bring our instruments with us." Andy didn't look too hopeful.

"I think I have that covered." Ethan finally got up from the floor, walked to the closet, and opened the door. Instrument cases were stuffed inside. "What's your pleasure, gentlemen?"

Andy started laughing as he stood. "Is this the wayward home for instruments, where they go to die?"

"Hey now, they're dusty, but not dead." Ethan rolled his eyes. He felt like that some days, dusty but not dead yet.

Andy puckered his lips in thought. "We'll practice our piece, but only if you play with us."

"Oh, Andy, no." Ethan began to stammer. "I don't, I don't play anymore." The last time was after Stephanie's funeral, when everything was packed away, except his memories of her.

Andy was going to lay a guilt trip on his uncle at the same time he was going to pay him a huge compliment. "I remember you playing. I was a lot younger then, but I do remember. You were great. You're the reason I can play the trumpet too." He glanced over to his brother. "You're too little to really remember, Nic."

"I am not!" Nic's face drew up, pouting. "I'm not little, Andy!"

"Guys, come on. Let's clean up, then we'll pull these out. Okay?" Was he really the reason Andy had picked up yet another instrument?

All three came back into the main room and began to clear dishes from the table. Jane silently queried her brother if everything was okay. He nodded ever so slightly, letting her know the boys were fine. Ethan would be grilling her later about Colin though.

"Don't get up, unless you want to. The boys and I are going to clean up. Then, if you're agreeable, Andy and Nic are going to play their recital piece for our listening pleasure this evening." Ethan ruffled Nic's hair.

Andy wasn't letting his Uncle off that easily. "And Uncle E's going to play with us."

The ladies all shared a look of surprise with that statement. The biggest surprise came from Mrs. Holiday. "Let us help then so we can get to the music faster!"

11

Hallelujah

Charlotte took a plate to Adam in the lobby after returning a missed call to Racheal. Then she called her brother and parents, who were eating together in Franklin, North Carolina. She came back into the apartment in time to see the boys unpacking instruments from dusty cases. Ethan's eyes caught hers as she walked toward the sofa.

"Racheal alright?" His eyes were concerned.

"She's fine. She wanted to say thank you for the meal I had sent over after lunch today. I had already told her it was coming, but apparently it went over really well. Everyone enjoyed a great meal and she looked like a rockstar hostess for her in-laws." Charlotte sat down, in a side chair, watching the boys.

Andy wiped down Ethan's silver trumpet. It was heavy, well made, and the epitome of a beautiful instrument. His own brass version wasn't this elegant. "This is a great trumpet, Uncle E. Wow!"

Ethan's face lit-up in a wide smile. "Wait until you hear it!"

Andy held up the trumpet, pursed his lips, and a cool, smooth note floated out. His lung capacity was excellent as well as his control. The note was solemn, haunting, and held. Then silence.

Nic strummed the bass guitar in his hand. He listened to the notes while standing in front of the small amp. A few more came out, and he began tuning.

Ethan set up two music stands, one for each of the boys.

Andy's eyes drilled into his uncle. "Where's yours?"

"I'll share with Nic." Ethan would rather just listen than participate, but Andy was having none of it.

"Okay. Which guitar do you want?" Andy put the trumpet down. His uncle would be participating tonight.

"The strings weren't great when I put the acoustic away. Bring both the cases. I'll see which one is in better shape."

"You'll need the other amp too, right?" Andy waited for him to answer.

"You're going to make me play tonight, aren't you?" Ethan's chin dropped in resignation.

"Oh, you better believe it! A chance to jam with my uncle finally? I'm not missing this." Andy grinned at him with delight.

When they returned and opened the cases on the living room floor, both guitars were shiny in their protective cases, but the acoustic now had a broken string. The resonating guitar had a string missing, when Ethan lifted it from the case.

"I'm sorry, Andy. You're just going to have to play without me. I glanced at Nic's music on his tablet, and a cello won't sound great with this arrangement. That's the only other stringed instrument I have in reasonable shape.

Mrs. Holiday had a great idea. "I have just the thing. I'll be back in a few minutes."

She practically sprinted for the door, leaving everyone questioning exactly what prompted her sudden departure. When she returned, as promised, in only a few minutes, they knew why. The case was almost more than she could handle, but Ethan recognized the shape. He met her a few steps inside the door, taking the weight from her arms. He laid the case gently on the floor and unlatched the sides. The contents greeted him with an unexpected surprise.

Andy and Nic stood beside him, sharing in the new delight. They all wore the same expression of awe. Ethan gently pulled the guitar from the case, handling it with great care.

Charlotte watched as Ethan's eyes caught hers. He looked like an excited child on Christmas morning who'd been given the best present ever. She didn't know what he was hanging around his neck and plugging into an amp, but she was happy in sharing his joy.

Mrs. Holiday sat down beside Jane once more, trying to catch her breath. "It's been packed away a little too long. And before you ask, Harold had it worked on before he died because it had a warped neck. That resonator is five years older than me, made in 1932. It's a National Style-O. He had Marc Schoenberger install a new truss rod, cone, tuners, and a cover plate. It's been refretted too. The fingerboard is ebony. It still has a few dings and wear, but the sound, oh the sound. Harold had it out, playing it, a few weeks before he died. You're holding the pride and joy of Harold Holiday, the jazz guitarist. He played with all the greats here in the city. I never missed a performance."

Ethan put his fingers on the frets and picked a few notes out, tuning up, before finding a rhythm with the instrument. The feel and sound were phenomenal. "I know you have a lot of great stories to tell." He winked at her. "Thank you for bringing this and sharing this incredible guitar with us, Mrs. Holiday."

All three musicians now had instruments in their hands. They discussed chords and progressions for a few minutes. Charlotte listened, but didn't understand their world at the moment. Jane and Mrs. Holiday seemed to understand perfectly. After a few bars were played by each, they decided to give it a go and play the piece.

Andy smirked, "This is going to be really rough. We just started playing this at home, so forgive us now."

The ladies smiled at his statement. Jane looked at her oldest, standing there with his uncle. Andy looked all grown up in a thirteen year old body. He'd seen and heard too much lately for it not to have changed him.

As they began, there was hesitancy by all, notes shorter and uncertain. The melody went on, transforming the evening into a shared experience they'd never forget. Music was transporting them all to a place of longing, grieving, and by the end, with Andy's last note, to healing. Hallelujah.

Mrs. Holiday grabbed Jane's hand and held it. Memories overtook her and she needed something to ground her here in this time.

Jane turned toward her on the sofa and put her other arm around the woman. "Are you okay?"

Tears ran down Mrs. Holiday's face. Charlotte retrieved some tissues from the hall bathroom. They all needed them, truth be told.

"Harold would be pleased with your command of that guitar, Mr. Cooper. And I cannot in good conscience put it back into a closet now. Sterling has told me to sell it, but I can't bear the thought of it landing in someone's hands I don't know. If it's all the same to you, keep it. Keep it and play it, please."

Ethan took the strap off and gently placed it on a guitar stand he'd brought out earlier. He knelt in front of her, taking her hands into his. "It would be my honor, Mrs. Holiday. My family and I will be having our annual gala, nearby at The Olmsted, to raise money for the arts in schools in a couple of weeks. The boys will be back here." He turned to smile at them. "What do you say we all practice this piece and play it, that night?"

They nodded, enthusiastically.

His focus returned to her. "Would you join us, that night, Mrs. Holiday?"

She squeezed his hands. "I'd be delighted."

Ethan let her hands go as she sat forward on the sofa, hugging him.

Mrs. Holiday looked around the room. "I cannot recall the last time I've been so blessed on Thanksgiving."

"Us too." Ethan felt her let go of him. He stood up, then took Charlotte's hand, pulling her close. He hugged her tightly and whispered in her ear. "Happy Thanksgiving, Charlotte."

She pulled away and realized everyone was staring at them. She didn't care. "Happy Thanksgiving, Ethan."

I do believe there is a turkey pot pie in our future, Ethan thought. The leftovers were great, but he couldn't handle eating more turkey unless it was a pot pie. He returned the butter to the refrigerator, after sweet potato pancakes, and glanced at what would become dinner tonight after some work making a crust later.

Breakfast was over, the dishes were finished, thanks to the boys, and they sat quietly chatting about music beside Charlotte at the kitchen island. Ethan leaned forward, pouring Charlotte more coffee into her cup, then refilling his own. She looked like her thoughts were a million miles away as she smiled, thanking him for the refill.

Jane was getting ready to leave, scurrying around the apartment, in and out of the bathroom.

Nic and Andy already had their suitcases rolled to the front door. Marcus was on his way to pick them up and take them to the airport. The weekend had flown by, and now Sunday was already here.

Ethan strode to the open guest room door with his cup in hand. "I'm glad you and the boys decided to stay a little longer. Will you let me know when you get settled back at home, later?"

Jane threw her slippers in the bag and pulled the zipper around her suitcase. "I am too. I'll text you when we're on the ground in Charleston. We've all had such a great time being here with you and Charlotte." She pulled her carry-on to the end of the bed. "The boys don't care if we ever go back. They've enjoyed playing music with you between plotting shopping excursions to pick-up groceries and cooking up great science with her. Good thing we've been walking everywhere because I think I gained five pounds between all the food and the birthday cake on Friday. Even Sugar whined at me when I went to get the boys from Mrs. Holiday's place last night. This trip has changed a lot of things." She sat the suitcase on the floor, pulled out the handle, and put the carry-on strap over it, rolling it to the door where he stood. "Thank you for discussing what's been happening with Colin after everyone went to bed Thursday night."

"Absolutely." Ethan sipped his coffee.

"I feel empowered to go home and take my life back again. I don't want the boys to grow-up thinking this kind of treatment is okay, when it most certainly is not." Jane reached up, putting her hand on Ethan's left shoulder. "I'm glad I have my brother back. I haven't seen him in years."

"I feel more like myself, my old self, since I met her." His cheeks pulled up as a bright smile erupted.

"Good. Don't lose him again. I like her, the boys adore her. She fits right in with our crazy family." She continued smiling at him. "You're falling for her, even if you won't admit it to yourself. I want you to remember that loving someone else isn't betraying Stephanie. Okay?"

He nodded, agreeing with her. "Okay." The cell phone buzzed with a text in his pocket. "Marcus is here."

Everyone began moving toward the door. Ethan left his coffee cup on the kitchen island as he walked back through. The boys were hugging their new friend. Charlotte promised to be there when they returned for the gala so they could talk games and science. They promised their uncle to practice a few more songs for the gala and be ready to jam again soon with him. All their hugs given, and so-longs said, they were out the door.

Charlotte stood there in silence, looking at Ethan. It was quiet in the apartment for the first time since Wednesday afternoon.

"I don't know whether to be happy we have the place back to ourselves or sad." Ethan truly felt a loss with his sister and nephews gone. "I didn't realize how much I missed having them around."

"They aren't even my family and I'll miss them." Charlotte walked back toward the kitchen. She picked up her coffee cup and went over to the patio doors, staring out on a cold Sunday morning. It was only nine-thirty.

Ethan came to stand beside her, gazing out on bare treetops in Central Park. "What are we going to do with ourselves today?"

"Maybe hit Central Park, scout some empty spots for the boutique, and walk off some of the weight I gained over the weekend?"

Charlotte wore the silliest expression he'd seen on her.

"Are you insinuating we've packed on a few pounds this weekend?"

Again with the silly face. "I'm not insinuating. I know I have." She used both her hands to pat her derrière. "Stretchy jeans are too forgiving, but my wool trousers and skirts aren't. I've had so much rich food. I've enjoyed every bite, but I need to walk. Are you with me, Cooper?"

Ethan didn't have to think on that one, at all. "I'd follow you anywhere, Rose." The response came out a little too quickly for him, but he really did mean that.

"What about this one?" Ethan spun around taking in all the shops surrounding them. "There's a bridal boutique on one side, a jewelry boutique there, women's shoe store over here, and look right there a furniture store for babies. Plus there's a restaurant over there, a coffee shop, and a doughnut shop. Seems to be good food traffic and these are higher end retail outlets."

Charlotte stood in front of an empty space, three blocks from Lexington Avenue, looking up. The front windows were large, the decorative detail on the building in great condition, and there were enough upscale retail stores nearby. "How could you tell about good foot traffic? Every sidewalk in the city is covered with people, constantly!"

She waded through the crowd and stood near the edge of the sidewalk, cars whizzing by behind her. Her head tilted back as she took in the full building. She stopped counting after ten stories. There would be plenty of foot traffic indeed. The neighborhood was full of upscale businesses and plenty of residents. Her eyes closed for a moment. Could she imagine her store here? Her eyes opened to Ethan standing right in front of her, very close.

He wore an inquisitive look. "What's going through that sharp mind of yours?"

She smiled at his comment. "I'm trying to decide if I like the location or not. It's difficult for me to get a feel for the spot outside with all the noise and distraction. I like the idea of a city, because goods and services are much more readily available, and I spend quite a bit of time in them working, but I go home. My nearest neighbors are cows, and I like it that way. Even as high up as your apartment is, on the top floor at sixty-sixth street, I can still hear traffic noise at times. Cars and taxi's everywhere just like people, and their smells intermingling. Expensive perfume goes up your nostrils one minute from a woman you pass on the street then it's followed by a breath of exhaust from a taxi. Litter blowing around on the streets between people's feet, rushing to get to the same destination they are. Even the trash is in a hurry here. The buildings are so tall they block out the sunlight, and don't you dare look up to admire the modern marvels of architecture because the residents will yell at you to get out of their way, tourist!" She looked over at the subway vent nearby as rush of air flowed over them, another train passing by beneath their feet. Her eyes drifted up again to his. "I know you and

Racheal love it here, but I'm just not sold on this place. One minute I think I can take it and the next-"

A car horn sounded directly behind her from a taxi, stuck behind a car that had abruptly stopped. The cabbie wasn't happy about it and let the other driver know it with another sound from the horn. It was loud! Ethan's face drew up in a scowl as he raised his left hand at them, making a fist. The city could bring out the best in him, but also the worst in people. He stepped away from her and smacked the hood of the yellow van, they were so close to them. "Get away from the curb! You shouldn't be driving this far over anyway!"

The silver sedan in front let someone out and pulled away. The taxi sounded their horn again and maneuvered around the sedan into another lane to pass, blowing his horn, again.

Ethan turned back around to see Charlotte's right hand pulled up, covering her heart. Her face was panicked, her eyes wide with terror. The taxi's horn had set off a bad reaction. The loud noise had hurt his ears. He could only imagine the sound for her, magnified, in both ears. From the look on her face, anxiety was rising up along with shots of adrenaline. She stood frozen in place as he hugged her. He put his face next to her right ear. "I'm sorry. Let's go over here to this coffee shop, get something to drink and thaw out. We can figure out where we want to go for lunch." He pulled his face away to look at her. "Are you okay? Can you move?"

She only nodded affirmatively. Now to get her feet moving. He stepped back and held out his hand to her. Once inside, and sitting at a table with two hot peppermint teas, he spoke to her again.

"Where did you go back there, in your mind?" Ethan waited for her speak.

Charlotte was staring at him. Her jaw opened, but nothing came out for another thirty seconds. Her eyes began to dart around the room, then returned to him. "The sound from the horn. Loud, sharp, close to me. I remember how my head felt when I woke up, after the bomb went off. I couldn't hear anything, but buzzing. People were talking to me, trying to help me. I was in and out. That's how I felt on the sidewalk. The noise, people talking, but not hearing them. I was back in that bubble for a split second, panicked with my ears buzzing. I don't know if I'll ever be able to live here in the city with all the triggers." Tears began to well up in her eyes. "I'm sorry, Ethan. I wanted to walk around and enjoy today. I didn't mean to freak out and shut down on you. I think I'm just tired."

"No apologies. Two years might have passed, but the trauma is still fresh. That will take time. Give yourself a chance to continue healing. We can rest this afternoon." Ethan pushed the tea cup aside and took her hands in his. He couldn't fathom what she'd been through. She let him in to the soft places of her heart and hurts. That meant the world to him.

"Our baby would have been about a year and half old now. We didn't find out if would be a boy or girl. We wanted a surprise. I lost our baby on December the eighth. I was due in May." Ethan handed her a handkerchief from his jacket pocket. It was bright white with his monogram embroidered into the corner in grey, what else. "Thank you." She blotted the moisture from her cheek as the tears were escaping. "It's not that I don't crave a new start with my life. I just don't know if New York City is the best place for me. I want to like it here. My printers are across the river in Jersey. I have many business clients here and wholesale accounts are picking up. Racheal is here." She paused and smiled at him. "And you're here."

He cupped her right cheek with his left hand, smiling back at her. "You'll figure it out. We will figure this out." He had emphasized the word 'we.' His hand dropped.

Fresh waves of patrons were stuffing the coffee shop. The crowd began to press in near their table. Ethan knew he needed to get Charlotte out and away from the noisy crowd. "What do you say we get takeout from Chow's down the street and ride the Subway back? I could use some lunch and my feet could use some heat."

She chuckled, "Mine are frozen too. Jeans, sweaters, and boots are just no match for this cold, even with a parka."

He took her hand, squeezing it gently. "I agree. Gotham is chilly today. Back to the bat cave!"

12

Peeling an Onion

Racheal took a bite from the Malasada, fresh from a Hawaiian style bakery. Every taste of the doughnut-like pastry sent her tastebuds into orbit. Her eyes glanced over at the nearly-full coffee mug within easy reach. The two bites left would easily fit into the wide mouth, Grey Cooper logo emblazoned mug. *Oh, why not?* The coconut cream filling remnants were still coating her lips. The coffee soaked Malasada would be the crowning glory of the last bites. Yes, that tasted every bit as good as she had imagined. Now she had sticky fingers on her right hand and simply didn't care. She wanted another one. And she kept lavender wipes in her desk that she most certainly needed after this.

Charlotte came into the office with Ethan hot on her heels, armed with the box that held the last three Malasadas. She was gripping a coffee cup in her left hand.

Racheal's eyes lit up. "You read my mind. Give me that evil deliciousness! How have I never had one of these?"

Charlotte put the box down on Racheal's desk, opening the lid. All three picked up a Malasada, emptying the box. "I had them when I spent two weeks at Hickam, in O'ahu. Malasadas might be Portuguese, but they're Hawaiian style now. If you're ever in Honolulu, you have try Liliha's or Leonard's. I couldn't bring back two boxes of Malasadas from up the street here without getting Kona coffee to brew up once we came back here. I wanted us to have the full experience."

Ethan and Charlotte sat across from Racheal, alternating bites of Malasada with sips of Kona coffee.

"Thank you. My skirt's not going to fit if I keep this up. So I take it both store fronts were a bust?" Racheal sunk her teeth into the creamy filling, coating her mouth in coconut once more.

"One was ridiculously over priced given the location and the other, well, the owner never showed up to open the space. When he finally did call, we were waiting on the order at the bakery for the malasadas. Come to find out, it's already rented." Charlotte exhaled in disgust.

Ethan knew how exasperated Charlotte was feeling. Over a dozen spaces looked at, so far, and nothing had panned out. "Let's not discuss this sore subject right now. Our toes haven't thawed out yet from waiting on the guy. We'll keep looking." His bite was greedily eaten of the coconut filled delight. "Found anything interesting, yet?" Ethan managed to get the words out between chewing. His mother would be horrified to see him speaking with his mouth full of food. In that moment, he grinned to himself at the mere thought of defying her.

"Plenty. I'll give him points for originality in picking laundry for laundering. There are irregularities between what is deposited in the bank account for the dry-cleaning businesses, which is the laundered drug cash, and what's reported on their sales tax, their Federal Tax returns, and more. That's what's tripped the IRS audit, no doubt. Every deposit is just under the radar with less than five grand per bank transaction made for each of the so-called branches of the thirty-two cleaners from all over town. Each one of them has their own bank account, with a dozen banks all over the five boroughs. This keeps any one account from tripping suspicious activity reports or SAR's. There are daily deposits, two a day, minimum. Then funds are drawn off to a series of bogus shell corporations for paying the bills for the cleaners. Spiffy Cleaning Supplies is the name I've seen the most. The other one is a hanger company, Dangle and Wood, who has a website and everything, but no actual contact information that's legit or online ordering. Then there is Empire's monthly draw, for accounting and taxes, and this one, this one is the kicker, Star of Persia Community Relief Fund of NY. It's listed as a non-profit! They're receiving hefty donations every month. The brokerage account is also coming out of the monthly deposits, managed via Empire as well."

Ethan swallowed, licking his lips, enjoying the final taste of the creamy filling. "It's barely ten-thirty, Racheal. You've found all this since nine?"

CHAPTER TWELVE

Her chest vibrated in quiet laughter. "Not exactly. I got bored listening to my in-laws over the long weekend. I went hunting this morning for the rest. Dangle and Wood is a registered corporation here in New York, but I kept digging about their bogus website. The domain is registered to a company, an Esther of Shiraz, in Shiraz, Iran. I'm terrible with geography. Where exactly is that?"

Charlotte cleared her throat, drawing the attention in the room. "Esther is Persian for star. Want to bet the non-profit isn't really a non-profit? Shiraz is in south central Iran. It's about four and a half hours from the Persian Gulf. I'd say about three hundred clicks."

"You want to translate that for those of us that aren't militarily inclined?" Ethan's eyes narrowed.

"Sorry. About a hundred and eighty miles. It's a beautiful city. There are lots of gardens and old sculptures. I was there once." Charlotte couldn't tell them she was there with a team to get a reconnaissance plane off the ground that had become disabled, crash landing outside the city. The pilot was injured, but not gravely. He'd flown back with Charlotte and the SEAL team, after they returned to the Gulf, onto a Zodiac, and to a carrier. What a trip! The plane made it out of the desert under the cover of darkness, with Caroline Blaine at the yoke. The team was in and out with the U.S. denying any knowledge of their whereabouts or the incident.

"What were you doing in Shiraz?" Ethan was entirely curious now.

She inhaled slowly, details of the mission still flashing before her eyes, wishing with all her might that she could share with them. "Need to know. It's classified."

Racheal bounced in her chair again, body shaking in silent laughter. Her best sarcastic comment was issued as she rolled in eyes playfully. "Military contractors!"

Charlotte stood up from her chair to avoid feeling any worse regarding her imposed silence. "I'm getting more coffee. You guys want a refill, too?"

Racheal was already caffeinated to the max. "I better pass, or I'll bounce my way out of this chair. Thanks."

Ethan eyed the mug in his hand. He could always drink more coffee. "Sure."

Her silhouette disappeared down the long hall with their mugs.

He scooted forward in his chair, closer to the desk, resting his arms there for a moment. "Nice job on ferreting out the financials. Let me know when you find something else worthy of sharing. I'm going to wash the Malasada off my fingers."

Ethan came back down the hall with Charlotte a few minutes later, both with freshly washed hands and refilled coffee mugs. They were passing the conference room when Racheal came up behind them, pulling slightly on Charlotte's elbow.

"You need to come back in here." Racheal, Charlotte, and Ethan all resumed their seats from before. Racheal spilled the last bit of gleaned information. "I checked the linked brokerage account that Ashem's been investing their money in. With all the brokerage transfers, there should be about ten million in there. I checked and there is less than a million."

"Ashem's committing securities fraud." Ethan felt his chin drop as his head turned to see the same reaction on Charlotte's face. Surprise! He closed his mouth finally. "He's duping this gang with a Ponzi scheme, and reporting false statements to them. Wow!" Detective Togo needed to hear this. They could arrest Ashem on securities fraud and take the time they needed to build the case out on remaining charges. Ethan knew he could lay this case out enough to get Ashem off the street. "I've got to call Detective Togo."

Charlotte grabbed Ethan's arm as he stood up, causing him to drop back down into the chair. "Wait! I have files to break the encryption on. I'm waiting for some help from overseas on a few things. Let's wrap this neatly and then present our findings. This is bigger than we thought."

"You're absolutely right, it is." Sitting on this kind of information made him even more fearful for Dānā's safety. When Ethan had read the NYPD's files on the full case, the gang had ties to a Mexican Cartel. No wonder they had killed off witnesses so readily. They'd do anything to protect their supply, and their money. "As soon as you break into those files, let me know. Dānā doesn't need to be in the building with this guy if he's ripping off a gang with cartel ties to Mexico. That's a deadly recipe. Ashem is extremely arrogant to do this right under their noses. When Club 13 figures it out, he's a dead man, and Dānā will be too."

Charlotte was still sitting on Ethan's sofa pouring over emails, and a few files they referenced that she could access from what she'd copied. Ethan was in a meeting with Racheal in the conference room, along with half a dozen other lawyers, over a longtime client's initial public offering. Racheal had the deal laid-out perfectly. Ethan was simply a managing partner's presence, listening as she spelled out the perfect plan. Their IPO would be rolled out soon and everything had to be in place beforehand. After this was finished, Ethan, Charlotte, and Racheal could return to peeling the Vidalia onion on Ashem.

The food digesting in Charlotte's belly coupled with the warm environment were doing a number on her concentration. They'd had a late lunch earlier. This was the last scheduled business for the day in the office. Her eyes were blinking, slower and slower as her breath evened out. Three o'clock was nap time after all.

Fuzzy thoughts were running rampant. Ashem was importing old books from Europe. Entire libraries in some cases. Money was trading hands over the books. Containers were coming into the port, full of books, then being stored in a warehouse in Queens. This spreadsheet wasn't connected to anything external, but it had thousands of entries.

Even slower blinking, head tilting forward. The room was now blurry.

Ashem was buying and selling old books.

Farsi to one buyer, then Arabic to another.

Books. Old books. More entries in the spreadsheet, names in one column numbers in another..

Back to Farsi.

Something felt warm and soft under her face now.

Ethan moved the laptop and closed the lid, placing it on his desk. She looked so cute napping on his sofa. He'd moved a pillow under her head as she'd sunk down onto the leather. Nancy came in to catch him looking at the sleeping woman.

"You had a call from your mother and Mr. Carter." Nancy glanced at Charlotte on the sofa. She looked like she could use a blanket, so a throw was pulled out of a covered storage ottoman at the end of the sofa. She caught Ethan's smile out of the corner of her eye as the large throw was spread over Charlotte. How many times had she covered up Ethan on this very sofa? "Let me know if you need anything. I'm leaving early to spend a little time with my son before he leaves in the morning."

Ethan spoke just as quietly as Nancy had. "Thanks for covering her up. Go. I'll see you in the morning."

Nancy's eyes gleamed at him as the corners of her mouth drew up in a knowing grin. He'd finally found someone. "Of course. I'll see you tomorrow."

Ethan looked up and over the stack of papers under his left hand. Racheal had outlined the fraud Ashem was executing. It was nearly four and his eyes needed a break from an hour of reading through this mess. Charlotte sat up abruptly, spooking him.

"It's a hawala!"

His brow furrowed. "It's a haw-whatta?"

She moved the blanket and stood up. "A hawala. It's how Ashem is moving money out of the country." Charlotte grabbed her phone laying nearby and dialed the Navy's ARES Command in Italy to speak to the head cyber analyst. "Hi. It's Charlotte. I didn't wake you, did I? I was just wondering if you'd gotten to the files yet? Did you break the encryption?" She paused for the man to answer on the other end. It was ten o'clock at night in Italy. "I understand you've had other assignments, but this is important. I realize it's late, but please get to those files as fast as you can. Call me when you know something. I don't care what time it is." Another pause. "You too, thanks. Bye."

Ethan watched her brow furrow as she sat back down, phone in hand, looking a bit dazed. "Are you alright?"

"Yes." She put her hands on either side of head, sliding them down to cover her eyes. She couldn't let it slip that there were other vague emails pointing to a larger long-term plan, an assault on American soil. "No, but I will be when the ARES Command analyst calls me back and tells me he's cracked the files. I have my suspicions about what they are, but I won't know for sure until then. You need to see this." She looked around for her laptop.

He came around the desk, picking up the laptop from the corner and handing it to her. "This what you're looking for? You were conked-out and it was sliding off, so I moved it."

"Thanks. Who tucked me in?" She waited for his reply, holding his gaze as he sat down beside her.

A sly grin erupted on his face. "Nancy. She took off early to spend some time with her son before he goes back out west."

Charlotte lifted the lid on the laptop, the Mac quickly coming back to life, just where she had left it. "I'm happy he's here for Nancy. Now, look at this spreadsheet with me."

Ethan scooted close beside her, putting his right arm around her. "What exactly am I looking at?"

Racheal came in to the office, noting just how cozy the two of them were. "I see you two are really putting your heads together over this."

He felt himself smile and roll his eyes at once. "Haven't you heard that two heads are better than one? In our case, three. Now get over here, Charlotte's about to explain something important."

"Oh yeah? What did you find, Charlie?" Racheal waited for them to make room for her before sitting on Charlotte's right side.

"Ashem is moving money out of the country using a hawala and that non-profit. I found his entries in this spreadsheet. The entries correlate to emails talking about antique books. I don't know if they are actually books or just the cover he's using. But I did find an email talking about a shipment coming in to the port on Friday, supposedly it's from a private library in Europe."

Racheal's posture straightened. "That makes complete sense. It's both according to what I've been seeing."

Ethan and Racheal listened as Charlotte went over the entries, explaining her hawala theory and just what it was; how a terrorist organization looks legitimate on paper to get around the Patriot Act.

Charlotte's legs grew restless. She excused herself, and slipped away to take a phone call from Italy.

She stepped into the dark conference room down the hall, and stood in front of the large windows, chatting with the ARES team. The lights below her twinkled in the late Fall evening. She stepped away from the glass and near one of the light fixtures at the end of the conference table. Something was interfering with her left hearing aid. She pulled the phone away, asking the team to wait a moment. She stepped away from the table and the noise went away. She stepped back, near the light fixture, the interference returned. The closer she leaned, the louder the noise became. This was the end of the table the Detective had been at with the ADA and the Police Commissioner. She held the phone up, telling them to call when they had something before hanging up. The flash light function on the phone was turned on, shining it intently on the base of the light fixture. She had to find the interference source or she was going to go deaf. There was nothing out of the ordinary on the outside of the base, but the inside lip of the bottom was another story. Her fingers hit something out of place on the smooth interior metal. She checked the other two fixtures. The base held the same surprise. The conference room had been bugged. She removed all three and put them inside a water glass, pouring it full of water from the courtesy bottles nearby on a cart. She placed the glass back on the cart, behind the empty glasses, where only Nancy would notice it's presence. She scanned the rest of the room, using her hearing aids as the great frequency detector they were, finding no more. But she did find a feature to the conference room they hadn't used before. The glass had the ability to go opaque when the door was closed. Why hadn't it been triggered before? Ethan and Racheal were still talking. They wouldn't mind is she fixed the glass, right? After visiting Nancy's desk, and finding a letter opener and some pliers, she fixed the circuit for the glass. When she returned the tools, Charlotte scribbled a note to leave the glass with water on the cart for her to deal with later. She returned finally to Ethan and Racheal, sitting on the sofa, to listen to their conclusions. Their conversation continued into the evening until Gabriel came by at eight thirty, looking for Racheal who wasn't answering her cell phone.

Lieutenant Commander Ben Gibson's eyes darted to the corner of his computer screen. He'd finally found the right way to break the encryption on files she'd sent him securely days before. Other high-priority tasks had been occupying his time and that of his team. His Commanding Officer, Captain Blaine, had just pushed this to the front of the line. The files were easy enough to crack for the head technology guru of the ARES team. Before joining the military after college he was a hacker, but after being brought into the Navy's fold he was all patriot. Now that the encryption was off, files were looking familiar to him. After Pink's call, roughly six hours before, his curiosity was up. Once he'd seen the contents of the first files sleep was out of the question. He'd been up all night chewing his way through them, armed with coffee and sugar, his preferred fuel. No civilian should be in possession of these files. Alarm bells were going off in his head with the last file he'd opened, missile transport schedules into Afghanistan. And now this file, the shipping manifest for a container coming into the port of New York on Friday. The contents were strange indeed. Pink had every cause for concern when she'd seen the vague details in an email, referencing files Commander Gibson had cracked. They had both agreed on the last phone call that Caroline needed to be brought up to speed, quickly. Blaine wouldn't be awake for another hour. Where the team resided, near Naples, Italy, it was only four thirty in the morning. After twelve years of living in the team's residence, Gibson knew his CO all too well. They were more like family than colleagues. She'd be upset with him if he didn't wake her up.

He left the command room, deep under the earth of a what looked like a normal villa on the outskirts of town to the eye that didn't know any better. Each flight he climbed reminded him to get more exercise in. Too much time behind a computer screen needed to be remedied with more cardio. He was slightly winded when he reached the bedroom door. He knocked gently, knowing he'd rouse her husband as well. David Reese, the Judge Advocate General Commanding Officer of the Naples office, was used to this after so many years. Gibson knocked again, a bit more insistent.

"Captain?"

Reese squeezed his wife, snuggled up to him under his right arm. "He doesn't mean me." His voice was rough, but playful.

Caroline moved Reese's arm and sat up. She knew the owner of that voice. "Yes, Commander?"

"I'm sorry to wake you, ma'am, but I have a situation. You're needed in the command room."

"Give me five minutes, Mr. Gibson."

"Yes, ma'am." Gibson walked away from the door, heading for the kitchen to make a fresh pot of coffee. They were going to need it.

Caroline's dry eyes were adjusting to being open. She pushed a button on her blue-faced watch, illuminating the dial. *Four-thirty in the morning, lovely. Happy Tuesday.*

13

Onion Soup

Charlotte was on her back, in the middle of the bed, pondering what Commander Gibson had found in the files. What looked like racketeering wrapped in a handmade suit was truly terrorism. The act of visiting New York to find a space for her stationery shop and spend time with Racheal seemed as though they were the last thing to focus her intentions upon. She had been sent here with a purpose greater than herself. God always had a plan. Now there were more questions than answers. Then again, there always were. Benjamin's face was in her mind just before the dreamy haze of sleep found her. His arms were around her, hugging her tightly to him. She missed him so. Her head was against his chest breathing him in. The scent on his clothes wasn't him although it was also familiar to her. She raised her head to kiss him only to find she was in Ethan's embrace. His right hand slipped away from her body, pulling her left hand up to kiss the back. As his lips pulled away, she could see an exquisite pear shaped diamond on her ring finger. The stone was brilliant, large, slightly pink, set in white gold with tiny diamonds outlining the shape.

When morning came, she awoke with the telling secret of her dream. God had shown her many things in dreams and visions. Charlotte wasn't afraid of these revelations even when they didn't always make complete sense at the time.

"I trust your plan for me," she whispered out into the room. "For your ways are not my ways, nor your thoughts my thoughts."

Her feet hit the floor, taking her from sleepy warmth into a new day of uncertainty.

Ten thirty came all too quickly. Charlotte's stomach growled loudly enough to get Racheal and Ethan's attention. They were sorting financial documents to build the case for securities fraud.

Racheal was lost in number-land, her forte. Piles of sorted statements, communications via email, bogus bills, phony corporations, and even charitable contributions lay in the growing stacks. More printed documents were coming from the copier soon and she wasn't even through the rolling cart load that had printed overnight, a quarter still occupying the shelves beside them.

Emails, emails, and more emails. Charlotte couldn't take any more emails. Then something else she hadn't seen before caught her attention in the file tree of the portable drive contents Dānā had garnered. These were videos according to the file extension, and there were lots of them. She muted the sound on her laptop and clicked on the first one in the list. The picture was in high definition, color, and made her stomach turn. She recognized the location. It was the dry cleaning building nearby she'd visited while touring properties. The realtor had been confused about the listing and Charlotte was concerned over the stacked barrels and chemical stockpile. Her suspicions were confirmed about the purpose of those barrels, chemicals, battery and suspension chain. These videos were a record of executions and torture. She stopped the video when the unknown male, hung by his arms on the chain, passed out from torture. Random clicks on videos yielded much the same. There were two hundred and twelve files in the folder. If Ashem was in possession of these videos then he most likely knew she had been in the building. Did the cameras stay on all the time or did they turn them on to bear witness with video when someone was killed? Did he have her face on camera? She hadn't seen his face in any of the footage yet either. Her stomach issued another loud growl.

"If you're hungry, we can take a break. We did only drink a small smoothie this morning." Ethan waited on Charlotte's answer.

"I think I'll take a break. My eyes are starting to cross from reading through all this. I'm going to get some air and get something up the street." She subtly moved her eyes and head, indicating he needed to follow her. Racheal was too engrossed in her sorting to notice.

He winked at her. Yes, he had taken the hint. "We'll be back, Rae. Can we bring you anything?"

"No, thanks." Racheal took a sip from her coffee mug. "I'm good. See you in a bit."

Barbara was pushing another loaded cart down the hall toward them, three more shelves full of printed documents.

Ethan paused at the entrance to a nearby bustling kosher bagel spot, Ess-A-Bagel. He noted Charlotte had changed her shoes from heels to winter boots before leaving the office and was sporting a heavier coat. The sidewalk had been flooded with people coming up from the subway when they passed by in the cold. This didn't seem to phase her today. There was no avoidance of the moving crowd and no panic when a taxi sped by, on two different blocks, blowing their horn incessantly. Despite the fact she had openly stated her disdain for the Big Apple, she was starting to act like a New Yorker, even incorporating more black into her wardrobe. They hadn't discussed where they were going, yet he'd followed blindly after her.

He held the door open for her.

"Thank you. I'd apologize for coming all the way down here in the cold, but I want a Melanie's Favorite. Racheal will eat one if we take her one back."

Both exclaiming, "Hold the onions!"

Ethan waited in line with her. They hadn't ordered ahead and knew it would take a few minutes. "These things are big enough to eat half now and save half for lunch. You walked here like you've been here before. I take it Racheal has schooled you on the Nova bagel selections?"

"Of course. She might not cook, but Rae eats well when she takes the time to eat. The first time I came to visit her after she left the

DA's office, we came here before she went to work at your firm that day."

"I see. So are you going to tell me what it is you found? The suspense is killing me. You didn't say a word about it in the elevator." His bright eyes were wide open and expectant.

Charlotte looked around them, eyeing the line. It was like watching a talking snake with flailing arms, all moving slowly toward a register. She heard each customer giving their order as they crept along, some holding papers and coffees, most staring into their phones, completely oblivious to the person next to them or their personal space. "Not here. Let's get this to go. We have a stop to make on the way back."

Her phone buzzed inside a well-insulated jacket pocket. She prayed it wasn't William again, asking her more questions about a contract or some other detail. They'd spoken three times already today. He'd never had so many questions about his job before. Now that he was taking over, she questioned whether he could really pull the task off. She held the phone up. It was Blaine. "Hello, Captain."

"Hello. I'm here. Where are we meeting up?"

Charlotte pursed her lips in thought. "I didn't expect you this soon. How about 601 Lexington Avenue, the offices of Grey Cooper, thirty-seventh floor. You hungry? I'll pick you something up."

"Sure. It's going to be a little while. Traffic is backed up in Teterboro City where I put the plane down."

"Okay. Call me when you get closer. I'll meet you in the lobby at Lexington." Charlotte noticed Ethan's eyebrows were scrunched up.

"Copy that. Bye."

Ethan was holding a large bag of food from the bagel shop. The smell was making his stomach growl in want. Charlotte was holding up her phone, passing what used to be the dry cleaners as everyone local knew it for the fifth time. They were walking in circles. "It's freezing out here. Why are we walking up and down the block, repeatedly? And who was that on the phone?"

She held up the phone a little higher. "There it is!"

"There what is?" His testy tone finally garnered her attention.

"I know you're cold. Come on, let's go!" She put her phone away and started walking.

He shook his head in surrender. Right now he wanted the feeling back in his fingers and toes, quickly catching up to her frantic pace.

Charlotte slowed down once they were away from the building, stopping near the plaza entrance to Ethan's building. People passing by had their own agenda and didn't care that two people were stopped, huddled together. She put her lips near Ethan's ear, spilling her secret about the videos she'd found and their horrific content. There was also the question of the many barrels occupying the facility that could be used to construct a bomb or possibly decaying bodies. When she pulled away, her hand was on their bag of food, supporting the weight, as the strength in his own hands gave way. The bag fell into her grasp. The shock he wore settled a few seconds later.

"You've been in that building. You told me so. If he's seen your face in a video, we can't let him see you again or you'll be a target."

"I have to get back inside that building. We need to know if those barrels contain what I think they do. Come on, I'm freezing too. I really just needed to see if there was a wireless signal broadcasting all the time from the building or not. That was the whole point of leaving the office. I knew you wouldn't let me leave alone though."

He took possession of the bag again. "You're correct. I wouldn't have. You found a signal. We can't chance having you go back in there."

"The lock on the security grate can be picked. I can bypass the security on the door. We can jam the signal."

"We can?" His voice rang with surprise.

"I'll need to use some tools and spare parts I saw on the work bench in your tech support area. I can build a quick jammer, but we'll have to figure out exactly what side of the building the router is on first. Then we can jam it. We have to be close because what I'll build won't have that far of a range, but we can do it." Charlotte was resolute in her statement.

Ethan's phone began to ring.

"Give me the bag. That's Detective Togo. Answer it. He's on his way over and he's not going to be happy." She smiled at him as they walked into the lobby.

He looked at the caller identification, the detective's number blaring at him. That same look of shock had returned to his face along with a furrowed brow.

Charlotte stood just outside the skyscraper's entrance, watching the hustle of those around her. Blowing snow hit the side of her left cheek, stinging before melting. The city was alive and had it's own pulse; never ceasing, always beating, all hours of the day and night. On the ground, one couldn't fully appreciate the beauty of the chaos. Above it, that was a different matter. Patterns became visible and you could make sense of it all. She dared to crane her neck, turning to look up at 601 Lexington Avenue. The building truly was a masterpiece of modern architecture, like so many in this burgeoning metropolis.

Captain Caroline Blaine cut through the throng of walkers on the sidewalk, invading Charlotte's personal space as only a spook could, quickly and with the art of surprise. "Tourist!"

Charlotte jerked her head down. The surprise of the moment caused her heart to skip a beat before turning to greet the owner of that voice. "You caught me." She chuckled, smiling at Captain Blaine. "It's good to see you."

Blaine smiled back at her. "You too. We really need to stop meeting like this and have a girls weekend sometime."

"Yes, we do! How many years have we been threatening to do that?" Charlotte thought that was a great idea.

"If only our lives were that simple." Blaine's expression indicating just what a fleeting thought 'simple' was in her life.

"Let's get inside. It's freezing and you're not wearing a hat. I like the pixie cut, by the way. Please don't take this the wrong way, but that haircut takes ten years off of you." Charlotte walked with

Blaine getting them through security and to the elevator bank. The Captain moved quickly, even with much shorter legs than Charlotte. Blaine's sensible Italian shoes complimented her hand-made dark gray trousers, suit jacket, and long black wool overcoat. The ensemble was part Italian, part French, but all Blaine, right down to the red tailored button up shirt.

Blaine ran her hand over the extremely short haircut. The number of silver and white hairs far outnumbered the brown now. At forty-seven, she'd earned every one of them the hard way. "Thanks. About three weeks ago I decided I was over fuzzy curls and hair dye. I don't have to stuff the fuzz under a cover if and when I do have to sport a Navy uniform. I'm too old for fussy hair anymore. I don't have the patience for products and diffusers in my life right now. You should try it. Coco Chanel did say that a woman who cuts her hair was about to change her life."

"If only I looked that good in short hair! I can only imagine the freedom." Charlotte was trying to imagine her own head with shorter blonde hair when the elevator came to rest. As the doors opened she decided having short hair would only expose her hearing aids even further. She tried to hide them as much as possible to elude questions about wearing them at her age. "So how is it that even in New York City you can pull off a sneak attack like a tiger stalking prey? Even with bionic ears, I never heard you approach."

They stepped inside the car, waiting on the doors to close.

Blaine's eyes narrowed in a tired smile, accentuating the fine lines around her gray eyes. "It's what I do, Pink." A yawn escaped before she could stifle it. "I read your emails from last week about the detective on this case with you. There are things you should know."

The elevator car was rapidly rising to the thirty-seventh floor.

"You too. He beat you here; arrived about ten minutes ago. We put him in the conference room and told him we'd be with him shortly. He was practically foaming at the mouth."

Blaine's nostrils flared, "Oh goody!"

Togo was silently fuming, pacing in the conference room. The bottle of water in his hand was losing the battle to his mood, the plastic giving way in his grip. The crunch garnered his attention as he finally turned up the nearly-empty vessel and drained it, tossing it into a nearby recycle bin. Voices were growing louder in the hall. His brow was deeply furrowed as Ethan, Racheal, and Nancy filed in. Nancy sat her notepad and pen on the table, just in case she might need it.

Togo drew a breath to launch into a tirade, but Ethan put his hand up.

"Don't. Sit down, Detective." Ethan saw Charlotte approaching through the glass with a woman by her side. "I heard enough on the phone." The posture he carried and the suit Ethan wore commanded attention wherever he went. When he spoke, people listened. Even the Detective remained quiet and it simply wasn't in his nature. This woman coming in with Charlotte carried a posture of power herself and the wardrobe to back it up. Charlotte could be bold, but she had softer side than the woman she entered with.

Charlotte closed the door behind them. The conference room glass went opaque as soon as the lock mechanism made contact, hiding them from anyone passing by in the hall.

The surprise on Ethan's face said it all. Clearly Charlotte had been busy. "When did you..."

"Last night. I got bored." Charlotte's body jiggled with suppressed laughter as she smiled at him. She walked to the hospitality cart, moving the glasses to gain access to something hidden under the shelf at the back. She pulled out a glass filled with water and something in the bottom. Her heels clicked as she walked around the table, placing the glass in front of the Detective. "I believe these belong to you."

Captain Blaine tried unsuccessfully to stifle a grin. Her team had done a deep dive into the detective and saw texts revealing the bugged conversations. Blaine didn't need to tell Pink anything. Pink knew exactly how to do her job.

The detective's eyes dropped to the water glass, full of liquid and the three bugs he'd left behind to gather intel. His jaw hung open slightly for a moment before his face drew up in a smug manor of incredulity. "You caught me. Exigent circumstances. I didn't know if I could trust you."

"That goes both ways." Ethan recognized what was in the glass. He wondered how on earth Charlotte had found them. She answered that question almost immediately for the group.

"I was on a phone call last night, with her," Charlotte's head turning to zero in on Captain Blaine, "when I had difficulty hearing our conversation from interference in my ears, I scanned the room. My hearing aids make excellent detectors of certain frequencies. You no doubt heard a little bit of what was said during my phone conversation until I abruptly terminated your eavesdropping." She sat down finally, beside Ethan with Blaine on her right.

"I was told there was nothing of value overheard." Togo knew he had been caught, there was no sense in trying to deny anything even though nothing was garnered from the illegal act. "I'll apologize then on behalf of the NYPD. The Commissioner gave the nod of the placement. So if you have any intention of taking legal action against your father-in-law, take it up with him."

Ethan felt his jaw slip forward, his teeth grinding over each other. His breathing was already faster than usual, nostrils flaring, eyes narrowing. Yes, it was fair to say he was good and angry. He drew a deep calming breath. If he'd learned anything over the years as an attorney, it was to clear your system as best you could of anger before engaging in litigation or discussion of any kind. It clouded your judgement and did not serve you well. "I know you were simply following an order, Detective. I'll take this up with the Commissioner. I have no intention of suing the department but visiting One PP to express my great disappointment, that is a resounding yes." He shifted his weight, titling the chair back slightly, shoulders posturing against the leather. "Any other invasion of privacy I should address with him, like phone taps?"

"Not that I'm aware of." Togo licked his lips, staring at Ethan before shifting his focus to Charlotte again as she began speaking.

Racheal silently watched the volley in the room, like a match-point tennis game on Centre Court at Wimbledon that made you uncomfortably nervous but you couldn't stop watching.

Charlotte drilled into Togo. "Continuing on with show and tell, would you like to explain why your narcotics guys aren't playing nicely with your counterterrorism squad?"

Togo was completely surprised by the question. How dare she question his department! "What are you talkin' about?"

Charlotte licked her lips, raising her eyebrows as she shared a look with Captain Blaine. "I didn't know who you were with either. I did some poking around on my own. I didn't like what I found. That's why I called in reinforcements. They have bigger guns than the NYPD with immunity and means to take down an assassin and an international terrorist without the red tape. Detective Togo, everybody, this is Captain Caroline Blaine, U.S. Navy with the Defense Intelligence Agency, and a real firecracker." She smiled at Blaine. If they only knew just how much of a firecracker Blaine really was. She did things her way, always.

Blaine's face colored slightly, returning the grin. "I'm not going to waste time, Detective. You won't have the Chief of Detectives breathing down your neck or the Commissioner giving you any grief over my presence here. So ditch the attitude, right now. Commissioner Fairchild has been brought up to speed on the situation and the NYPD is fully cooperating with my team, which you all are now a part of. To be blunt, you have dirty cops in your narcotics unit. There is no way that many seasoned cops let their mark slip past them only to have him kill a rival gang off within a few hours. But you knew that already, didn't you?"

Togo's face dropped. "Yes. The trouble is, I can't prove it and I don't know how many people are involved yet. I find out too many things after the fact."

"That's where I can help you. You have three men who have been making a little too much money, but hiding it extremely well, in multiple accounts, so that one large sum doesn't trip federal banking measures in place to point the finger at them. But there's more. Do you want to tell them or shall I?" Captain Blaine's demeanor changed. This case was very personal to Detective Togo.

"Six weeks ago my niece witnessed a Club Thirteen shakedown. She called me. I told her to put a bag together and get out. I told her I'd meet her and hide her. Before she could get out of her apartment, they swarmed and she became another tied-up loose end to them. She was twenty-three years old. They got her roommates too. Three girls, minding their own business, gunned down before they really even lived. I started digging in to the case and why nothing had been happening on any leads. I felt like I'd fallen down a rabbit hole when I started running down all the ties this gang has in the city, all very quietly, with minimal department involvement so I didn't tip off the wrong people. High powered attorneys, accountant firms, and an assassin comes back to town via backchannel because he didn't come through customs and have his passport stamped. I couldn't fathom why or how all this was still happening. Then I got a phone call from the very firm they were using for accounting. I found his tie to this firm. So I went straight to the Commissioner's office. He told me to call you, Mr. Cooper, and get busy. So I did. And now here we are."

Charlotte's heart strings were tugged for Togo's situation. He obviously cared greatly for his niece. "I'm sorry about your niece."

"As am I." Ethan immediately followed her condolences.

Blaine knew what it was like to lose family members for such nefarious reasons. "You'll have to stay out of what we're going to execute, Detective, as far as the NYPD officer's involved in padding their own pockets or you'll be labeled as a snitch with the department. That stigma stays with you even if the bust was warranted."

Togo nodded, silently, in agreement.

Captain Blaine was ready to get down to it. "After my team brought me up to speed VERY early this morning, I hopped on a plane at sixty-thirty hours my time at an airfield near Naples. With the six hours time difference, and eight hours to get here, I'm tired. I'm hungry, and I'm aggravated that this has been allowed to go on this long for Mr. Cooper and Mr. Togo. This ends. This ends with us. We start with the dirty cops, then we go to the gang. We move to Ashem and the assassin. We take out one of the heads of an international terrorist organization that has deep ties in this country. It's going to be messy. It's going to be complicated. It's going to be dangerous. It's going to be difficult on all of us. Either you're in or your out, right now. If you're out, there's no hard feelings just leave the room and you still have plausible deniability if you're questioned."

No one left the room. Ethan, Charlotte, Racheal, Nancy, and Detective Togo all craned their heads around, looking at each other. The Captain gave them a full minute of silence after she stood. Togo's eyes went to the bulge in Blaine's clothing at her right hip. She was armed and probably wearing a vest.

Blaine's stomach was growling. "Before we get started, please tell me where you put that something you promised me to eat."

14

Bits and Pieces

Charlotte was the only person siting at the bench in the tech support area and the only woman in the room of three men in their twenties, completely ignoring her. The soldering iron was on, hot, and ready. Circuit boards, duct tape, and pieces from an old router were laying in front of her. She was stripping off wire to make connections when a familiar scent and energy came up behind her. Ethan's shoes made a certain sound along with the cadence of his stride.

"I'm almost finished, Ethan." She pulled the hot soldering iron out of it's holder, pressing the tip to the end of a wire on a circuit board.

He looked at the pieces strewn in front of her. He recognized the remains of what was once a small wireless router. "Blaine's still upstairs with Togo, discussing things. They're waiting on you." He watched her pick points on the boards and keep touching the hot tip, melting portions of a wire to places on the boards. Ethan was impressed with her and her abilities. He wondered what it was like to be in her mind, always going, always thinking of solutions to what was in front of her. "You're sure this is going to jam the signal?"

"I'm positive. Hand me that antenna piece, will you?" She pointed to a loose black object lying beside the old wireless router case.

His left hand grasped the object and passed it over. The tech guys were discussing a problem with the server in the law library and how to fix the issue. He liked watching her work although he didn't understand what she was doing. She had great confidence, which drew him in, and kindness in her eyes. Charlotte was just the breath of fresh air he needed in his life, surprising him every day in some way. He admired her for pursuing exactly what she wanted, a stationery store, even though she was clearly talented mechanically. He'd always wanted to paint and give music lessons. And yet, here he was, managing partner at his own firm, grooming Racheal. His mother wouldn't have allowed her son to be the vagabond artist who had a parade of students in and out. *Success isn't always what you thought it would be and it comes with a price, your dreams*, he thought.

Charlotte pursed her lips as she brought together the last piece. "Let's get our coats. We're going to make sure this works." She could hear the network technicians making assumptions about the library server. The soldering iron was replaced, unplugged, and the excess parts put away in a box under the bench. As she walked away with Ethan to leave the room, she paused at the door with him. These techs were afraid of the lawyers from the comments they were making. "Guys, you can postulate all day on what's wrong with the server, but until you actually leave the room and troubleshoot, you're never going to know. If the partners make you that uncomfortable, go unplug the machine and bring it down here. Just post a sign that it's out of order and send an email to the company address book. The faster you get it fixed, the faster you'll stop receiving emails that it's broken."

They exchanged looks with each other, deciding who would leave the room and actually invade the law library.

Ethan was getting aggravated. "Oh for heavens sake! She's right. One of you just go! And if someone gives you a hard time, tell them I sent you to get the machine. Then come and tell me who it was and I'll have a chat with them." As he and Charlotte approached the elevator, Ethan watched the youngest tech leave for the stairs. "Those guys take socially awkward up to a new level. I didn't think my firm was that scary."

They walked to the elevator.

"If I didn't know you, I'd be intimidated by you." She said it very succinctly.

"Really?" He was puzzled.

"Yes. Your posture, your hand-made suit, your tone. You have a way of commanding someone's attention completely. You get what you want."

The elevator car arrived, the doors opening before them.

He turned to her once inside, staring directly into her eyes. Ethan inhaled slowly, breathing in her scent he was so close. The more time he spent around her, the more he knew exactly what he wanted. Her. "I go after what I want."

Charlotte swallowed as she remembered to breathe, her cheeks flushing. Her brown eyes were locked on him. He really meant that. There was no question in her mind now exactly how he felt about her. She wanted very much to give in to the growing feelings she had for him. Letting him in was dangerous to her heart.

The elevator doors closed. Thoughts and ideas were running amok.

Ethan sat behind his desk, watching Captain Blaine and Charlotte speak in a kind of short hand he didn't understand. Too many military abbreviations? Jargon he didn't recognize? The techs from earlier were still on his mind. They seemed so intimidated by him and the attorneys at the firm that they feared the repercussions of fixing a server because of a confrontation with a firm member. What kind of culture had he allowed to propagate at this firm? It was us and them? If you weren't a partner then you were nothing? The associates were clearly upset when the document center was out of order and the partners had scolded them for sending jobs to their wing. Technology helped a firm to succeed. Great associates who felt they contributed and were allowed to flourish made a firm or could break a firm. Clearly, something needed to change at this one. He stood up.

"Ladies, I'll be back in a few minutes." He stepped over to Nancy's desk. "Pardon the interruption."

"Of course, Mr. Cooper."

"Nancy, do you feel like the other partners exclude or harass our associates and other employees because only they contribute to the bottom line with enough billable hours?"

"Racheal is the only partner that makes me feel wanted here. I stay on this side of the building for a reason. Barbara and I both stay over here unless we absolutely have to go to the other wing."

His shoulders sunk down inside his suit. "How have I been so blind to this? Why didn't you hit me over the head and tell me?"

"Because you have enough to deal with already." Nancy was very matter of fact. "I learned years ago to keep my head down and my mouth shut. I work for you. I don't worry about them. I'm a grown woman. So is Barbara. We'd tell you or Racheal if there was something we couldn't handle."

"But you shouldn't have to handle it. I don't want a law firm where the partners make everyone else feel less than adequate because they don't have juris doctorate after their name. Charles and I always wanted this place to feel like a family."

"This isn't anything new, Mr. Cooper. Certain long-time members of this family are going to need their butt busted if they don't cease their belittling actions." Her tone matched the motherly warning given if you didn't stop what you were doing.

Ethan cracked a silly smile as Nancy made a face only a mother could flash with that line, eyes that clearly meant the warning that made you wonder if you shouldn't listen to her or else. Yes, apparently they did need some butt busting. As the managing partner, he was just the one to give it to them.

She winked at him. Obviously, she'd given him food for thought. "We can discuss this further when you're not up to your elbows with other important things. Please let Captain Blaine know I've arranged what she asked for earlier. Racheal and the Detective are on their way back now from the Judge's chambers. She said they were successful."

"That's wonderful news, Nancy. Thank you." He was troubled over the firm but relieved the team now had the legal side of the ball rolling toward executing their plan.

Thirty minutes later, at four-forty-five, Racheal and Detective Togo raced from the elevator toward the conference room. They walked by Ethan's office at their determined pace, Racheal waving at everyone, silently, to join them through the glass.

"We got'em! All of them! It's been years since I've looked at warrants this closely or used my legs so effectively with Judge Helmsley." Her body racked with audible laughter. "Now to get these shoes off my feet and a hot cup of coffee in my hand. I'm freezing!"

"I've got that one covered." Barbara stepped into the conference room with coffee in both hands for the Detective and Racheal. "Anything else, Ms. Maxwell?"

"Oh, thank you, Barbara!" Racheal wrapped her frozen fingers around the ceramic cup in relief. "That's all for now. For your own safety, shut that door behind you. If you're caught up, have a great night, Barbara. See you tomorrow."

"Yes, ma'am. Happy to help with the cloak and dagger. I haven't seen you this excited about a case in a while." Barbara actually looked pleased as she turned to leave.

The door clicked shut, the glass walls turning milky white. Orders were about to be given and divided up amongst the team. The plans were falling into place quickly and justice was going to be served.

Charlotte's mind hadn't shut down since Blaine had landed. Who was she kidding? Did her mind ever shut down? This heightened time of critical thinking had been good for one thing, no panic attacks. They had abated with all the business of the days and nights keeping her mind occupied. She had a great sense of purpose again, instead of going from phone call to phone call with vendors, meeting to meeting with key military personnel, and once alone, her mind flashing back to the horrors on the day she had lost Benjamin. Now, there was clarity, focus for what immediately lay ahead. Their plan was like a great poker game. For now, they were stacking the deck in their favor. Blaine never played poker without an ace up her sleeve. Charlotte had seen that over the years.

Over a week had passed in a blur of caffeine, naps, more caffeine, and enough adrenaline to keep them all going on little sleep. The first week of December was merely a memory. Meals were eaten together over the conference room table. More of Blaine's team had presented themselves, George Winter and Leilani Kekoa had headed for Savannah, Georgia. That left Harry Ashby, Noah Wheaton, and Daniel Wheaton in New York. The family resemblance with Daniel was undeniable. He had been the last team member to fly up from Washington to meet them. They had paired off to the dry cleaner building with Charlotte's gizmo to jam the signal and conduct surveillance. Several gang members were also tailed after being seen going in and out. Data transmissions occurred when there were people inside the dry cleaners. The cameras were motion activated. There was no certainty of Charlotte's safety now if Ashem had watched the transmissions from the cameras, which she had seen on his garnered files. The gang had to be suspicious of her poking around inside the building if they were also keeping an eye on the place. She was staring out the windows from Ethan's office, the Empire State Building was a faint outline in the distance. The sun was setting on another Thursday very quickly. Warrants were in place for arrests, for seizure of Ashem's computers, and they had probable cause for a warrant to enter the dry cleaners. The shipment that would be in the port would also be searched, most likely seized, with the warrants being signed off on as the rest of the team waited. This was no longer a quiet NYPD investigation. It had passed over to the U.S. Attorney's office once Blaine and her team were fully in charge. Now alphabet soup was involved, DEA, FBI, Homeland Security, and the Navy. They all cooperated and coordinated with Blaine's team, who had agreed to be the lead on this circus since it involved stolen Navy intelligence and real property. Each government agency would have their pickings on what was divided up after arrests were made.

Charlotte turned away from the windows to find Ethan standing in the office doorway, staring at her. "Is she ready for us to come back in?"

He simply nodded affirmatively. The circles under his eyes had grown since this morning.

Blaine was sure to include everyone involved at the law firm and Detective Togo on any update, regardless of how small. They were sitting and standing in the conference room. Lewis had picked up Chinese for them and disappeared with Marcus to eat their portions before fetching them all dessert from Baby Cakes. Chinese food containers covered the table as everyone grabbed a plate and their choice of utensils. Ethan found a container of garlic chicken near the middle of the heap. He tipped it slightly to the right where Charlotte could see the contents. She grinned at him, then winked in her approval. There was a bag of four eggrolls in her hand. He returned the wink at her regarding the eggrolls for them to eat. She grabbed two sets of chopsticks as they sat down near the end to dig in to the garlic chicken together. As everyone settled in around the table with their preferred choices, Blaine whistled to knock the din of noise down, then looked to Ethan. He offered a quick prayer for the blessing of the food.

Charlotte waited for Ethan to have a few bites of the chicken first. She quickly devoured an egg roll and picked up her chopsticks. The two traded off in silence for possession of the garlic chicken box.

"Don't eat all of it. I want some more." Ethan bit off the end of a second egg roll.

"I won't. I promise." Charlotte brought the chopsticks back to her mouth. The hot pepper and garlic in the sauce were beginning to make her sweat, a fine sheen breaking out across her lip. "This is hotter than the garlic chicken I have at home."

Blaine countered her statement. "But it's really good! Thank you, Ethan, for feeding my team and taking such good care of us. The Olmsted Hotel has been a dream, what little I've been there. I'm looking forward to a hot bath and some sleep soon."

Ethan swallowed his bite of egg roll. "You're welcome. We cannot thank you enough for the help."

Blaine put down her chopsticks and a box of Hunan Beef. "Absolutely. It's what we do. I know you're ready for some closure." She licked her lips where the sauce still remained in the corners of her mouth. "Let's all go get some rest so we can hit the ground running, early. Detective, you will be staying with us at the hotel tonight. No one stays alone." She turned to Racheal. "Including you. Ashem has eyes and ears all over the place, high up on the food chain and payrolls."

Daniel Wheaton, Captain Blaine's son, sitting beside her, paused his aggressive attack on a box of chow mein. "We ready to run this?" He was the youngest of Blaine's team at thirty-one.

Everyone's eyes focused on Blaine. Charlotte was the person who began speaking, however.

"We break after eating. We're all short on sleep. Get as much as possible. We all meet back here at zero four hundred hours. ARES team, you have your assignments. Lewis and Marcus will be assisting. Just remember folks, they are civilians. If you have to leave your vehicles, make sure they're protected with a vest and they remain behind cover. Daniel, are the DEA agents up to speed and ready?"

"Yes, ma'am. They're standing by for our cue."

"Great. Dānā signed off on the building purchase yesterday afternoon. Now that Ashem, well technically Empire, no longer owns the building we have unfettered access to clean out and clean up. Vests handed out earlier today are not optional. You eat in them. You sleep in them. The minute you walk outside this place, they better be on under your clothing. When the jammer finally died yesterday, while we were pulling out most of the barrels in the old dry cleaning building, anyone on camera with me became targets. Ashem's passport has been flagged. His personal accounts have been frozen. Without assets at his disposal, he's not going anywhere. The securities fraud case is a lock, thanks to my brilliant friend, Racheal." Charlotte paused as light applause was given. "Classified Navy materials and weapons have been and will be recovered from the information off of Ashem's hard drive. George and Leilani are tightening up loose ends in Savannah."

Daniel, Harry, and Blaine all issued a Navy "Hoo-yah!"

"Once we wrap this up with a bow for the NYPD, the DEA, Homeland Security, and the Navy, we're home free. Any questions?"

No one spoke up immediately. They were continuing to eat and enjoy a moment of normalcy. Ethan now understood why Charlotte had spent most of the day with Blaine. She was here because Charlotte had called, but Charlotte was helping to call the plays.

Charlotte needed another egg roll. "Alright then. Eat up! Curtain goes up at zero four hundred."

Noah Wheaton put his dinner aside for a moment. He pulled a folded flat badge out of his jacket pocket and slid it down the table to Charlotte, near the end with Ethan. Charlotte lifted the cover to see an updated photo on government credentials for the DIA.

Blaine picked up an egg roll from the middle of the table. They were almost gone now. "Your updated credentials. I'm glad to have you back, Pink."

Charlotte swallowed another bite. "I'm not back. Just on loan again."

A knowing smile graced Blaine's lips. "Uh huh. We both know you don't walk away from this. One way or another it follows you, wherever you go. Those have been on ice since the accident. I didn't want to pull you back in too soon. I know it's not permanent, but it's nice to know I can call you when I need you."

"Anytime." Charlotte meant that. She was a civilian, but honored to serve alongside those in uniform when her country or service members needed her.

Ethan leaned forward to see Charlotte's photo on Defense Intelligence Agency credentials. His brow furrowed. "Are you a spook?"

A laugh escaped her throat. "I can neither confirm nor deny." She flashed him a quick grin. "I'm kidding. I just assist them when I'm needed. I relinquished my credentials after the accident. With the panic attacks and the PTSD, I couldn't go out in the field anymore. If I have to carry a weapon, especially here in New York, the credentials make it easier."

Detective Togo leaned across the table. "I heard that!"

"No offense, Detective."

His belly shook under the Chinese container resting on it. "None taken. I understand."

Charlotte leaned forward so only Ethan could hear her words. "I spent some time on the phone today with Blaine's team psychologist. I had to pass the muster before I could be handed credentials again or go out with her in the field. If I'm not fit, I have no business putting myself or someone else in danger. I'm cleared for duty again if they need me, hearing aids and all. Blaine worked with me today on box breathing techniques too. I haven't employed them in a while."

Ethan squeezed her knee and smiled. She was a woman of many mysteries and talents. "She called you Pink. Is that your code name?"

Another chuckle. "Yes, it is, because I'm always wearing it. Blaine chose it for me."

"It suits you perfectly. Especially since you're wearing a pink shirt right now."

15

The Enemy of My Enemy

Daylight was only beginning to peek through the cloudy skies hovering over Harlem. The borough was just waking up to a frigid late Fall day. Christmas lights were still on in a few of the apartment windows on the street, their twinkling strands plugged in from the evening before. Harry Ashby gripped an insulated coffee cup through tactical gloves, watching one apartment in particular. The dark van he was in driven by Marcus, Ethan's longtime driver, was parked across from a multi-story building, watching the dark window of dirty vice cop. Harry sat waiting for him, like a lion, watching the door for his prey. He knew the cop had a routine as he had been sitting on this guy for a few days now. Steam billowed away from the coffee cup's lid as he took a sip. He was usually quite the joker, but this morning chose to remain silent, concentrating on the job at hand. The cop finally came outside. Marcus crept up the street with the van, coming alongside the cop's SUV parked at the curb. Harry exited the van quietly from the now

287

open side door. A black hood was pulled down over the cop's head as Harry's arms went around his neck. He never knew what hit him from behind. Within moments, the target passed out and was pulled into the van. Harry's snatch and grab job was complete. He looked down at the ground to the smashed pieces of his earwig. In his haste to capture the cop he'd lost his communication with the team. He tried calling Blaine, no answer.

To the southeast, in the borough of Queens, another dark van, driven by Lewis, sat parked outside a small home, clad in brick, with Noah Wheaton in the passenger seat surveilling the entrance of the home. There was only one car parked at the curb, as the cop on the take was divorced with one child who visited only on the weekends. Christmas lights on the house closest to them were intermittently flashing on the roofline. It was cold here in New York, not like the temperatures near Naples, Italy, where he'd been based out of with Captain Blaine for the last twelve years with the rest of the team. He had been discussing wines with Lewis since four thirty in the morning. Primitivo grapes versus softer American grapes seemed to keep them awake over their coffee, now all but gone. Dawn was breaking. They were both quiet again, watching the lights come on in the home. Somebody was awake and would be in custody without a hiccup as soon as they exited the home.

Captain Blaine was dozing in the passenger seat of the Mercedes Lewis usually piloted daily through traffic for Racheal. Charlotte put the night vision binoculars back down on her lap, narrowly avoiding the steering wheel she'd moved up for the time being. They were practically useless because of the lights here in the city. Chelsea, the cop's neighborhood, was waking up for the day. She reached for the lukewarm coffee left in the insulated tumbler. The cup was empty, again. Dawn was coming but the city lights and looming outlines of tall buildings blocked out the first rays of the day. Detective Togo and Ethan could be heard snoring in the back seat, further proof that Blaine literally could sleep though anything. Even with only one hearing aid in her right ear, with the worst hearing damage, the snoring was loud enough. It was echoing in her left ear, where the team earwig resided. The Chief of the vice squad came around the corner of the apartment building at five minutes after six for his daily run. Charlotte drew a breath. As soon as she spoke, everyone in the car was awake.

"The target is approaching your location, Lieutenant."

Daniel was sitting in a coffee shop, using a newspaper as a prop. He ditched the paper and sprang into action with her words in his earwig.

"He's wearing an NYPD sweatshirt, black beanie. You can't miss him." Charlotte cranked the car and inched out into traffic from the side street. She tossed the radio at Blaine, now wide awake.

"You let me fall asleep?" Blaine was appalled she had been dozing.

"It's a boring detail. There was no sense in all of us being awake until warranted." Charlotte turned the steering wheel more bringing the car closer to the action.

Daniel timed his move perfectly, opening the coffee shop door into the target with some force. The chief grabbed his nose, no doubt broken by the impact of the glass on his face. His hands came up to meet blood, now gushing from his nose. Before he knew it, Daniel had him on the ground to bleed on the sidewalk.

"Target acquired. Can you call me a bus? He's going to need some medical attention."

Blaine depressed the button on the radio. "You got it." Her cell phone buzzed with two text messages from Noah and a missed call from Harry. She keyed the police radio to call an ambulance for the chief, now in custody.

Daniel was handcuffing the dirty cop as the Mercedes came to a slow stop. The tinted passenger window rolled down a couple of inches, exposing Blaine to the cold air but hiding the backseat occupants.

"Looks like you've got him in hand, Mr. Wheaton. Bus is on the way, courtesy FDNY. Marshals are on the way too. Noah acquired his target. I haven't heard from Harry. Just a missed call. See if you can get in touch with him. I'll meet up with you later. You stay with them, follow them through processing."

Daniel's breath was forming puffs in the chilly morning air with each exhale. "See you then. I'll get the paperwork going." The cop was on his belly, moaning and wiggling in the cuffs. "Pipe down, sweetheart. You're not going anywhere."

"I'm an NYPD-"

"Lieutenant Daniel Wheaton, U.S. Naval Intelligence. Now that we've been formally introduced. I have a warrant for your arrest, Chief, by order of the U.S. Attorney. On behalf of the United

States, let me read you your rights. Oh wait! You're involved with an organization that supports terrorism, so as of now, under the Patriot Act and ratified by the Supreme Court, kiss your rights goodbye. Now sit up. Here comes the calvary to take a look at your nose."

Charlotte pulled away from the curb to head toward the parking garage near the firm. "Three down, only a gang and terrorist to go. I need to get back across town and find a restroom. I've had WAY too much coffee." Ethan had to get to East Harlem and she had to get to the old dry cleaners to complete their part of the mission.

Charlotte opened the front door of the old dry cleaners without any issue from the security system. The building had belonged to Empire, unbeknownst to Dānā until he was made fully aware. After full disclosure, Dānā was more than willing to divest the property. Ethan and Racheal drew up the paperwork quickly. After a hasty purchase, the building was now hers, at least legally for the tidy sum of one dollar. What was inside the building now belonged to Charlotte, regardless of the nefarious nature of the contents. She began to pull the lids off of drums, already known to contain large sums of cash. The cameras inside were still running, Blaine's team monitoring the signal and outgoing data. Outside, agents from the Drug Enforcement Agency in cooperation with the NYPD, and Captain Blaine's ARES unit, with the Defense Intelligence Agency, surrounded the building. The three dirty cops were now occupying federal cells under the watchful eyes of the U.S. Marshal Service to be taken to a rendition site for further questioning at Blaine's discretion. The DEA wanted the gang members, Detective Togo wanted the assassin, and Blaine wanted Ashem so badly she could taste it. Their paths had fully converged.

The cameras usefulness had been exploited. They now had footage of her quintessentially robbing the stateside branch of a Mexican drug cartel. She looked right into the camera, daring whomever was watching to stop her.

"Do you have what you need, Blaine?" Charlotte put the drum lid in her hand on the floor.

"We do. You can come out now." Blaine was watching a mobile feed on an iPad inside a surveillance van a block away.

Charlotte remembered the chemical containers near the rear entrance of the building. The door was locked from both sides when she had tried opening it before. It didn't seem to be on the digital lock circuit with the others. She pulled off what looked like a fire door bumper mechanism to reveal an old-fashioned dead bolt securing the door.

"What are you doing, Pink?" Blaine was curious about her friend's actions.

"I'm setting up a little insurance. You always taught me to never play poker without an ace up my sleeve. I'm taking care of that ace." Charlotte looked around her at all the other tools, mechanically and chemically, at her disposal. The car battery on a moving dolly was wheeled over. By using the available parts on hand, the battery was turned into an electromagnet. In a few moments, she had the lock disabled and the door could move freely. Charlotte disabled the magnet, but left the battery near the door re-attaching the cables in a such a way as to electrify the door. Anyone who grabbed it from the other side would get a big enough zap to propel them backwards, giving authorities enough time to seize them. "Are you following me, Captain?"

Blaine smirked over the scene she was watching in her hands. "I see it." She let everyone listening on their team in on the action. "Be advised, everyone, the rear door is not approachable, repeat, do not touch or go near the rear door on the building." She continued to speak with Charlotte via her team earwig. "So advised." A grin erupted on her face. "How fast is that brain of yours working right now?" Laughter left her body. "Just how many cards do you have up your sleeve, Pink?"

"Enough to stack the deck in our favor." Charlotte continued to pull containers from shelves setting up the rest of the insurance policy. When she was satisfied, she looked up at the camera Blaine was watching currently. She smirked, then winked at the camera. "Aces."

Detective Togo came over their earwigs. "We have a lone marked Club Thirteen dark gray Range Rover approaching from the northeast. GET OUTTA THERE, NOW!"

Charlotte ran toward the front, killing the lights in the building. "I cannot make the front door. They'll see me!" She ran toward a utility closet near the rear of the building. "I'm hiding instead. I'm in a utility closet in the northwest corner. Let me know when I'm clear. Where did these guys come from?"

Harry Ashby climbed into the van with Blaine. "From the port. I followed them after we picked up our target. My earwig is dead or I would've told you. Target acquired, by the way."

"Why didn't you just call me?" Leave it to Harry to always have issues. Blaine waited on his answer.

"I did, from my phone and two others. I've been trying for more than an hour. I sent texts too." Harry gave her a look that said it all.

Blaine pulled her phone out. It was on silent. She didn't remember switching it to silent. Fifteen missed calls from Harry shown in large letters on her phone, another twelve from two different numbers she didn't recognize. The screen was dim although the battery was nearly fully charged. She held the button down to reboot the phone. "Yes, you did. What have we missed?"

Harry took off his gloves, rubbing his hands together. "If it can go wrong, it will." He pulled another earwig out of a briefcase in the van, placing it in his ear. "Four occupants. They kept taking boxes from a container at the port and loading them into the back of that Rover. I don't know what's inside, but it's important enough that they haven't been to bed yet. Your Butcher is inside that SUV. He was the one barking orders. Everyone else is lower level. Don't let him out of your sight."

Togo piped up, his fists clenching. "We won't."

Lewis and Noah sat in the Benz, parked across the street from a multi-story East Harlem building, off of the northeast corner of Central Park. The facade was rough, crumbling in some places, and had weathered many tenants. Most of the block had undergone preservation renewal. New brick, new paint, new sidewalks, new railing, but this building stood out in a worn-down manner. The structure seemed to emanate a vibe that kept you away. Traffic was picking up for the day. Delivery trucks were passing by, taxi cabs, and even more pedestrians were stirring. Somewhere nearby a dog was barking loudly. Vehicle exhaust mixed with the smell of fresh baked goods from a corner store caught on the stiff breeze whistling between the buildings.

Ethan stood in front of the property peering up at what once would have been a beautiful building. Even in the dim morning light, the moulding along the roofline could be made out along with the details around the windows. Now it housed an entire empire of it's own, Club Thirteen. They owned East Harlem and had for years. *What must it be like living near them on a daily basis?* He took the stairs and rapped loudly on the front door. It too was worn with peeling black paint. He turned to see the tinted car windows on the passenger side of the Benz, facing him. He knew there was a laser microphone pointed toward him and the building, listening, from behind that dark tint. He had volunteered to do this despite Charlotte, Nancy, and Racheal trying to talk him out of it.

Noah spoke up in his ear. "Deep breath. You got this. If they've even gone to bed, it may take a minute to roust them. Keep knocking. Guys like this are not up before mid-afternoon usually." The microphone in his hand was picking up someone coming to the door. "Someone is heading your way."

Ethan sucked in a short breath as the door opened just a little bit. He tried to steady his nerves.

A twenty-something, barely shoulder-high, hispanic male peered back at him through the crack, his coal black short hair sticking up in several places. He'd obviously been rousted from sleep. *Who does this guy think he is knocking on OUR door this time of day?* His thick accent came out with a sharp tone. "Leave now and I might forget you woke me up."

Ethan tried not let his words come out shaky. "I need to speak with Lalo."

"And just what business do you have with him?" The man eyed Ethan's obviously tailored suit, impeccable shoes, and silk tie showing somewhat underneath his black wool car coat. He was dressed too well to be a cop.

"Tell him if he wants to live, he needs to speak with me. His boss in Mexico City is going to want his money for the shipment coming into the port. Lalo's money is not where he thinks it is. He's been robbed."

Narrow sleep-deprived eyes on the other side of the door suddenly went wide. "You serious? Give me a minute, man."

The door was abruptly shut in Ethan's face. He stood there on the stoop, waiting, for several minutes. The wind was picking up; a storm was coming. His gloved hands retreated to his coat pockets. He could feel his heart beating in his ears. *Please let this come to an end without anyone getting hurt,* he silently prayed.

Noah's voice came back in his ear. "You're doing great. Good job on not oversharing with the door man. Sounds like a couple of people are approaching the door. We've got a small army sitting out here between the NYPD and the DEA. We're listening. If it should go south, we will breach the door. Watch your six."

Ethan's brow furrowed. "Huh?"

"Be careful." Noah had been working with the Navy for so long he'd picked up that phrase for watching your rear-end.

The door opened a bit wider this time and a hefty arm came out, pulling Ethan's car coat forward before the rest of his body followed with a sudden jerk. The heavy, worn door shut quickly to keep the cold air outside. Ethan looked up in the nearly dark entry to see Lalo Becerra descending the stairs, rubbing his eyes. The closer he came, the heavier the smell of stale alcohol became. The man Ethan had blamed as the instigator for his wife's death was walking toward him. The heartbeat in his ears was fading. His nostrils were beginning to flair, his breath deepening. Slow rage was warming him quite nicely. *Calm down. You have a job to do.*

Noah piped up in his ear again. "I know you want to tackle this man and beat him to a pulp. I understand that urge. I've been there. Deep breaths, let that anger be useful. Remember, you're the man standing in between him and his money. You've got the power."

Two taller, well built men who'd escorted him inside began to pat him down roughly.

"I'm not armed." Ethan had never carried a gun but today he wished that he did standing feet from a man he'd grown to abhor.

Lalo titled his head back, chin out, dismissing them from their task. *This fool wouldn't dare come armed or wearing a wire.* From his relaxed posture, he didn't feel threatened in the slightest. "You shouldn't be here. You might wind up like that pretty little wife of yours."

Yes, it was safe to say they were familiar with each other. It was like high-noon between two unarmed cowboys.

"You got us outta bed. You got something to say, say it!" Lalo propped himself up on the stair rail, his crew filling up the entryway, rousted from their sleep by raised voices.

Ethan felt his lower jaw retreat, his teeth grinding together. "Do you know where your money is?"

"That's a stupid question, GQ. I know where **all** my money is. I got an accountant and an investment firm takes care of my family. Empire. It's all legit now too. Ain't nothing you can do about it."

"My firm went through your firm's records because of suspected securities fraud and money laundering. He's taking care of your money alright and taking you to the cleaners. Pun intended."

Lalo's eyes narrowed. "You have my attention, GQ. Now make it quick because I have a short attention span."

"Don't take my word for it. Look at your books for yourself. You know how much you take in, roughly, from your dealers every month."

"Downsizing. There's just ten of us now and our ladies." Lalo motioned to everyone present then waved a hand at the rest of the house.

"Look at the statements Ashem's giving to you. I'm not an accountant or an investment banker, but even I figured out he's playing you. He's siphoning off your money. It's been small amounts over time, but it's added up to a big payday for him. Ever heard of a broken arrow? There's one off the coast of Savannah, Georgia. He's using your money to help his own 'gang' to find a lost bomb and harvest the uranium. They're planning something as we speak. And the cash you've been keeping in the closed dry cleaners, that's gone too. The building was sold off. The new owner is there now, moving barrels and discovering a treasure trove inside."

"How do you know about that?"

"I had a friend who wanted to lease the space. She found it curious that the owner had the building for sale but had no interest in selling it. We did a little digging. Imagine our surprise when we found fifty-five gallon drums that used to hold solvents and detergents now full of cash. I guess that's where you were keeping it all until Ashem could deal with it, right?" Ethan pulled out his phone to show Lalo the video Blaine's team had pushed to his phone minutes before of Charlotte inside opening barrels.

"So much for the state-of-the-art security system you just had to have installed, Pee Wee." The short hispanic who'd initially opened the door to Ethan walked back into the entry from another room after hearing the chastisement.

"I forgot to pull the grate back down again. Sorry. I believe him, Lalo. I thought the statements were a little odd, but they have been off. I thought it was just market fluctuation." Pee Wee wasn't sure if he was going to be hit or killed by the statement.

"You knew this and didn't tell me? Get the guys and let's roll. We're checking out the cleaners with GQ. If this is real, Empire is going down. We worked too hard to get into this country to have it wasted by some desert rag America hater. I ain't forgot nine eleven man."

"None of us ever will, but they aren't all America haters. The principal owner, Dānā, whom I'm sure you've seen, is who drew our attention to the fraud. He did you a big favor."

"It's gone. All of it, gone!" Pee Wee began shrieking as he continued to watch the phone Ethan was holding. The older video feed, timestamped to current, showed the barrels that once held money were now devoid of their cargo.

"What if I can help you get it back?"

Lalo pondered the idea. "Why would you do that, GQ? We sent the man to kill the witness your wife was riding with."

Ethan sucked in a breath before answering. "Because you didn't order El Carnicero to kill her, did you?"

Lalo rubbed his eyes. "No, just our blabbing former family. It came down from Mexico City. Killing is Ferrara's thing. Not mine. He has a thing for a Persian lady up the street. So he visits, often. I can't help it if bodies pile up when he's in town. He freaks me out actually."

Noah, still listening with the microphone from outside, turned to issue a big grin to Lewis. "We got him! He just incriminated himself and his crew."

Ethan prayed Noah had recorded every word the laser was yielding from outside for use later at trial. "The enemy of my enemy is my friend. I want the hitman who killed my wife. You want the man who's taking your money. I despise a liar and thief. Ashem is both."

Lalo rubbed his chin, then pursed his lips. "Ay, yo. What you say?"

One by one, the gang all agreed.

Ethan nodded once in agreement. "Have Ashem meet us at the old dry cleaners in thirty minutes."

Lalo tilted his head to look at Ethan through squinted eyes. "Us?"

Ethan froze in place. "Bring whomever you want. Although the place is small. My car is out front. I have room for two more. My driver is waiting. I am only assuming you'd want me there since my firm documented his malfeasance."

Noah breathed a sigh of relief. "Nice save."

"Whoa, GQ! Cool it with the five dollar words. We don't need you and your chauffeur there. We'll handle it our way, city boy." Lalo locked eyes on him as a plan was forming in his head.

Now that is frightening. "You cannot kill him if you want your money back. This man has financial accounts in foreign countries, properties, friends in high places, and a fake paper trail. If you want your money back, we need him alive."

"You're no fun. Can I make him sweat, just a little?" Lalo could see his valid point.

Ethan couldn't help but smile. "I think this occasion definitely calls for that."

"Go get in your car. What is it, a Bentley?" Lalo teased, waiting.

"No, black Mercedes across the street. We'll wait and follow you." Ethan hoped they'd let him just walk out. He didn't relish the thought of riding anywhere with this gang.

"Show our friend here the door. Pee Wee, make the call." Lalo ascended the stairs as Ethan was escorted out. They needed heavy clothes. It was too cold outside and too early for all this. He hadn't been asleep nearly long enough.

Ethan tried to walk calmly from the building to the car. The icy wind was numbing to the face. Marcus got out and opened the rear passenger door to keep up appearances in case someone was watching from the gang.

Noah remained quiet until Marcus was inside the car as well. "You did it, GQ." He chuckled at overemphasizing the GQ, "The fact that you dressed the part and played to their weakness did the trick. Nice job."

"When he turned on me after I said 'us' I thought that was it." Ethan put his seatbelt on and settled.

"No, you saved it quite brilliantly." Noah listened to the sounds of Spanish mixed with English, clothes being donned, and no doubt weapons being gathered. Minutes passed and only five people exited the building, headed for a late model Cadillac Escalade. Noah piped up to let Blaine know they were on the move. "Headed your way with four in a black Escalade." Noah keyed another frequency to talk to the DEA again. "Robby, it's your show now, man."

The DEA car stayed behind to monitor the gang along with an unmarked NYPD unit. Now that Lalo was no longer in the building, more DEA agents would be swarming shortly to arrest the remaining occupants. Club Thirteen would be shut down in East Harlem.

16

Bait and Switch

The wind seemed to propel the black Mercedes Benz faster as it passed Detective Togo's location in an unmarked NYPD cruiser. The car came to a stop behind the Range Rover, already parked in front of the old dry cleaners.

Captain Blaine's voice cut through everyone's channels. "Stay alert! That is not Ethan Cooper's car. His won't arrive at our location for a few more minutes. Somebody with infrared tell me how many people are in that car!"

El Carnicero opened the driver's door of the Range Rover and stepped out into the breezy December morning. Despite the cold, his head was completely exposed, showing extensive tattooing. Dark ink covered the back, sides, and top; everywhere but his face. The goatee around his mouth was the only adornment. The long, thick black duster covering his body came within a few inches of touching the ground. Only three strides with his long legs and he opened the rear passenger door of the Mercedes.

"Two people in the car. One exiting now and a driver. Ferrara was the only passenger in the Rover." The disembodied voice belonged to a DEA agent helping them.

"Copy that." Blaine was watching this new development carefully.

Ashem stepped out of the vehicle onto the sidewalk, gesticulating wildly as he spoke in Farsi to someone on the phone.

Blaine could hear every word but Farsi wasn't her strongest foreign language. That was Pink's wheelhouse. "Are you hearing this, Pink?"

"Not really." Charlotte strained to hear what was being said through the com in her ear, turned up as loud as possible, and the one remaining hearing aid she was wearing in her left ear.

"They're coming your way. Stay put." Blaine let out a slow breath before her face scrunched up in slight frustration. "Harry, see if you can get playback on that conversation to Pink."

"Copy that." Harry sprang to work in the back of the van.

Ashem stood behind El Carnicero, waiting for him to open the door to the building. His conversation wrapped up finally, tucking his phone away inside his coat. "Hurry up! They'll be here soon."

"I can't imagine Lalo coming down here himself at this time of day." Ferrara held the door open for Ashem.

Echoes of heel clicks from Ashem's Italian hand-made shoes circled the empty building as he walked forward, deeper into the space. The sound was more resonant than usual. As the lights came on, under his right hand, he knew why. The many barrels that once occupied the middle of the space were now almost gone. Only three barrels, sitting together, were left. The room was devoid of any sound dampening materials as well. He turned around completely, looking for some explanation for what should have been here.

Ashem faced Ferrara, his eyebrows drawn completely up under his wool fedora. "What is the meaning of all this? Did you remove the containers?"

"I've done nothing of the sort!" Ferrara was insulted at the allegation he was responsible. He stepped forward and pulled the handle of the barrel closest to him. Once the ring popped off, the lid was removed. There was glycerin inside, exactly as it was marked. "Where's the money?"

"You're asking me?" Ashem's nose turned up slightly, his lips pursing in disdain. "It was supposed to be here. You have unfettered access to this place. And the grate was up when we arrived." His eyes rolled as his gloved hands came up to cover his face. He exhaled forcefully, his hands dropping to pound on the top of the barrel to the right of the glycerin.

Charlotte tried to be as still as possible and control her breathing, listening to the men. They were loud enough to easily hear the expletives issued by Ashem in Farsi, then more words. She smiled, her eyes squeezing shut, trying not to laugh at his frustration. *Could it be? He's afraid of the gang and the Mexican cartel the money belonged to. What would he tell his sister?*

Ferrara shoved him aside, pulling the ring off both the remaining barrels. One was empty, one contained potassium permanganate.

"Pink, he's pulling the tops off the barrels you left in the middle of the room. I'm no engineer, but that's not good, right?" Blaine knew both chemicals were traditionally used for softening water and to help with cleaning laundry. Pink had said so earlier, but she had also stated they were explosive if combined.

Charlotte couldn't reply. She tapped on her com link twice signifying a response of no. Her taps wouldn't be heard behind the heavy steel door, protecting her in the closet.

Togo's voice cut through. "13's Escalade just dropped three at the end of the block to walk up. Looks like the car's heading around the block to the back I think."

Harry was checking the plate he'd garnered earlier on the Range Rover. "Rover belongs to Esther Samadhi."

Blaine traded a look of surprise with Harry, as they continued to listen and watch.

Ashem exhaled again. "You must go. They'll be wondering why you're here." He pulled the fedora from his head using his left hand, his right reaching into his pocket to answer a buzzing cell phone.

Ferrara exited the dry cleaners shaking his head, as he walked down the back alley trying to get away from the building. Too late, Club 13's Escalade was parking behind the building. He'd walked right into their path.

"Keep your head down, Pink. This is about to get interesting. Everybody, stay sharp. This could go south quickly." Blaine watched three gang members enter the front door, just missing Ferrara as he'd left and headed opposite their direction. Lalo and Pee Wee shared a glance as Ferrara now stood before the vehicle. They exited, walking forward together as he slowly backed up. Tito, their driver, closed the door, locking their ride.

"What are you doing here with the enemy, El Carnicero?" Lalo put the pieces together. Ferrara was playing both sides.

"I didn't know he was the enemy." El Carnicero had gone completely ashen.

"You were supposed to protect the family, not betray us all. Do you know this man is a thief?" Pee Wee stepped between El Carnicero and Lalo.

"I go where the money is. He paid more." Ferrara smiled, unapologetic, looking back and forth between them, backing up slowly toward the building. His body made contact with the metal rear door Pink had rigged up earlier. The hiss and sizzle of electricity filled the air as Ferrara was repelled away from the door. The shock was enough for him to lose consciousness as his heavy body made contact with the pavement. He lay sprawled-out before them.

Pee Wee and Lalo stood at the rear door, waiting on Ethan to exit his vehicle, pulling up behind the Escalade. Marcus kept up appearances, opening the door, and waiting. Both were laughing at Ferrara's plight when Ethan looked down at their feet to his body.

"What happened to him?" He recognized El Carnicero. *Stay calm.* He could feel his nostrils flare, his body heating with anger again just looking at this man lying on the ground.

"He got what was comin' to him. Come on, GQ. We goin' in the front. Tito, stay back here and watch him." Lalo pointed to Ferrara's prone body, stepping over him as the three headed toward the front door. "You can stay or you can go. The fact you showed up here is enough. You're legit."

"You're telling me to leave?" Ethan was confused.

"Unless you like watching things get painful, you can go. I don't want to pay your dry cleaning bill. I'm not sure if you can get blood out of wool easily. That coat ain't cheap and I know your shoes ain't either."

"Alright then, I'll stay out front." Ethan stopped at the front door and waited as Lalo paused.

Lalo turned to him, holding out his gloved hand in the cold. "You're alright, GQ. And for what's it worth, I'm sorry about what *he* did to your wife. I have a pistol if you'd like to do the honors now. Or we can take care of business later."

Noah's voice piped up in Ethan's ear. "Take the pistol. It's one less gun they'll have inside. Come back toward us."

Ethan held his hand out. Lalo nodded affirmatively, shaking his gloved hand, placing his personal Glock nineteen in Ethan's gloved hand. There was no telling how many times this gun had been used in committing a crime.

"There is no safety, just the trigger. Give it to Tito when you're done."

Ethan issued one nod in silence, turning to walk back down the alley to the rear of the building.

Blaine's voice came through all their com links. "They're all inside now! Exterior teams, move in!"

Tito and Ferrara were scooped up by team members, Ethan himself being pushed back into the car he'd arrived inside. Noah took possession of the Glock in Ethan's hands before disappearing into the mix of team members now swarming the exterior of the building quietly. Marcus backed up and pulled away from the building to safety, a block away, behind the van Blaine and Harry now occupied. Togo was already pulling away with El Carnicero, his prize, still unconscious from a bump on the head as he hit the pavement apparently.

Marcus waited in the car. Ethan climbed into the back of the van with Blaine and Harry.

"Where is Charlotte? Is she safe?" Ethan was breathing heavier than he should be out of nervousness.

"She's in a closet at the back of the building. They surprised her." Blaine was trying to listen to what was going on inside. "Ethan, sit down." She leveled him with just a look. Now he knew how that felt. "Pink, it's all you now. Ethan is with me."

They were listening along with the other team members.

Charlotte exhaled loud enough to be heard in the van through her com link. Ethan was safe. *Thank you, God!* She kept her eyes closed and concentrated on the voices in the room.

Ashem was smug as he continued speaking to Lalo. "That arms shipment brokered for your boss was stolen Navy property from a Guantanamo warehouse. You're not evading the NYPD and the DEA anymore. Now you've got the U.S. Navy involved. The guns aren't at the port anymore. I have them now. The paper trail is clean from my side. All roads lead back to you, I'm afraid."

"So you're the one bumping off rival gangs in Harlem and the Bronx!" Pee Wee had discussed this with Lalo before. It was all well and fine to have your competition eliminated, but they knew it wasn't them issuing the decrees. They thought they were next.

"Aren't you a quick study!" Ashem sniggered, "Our Butcher friend has proven quite useful. You see, you all were a means to an end. I take your money, a little here and there, and I put it toward a worthy cause, like destabilizing the community using the old books I buy to print currency. I take more of your money and I buy friends in Washington who look the other way to give me codes, plans, lists of agents, when their bosses are busy with dinners and politics. A little more to find the components to bring a port city to it's knees with a bomb the United States built themselves, and lost. Still, more of your money buys me what I want, and that is to see the great satan wither from within." His eyes danced before them, turning coal black. His soul was just as cold as the room.

Lalo stepped forward, decking Ashem with a right cross. Lalo knew what evil was, and this man was biblically evil. Only demonic influence could change your eyes like that. "I fought too hard to get to this country, for the freedoms I wanted. My family came here one by one, as we could afford, legally, earning money via favors for the cartel. Freedom comes with a price. I will not tolerate thieves and the kind of bloodshed that happened on nine-eleven."

Another punch. Ashem's hat dropped to the ground, blood running freely from his lower lip and nose. "I abhor bloodshed."

Lalo knocked him down to the ground. "Yeah, your own."

Ashem looked up to a ring of Club Thirteen members surrounding him.

Pee Wee remembered the battery on the rolling dolly by the back door. He stepped away to get it, unhooking the cable from the door and breaking the circuit. Ashem was pinned to a wall when he returned.

"Where's the rest of our money? The barrels are gone." Lalo was inches from him, prepared to strike again. Normally, he would leave this to another member, but this was too personal for him. Pee Wee came into this peripheral vision. "I like the way you think."

Blaine saw the chance she'd been waiting for. Everyone was focused on another task. "Pink! Get out now. They're focused on Ashem. The back door is clear."

Charlotte opened the heavy steel door of the supply closet a mere crack to hear the sound of clothing being torn.

"Where's all our money? Allah can't help you now." Lalo reached forward with a jumper cable in each hand, completely focused on Ashem. They were going to sit him on top of the barrel of potassium permanganate, dragging the barrel across the floor along with the metal lid, away from Charlotte.

The sound of pain and burnt flesh was about to fill the room. Charlotte stayed low to the ground, moving toward the rear door. She heard screams as gang members held him up, deciding to use the hook above their heads instead. As they hung him up, a struggle between Ashem and his captors broke out, the barrel turning over to spill it's contents all over the floor. She paused, looking toward them, not sure if she'd been caught.

Someone in the gang had seen her.

"Hey! Stop her!" Gunfire in her direction ensued leaving her grateful for the vest she was wearing. She locked eyes with Lalo and his gang for a moment to see them covered in blue potassium permanganate, the fine powder all over the floor surrounding them. She lunged for the barrel containing the glycerin, using all her might, tipping it over onto the floor. They stopped firing as the liquid came closer quickly. Charlotte yanked the back door open, running with as fast as she could.

"Run now! Everybody get clear! It's cold. The reaction will take longer. You've got ten seconds!" Charlotte ran toward the van down the block.

Blaine was screaming into their com links. "Run, run, run! Now!"

The gang members, hearing the woman as she left, ran toward the front door, not really understanding what was about to occur. Ashem was left screaming, dangling from the hook, as the glycerin met the blue powder on him and everything below his feet.

Charlotte was in the street running toward them when the shockwave from the blast hit her, knocking her down onto the pavement.

Glass and pieces of the building were blown over a blast radius large enough to make Blaine thankful they had evacuated a two block radius during the night. She leapt from the van, along with

Harry, scurrying away to capture gang members now laying flat in the street. Ethan was running toward Charlotte, laying face down on the pavement.

"Charlotte!"

As he rolled her over into his lap to hold her, he noticed at least four holes in her coat and blouse, the vest she wore showing beneath. He was panicking on the inside from the moment he saw her leave the closet on the video feed they were watching. She came to life in his arms, drawing a deep breath, coughing, her eyes blinking rapidly. He was shaking all over but not from the cold morning air. "Charlotte!"

All she heard was high pitched buzzing, first from the indoor gun fire and then from the blast. His lips were moving, but she couldn't hear anything. She sat up in his arms, hugging him tightly in the street.

Blaine came upon them and smiled. Club Thirteen was now the DEA's problem. Unfortunately, there wasn't much left of Ashem to question. She bent down, seeing a glimmer on the pavement. The blast and fall had knocked out Charlotte's hearing aid and com link. The com link looked to be dead, flatter than normal. She kept walking toward Ethan and Pink.

"Are you okay?" Ethan kept asking her that.

She held his tear-streaked face in her hands, reading his lips. "I'm fine. I just cannot hear anything from the blast."

He swallowed and pulled her close again.

Blaine reached down and took one of Ethan's hands, dropping Charlotte's hearing aid into it. "She'll need this when the buzz dies down in her ears from the explosion. She's alright. We'll get her checked out by a unit around the corner."

Ethan peered at the hearing aid in his hand. "Thank you."

Blaine winked at him. "Thank you." She reached down and patted Charlotte on the back, getting her attention. She gave a thumbs up to Pink which was returned, signifying she was alright.

Snow flurries began to fly by on the cold breeze.

Charlotte sat on the back of the ambulance, wrapped in a blankets. Blaine had found her an NYPD t-shirt from someone helping out. The now expended vest, riddled with bullet holes, three of nine millimeter and two of forty caliber shots, was on her lap. It would be evidence now. Ethan stood to her right, closely monitoring the activity of the EMT. Finally, she got up from the back of the bay. Blaine waved at them as she came closer.

"We're wrapping it up quickly. I gotta go. I have to get our plane out of here before this storm sets in and down to D.C. by lunch time."

"You flew yourself?" The surprise was all over Ethan's face.

"Yes. Whenever I get an opportunity to handle a yoke now, I do."

"You're a woman of many talents, Blaine." Ethan was impressed.

"And even more secrets." Charlotte hugged her friend. "Thanks, lady."

"You're welcome, Pink. And for the record, if I ever need obsolete jet engines shipped to parts unknown, I'll still call you. I like your brother, but he's not you. There are a lot of people that feel the same way I do. You don't walk away from this business once you're in. Believe me, I've tried. It's a part of you. You're a patriot, just like I am. It's in our blood. Plus, William can't make the stationery Isabella and I both like."

Charlotte tried to laugh, then her torso reminded her not to do so. "True. See ya next time."

There would always be a next time, because evil didn't sleep and Blaine would stop at nothing to protect her country and it's freedoms. They were hugging and saying their goodbyes.

The EMT's were closing the ambulance bay doors.

"Is she okay to go home?" Ethan waited for their response.

"She needs to rest for a few days. Use over the counter pain meds if she needs them. Keep an eye on her for any breathing issues. Nothing made it through the vest, but she's going to have some fantastic bruises. Once the buzzing fully subsides, I think she'll be just fine."

"Thank you." He walked over to Charlotte, waving at Blaine as she disappeared down the street with Harry and Noah. Ethan kissed the side of her face. He looked up into the cold, gray sky now swirling with more flakes. "Let's get out of here. It's starting to snow harder."

"Snow!" Charlotte looked up into the sky as well.

"Yes, snow. There was a nor'easter in the forecast. Lots of snow!" Ethan put his arm around her, hugging her gingerly. "Lots and lots of snow!"

On the way back to the apartment, Marcus took the long way around so they could enjoy Christmas decorations. They called Racheal and Nancy to let them know how everything had gone. Jane also was now aware that Stephanie had finally received the justice she deserved. The car passed by the antique shop as well. Charlotte's dress was hanging on a mannequin in the window.

Ethan made them a quick tomato soup and grilled cheese, with gruyere, while Charlotte was taking her time getting cleaned up. He called Nancy and Racheal, again, when he heard the shower come alive finally.

"Yes, we're back at the apartment but I need your help with something. You know that antique store we like to poke around in, Racheal? Callahan's Vintage Market? It's near Upland, where we went to brunch that day. Charlotte found a vintage pink dress she's crazy about there. It's hanging in the window. I want to get her the dress for the gala, she's going to need shoes. I don't know another woman on earth who is as crazy about shoes as you are. Thank you, both." Ethan exhaled with relief. "Oh, and Nancy, while you're on the phone with them at the store, they had old fashioned tree decor the last time we were in there. I want all of their mercury ornaments, beaded snowflakes, and the pink and green large bulb lights they had hanging across an old mirror. I need enough decorations for the ten foot flocked tree you're going to help me buy from them. Marcus and Lewis are going to have to deliver it. Just store everything they pick-up until Thursday morning. Then clear my days on Thursday and Friday. I'm taking them off. I have decorating to do. I want the house to feel like Christmas when Jane and the boys are here."

Nancy and Racheal were switching off telling him things were going well at the office. He walked over to the coat hanging by the door, putting his fingers through bullet holes in Charlotte's long winter white coat. Good thing she had another winter coat while here. He was lost in the thought of the possibility Charlotte could have been killed earlier. Life was too short to have regrets and not spending enough time with those you love. "And go home. Send everyone home. Yes, I said go home. The storm is coming in. Make sure you have enough to eat on and plenty of water. I figure it will knock the power out like last time. Enjoy some time to rest. Work will be there for later. See you soon. Bye."

Lunch was in the warming drawer as Ethan stood at the windows, watching big, fluffy flakes falling. They were adding up quickly on the balcony. It wouldn't be long before the view of Central Park would be white as well.

He wasn't certain how long he'd been standing there, thanking God that they were alright. Ethan turned when he heard her approach. "Are you hungry?"

"Starving."

Before he knew it, the bowls were empty, the sandwiches eaten, and their mugs devoid of hot peppermint tea.

Charlotte opened her mouth wide, trying to clear her ears and make them pop while holding both hearing aids in place with her hands.

Ethan picked up their spoons and headed for the dishwasher. "Are you alright?"

She lowered her arms, handing him their bowls from across the island, where they had been sitting. "Yes, I am. I think we're even now in that we've both cost each other a decade off our lives. Don't volunteer to go into a known drug lord's house again to lure him into a trap, please."

He smirked at her. Picking up the tea kettle and refilling their cups. He raised his mug toward hers, their rims touching.

"Deal. I'm just still trying to process everything that's happened today, in the last few days actually." Ethan's brow furrowed. "My body is fine, but my mind...I looked at your ruined coat."

"I know how you feel. If you want to talk about it, we will. I'm sure we will, eventually. The coat is a casualty that's easy to replace. I keep seeing the flashes of gunfire. I felt them hitting, but it acted as fuel to make me focus. I knew what I had to do to survive and get out of there." Charlotte stood up and came around the kitchen island to stand beside him. "What do you say to enjoying more tea and watching it snow?"

He sat the mug down, putting both arms around her, burying his face in her hair. "Yes." It's the only word that would come out.

CHAPTER SIXTEEN

They stood there in the kitchen, letting their relief seep over each other; grateful to have this moment lost in time.

17

Snow in Central Park

The snow had fallen all afternoon and was still falling at more than two inches an hour. The landscape was covered with a white blanket. They had taken a moment to venture out across the street to Central Park and enjoy the flakes before it was too dangerous to remain outside. The worst of the storm would soon be bearing down on them. Wet spots were growing larger on their knitted caps and parkas. The noise of the city was a quiet roar against the falling snow as people rushed home. They dropped and made snow angels, rolling around gently, laughing like kids, in a world of their very own. Finally, back to their feet they went.

"Oh, no, you didn't!" A snowball had smacked into Ethan's chest as he fiddled with his phone, taking photos of the falling snow in the park.

Charlotte stood there, another snowball in hand. "Oh, yes, I did! I might be too sore this weekend to do this, so I have to get them in now."

SMACK! Another well aimed shot closed the distance between them. "If you think you can give up the well-executed snowball assault on me for a moment and come here, I'd like to take our picture." He waited on her to step toward him.

"Ah, fine then. Cease fire it is." She laughed, even though she felt it in her ribs, and stepped forward.

He caught her elbow and pulled her against him. Multiple snaps of selfies later and the phone was put back into his pocket. She took a step away from him, facing him. Charlotte looked up into the sky for a brief moment. The sting of snowflake crystals was pleasant to her rapidly cooling face. Her warm breath billowed up into the barrage of falling flakes. As her face tilted back down Ethan was suddenly upon her, a look of longing in his eyes mixed with welled-up tears echoing her own sentiment. Snow. It evoked so many pleasant memories for both of them, and just as many reminders that life had changed while enduring their grief. This morning had entwined them irrevocably. Old wounds and dealing with shared memories together could now occur.

If he was ever going to kiss her, it was now, if he didn't lose his nerve. Why was he so nervous about kissing her? Because she might be leaving if she couldn't get the boutique a home. Her best chance had been blown up earlier today. He'd thought about it a thousand times in last few days. *Just do it*, he chided himself. *What are you afraid of?*

Before another thought could cross her mind, his mouth was upon her lips, stealing her breath, but lending his own warmth. His lips were insistent, the urgency to possess her mouth and more was building. His hands found their way around her coat, cradling her against him. The need for more air finally caused him to pull away. Her head rested against his as she stood there, breathing heavily, eyes closed. He moved his face a bit to whisper in her ear, which she could easily hear with her bionic ears.

"Let's get inside." Ethan pulled away keeping her right hand clutched in his left for dear life. Letting her go right now would be like letting his lifeline fall away. His thoughts warred with his faith as they reentered the apartment. They needed to shed the wet clothes, making it easy to pull her along to his bed or into a hot shower. Her hand inched away.

Charlotte pulled her jacket and wet hat off to hang on the coat rack alongside his. She stood in front of him shivering. Overhead, the heat came to life. Neither moved as their gazes were fixed on the other, faces flushed from the warmer temperatures. After such a searing kiss there would be no returning to mere friendship.

Ethan managed to speak, his mouth feeling parched. "I think we both need to shed these wet clothes. I'll be back in a few minutes. How about I make us some hot cocoa?"

She simply nodded affirmatively and turned to pass through the open double doors. A few more steps to the bedroom. Charlotte stood clutching the bathroom door handle in her right hand, her back to the now closed door. Emotions were erupting vacillating between guilt and the fluttering feeling of falling deeper for this southern gentleman smack dab in the heart of New York City.

Several minutes passed before she let go of the door. It felt like the building was literally moving from the howling wind. One look into the toilet before she sat down told her she wasn't wrong. The water was swirling in the bowl from the movement of the building. Her skin was wet as she peeled off clothes now hung across the shower door and towel bars to dry. Even her underwear was wet due to rolling around in the snow with him and her ribs told her so as well. Their laughter had echoed around them she recalled. Being happy and having fun was easy with him, almost second nature in such a short time. Her heart ached to tell Benjamin just how much she had enjoyed the snow. Fresh tears came, quickly wiped away with a tissue. Benjamin. She thought she saw him this morning, as the world went black and the pavement came up to meet her face when the shockwave hit. Her reflection in the bathroom mirror suddenly went dark. The power had gone out.

Now dressed again, this time in warm pink pajamas and a robe, she padded back toward Ethan's side. He was pouring boiling water into two cups. "I just knew the power would go out. The generators for the building will keep the refrigerators, the oven and plumbing going."

"No heat then?" Her eyes went wide with concern. She was already frozen, her skin icy cold under the pink pajamas.

"We will have to use the gas logs instead. The temperature keeps dropping and is supposed to be down near zero tonight. We're going to have to close the doors to your place and stay in here where the heat is, between the kitchen and living room." He joined her at the French doors, overlooking the large balcony, passing a mug to her. "Don't worry. We'll be okay. We just need to get the pilot light going on the logs. I haven't used them in some time and frankly, the pilot light needs looked over. Most of the time I use a barbecue lighter after I turn the gas on because the darn pilot light won't come on otherwise. The button doesn't work anymore."

Her numb fingers gripped the mug, the heat infiltrating her skin. After fifteen minutes passed of him searching everywhere for the barbecue lighter, he returned to her at the doors to the balcony. The snow was falling quickly in the fading light with the wind whistling around the panes. The tops of the trees looking into Central Park, visible when they had left earlier, were now blurry and faint in the gray light. The nor'easter was bearing down on them.

"I can't seem to find the lighter." His brow furrowed with the admission.

Charlotte sipped her hot chocolate thoughtfully. She walked to the kitchen, opening a cabinet underneath the sink. Pushing bottles of cleaner aside, a box of steel wool scrubbing pads were located. She remembered seeing a radio on the bookshelves in the guest room. A few minutes later, Ethan stood nearby watching her pull a nine volt battery out of the radio and leaving the back open on the kitchen island.

"What are you doing?" He was curious.

She grinned broadly at him. "You need a spark to get the pilot light going." Steel wool was held up in her left hand, the nine volt battery in her right. "You turn the gas on, I'll take care of the spark."

The battery was held to the coated steel wool scrubbing pad in several places, causing it spark and light for just a moment. She was holding it away from her clothes with his kitchen tongs. He knelt down and turned the gas on as the lit steel wool came close to the open gas line. Hissing began as the gas built, then the pilot light flickered to life as the tongs were held near. She moved the tongs away as Ethan turned the logs on. They now had heat.

He felt laughter bubble up from his chest. "You're amazing." He quickly kissed her right cheek. "I'm going to go check on Mrs. Holiday to make sure she has heat and what she needs. I'll be back. Shut the doors to the bedrooms and the suite. Let's keep the heat on this side as much as possible. "

Leaving the main living area wasn't going to be an option tonight as the temperature was dropping rapidly outside. Only trips to the bathroom would have them leaving the main area. Ethan sat down on the sofa with his mug, joining Charlotte, after putting the steel wool into the kitchen sink.

"She's got three sets of gas logs going, plenty of groceries. I told her to let us know if she needed us. She gave me her extra barbecue lighter. So I guess it will be a pajama party in front of the fireplace here tonight." He put his left arm around her, pulling her close. "It's a very exclusive guest list."

She laughed into her mug. "We're both adults. We can share the pull-out. I suppose we should go ahead and make the bed up before it gets completely dark in here."

"It won't be completely dark. I do have some candles."

The guest bedroom was robbed of the goose down comforter, a blanket, and two pillows from the top of the closet. Fresh sheets came from the linen closet. Before long they were snuggled up under the covers, their cocoa finished and bourbon taking it's place. Glasses rested on end tables on either side of the sofa. Charlotte was still cold. She buried herself in the warm cover and new found comfort at Ethan's side.

He could feel her temperature through the pajamas as he held her near. They were propped up on pillows against the back of the sofa, legs stretched out beneath the cozy covers. He rubbed his hand up and down her arm. "You're still cold. I'm sorry."

"I'm alright. I'll get warm. I didn't realize how much heat I lost out there ducking snow balls and rolling around in the snow after I was tackled. You're a sore loser."

"You've got a fast arm on those snowballs even with bruised ribs. You're tough. I think I'm going to have bruises to match yours."

She smirked, a playful tone in her voice. "Oh, poor baby. How about a rematch?"

"Different game though. How ticklish are you?" He held his breath waiting on the answer.

"I'm not." She looked up at him in firelight, suddenly serious, the flames reflecting in his eyes. She hesitated to act on the impulse her body was screaming at her. His lips were wet with the last sip of bourbon he had imbibed. She wondered what Ethan's lips tasted like mingled with the bourbon.

His eyes were now focused on her mouth, lips still damp with the last drops of bourbon from her own glass waiting on the end table. He could only hear her breath as she raised up slightly in his arms, hesitantly leaning forward to kiss him. She licked her bottom lip and drew another breath before closing the distance between them. She had casually liked bourbon before tasting the amber liquid mingled with his soft lips. Bourbon would be her preference from now on as it would remind her of this moment.

The kiss wasn't rushed. They weren't teenagers. At first it was sweet sorrow for both of them, recalling the last time a kiss was shared with their spouse. Then still more languid kisses, slow breaths, and learning how to kiss someone anew. Charlotte pulled away slightly, breathing in his scent, now thick in her nostrils. "We're going to need lip balm by morning because I'm going to enjoy kissing you, all night, Mr. Cooper."

He inhaled deeply at her words. They echoed his own thoughts. His arms pulled her down under the covers farther with him, both now lying on their sides. Each kiss pulled warmth back into their souls, hope rising up that love had found them both again. Her head fell back slightly as his warm mouth found the side of her neck, heat pooling into her cool skin. The more he kissed her, the more remembrance of this with Ben flooded her mind. She hadn't felt the touch of a man in a while and she liked this time with Ethan. His touch wasn't hurried, neither were his lips.

Charlotte pushed Ethan onto his back after a while. She had enjoyed his ministrations over her neck, face, and lips. She sat on his stomach, feeling his taut abdominals tighten even more. She looked down on him in the soft glow of the fireplace and nearby candles he'd managed to find. He was beautiful. Light illuminated his face showing the earned lines in his forehead, the silver hair mixed into the dark blonde at his temples and full hairline, even the soft lines around his expressive eyes and the longest lashes batting down. She unbuttoned his pajama top only two buttons, allowing her greater purchase to draw out her own plied kisses on him.

Hours passed with the two of them trading places many times in this new dance beneath a down comforter. This wasn't about sex for either of them. It was about enjoying the touch of another, true intimacy and learning to appreciate being in another's arms once more. They talked about what had happened earlier in the day, enjoyed periods of quietness, and stints of laughter before more kisses. The shared trauma of the day was now a healing memory for the both of them. Near dawn, snuggled against each other, sleep came.

How could it already be Monday? Ethan kept asking himself that question all morning. The weekend had flown by, snuggled up with Charlotte at every opportunity. He hadn't wanted to leave her today, nestled under the down comforter on the sofa where they seemed to gravitate toward at every opportunity. The office was nearly devoid of employees. The power at 601 Lexington Avenue had been fully restored along with rest of Manhattan late Sunday evening. The outer burroughs had come back online during the night. The storm had bombed out Saturday afternoon, leaving behind four feet of snow, five feet in East Hampton, where Charles Grey lived. Racheal came down the hall in snow boots, Gabriel in tow, carrying her briefcase and a bag for changing her clunky shoes out. Ethan and Nancy were the only two people on that side of the building until then. As if right on cue at ten minutes after nine, more associates started filing in, paralegals as well. The city was finding it's way as the snow ploughs and workers put so much effort into clearing and safety. He had sent Marcus out to get breakfast for everyone if they needed a meal.

"Morning! What are you doing here? I thought you were coming in at ten?" Ethan leaned back in his office chair as Racheal paused at his door, Gabriel stopping behind her.

"Morning! We wanted to get something to eat but the place wasn't open yet. Did you eat already?" Racheal took the shoe bag from Gabriel's hand.

Ethan came toward the door. "Go, change your shoes and settle in. I'll get us some coffee and meet you in your office. Breakfast is on the way." He took a few more bouncy steps and stopped in front of Nancy. "Coffee or cocoa?"

Nancy giggled like a school girl. "Cocoa, extra marshmallows, please."

Everyone's neck craned around to see Ethan's perky, retreating form. He was whistling. And not just any tune, *Frosty The Snowman*. The entire wing of the building could hear him make it through the verse and the chorus, then continue to repeat.

Grey Cooper mugs were lined up, ready for filling. Marcus walked in as Ethan started to pour coffee from the fresh pot.

"I'll take one of those, please." Marcus had large trays of food stacked up and a bag hanging on each arm. "Take this to the conference room next to your office?"

"Please. I'll meet you all down there soon." Ethan pulled a tray from a cabinet carefully placing each filled mug for transport. He mixed the hot chocolate for Nancy, adding plenty of marshmallows before rinsing the spoon, placing it into the dishwasher. He pulled the heavy cream out of the fridge, topping each coffee off for those that liked cream. Down the hall he went, whistling again, *The Happy Elf* by Harry Connick, Junior.

Nancy followed him into the conference room, taking the mug of cocoa from the tray as he placed it on the table end. Marcus was arranging trays, pulling off the lids. Bagels, condiments, utensils, and napkins were in the two bags. Nancy took a sip from her mug and went to work helping Marcus. Ethan took his mug along with a Lox bagel to his office. More whistling as he walked back down the hall. He stuck his head into Racheal's office. "Breakfast is here. Come and get something before it disappears, then meet me in my office."

The associates, paralegals, and assistants were swarming the conference room as Ethan, Racheal, and Gabriel sat in his office eating and chatting.

Gabriel finished his bagel and wadded-up the napkin it had been in, crumpling it into a small ball before it sailed into Ethan's nearby trash can. "I received a phone call early this morning that my firm is downsizing and I'm out of a job, right before Christmas."

Ethan was still chewing a bite. He began to nod as he swallowed. "Jarrett and Fields filed for bankruptcy and are being investigated for fraud. I heard it last week."

Racheal had already inhaled her bagel and was to the bottom of her coffee as well. "I figured you knew. You didn't even blink when Gabriel said something. I know we were up to our eyeballs in our issues but a heads-up would have been nice!" Her head tilted slightly as her eyes drilled into him.

"Cool your jets, Rae." Ethan held up a finger for her to pause that thought. Nancy was waiting outside the glass door. "Nancy, is he here?"

"Yes, early. Would you like me to show him in now?"

"Please." Ethan rose from behind his desk as Dānā came walking in. "Good morning!"

Racheal was starting to simmer but stood up as well to shake Dānā's hand. "Good morning!"

Dānā looked at the man now standing beside Racheal.

"Mr. Darbandi, this is my husband, Gabriel Rodriguez."

Gabriel stepped forward to also shake Dānā's hand. "Hello. Nice to meet you."

"Please call me Dānā." He turned to look at Ethan. "This is the man you spoke of?"

"Yes, this is he." Ethan sat down again at his desk. "Would you like something to drink before we start discussing the terms of the partnership?"

Racheal and Gabriel both wore looks of bewilderment echoing the same word. "Partnership?"

"Nothing to drink, please." Dānā sat down in one of the chairs near Gabriel and Racheal, now resuming their spots on the sofa. "You came very highly recommended, Mr. Rodriguez. After all this scandal, I don't know how much more I can handle. I need someone solid with years of experience in wealth management and accounting who knows how to maintain the strongest relationships with our clients. It comes with a seven figure salary plus more when we do well. In two weeks, you can move into the apartment formerly occupied by my old partner, whom you know is deceased. According to your wife it is owned by Empire, unbeknownst to me until recently. The apartment's view is Central Park west, near the top floor, three bedrooms, three bathrooms, two levels, with lots of space. It will be empty, cleaned and ready to go. The apartment is yours provided it suits your wife and the salary is agreeable. Apparently we own many properties to which I had no knowledge. I demand upmost honesty, trust, and a willingness to work. Our clients need to know they can depend on us, even in the midst of trials. We have an uphill battle on our hands to clean this up. Are you agreeable to hard work and to help me straighten out this mess?"

Gabriel began to sputter. Racheal had been squeezing his hand while Dānā was listing off the perks and perils of the job. "Yyyess. Yes. When do I start?"

"Next Monday. I want the authorities to finish getting everything they need cleared out first."

Racheal and Gabriel shared a hug before both rose to shake Dānā's hand once more. She went behind the desk and hugged Ethan too.

"You're maddening! Thank you, you sneaky little elf." Racheal squeezed him again.

"You're welcome. We have to have each other's backs. And you should know by now I've always had yours."

"I do. I hear we're having dinner together tonight. Charlotte called me a few minutes before we came in here."

"We are? Sounds good to me. She was supposed to meet the Realtor this morning to look at a few more properties, but I think that might be cancelled given the state of things."

"The meeting was cancelled. She also said you two had a great weekend. Care to elaborate? She wouldn't tell me anything beyond that. Is that why you're Mr. Happy and whistling this morning?" Racheal was too curious.

Ethan couldn't fight the big grin erupting on his face. "First year law school rule, never ask a question you don't already know the answer to."

Racheal's chin dipped down. "Oh please. The answer is written all over your face. How many years have we known each other? How long have I wanted you both to be happy again?" She waited on a reply.

"We discussed what happened during the operation with Captain Blaine, enjoyed the snow, and rested." Ethan cleared his throat quietly. "It would be ungentlemanly of me to elaborate more."

"Hmm. I'll get more of out of both of you, later. Nancy and I pulled our James Bond act on Friday before the storm hit. We have a dress and shoes to hide in your closet." Racheal's eyes were dancing. There was more to this story. For now she was elated that Gabriel would finally have the position he was worthy of and had worked so long to achieve. Now they'd live in the same city, sharing a fulfilling life together finally.

18

O Christmas Tree

Dinner with Racheal and Gabriel on Monday evening had them all laughing, including Marcus and Lewis, who joined them for a festive celebration. They chased each other through lower Manhattan in cars looking at Christmas decorations, passing by the antique market, before finishing the night off at Ethan's apartment with drinks. Charlotte noticed the dress was missing from the window at the store during their drive. Racheal had done well to curb her response, hiding the surprise just a bit longer.

By Thursday morning, Charlotte had spent her days on the phone with her brother and company, fulfilling orders for stationery that had piled up, and scanning documents to send to her family business using the office with Racheal and Ethan. She was becoming a regular fixture there. Nancy had made the comment to Ethan that if she stayed much longer he would need to find her an office instead of the conference room. They all appreciated having her there. Her mechanical dexterity and knowledge proved useful each day.

Ethan stood in the kitchen at five minutes until seven, still wearing pajamas. He could hear Charlotte in the shower, preparing for the day. Marcus and Lewis were escorted up by the doorman, hauling the ten foot flocked artificial Christmas tree into the apartment. The market had boxed up all the decorations into clear tubs for easy transport and storage. Tubs just kept piling up in the living room. Lewis placed the tree base at the end of the glass doors, near the sofa. Marcus made sure the tree was straight after the last piece was snapped on. The remaining items to come up were the dress and a shoebox. Ethan put those in his closet and returned to the living room. He prayed they'd get it all in the apartment before Charlotte came through the doors for the morning.

Lewis clapped Ethan on the back as they hurried to leave, lest they spoil the surprise. "Have fun! Enjoy the time off. Be happy. It's wonderful to see a smile on your face again."

Marcus smiled at Ethan. "I agree. You need it and you deserve it. I'll be by with lunch at eleven thirty. I have the SUV reserved for the rest of the week and the weekend. I'll be picking up Mrs. Jane and the boys around four, when their flight is expected. And I will get your mother in the car tomorrow when she arrives. Soak up every minute with your family. I'll see you later."

"Thank you for your help with the surprise. I literally couldn't have done this without you two. I appreciate you both." He paused, "And Merry Christmas."

"Merry Christmas." And they were gone.

Right on cue, a moment passed and Charlotte was walking through the open doors in a sweater and skirt. "Why are you not dressed yet? We're going to be late." Her speech dropped off when her eyes spied the imposing flocked tree now standing in the living room. A grin erupted on her face, growing wider by the minute as they walked toward the tree. "I thought I heard Marcus and Lewis out here!"

She turned around and Ethan was beside her. "Merry Christmas." He leaned forward and planted a soft kiss on her lips. "We're not going into the office today."

"We're not?" Charlotte was shocked.

"No, I'm taking some time off." Ethan eyes were bright and clear, happy. He did something unprecedented, turning on Christmas music. "Now let's get these boxes open. We need a little Christmas in here. I'll go get some more appropriate clothes on after a shower. You go change into something comfortable for all of this."

By eleven, they were now surrounded by empty boxes. The tree was already wired with warm white LED lights, plentiful enough that the entire living room was illuminated on this gray Thursday morning. Boxes of mercury ornaments were now on the tree, along with beaded snowflakes, and pastel glass orbs. Garland adorned the fireplace, complete with vintage pink and green bulbs to match the glass ornaments on the tree. The living room looked like a winter Christmas dream. Nancy had purchased everything the vintage market had put out in the display. There was even a wreath on the front door to the apartment that matched the tree decorations. Tiny flocked bottle brush trees in groups of three sat on the kitchen island, end tables, and a winter arrangement sat in the middle of the kitchen table.

Ethan and Charlotte sat down on the sofa for a break, coffee mugs in hand, clinking them together in a job well done.

Jane approached the apartment door, pausing to look at the flocked Christmas wreath before knocking. The boys also noticed the wreath. Ella Fitzgerald could be heard crooning *Have Yourself a Merry Little Christmas.*

Andy looked to his mother, pleasantly surprised. "A Christmas wreath on the door?"

Jane smiled at him, juggling a bag over her arm and pushing it up to her shoulder while holding another in her hands. "And a nice one at that."

Ethan and Charlotte greeted them at the door. "Merry Christmas!"

Nic stepped forward as the door opened. "I think it's nice. Merry Christmas, Uncle Ethan!" He burst through the open door. "We like your wreath! Charlotte!"

Andy rolled two suitcases in behind him, letting his mother pass through the door ahead of him. The smell of cinnamon filled the air, along with a sweet smell, all swirled up to meet his nostrils drawing him further into the room. He inhaled deeply. "What is that? It's smells so good in here."

The boys were both talking non-stop to Charlotte, right over the top of each other. She didn't seem to mind in the least, answering them both and not missing a beat.

Ethan took a bag from Jane's hands and a suitcase from Andy. Charlotte pulled the other bag from Jane's shoulder, ushering them all further into the room. Jane took a few more steps, standing in the middle of the floor, head tilted, surveying the apartment in all of it's Christmas grandeur. She had never seen it decorated for Christmas, especially like this. Her feet stood rooted to the spot for several minutes taking it all in. There was a new painting of a Central Park snow scene hanging above the mantel, the logs on, warming the room. There were five creamy satin stockings decorated with pearls hanging from weighted snowflake hooks mixed in the greenery reflecting vintage large bulb pastel green and pink lights. Jane had seen the painting years before, covered, incomplete until now apparently. What had changed so markedly to affect her brother so? *Charlotte.*

"Oh, Ethan, it's resplendent." Jane inhaled the aromas floating through the air. She was transported back to the kitchen as a child. Two loaves of Mrs. Icey's spiced bread cooling on the counter in her mind. She turned to find herself wrapped in a hug from her brother.

"Come on, let's get your coat off and some cider in your hands." Ethan turned Jane, spinning her out of her coat and scarf.

Andy, Nic, and Charlotte were behind the kitchen island carefully ladling spiced cider into mugs, complete with a stick of cinnamon sticking out the top. Jane noticed how Charlotte always included the boys in everything. She was so good with them.

"Here, Momma." Nic handed Jane a mug as he came around the island.

Jane took the mug, lifting it to her face as she breathed in the aroma. She paused, seeing two loaves of what looked like spiced bread cooling on the counter. "Ethan! You made spiced bread too?"

"I thought it was appropriate. It wouldn't feel like Christmas without Mrs. Icey's spiced bread. They should be cool enough now to cut."

Jane rounded the island, eager to taste a slice of her childhood. "I haven't had this in years. Thank you. I want the recipe. I don't have her recipe box and you do." Ethan placed the first slice into her hands. The mug cooling on the counter, her teeth sank into the crumbs of the spiced bread. As the bite was savored, each morsel transported her to a different time. It tasted like gingerbread in a loaf. She could just feel the ginger's slight heat coming through with the brown sugar, cinnamon, clove, and allspice. Mrs. Icey always made Christmas special for them, taking the time to bake with them and decorate. The kitchen in her childhood home always had sugar cookies and gingerbread for them to decorate, and pomanders scenting the air on the counter in a bowl. Then there was spending days with Aunt Effie at her house. Sugared fruit, peppermint sticks, cinnamon red hots, and evergreens filling the air with their freshness. Tears welled up in her eyes as she finished the slice. Emotions bubbled up inside overflowing down her cheeks. The last few weeks of turmoil and her new resolve washed over her.

Charlotte came to her side, hugging her and remaining. Jane lost it, tears now freely flowing. Ethan took the boys into the bedroom to unpack some of the their things, leaving Jane and Charlotte standing in front of the kitchen. If Charlotte hadn't been holding Jane, she'd have sunk to the floor.

Still sniffling, she finally let go of Charlotte. "I'm a complete blubbering mess. I'm so sorry."

"No, no, honey, let it out. Come on, let's go use my side of the partition and let you get cleaned up in my bathroom. I'll get you a fresh washcloth for your face."

Charlotte left Jane to recover her composure and get Jane's bag if she needed something from it.

Andy met her at the bedroom door, handing it over. "I'm glad she finally cried. She thinks we don't know, but we do. And we're okay with it. All of it."

Nic pulled out his tablet. "I just want her to be happy again."

Ethan and Charlotte exchanged concerned glances. Ethan stepped around the boys coming toward Charlotte. "You take care of her. I'll get them occupied with some games before we head out and get some dinner."

"On it." Charlotte walked back into her side of the apartment, meeting Jane outside the bathroom door with her bag and a washcloth from the laundry room. "Take your time. The boys are getting settled in."

"Thank you, Charlotte." Jane had stopped crying. She emerged several minutes later and dropped her bag in the guest bedroom before returning to the living room on Ethan's side. She laid her phone down on the ottoman. "I'm sorry for losing it in your kitchen. I have a lot to discuss with you before we leave on Sunday."

"No apologies. You're only staying through Sunday afternoon?" Ethan seemed disappointed.

"If the boys were already out of school for Christmas I'd just stay up here for a while with you. But they have class again on Monday, clear through to December twentieth."

Charlotte sensed there was so much more to Jane's rattled nature at the moment. "Do you want to talk about it now? It might help."

Jane exhaled and sat down on the sofa. "I could use a drink of your bourbon."

Ethan knew that thought. He'd been plying his days with more bourbon than he should have for the last five years. Now it was just the occasional drink, not even everyday, with Charlotte. He poured Jane a little in a glass and handed it to her. "What's going on, Jane?"

She looked over at the boys, sitting at the kitchen island playing games on their tablets. "Marcy fired me yesterday morning over a job. It's not the money, I just don't need the added stress right now."

Charlotte exchanged another concerned look with Ethan.

"Not that you need to know the entire story, but here it is for the both of you." Jane paused for a moment and took a sip from her glass. "I don't blame the customer. I blame Marcy. Metallics mixed with blue and purple are hideous at Christmas! The house is low country traditional. When they drove in for the holidays and saw that mess, no greenery, no red, they were furious. The Hehn's knew she wouldn't back down from her design. Marc and Betsy called me to fix it before their daughter drove in from Ohio. I obliged. Then when Marcy found out, she fired me for going behind her back with a client. I started tuning her out when she started to defend her modern take on Christmas. I must have had a blank stare to match my listening skills because the last thing I remember was her saying something about I didn't have my name on the door and who did I think I was." Jane's eyes rolled. "Let me think. I'm from Charleston and I have better decorating taste in my pinky than she does in her whole Washington, D.C., contact list. She should have stayed in Washington. I'm five years older than Marcy. I know the families she's been courting for business because I introduced that little witch to every single one of them. I don't have my name on a door because I only work part time. Marcy doesn't have two boys with crazy music lesson schedules, activities, and an entire house to look after by herself."

Jane waited on their reactions as she unloaded. She felt awkward enough pouring out her problems to anyone, much less Charlotte, but she was sort of family now too. At least, Jane thought of her that way. Oh great! Now her phone was ringing. It was her estranged husband. She sat the glass down and grabbed the phone from the ottoman, walking toward the patio doors. Ethan and Charlotte would still be privy to every word. The boys put down their tablets and sat completely still, listening.

"Sign them. I have proof you've been living apart for over a year at another address because your name is on the lease you're living at with her! We'll be back Sunday, Colin. Get your things and be gone by then. I'm selling the house. It'll be listed by the end of the next week." She paused, listening to his response. "No, no, you don't. There is an infidelity clause and this is the third time. What's mine is still mine, and what's yours is half mine because of the taking care of the boys. I hope she's worth it because she'll be the one paying for everything now. Could you have not been a little more original, Colin? My oldest school friend? We all go to church together. Find a new church home because I don't want to see you there anymore. And not that it matters to you, since you think the world revolves around your pecker, I'm petitioning for sole custody."

Andy and Nic stifled a laugh at their mother's use of a word they were not allowed to repeat.

Jane continued, "You never attend their recitals, you never show up period. You might as well be a stranger to them. When you drink, you get violent. I don't want the boys around that anymore. I don't want them exposed to a man who thinks violence against their mother is allowable. When you gave me the last black eye over a bottle of cheap whiskey, I swore I'd never let you hit me again. We're through. You have until Tuesday to messenger them back to the attorney's office. Goodbye, Colin."

Ethan stood up and walked over to Jane along with Charlotte. They stood there in an group hug for several moments. The boys got up to pile in on the hug.

Andy squeezed his brother too before he let go of everyone. "We're proud of you, Momma. It's time for a fresh start for all of us."

Nic agreed, "We've been waiting for you to make up your mind."

Jane hugged each boy to her. "You knew?"

Andy grinned, "We're not babies anymore."

Relief washed over Jane. "You'll always be my babies." She let them go after a moment. "Go play for a few more minutes. Then we'll get some dinner." She returned to the sofa and chair with Ethan and Charlotte. "I wondered how I was going to tell him. I feel like I just lost fifty pounds." Jane began to shake with laughter. "Wow! I don't know if that's the bourbon talking or giving him the kiss-off that's been coming for years, but I feel so much better." She felt a smile grace the corners of her mouth. It was genuine and wasn't the forced smile she'd been wearing for so long now to the world.

Ethan leaned forward to squeeze Jane's hand for a moment. "When you move out, go to Aunt Effie's place. You've been managing the house for me for years. Use it. Decorate it for Christmas any way you like."

"I'll do that. Thank you. And it's already decorated." Jane sighed, "No one's rented it for a vacation since the end of October, but I wanted it ready, just in case. Truth is, I've already found us a little house out near Folly Beach. It's closer to their school. It's quiet and charming. It's perfect for us. I've started putting things into storage and packing up closets. We should be moved in by Christmas."

"And you could open your own place. Why haven't you? You're great at what you do." Ethan had wondered the same thing for years. "Oh, wait! I know. Mother's been in your ear about how working is just beneath the Coopers. We hire people for that." He shook his hand in a dismissive manner, mocking his mother's gesture he and Jane had seen a thousand times.

"That's part of it." Jane bit her lip. Who was she kidding? The thought of having her own business was something she'd considered since graduation from the Savannah College of Art and Design. "I've always dreamed of having my own place. But the boys need me and I wanted to have the ability to be there for them."

"Make your own schedule. Buy that old building on King Street you're so in love with and do it. It's what you want, right?" Ethan waited on her response.

"Yes, but it's too big for just me." She did adore that building. It had three floors, plenty of space, charming, great light, and she'd seen the interior of the place. Oh, what a dream! The second floor had a great spot for her mahogany desk. She had no intention of opening a retail space on the bottom floor. What would she do with that? "I clearly have some thinking to do. I don't want this evening to be about my mess. It's almost five-thirty. I need to eat something and I know the boys are hungry."

Charlotte grinned, "Boys are always hungry."

Jane laughed, "Yes, they are. I'm at the grocery store every single day."

Ethan knew Charlotte had wanted to visit Ladurée, near them, and they hadn't managed to stop there yet. "How about we stay close by? I know just the spot." He smiled at them both. "Get your coats. Dress warmly everybody."

They walked a block to get the best hot dogs Jane had EVER eaten. She couldn't remember the last time she'd had three hot dogs for a meal. But Charlotte was correct, they were fabulous. Ethan had introduced them all to hot dogs all over again. She'd officially been converted to New York dogs. The boys kept eating them and now they wanted dessert. It was a welcomed new departure from the burgers the boys always insisted upon. A little more walking and they had a box of French macarons from Ladurée to share. They walked south, nibbling, down Madison Avenue to Fifth Avenue and finally to Wollman Rink, in the heart of Central Park. The rink was a popular destination, but tonight was surprisingly empty. Ethan rented them all ice skates.

Charlotte wore a panicked expression as she donned the skates.

Andy took her hand as she gingerly stood up. "Come on, Aunt Charlotte!"

Charlotte held on for dear life as she took a step forward. She froze at Andy's words, looking at Ethan and then Jane. Ethan squeezed his sister in a standing side-hug, both smiling back at her. Charlotte waited to see what they'd say about Andy's words. Her heart swelled at the affection Andy obviously had toward her by referring to her as 'Aunt Charlotte.' Southerners referred to older adults as Aunt or Uncle so-and-so even if they weren't related as a term of endearment and respect.

Jane pulled Nic up on his skate edges. She smiled widely at Charlotte. "Come on boys! Let's show Aunt Charlotte how it's done!"

Ethan lunged forward to help Charlotte steady her confidence. Andy and Nic were heading toward the ice with Jane. They waited for Ethan to guide Charlotte onto the ice. She watched the boys come toward, gliding easily. With a boy on each arm, they pushed off with Charlotte between them.

"Boys, take care of her. Don't you let her fall!" Jane skated slowly next to Ethan watching the boys stay right with Charlotte, going slower than they normally would have. "All I heard once we left at Thanksgiving was Charlotte, Charlotte, Charlotte."

Ethan took a breath. He was waiting for this. "Yes, she told me they've called her a few times."

"She called them too. She called the day of Andy's and Nic's big recital and then after to see how it went, just like you did." Jane watched his eyes for the response. "I know she's coming to the fundraiser. You know what you have to do, right?"

"I see the love of gossip hasn't skipped a generation. Yes, I know." Ethan took a deep breath, blowing out visible mist in the cold air. "I think I want your help with that too. She needs to understand why or it may frighten her."

"Trust me. When I see the way you look at each other, since the first day I met her, she just might surprise you. Now, meeting mother on the other hand, that is the frightening thought."

They shared a sibling laugh.

"Ethan, I know you love her. Have you told her that?"

He swallowed, then answered. "I love her a little more every day. She's been here right at a month, but I feel like I've always known her. Loving her is as easy as breathing."

Jane looked at him, his eyes focused on Charlotte across the rink with the boys who were pulling her along carefully. "That's how it should be. We love her too. She's family now. I can totally see a difference in you. Taking time off, the casual clothes, the music, the Christmas decor. You're in love. Tell her." She turned, skating backward facing her brother. "Let's go rescue her from the boys. Race ya!"

The boys let go of Charlotte when Ethan took over their post. Jane zipped past them with the boys several times as they made their way around in the cold night air.

"Looks like you're getting the hang of this tradition of ours. We always go skating before the fundraiser." Ethan squeezed her gloved hand. She was quiet. "Are you alright?"

"I'm fine. It's been a long time since I've been on any kind of skates."

"And?" He waited.

"And I'm still processing being called Aunt Charlotte by your nephews." Charlotte wore an uncertain look in her eyes.

350

"It's fitting, since they think of you as family now too." There. He had said it. He came to a stop easily on the ice with her, pulling her into an embrace. Leaning into her ear, he decided to go for broke. "I'm in love with you, Ms. Rose. I think I have been since the day I met you in The Boxwood, over bourbon and bacon.

Her cheeks drew up in a smile, eyes narrowing, dancing in the lights shining around the rink. Her head pulled back, looking deeply into his eyes. "I've fallen in love with you too, Mr. Cooper. I lost my heart to you over bourbon and bacon."

He chuckled and squeezed her gently, keeping in mind she still had bruises. His breath billowed out into the cold. "Remember that for later, alright?"

She looked at him, puzzled, her right eyebrow drawn up. "Alright." *What on earth is he talking about?*

Jane and the boys caught up to them again. "You two are looking awfully serious over here. Who's ready for hot chocolate and maybe an adult beverage for Momma?"

"Ooo! Me!" Nic was already skating toward the side to leave.

"I think he wants to some hot chocolate." Andy shook his head, laughing just a bit at his little brother. He was quiet until they were leaving the rink. "How is Mrs. Holiday? Can we go see Sugar?"

"Andy it's almost eight. Let's call on her tomorrow." Jane looked at Ethan as they walked back to the apartment on sixty-sixth.

They made it across the street safely as a car pulled away from the curb at the building. Mrs. Holiday was almost to the door where Mr. Adam Rodale awaited.

"Good evening, Mrs. Holiday!"

The door was pulled open for her. "Good evening, Mr. Rodale."

"And how was dinner this evening, ma'am?" He depressed the elevator button for her.

"Quite good, thank you." She walked slowly toward the elevator. "The lobby looks beautiful, by the way. You've done a wonderful job decorating as usual. I especially like all the amaryllis."

"Thank you, ma'am." His head dipped a bit at the recognition. "I enjoy it immensely."

Ethan opened the door for Jane and Charlotte, then the boys followed.

"Sorry, sir." Adam quickly stepped away from the elevator.

"No apologies. You're busy." Ethan caught the elevator with his hand. "Good evening, Mrs. Holiday. Do you mind if we ride up with you?"

The boys and Jane came into her view. Her face brightened more than usual. She'd seemed more happy lately. "Good evening, everyone! Of course not, please."

Mrs. Holiday was happy to see them. Andy and Nic stepped forward to hug her without thinking. At first she stiffened. She did something she didn't normally do. She relaxed and hugged them back, her stodgy countenance melting at their unconditional affection.

Ethan didn't know how to take her new demeanor with them since Thanksgiving, but he was glad she was in a good mood. They'd had music on several times lately and she had not made any comments about the volume at all.

Andy turned to his mother, "Can we please go see Sugar tomorrow?"

"It's fine with me. Mrs. Holiday?"

Mrs. Holiday looked back at Nic, then Andy. "Why not for a short visit tonight? I know Sugar will be happy to see you."

"Oh, no. We don't want to impose upon your evening." Jane pulled Andy's shoulders toward her just a bit.

"I insist. Give me a few moments to get settled and send them down. I'll get Sugar out of his crate. He'll need a visit outside and the boys can mind him for me."

Jane conceded as the boys both pleaded. "Alright. Half an hour, then we need to get settled for bed, okay? It's been a long day."

Ethan poured them a night cap of bourbon. The hot cocoa for the boys was all but forgotten in lieu of a visit with Sugar.

"No running down the hall to the elevator. And remember, thirty minutes, okay? I want you back up here no later than nine." Jane shut the door and walked over to the sofa.

There they all sat, Charlotte in the middle, with their feet up staring at the flames in the fireplace, which had not been turned off since the storm. The pilot light had also been addressed.

"Thank you, both, for taking such good care of us." Jane's shoulders truly relaxed for the first time in months.

Charlotte squeezed Jane's elbow with her free hand for just a moment. She pulled the glass up to her lips, taking a sip.

They enjoyed some silence before finally stirring for Ethan to refill their glasses. He focused on the stocking hanging on the mantel. He'd put something in there earlier in the day while they were decorating. Charlotte hadn't seemed to notice as they had been very busy elves.

Jane looked at Ethan upon his return to the sofa with them, taking her glass back in hand. "Our mother will be here tomorrow. I'm going to apologize for her right now."

Charlotte's eyes grew wide. "To hear the two of you talk it's like she has horns and a tail."

Everyone chuckled.

Jane tilted her head. "Sometimes I think she does. Our mother thinks herself as proper as they come. She will spout off our lineage as descendants from the reigning family in England. And as such, for functions, she insists that if you bring someone along that's publicly photographed for posterity they must either already be your spouse or your intended."

Charlotte's eyebrow went up again as she turned her head toward Ethan. "So you mean I can't go to the fundraiser with you because we're not married or engaged?"

Ethan sipped his bourbon. "As our mother would say, 'No ring, no bring.' Although not using those exact words."

Jane bumped her shoulder against Charlotte. "Don't worry. My brother and I have already talked. He's figured out how to circumvent the issue."

"What?" Charlotte was now extremely confused. "Is that what you meant earlier, before we left the rink?"

Ethan cleared his throat after finishing what was left in the glass of the Woodford Reserve in one swallow. He stood up, taking Charlotte's hand and leading her to the stocking. He pulled the stocking off the snowflake hanger, holding it front of her. She stuck her hand in, feeling a small box, then pulling it out.

"Charlotte Dreyton Rose, would you honor me by wearing my Aunt Effie's ring and accompanying me to the Hearts for Arts East fundraiser gala?"

Her lips parted, jaw slack, eyes wide. Charlotte closed her mouth, inhaling sharply as she opened the box. Inside was the most magnificent tear-drop-shaped diamond set in a thin platinum band she'd ever seen. It was similar to the ring she had seen in her dream, only this one had three small diamonds on either side. It seemed to be slightly colored pink, glimmering in the fire and tree light, casting shapes onto the ceiling and her face. She swallowed, taking short breaths.

Ethan shared a nervous look with Jane before returning his gaze to Charlotte. He hung the stocking back up before taking the box from her hand. He pulled the ring from the box, placing it on her left hand with absolutely no resistance. Ethan had used a ring of hers a week ago to check the size. And with Nancy's help calling upon a trusted jeweler, it fit perfectly. "I know I'm a complicated package, but we all want you to be there."

Charlotte looked up into his eyes, hers filled with tears, nearly spilling over. She smothered him with a hug, holding onto him for several moments before she remembered Jane was in the room. She was speechless. *Was this for real or just for the gala fundraiser?* Either way, she was in, even if only for pretend.

"I think that's a yes." Jane chuckled as she got up, sitting her now empty glass down. She put her arms around the two of them. "Looks like you have a date for the fundraiser, Ethan. And I have the sister I've always wanted, even if it's just to keep mother off kilter and guessing so Charlotte can be there with us."

Ethan pulled away from Charlotte slightly. Jane let them go. He took Charlotte's hand, leading her to his bedroom, then the closet. Jane took this as her cue to dress the sofa with bed covers so the boys could go to sleep soon for the night. They would be returning from Mrs. Holiday's soon.

"Why are we in your closet, Ethan?"

"This." He stepped toward a long garment bag, touching the floor from the highest clothes rack. It was hung on the edge of the rack, turned toward them. As he unzipped the bag, Charlotte squealed as the dress fell out and on to the floor.

"My dress! Oh Ethan! I thought it was gone, that I'd missed it forever."

"Not a chance. This dress couldn't be worn by anyone but you. It was made for you. Racheal and Nancy helped me out with this and the decorations."

Her face was pink, flushed with excitement. "I figured. You're good at surprising a woman. And Racheal! How did she keep a straight face the other night when I went on and on about the dress missing from the window? She's got a better poker face than I remember."

Ethan laughed, "She's had to develop one dealing with all the clients we have. And Racheal left shoes too. They're under my bed." He pulled the hanging straps free of the wooden hanger, handing the dress over to her.

Charlotte held it against her body, turning in front of the mirror to see it. "It's perfect. Thank you, Mr. Cooper."

"You're entirely welcome, Ms. Rose." He leaned over and kissed her softly. He stood there, looking into the mirror with her. "I can hear my mother now, in that higher pitched un-approving tone of hers. 'She was wearing the entirely wrong shade of pink.'" He kissed her again, this time on the temple. "Mostly black ball gowns will be the norm. You'll be the bell of the ball in pink, my belle, my sweet southern belle."

19

Godzilla Has Landed

Marcus waved at Margaret Cooper as he approached the baggage carousel with a folding, rolling cart he kept in-service at all times. Today he prayed it wouldn't break when he used it to collect her luggage. The wheels were reinforced for heavy loads. No matter how abbreviated the stay, she consistently overpacked. Even though Marcus enjoyed his job, working for Ethan a decade now, generously compensated already, there would be a large tip after Mrs. Cooper left. Marcus knew the type. He'd served them as a driver before permanently being added to the firm's contracted car service as Ethan's personal driver. Lewis had been the convincing factor, stealing Marcus away from another underpaid position at a rival car service.

Godzilla has arrived, he thought.

"Good afternoon, Mrs. Cooper. How was your flight?"

"You're late. Good afternoon, Marty." She stood there, waiting by the carousel, impatiently tapping her foot. She motioned for him to pick the bags up off the carousel.

"It's Marcus. And I had to wait in line to park the car so it wouldn't be towed." The woman had been calling him everything but Marcus for ten years now. *Thank God she only visits once or twice a year.* Four suitcases, a bandouliére, and a vanity case filled the cart. The wheels squeaked on take off under the load. It bounced along grunting due to the weight.

She walked along slowly behind him, carrying the largest Kate Spade black bag for a purse he'd ever seen. Obviously, Margaret had used it for her carry-on necessities. It perfectly matched her outfit, before she buttoned up the black wool car coat she was wearing, her Louboutin's clicking on the commercial tile.

"Careful you don't damage my vintage Louis Vuitton. It's worth more than you make in a month."

"Yes, ma'am." He bit his lip, smiling at her, pushing the cart toward the exit. *I highly doubt that because your son realizes my worth and appreciates me.*

Marcus drove along bustling streets, finally reaching Central Park West and stopping the black Mercedes in front of The Olmsted Hotel. He opened the door to get out.

"Why are you stopping here? My room is at The Plaza."

"My apologies, Mrs. Cooper. I was told by Mr. Cooper to take you to The Olmsted."

"Absolutely not. Take me to The Plaza." She crossed her arms, staring at him in the rear-view mirror.

Forty-five minutes later, Marcus pulled up once again at The Olmsted Hotel. He opened the rear door, on the driver's side. She held out her hand for assistance.

"I suppose this will have to do since there seems to have been some sort of mix-up at The Plaza. I'll have to get Ethan to address this with Nancy. I hope she didn't neglect the details of the gala like she did securing my hotel room. I'll have a ride to Ethan's apartment once I've checked in."

"Yes, ma'am. I'll wait."

The bellman at the hotel rolled out a brass cart to get her luggage from Marcus at the curb. "Good afternoon. Checking in, ma'am?"

"Obviously I'm checking in. Why else would I possess this much luggage?"

"Yes, ma'am. I'll meet you inside." The bellman shared a look with Marcus while they loaded the cart. "Is she always this nice?" He waited until she disappeared inside.

"That's her usual, charming self. That is Mrs. Margaret Cooper, mother to Mr. Ethan Cooper, frat brother to your hotel's owner, Mr. Jared Carter." Marcus reached into his pocket and handed the bellman three crisp new one hundred dollar bills paper-clipped to a Grey Cooper business card, Ethan's cell phone number written on the front, Marcus's on the other. "From him, for your trouble. If she needs a car, you call me. If you she gives you a fit, you call him. Gird your loins is all I can say. Don't bother giving her your name, she won't remember it. And don't expect a kind word or a tip." Marcus shut the trunk lid and opened the rear passenger door to retrieve two of the smaller suitcases. I have two pieces in the front seat, her vanity case and the bandouliére. All of it wouldn't fit into the trunk. Watch the corners when you're wheeling her things around. If one of these gets damaged I have a feeling she'd get you fired."

"Thanks for the heads-up." The bellman swallowed, his eyes wide with concern as he rolled the cart forward extra gently.

Ten minutes later she re-appeared and was dropped off at Ethan's building. Adam Rodale sucked in a breath. "Button your collar, Donald. Here she comes!" He pulled the door open, greeting her. "Good afternoon, Mrs. Cooper. It's nice to see you again."

She made an indistinguishable noise in her throat. "Hello." She stood in front of the elevator doors glaring at him. She cleared her throat finally.

Adam pushed the button to call the car. "Enjoy your afternoon ma'am."

Once the doors closed behind her, Donald and Adam both exhaled labored breaths of relief. "Donald, let Mr. Cooper know she's on her way up."

Margaret approached the door to the apartment, her lips pursed. *A flocked wreath with pastel pink and green glass balls. How tacky!* She could hear Louis Armstong's *Cool Yule* playing inside.

Ethan opened the door. "Hello, Mother." He had a mug of something in his hand as he stepped aside to allow her entry.

She stepped inside and all the air in the room seemed to be sucked out at once. Jane reached for the music remote to cut it off completely. The boy's laughter ceased. Mrs. Holiday, sitting in a chair near the tree, turned her head toward the door. Sugar was at her feet and immediately began to growl very low. The boys were making Christmas cards on the kitchen island, art supplies strewn everywhere along with glitter and glue.

Nic still had glitter on his hands from making a card for Mrs. Holiday among others. He had forgotten to wash them as he headed toward his grandmother.

"Hi Granny!"

Margaret visibly cringed at the word *granny*. "Child, go wash your hands. You're covered in glitter. Don't touch me until you've changed clothes." Margaret recoiled as Nic stopped in his tracks, his eyes dropping.

"Yes, ma'am." Nic went to the sink to was his hands, then to the bedroom to change.

"Andy, do you have a kiss for your grandmother?" She pulled off her coat, handing it to Ethan as if he were the valet.

Ethan rolled his eyes then hung the coat up, stuffing her gloves into the pockets.

Andy obediently went to kiss his grandmother's cheek, then quietly returned to clean up the island and their mess.

Ethan strolled into the kitchen, mug still in hand to refill it with cider, simmering on the stove. "Can I offer you some spiced cider, Mother? Margaret Cooper, this is my neighbor, Mrs. Edith Holiday"

"No." Her reply was flat and sharp.

"How about you, Mrs. Holiday?"

"I believe I've had enough. Sugar and I need to be getting back. The cider and the jazz were lovely. Boys, I'm hanging my cards on the refrigerator. Thank you. I've enjoyed myself immensely. We can show ourselves out." The dog walked by Mrs. Holiday's side, growling loudly as he passed Margaret. "Sugar, come."

The door clicked shut behind them. Margaret stepped further into the room, surveying the decorations. She looked through the open doors into the corporate suite. There was a large bouquet of light pink roses sitting on the coffee table, a pink throw across the back of a chair, and pairs of heels sitting by the other exit door. The length of the shoe sizes told her they didn't belong to Jane and would explain the pink theme running in the rooms.

"I take it someone is staying in the suite?" She looked around before walking toward the chair Mrs. Holiday had been in.

"Yes, she's at the office now taking care of more pressing matters. Charlotte Rose, whom you'll meet later at dinner." Ethan came to the sofa, setting down his own mug, and picking up Jane's to refill. "How was your flight?"

"Uneventful. Why would I meet the help later at dinner? And why are the doors open wide between the two spaces?" Margaret's eyes drifted to the canvas over the fireplace as she sat down. "Where did you buy that painting? It's terribly unoriginal."

Ethan gritted his teeth, thinking back to the nor'easter he'd been through days before with Charlotte. He'd watched her fall asleep one evening before pulling it out to finish. He'd used the photos taken during their trip into the park as his inspiration. The memory and the painting made him smile, regardless of what his mother thought. "She's been instrumental in helping me the last few weeks."

"I'm in the presidential suite at The Olmsted instead of a suite at The Plaza. Nancy needs to know there was a mix-up." She straightened her trousers.

Nic slipped quietly back into the room to help Andy finish the clean up. He'd been told repeatedly by his grandmother that children should be seen and not heard.

"There was no mix-up. Jared comped the suite since we're having the gala there. We thought it would be nice for you to already be there and not have to travel back and forth the night of the event." Ethan sat down on the sofa with Jane. "We've changed things up a bit this year. Because of Charlotte, there will be several high-ranking military officials from Washington, D.C., there to present children of active and deceased service members scholarships and instruments. Jared arranged local and regional wines for auction. Charlotte also arranged a dozen Frazier Fir trees to be shipped from Cashiers, North Carolina, near where she lives in Franklin, so the event room smells like evergreen. We've spent the day decorating the trees with kids from all over the city who have benefited from the fundraisers. Each tree has a different theme. At the end of the night, the trees will be auctioned off to the highest bidders. All of the auctions are going through a digital app Charlotte set up. Nancy helped me and Jane with all the coordination for the colors and theme, Winterland. We've had trips donated by cruise lines when people found out that military service members kids would benefit from this. There's been an enormous amount of support because of adding scholarships for military families to this program, no matter where they are stationed. Finally, we're giving back, so much better than I ever dreamed we could." He exhaled, waiting for her reaction.

"This Charlotte," she said her name through clenched teeth, "sounds like a very charismatic person. Obviously, she's affected your taste." Margaret looked around the room at the very festive apartment. She couldn't admit that the place was really lovely. "I'm a bit tired. I believe I'll return to the hotel. I'll see you all at The Carlyle at six."

Marcus had circled the block a few times, pulling up in front of the building just as Margaret Cooper walked outside. He had set a timer for fifteen minutes. It had been eleven.

Her name kept rolling around in Margaret's mind, Charlotte Rose. She obviously liked pink. It was everywhere. And then there was Ethan. His eyes lit up each time he said her name. If she didn't know any better, she'd swear he was in love with the woman. He had to be. Why else would he allow her to stay in his corporate suite with the doors open between them, and to dictate his decorating choices? She pulled out her cell phone, dialing a longtime family friend who happened to be an attorney in Charleston. She walked to the window looking out onto Central Park. The view was breathtaking and the room posh enough to please a president.

"Hello Perry. I'm sorry to disturb your evening, but I need your help with something. I'd like you to run a background check for me. Her name is Charlotte Rose. I believe from North Carolina. I'm not certain of the town. Somewhere near Christmas trees. Yes, email is fine. Thank you. Bye."

Margaret had been unpacked by a floor attendant while she was away from the room at Ethan's. She sipped sparkling cold water from a crystal glass, a slice of lime floating amongst the bubbles. *Airplanes dry you out so much. I cannot drink at dinner until I've rehydrated. I think I'll take a bath and then dress.* Even with the world at her fingertips for years, she felt hallow and empty inside. She needed a change.

Jane straightened Andy's jacket lapels and pulled Nic's shirt collar straight. "Best behavior tonight, okay? No loud talking. Sit up at the table, no elbows, use your napkins. Small bites, don't talk with your mouth full."

Both nodded at her affirmatively, tugging at their dress coats.

Ethan smiled at them. "Let's enjoy our dinner. You know how to behave." He checked his watch, five fifty-five.

"Mr. Cooper. Nice to see you again this evening. Your mother is waiting." The maître d'hôtel led them through the tables to be seated in a private section.

"Hello again. You're late." Margaret put her napkin into her lap laying the menu off to the side.

"It's five til. And it's fine, Mother." Ethan pursed his lips.

Nic approached Margaret, kissing one cheek, since he'd missed the opportunity from earlier. He sat down, next to her, his brother also seating himself on that side of the large rectangular table for six, covered in a long white table cloth. Ethan sat down opposite his mother, Jane leaving a space for Charlotte to join them in-between the two. She faced Andy, picking up her napkin and laying it into her lap. The boys followed her lead.

Their waiter arrived. The evening's specialties were discussed as was the wine selection. Margaret insisted on having her favorite, Cristal Champagne from 1969. Ethan ordered two bourbons for himself and Jane, sparkling water for the boys. Their amuse bouche had been a large charcuterie board which included caviar. Margaret chose lobster for her entrée. The boys of course picked burgers to her disdain. Jane wanted to try what Ethan recommended, the filet mignon.

They managed to almost make it through the meal without an insult being hurled. The boys were finished, getting restless at the table. Ethan kept checking his watch wondering what was keeping Charlotte. Finally, she arrived at twenty minutes after seven. He stood up to greet her.

"I'm so sorry, everyone. Please excuse my tardiness." She kissed Ethan's cheek.

"Is everything alright?" Ethan didn't blame her. Given the choice, he would have avoided this prickly-as-a-cactus meal.

"For now." She smiled at him and sat down. "Hello, Mrs. Cooper. I'm Charlotte-"

"Rose. Yes, I know." Margaret swallowed one bite off of the cheesecake in front of her, pushing the rest over to Nic and Andy. "What could have possibly kept you? We're almost finished." Her eyes had studied Charlotte's appearance from the moment she approached the table. *She's very tall. He could do worse. She's dressed well, groomed well, although her hair down is messy. It's a bit long for someone her age.*

Charlotte watched the boys push the plate back and forth. *They don't want cheesecake.* "If you must know, the Prime Minister of Israel. Their short range missile defense system outside of Tel Aviv went down last night. I've been on the phone and video chat most of the day at the office to help get them back online." She leveled Margaret with her response.

Margaret truly didn't have a reply for that.

Ethan leaned over. "William couldn't help? I thought he sent them circuit boards, overnight."

Charlotte took a sip from the water glass in front of her, condensation running down the sides to her fingers. She dried them on the napkin in her lap. "He did. I reprogrammed them remotely. It's fixed, finally."

Margaret spoke up. "I understand you'll be attending the gala fundraiser tomorrow night since you're helping with the event."

"I have helped, all that I could. I'm excited to hear the talent that will be showcased tomorrow evening by the young musicians playing alongside the band. Seeing all the artwork from the students displayed will be great. Sitting with you all, enjoying the evening, resting a little. It's been a busy couple of weeks."

"Sitting with us? You're attending as Ethan's guest?" Margaret couldn't believe her ears.

"That's right." Charlotte waived the menu away. She wasn't hungry anyway.

Jane changed the subject. "You missed an amazing filet. Perfectly cooked and I enjoyed every bite. How was your lobster, Mother?"

"Overcooked." Margaret sipped from her Champagne glass, finishing the second glass.

The boys were getting a little louder over their objection to the cheesecake. They had finished their meal and stayed mostly quiet for as long as they could. They were bored. Andy stood up to excuse himself, his napkin falling into the floor.

Jane leaned over and picked it up, the waiter taking it from her almost immediately. "Where is your restroom? Nic, do you need to go too?"

Nic stood up a bit zealously, dragging the tablecloth down the table before it could be stopped. The water glass in front of Charlotte tipped over into her lap. Nic's eyes grew wide in horror.

"Clumsy, clumsy, clumsy, Nicholas!" Margaret's words were biting toward her grandson.

Nic's jaw was slack, unsure of the repercussions since his grandmother was there.

Jane started apologizing. "I'm so sorry, Charlotte. Nic, apologize to her."

"I'm sorry, Aunt Charlotte."

Margaret was completely taken aback. *Aunt Charlotte?*

Charlotte stood up which caused Ethan to stand up. She glared daggers at Margaret for chastising Nic so vehemently. "No harm done, Nic. It's just water. Come on boys, let's go to the restroom."

Ethan watched as she put her hand on Nic's shoulder, guiding him along, then winking at him while smiling. He motioned to the waiter handing him a credit card. "I've had all the fun I can stand for one night. Enjoy the rest of your evening, Mother. Jane?"

"Did I say something?" Margaret looked back and forth between her children. "Ethan Ashley Cooper, if that woman thinks she's coming to the gala with you, she's got another think coming. You're not married to her. You know nothing about her lineage. She works for a living, obviously. That's not our class dear."

Ethan felt his nostrils flare, breathing deeply before issuing his response. He closed his eyes for a brief moment, regaining his composure. "She has more class than you ever will. She doesn't belittle people around her for sport to just make herself feel important. Her family comes from Charleston. Dreyton. I think you've heard of them. And for your information, she is the president of a multi-billion dollar private engineering and defense company. She's the smartest woman I've ever known. She will be by my side tomorrow night, making our family look better than you ever could. Now put that in your Louis Vuitton and stuff it! Good night, Mother."

20

The Gala

      "The bellman visibly shrank in his uniform when I dropped her off. The entire staff was more than happy to have me pick her up earlier to get her hair and makeup taken care of for the gala. They seemed to deflate when I returned with her." Marcus looked up in the rear view mirror to see Ethan's face cringe. Marcus came to a stop in front of The Olmsted Hotel, opening the front door for Jane, and then the back door for Charlotte to get out of the large Mercedes SUV.

Jane patted his arm. "You're a good man, Marcus. Thank you." She stood there on a red carpet, straightening her dress as other guests for the gala were arriving.

"Happy to help, ma'am." Marcus waited for the boys and Ethan to get out from the far back seat.

Lewis was right behind him, letting Gabriel and Racheal out as well.

Ethan pulled two invitations out of his coat pocket, walking them to Lewis and Marcus. "Don't go anywhere. You're just as welcome inside tonight, as always. So park these and come on in. You're already dressed for it."

Marcus thanked him, looking at the invitation in his hand.

Lewis smiled, "I always knew you were a class act. Thank you."

"I've given you these every year. This year, I do hope you'll come inside." Ethan smiled at them both.

Marcus watched their retreating forms as they all converged to enter together, standing there for a moment with Lewis.

"That's no rubber chicken dinner this year. He's completely changed the format. And that's a ten thousand dollar sought after invitation in your hand. Come on." His eyes danced. "This should be fun!"

Ethan noticed the time as they entered the Grand Oak Hall inside The Olmsted. Six thirty on the nose. The gala didn't officially begin until seven. The hall was flooded with attendants, dressed in the best finery. People were dancing, laughing, drinking, and chatting, not sitting at tables bored to death once more. Nancy and Mrs. Holiday waved at him from across the room as they spoke to someone in a military uniform, enjoying the champagne that was flowing freely. It was, after all, a night to celebrate the arts as well as support them. Right on cue, Margaret wandered over in her black evening gown.

"Late to your own party, son? Hello, everyone." Margaret looked at Charlotte's pink dress. It perfectly suited her yet it truly marked her as a standout in the sea of black this evening. Even Ethan wore a pink tie with his black tuxedo. "Pink at a black tie event?"

"Good evening, Mother." He ignored her commentary and kissed her cheek. "You remember Racheal and Gabriel?"

"Of course, nice to see you again." The words were there on her lips but their meaning was entirely absent. Margaret leaned in a bit so only Ethan could hear her over the noise of music and chatter in the hall. "You'll have to excuse my provocation last night. I was simply taken aback that you're dating the help, practically living with her actually." Then her eyes dropped to the ring on Charlotte's hand, draped over Ethan's right arm.

The event photographer, coupled with members of the press were wandering around. Three with cameras stopped to take photos of the throng of people who had entered.

Much to Margaret's dismay, Ethan was being photographed for posterity standing next to Charlotte. She leaned in to his left ear once more while smiling for the cameras. "Ethan, that's a rather large skating rink Charlotte is wearing on a very important finger."

"Yes, we're not going to have a large wedding, just a few friends and family in Charleston on New Years. Hopefully the Planter's Inn will be able to accommodate us on such short notice." He said it louder than usual so the reporters would take note.

Charlotte bit her lip to keep from cracking up. Racheal's eyes lit up as she noticed the ring for the first time. Charlotte caught the reaction, issuing a slight shake of her head to Racheal, indicating

Ethan was simply kidding. Then Charlotte leaned over to Ethan. "Hamming it up, aren't you?"

He grinned, spinning her around on the floor to dance, smiling broadly at his mother as they twirled away. "I'm done tip toeing around her. I've resolved that I'm living my life. I'm not ashamed of who I am, a musician, some time painter, and an attorney."

Everyone seemed to turn and look their way as Ethan spun Charlotte around the dance floor, her long pink gown lifting and flowing outward as they turned. The sea of attendees parted as he swept her around, again and again, to *The Christmas Waltz*. As the music ceased, there was clapping to be heard. She blushed in his arms, perfectly matching her signature color this evening. He took her hand and kissed it before pulling her onto the stage with him. Someone handed him a wireless microphone.

He gently tapped the end to verify the disposition of the mic. "Good evening, everyone. Thank you for honoring this worthy cause with your attendance and continued support. I hope you're enjoying the new format this year. If you haven't already noticed the signs to download the auction app, then you need to get your glasses out." Laughter came from the crowd to meet them on the stage. "There are too many people I'd like to thank for making this happen tonight. They're all listed in the souvenir program, along with photographs of the art on display tonight, a testament of what your support has made possible for these kids. Our endeavor is reaching more families than ever, adding currently active and veteran's families to our list of recipients. You'll hear from them tonight, along with special guests from all branches of the armed services with us this evening. Thank you for your service to this country, and thank you everyone for being here. Let's dance!" Ethan turned to smile at Charlotte. She clapped along with the crowd.

The applause continued as they descended the steps from the stage.

"Nice speech. I think you've done that a time or two."

He continued to grin at her. "Maybe." Laughter escaped him. *So this is what happy feels like again.* The evening continued on with Charlotte introducing him to decorated military officers and enlisted alike wearing their dress uniforms. He paused, whispering a question to her. "This insignia is the same, a bird, like the Colonel's you've addressed tonight. You just called this person Captain. Why?"

Charlotte smiled at him and softly said, "The Navy and the Coast Guard are different. You met Captain Blaine. She's the same rank as a Colonel. The Navy and the Coast Guard have a different ranking system than the other branches. The titles are different even thought the insignia is the same. That bird represents years of service and dedication. Only a select few women rise above the rank of Lieutenant Commander, that's the same rank as Major in the other branches. You've met women that are Rear Admirals and Generals tonight as they presented awards, even a couple of Master Chiefs."

Ethan looked at the different uniforms surrounding him. Each of them dedicated themselves to preserving and defending the freedoms many people took for granted. "I'm just grateful they serve this nation so admirably and willingly. They sacrifice so much for us." He remembered a Bible verse that was appropriate from John, chapter fifteen, verse thirteen. He said it, out loud. "Greater love has no one than this: to lay down one's life for one's friends."

She smiled at him. "Amen. They certainly do. All service is important."

Jared Carter walked up to Charlotte, kissing her cheek. "Who is this lovely woman in pink?"

Charlotte let go of Ethan's arm to hug Jared.

"That's quite a wonderful sight in a sea of black." Jared shook Ethan's hand, smiling. "And look at your tie!"

Ethan put his arm around Charlotte's waist, laughing. "I don't believe there was a dress code that specified black."

"Ha! This is New York City! The dress code is black any day of the work week and weekends too." Jared continued to chat with them.

They had all largely avoided sitting down with Margaret at a table. Only Mrs. Holiday, who couldn't have stood up as they had all managed for the evening, sat two chairs over from her. Margaret had been largely ignored by the family. She sat sipping champagne, her eyes wandering around the room. People had stopped to speak with Mrs. Holiday all evening. Margaret found it interesting that many knew Edith and commented on how her husband's music had touched their lives. Margaret had been a captive audience, watching and listening to the woman. Mrs. Holiday seemed to be highly revered even though she had been married to a musician, of all vocations.

Mrs. Holiday got up and brought a cup of tea, along with her own, and sat down on Margaret's left. "I know how you feel about me. I can see it in your face. I knew who you were the minute I laid eyes on you. I know because I was you. Part of me still is. She surfaces from time to time when I'm uncertain of my surroundings." She held up her hand for Margaret to be quiet as she continued. "I had nothing but derision for those that surrounded me. No one understood how things were supposed to be properly done. You weren't supposed to associate with other people that weren't the same class. I thought myself to be above the rest." She looked down into her tea cup and exhaled. "And then I met Harold Holiday. He was everything my family wasn't, everything I thought was deplorable. He was a musician, with an eighth grade education. He had no table manners and wouldn't have known a charger from a cake plate. But I fell head-over-heels for that man. He opened my eyes to the value of everyone around me. He taught me to love myself and that I was enough. Be proud of your heritage, but know that you're no more important than anyone in this room. None of us is. Your value lies in the ability to serve others. That's the heart of hospitality. Meet people on their level, where they are. Love them for where they are, and be proud of them for who they are. I had to learn that the hard way when I raised my granddaughter, Sterling."

Margaret had tears welling up in her eyes, at the point of spilling over. She intently listened to Edith.

"Oh what a handful Sterling was! I let her name me instead of imposing a title on her. To her I was Ninny." Edith took Margaret's hands in hers without reservation. "Love them, while you still can." Edith turned her head toward Nic and Andy, standing near their mother, Jane's arm draped over Nic's shoulder. Edith waved at the boys. They eagerly waved back at her as she rose to go to them, leaving Margaret to ponder her words. Edith hugged the boys and encouraged them to follow their Uncle.

Margaret was stunned to complete silence. Her chin shook as she struggled to hold back tears. She watched as Ethan climbed the stairs to the stage, once more, at almost eight thirty. He was followed by Nic and Andy, who now held a bright silver trumpet. They stood together chatting for a few minutes, then music stands were shuffled around to them. Nic sat down at the piano. Ethan took some sort of guitar from a man off the side. He tilted his head, listening carefully while tuning the instrument. He walked back to Andy, standing next to Nic at the piano. As the band wound down their current tune, Ethan counted off into a mic near him so Andy and Nic could hear. Mrs. Holiday, Charlotte, Jane, Racheal, and Gabriel stood around the stage smiling at them.

Each one had been practicing intently for their part, even after the boy's recital. Ethan's fingers slid over the frets on the resonator guitar that had once belonged to Harry Holiday. Andy put his lips to the trumpet and began. The tune wound around them all, haunting and provocative, evoking a change in Margaret. The melody reached into her soul, prompting tears to flow from her closed eyes, streaming down her face. The old Margaret passed away, right there at the table that night. The song felt like a catharsis in her heart.

Something felt like it physically broke loose inside of her, coming to the surface as the façade crackled like the glaze on old porcelain. She looked around the room. All the attention was focused on her family, playing music in public, serving others with a beautiful song. Those were her grandchildren getting a standing ovation, and her son. Her son, who despite her demanding efforts, put this together himself. Pride for them swelled into her heart. Hallelujah.

Ethan approached the mic once more. "Thank you everyone for coming and your graciousness. Have a wonderful evening! Merry Christmas!"

Revelation twenty-one, verse five. "Behold, I make all things new." Margaret wiped her face using a napkin, checking her makeup quickly in a compact. *No mascara tracks. I can get up now.* She charged forward coming right up behind Jane. The instruments were being handed off. She looked at Mrs. Holiday as she opened her mouth. "Carlye Jane Cooper-Bishop!"

Jane spun around, wide-eyed at the use of her full name.

Margaret's face broke into a smile Jane hadn't seen since she was a child. "Why didn't you tell me my boys were so talented?" Her voice broke with emotion as fresh tears filled her eyes.

Charlotte had turned around hearing Margaret's voice. Ethan and the boys came down from the stage, fearing the worst as he knew she disapproved of them playing in public.

Margaret stepped back and opened her arms to Andy and Nic, who had never seen their grandmother cry like this. She held one in each arm, kissing the top of their heads. "You were wonderful! I'm so proud of you."

Ethan exchanged worried looks with Jane.

Jane didn't know what to do other than pat her mother's back carefully. *Has she suffered a breakdown? Maybe a stroke?*

Mrs. Holiday wore a knowing smile that she shared silently with Margaret.

Charlotte smiled at Ethan, her heart still beaming over their performance. All eyes were focused on Margaret.

Andy squeezed Margaret in a hug before pulling away to look up at her. "We've been practicing for weeks."

"It shows. It was marvelous." She held Nic right where he was.

"Did you really like it, Granny? I mean, Grandmother." Nic looked up at her.

"It was fantastic. And it's Granny from now on. If it's good enough for Queen Elizabeth, it's more than good enough for me."

Ethan held out a handkerchief to his mother to wipe her face. She let go of Nic to take it from his hand. After wiping her face once more, she took a few breaths. "I realized tonight I really don't know my children, or my grandchildren. I want to, if you'll let me. I ask your forgiveness, please."

Andy and Nic swarmed her sides again, hugging her to their hearts were content.

Charlotte squeezed Ethan's hand as she held it now.

Margaret stepped forward, clutching the handkerchief as she stood in front of Charlotte and Ethan. "And you, you've proven your point. I don't agree with your timing but I cannot say I disprove of your choice."

Ethan could have picked his jaw up from the floor.

"I did a background check on you, Ms. Rose. Or is it Mrs. David?"

"You did what, Mother?"

"I had to know who you were going to marry next, since I didn't have the opportunity to even meet Stephanie before you'd married her. I approve." Then she smirked at him. "Not just anyone can tell me off so well and get by with it." Her attention focused once more on Charlotte. "I knew the moment I saw you with Ethan tonight that he would marry you."

Ethan seemed skeptical, exchanging looks with Jane and Charlotte. Then he felt guilty about the deception.

"Don't look at me like that. I have done you both a great disservice as a mother, leaving my late sister to encourage you and the housekeeper to raise you. But I can tell when two people are meant to be together. So, congratulations!" She exhaled and ruffled Nic's hair. "It's getting late and I'm tired. Good night everyone."

Ethan settled with Charlotte on her sofa after they all returned to the apartment by ten. The party was still going strong, but the boys were tired, including Ethan. The boys were asleep on the sofa and Jane tucked in as well. The place was quiet.

"I have had way too much to drink tonight." Ethan was drinking another glass of water as Charlotte handed him some pain reliever.

"Head still aching?" Charlotte rubbed his shoulders slightly.

He rubbed his temples after downing the rest of the glass with the pills. "I don't know what universe I'm in. My mother turned into a human being tonight. We'll see if it was a Cinderella transformation come midnight."

They both shook with silent laughter.

Ethan had already pulled his tie loose on the way home. He arched his neck to right, then to left, the musculature and vertebrae issuing a pop. He picked up her left hand in his right, kissing it before tracing her fingers one by one, stopping at the ring. She reached over to take it off, unsure if the ruse was over or exactly what he intended. He squeezed her hand gently.

"No, leave it on. It's not been on anyone else's hand but Aunt Effie's and now yours." His eyes squinted as his temples continued to pound. He was unaware she had slipped away to change clothes until he felt her return to his side on the corporate suite's sofa. He must have dozed off.

"Come on. Let's get you to bed." She led him to his bedroom, helping his fingers pry the button studs from the tuxedo shirt as he fumbled with the cuff links. There he stood in the closet with her, bedroom door shut. He leaned forward and kissed her deeply. "You looked wonderful tonight."

She pushed his shirt off from from his shoulders, pulling the white t-shirt over his head, for the first time seeing his naked torso. She reached for his pajama top, hanging on a hook nearby. He took it from her hand, pulling it on gingerly. He'd have preferred to leave it off entirely and whisk her off to his bed. Sobriety from all the drinks was kicking in along with the still small voice telling him to save that for their honeymoon. He pulled away from kissing her again, pulling the bottoms from the apparel hook. He stepped into the bathroom, emerging a few minutes later dressed fully in pajamas. Charlotte was standing near the bed, looking out the windows at the New York skyline. She pulled back his covers, waiting on him to get in. He held on to her hand as she kissed his forehead, tucking him in. He tugged her back, pulling her down onto the bed. She stayed with him, running her fingers through his hair until his breath evened out in sleep. Charlotte carefully got up, looking at his form once more before slipping out the door to her own bed.

21

Duty First

Sunday. Ten days until Christmas. Ethan rolled over to the sound of the boys being shushed by Jane. They were still laughing, just quieter. He laid there listening. *Is that my mother laughing?* There it was again. *Yes, it is her.* Laughter was usually cause for joy instead of alarm, but this was his mother after all.

Ethan grabbed his robe and went bounding out into the kitchen.

Charlotte, Jane, and the boys were all laughing, even his mother. There were bowls on the counter, in the sink, the griddle on the range was covered in pancakes. Nic stood guard with a turner overseen by Charlotte's hands, helping him flip each one. He looked again and there was a container of flour laying sideways on the island spilling it's contents, flour on Andy's face, flour in the floor, and all over the front of the apron Margaret was wearing. Her face was also covered. Jane handed her a damp towel as they continued to laugh.

Ethan looked at the scene before him, amused. "What are you doing to my kitchen?"

"I was a bit zealous filling up the flour container after we made batter. Andy warned me. I suppose I'll need to take another bath now." Margaret pulled the apron off, holding it away from her body. "Jane, do you have a shirt I might borrow?"

"I'll get you one. Come on."

"Morning, Uncle E! I hope you're hungry." Andy raked off as much flour as he could into the trash can along with the bag before putting the partially filled container away. Then stuck his hands down into the dish water, rinsing the sponge he was using to clean up.

"Morning!" Ethan walked over, kissed Charlotte lightly, and patted Andy's shoulder. "How are my chefs this morning?"

Charlotte smiled, "Andy has cooked bacon in the oven. Jane helped me poach eggs. We've made hollandaise in your blender, and Margaret helped to stir up pancake batter. Grab yourself a cup of coffee and get the maple syrup from the fridge, please. We're almost ready to eat."

He stumbled toward the table, coffee in hand, not quite awake. He wondered if the scene before him was something out of a dream. His mother was acting like a normal person. The paper was already on the table. Margaret walked back in with Jane, no makeup on, in casual clothes she'd borrowed from Jane. Ethan looked at her again.

"What?" Margaret looked down to see if something was wrong with the outfit.

"Nothing. That's much better." Ethan sipped his coffee and opened the paper.

Margaret put the butter on the table and refilled Jane and Charlotte's coffee mugs. "Check out page eleven. Your fundraiser made the front page of the social section. There's a great shot of you and Charlotte and one of the boys with you on stage too." Margaret topped off her own coffee and sat down at the table with him. "I was beginning to think you were going to sleep the day away. It's almost nine." She winked at him.

Ethan smiled and rolled his eyes. He was still waiting for her to morph back into Margaret The Hun, the horrible name Jane and Ethan had called her for years behind her back. All the food was carried to the table where they ate family style.

Margaret put her makeshift napkin, a paper towel, on the table and pushed her chair back. "I think I'm going to slip into a carb coma from all those pancakes. Those were great, boys."

Charlotte's phone started ringing. She ignored it, at first. Then as they were clearing the table, it rang again. Then she heard Ethan's phone start ringing. Then her own again before she reached it on the kitchen island of the corporate suite. She answered as she saw the name, Captain Blaine. All activity ceased in the other room. They could hear every word.

"Hello." Charlotte went pale as she turned to face Ethan, eyes wide. He walked over to her, brow furrowed, not knowing exactly what was wrong, but he knew something was amiss. Her lower jaw went slack as she inhaled sharply. "I understand. Yes, ma'am, need to know. Bye."

Charlotte lowered the phone and put it back on the island. "That was Captain Blaine. I have to go, there's a situation I'm being flown in to deal with."

"You have to leave right now?" Ethan put his hands on her shoulders in concern. "Is this connected to Ashem?"

"Need to know. I can't say more than that. I'm sorry." Charlotte's eyes dropped.

The boys were coming over to them when Jane stopped Andy and Margaret caught Nic's arm. They all stood in the open doorway, looking at Ethan and Charlotte.

"Well, how long will you be gone?" Ethan hugged her for dear life.

"I don't know. I will let you know what's what as soon I can. I'm just not sure when that will be."

"Nine days before Christmas and I don't want you to go." Ethan squeezed her to him, before he let go. "I wish you weren't leaving."

Jane spoke up, standing beside her mother with the boys. "I do too. Will you let us know you're safe please?"

"I will call or text when I'm able. I'm not entirely certain what I'm going in to. I have to get to the heliport at thirtieth as quickly as possible. There's a plane waiting for me at Teterboro City. Beyond that, I won't know everything until I'm boots on the ground."

Margaret pulled away from the boys and used her own phone. "Marcus, this is Margaret. Good morning. I need you to bring the car to Ethan's apartment as quickly as possible. Charlotte needs a ride." She knew the driver would be bowled over that she used his name. She'd decided to give him the morning off and instead had taken a brisk walk to the apartment today. It was only a few blocks from the hotel. She walked back into the corporate suite side, pulling Jane with her. "Marcus is on the way. Alright, Jane you help Charlotte get her closet back into her suitcase. Ethan, you grab her bag for toiletries. Boys, bring the shoes into the bedroom. I'll get her outerwear ready as soon as she tells me where her coats are located." Margaret waved her hands about until Ethan spoke up.

"They're hanging by the door on the other side."

Everyone mobilized at once. Margaret pulled two wool car coats, parka, a hat, and gloves from the rack. She noticed three holes in the winter white coat as she threw it over her arm. "Do I want to know what happened here?"

Ethan shared a look with Charlotte and Jane, then licked his lips to face his mom. He exhaled slowly before answering. "Nine millimeter and forty caliber hollowpoint bullets. There were five total, three made holes in the coat. And I'll fill you in on exactly what happened later. I promise."

Margaret held the coat up, putting her index finger through the holes. They were large holes. "I don't understand all of this, but I admire your blind tenacity with whatever this is. Who is Captain Blaine?"

Ethan was turning pairs of heels to fit into a bag as the boys hand-ed them to him. He thought quickly as he answered. "Um, Captain is the equivalent of Colonel to the other branches. Blaine is the commanding officer with an elite branch of Naval Intelligence. And when the Navy calls, you answer." He looked up to see Charlotte smiling back at him, then winking with her right eye.

Jane and Charlotte had everything tucked away. Charlotte had finished her toiletries and took a coat, hat and gloves from Margaret.

"Thank you. I believe it is best that we retire my winter white favorite." She laughed, but Margaret seemed to agree.

Minutes later the doorman called up to announce Marcus's arriv-al. The whole family followed her downstairs, carrying bags. Hugs were exchanged and a few tears by the boys. Ethan climbed in to ride with her until she boarded the helicopter. The car ride was utter silence as he held her hand.

When they arrived at the heliport the Robinson Raven's rotors were starting to turn. The bags were handed off by Marcus and Ethan. This was it. She turned one last time to kiss him.

Charlotte's lips pulled away. "I love you."

She might as well of punched him in the gut.

His eyes closed, his lips pursed, chin quivering. Tears were form-ing. "I love you, too."

The pilot waved his hand at them. Charlotte turned and ran to-ward the side, hopping in. Ethan felt tears fly away from his face with the turbulence stirred up by the helicopter taking off. He stood there with his arms crossed until it was out of sight.

Just like that, Charlotte was gone.

Charlotte felt a handkerchief in her pocket. Ethan had put it there for her in the chaos of packing so quickly. She inhaled his scent on the folded square trying not to use it to wipe the tears from her own face. The neatly folded square would be a reminder of him, to smell, while she was away from him, however long that might by. Her fingers traced his monogram. She put it back in her left pocket, pulling her hand back to her lap. The five-carat light pink diamond was still there.

All they had received was a text the same day she had left. It read: safe and sound and on the ground. One week had gone by. It was now two days until Christmas.

Ethan was sharing a late afternoon drink with Charles Grey. He was in the office cleaning out the remainder of his things, retiring for good. Charles noticed the distracted look on Ethan's face.

"Racheal apprised me of the last weeks excitement around here. I'm sorry I missed the gala, but we enjoyed our time in Nantucket with some extended family." Charles sat his empty glass down.

Ethan was sitting behind his desk, noticing that the winter sun was dropping rapidly. It would be hidden behind the tall buildings by four-thirty and dark by five o'clock.

"So the new frame on your desk there. Is that *the* Charlotte I've heard so much about?" Charles pointed to the silver picture frame.

The photo of Stephanie that once sat there was now beside Ethan's bourbon decanter. Still in the room, but located elsewhere. The boys had printed out photos from Ethan's phone before they left, giving him a photo he'd taken of the snowy day in Central Park. Nancy gifted him a picture frame when she saw the photo, mixed in with his papers lying on his desk. He pulled it out to stay on top before it was put into the frame. Each day he'd grown more sullen with Charlotte's absence.

"Yes, Charlotte Rose. I feel like the last month or so with her was a dream. Then she had to leave for a military obligation. It's like I'm walking around in a fog. I don't want to be here right now. I want to be near Jane and the boys. Even things with my mother have stabilized. I need to be near my family if I can't be with Charlotte. My heart aches."

Charles gave him a knowing look. "You're in love, Ethan. Go. Be with your family. This will still be here when you return."

Ethan pondered the notion of flying home to Charleston for Christmas.

Charles got up from the sofa. "It's time for you to let your carefully hand-selected stars shine, just like I did with you. We cannot do it all. The time for fourteen and sixteen hour days is over. We handle corporate clients as our bread and butter. We do our jobs so well we don't have to go to court. You've been grooming Racheal and others for this. Let them shine! I think of you as a son so I'm going to give you some sage advice. Go find your life again, with Charlotte. You've caught a glimpse of what life with her could be like. That's why you're miserable without her, without her love. Have Racheal run the firm as you've done for me for years now, and you can be somewhere else as oversight. There isn't another partner here that's interested in running the day-to-day. They all have another life, outside of here. Racheal's young. She's the most capable. Everyone here knows it." He could see the wheels turning in Ethan's mind. The possibilities were starting to form. "I expect I'll see you well after New Year's. I'll sign the paperwork for the buyout and leave it with Nancy today."

Instead of shaking hands with Ethan as usual, he walked around the desk as Ethan stood. Charles pulled him into a hug. "I'm leaving with great expectations for this firm as there will be a changing of the guard. Happy Christmas, Ethan."

"Yes, sir. You too."

Ethan came out of his office at five thirty, each foot planted loudly, stopping at Nancy's desk. "Thank you for staying to wait on Charles."

Nancy patted the folder on her desk. "You're welcome. It's done. It's all here, Mr. Cooper."

He exhaled loudly, tilting his head back. His lips pursed as he looked at her. "You never told me what you wanted for Christmas this year."

"Something simple, time off." Nancy opened the file with the buyout paperwork. "I'm going to make some copies of this, then I'm going home. Do you need anything else?"

"Just for you to enjoy tomorrow through the day after New Year's off, paid vacation. And if you check your email, there is a first class ticket to go see your son. The plane leaves at nine thirty tonight. Merry Christmas!"

Nancy put the paperwork down and hugged him. "Thank you, Mr. Cooper. Merry Christmas!"

"Now go! I don't want you to miss that plane." Ethan left her to walk into Racheal's office. She was packing her briefcase to leave. "You got a minute for me?"

Racheal moved her bag and sat down. "As long as you don't turn totally back into Mr. Grumpy pants."

He held up three fingers, together. "Scouts honor."

"What's on that Harvard mind of yours? Have you heard from her?" Racheal closed the lid to her laptop.

"Haven't heard a peep. You?"

Rachel shook her head negatively. "I miss her."

Ethan closed his eyes, his head dropping a moment before raising it again. "Me too. I'm going to catch a flight south and head to Charleston. I don't want to spend Christmas alone this year. I don't think I could bear it."

"Go. I'll look after things here. Take some time. There aren't going to be that many of us here between Christmas and New Year's anyway. I'll be working from home mostly if there is anything that comes up. Otherwise, there's nothing that pressing. See you next year."

"Thank you. Merry Christmas, Racheal."

"Merry Christmas. Now get out of here!" She smiled at him.

He wasted no time, getting his things together and leaving 601 Lexington Avenue that night. He hadn't been home for Christmas in so long he couldn't remember.

22

I'll Be Home For Christmas

E than was pulling two large rolling suitcases, with a hard case tied to the top of one, over uneven cobblestones toward Aunt Effie's home on Rainbow Row in Charleston, South Carolina. It was a cool night, with the temperatures in the middle fifties, with blooming camellias on the night breeze. There was a real evergreen wreath on the front door along with a smaller wreath hanging on each of the lower windows. He felt odd knocking on the front door of what was his house, but he knew Jane and the boys wouldn't be expecting him. He couldn't use his key.

Andy answered the door in his pajamas. It was almost nine and the boys would be heading for bed.

"Merry Christmas!" Ethan stepped inside, smothering Andy with a hug. Jane came from the direction of the rear kitchen. "Merry Christmas, Janie."

"Ethan! You're here!" Jane sprinted to hug him, sandwiching Andy between them.

"I can't breathe, Momma."

Nic came bounding down the stairs when he heard his Uncle's voice, launching himself at him from the last step. He felt himself spinning around in the air for a moment before Ethan sat him down. "You're here," he squealed.

"I couldn't very well spend Christmas without all of you." Ethan wore a wistful expression. Jane squeezed her brother's hand.

"Still no word?" Jane was hopping for news.

"Nothing."

"No news is good news, right?" Andy's eyebrows rose with the question.

They pulled the suitcases inside. After a few minutes, one was rolled into the living room near a real Christmas tree. Ethan unzipped the case, presents spilling out. The boys picked them up immediately.

Jane interceded, "Those go under the tree, please."

They were disappointed, but heeded her instruction.

"Now, go brush your teeth and get ready for bed."

Andy's face scrunched up with objection. "But Uncle E's here!"

Nic chimed in. "And it's Christmas! Can we stay up a little later, please?"

The sing song chorus of please came from the boys and Ethan too, which made her laugh before conceding. "Oh alright. Ten o'clock and then it's off to bed with you two." Her index finger pointed back and forth between the two boys. Ethan sat down on the sofa, Andy to his right, Nic to his left. Jane sat in a chair across from them. The little house on Folly Beach wouldn't be ready for them until after New Years and their over-sized country club house had sold in a weeks time, above asking price. Their mother hadn't morphed back into her old self either. They were supposed to have breakfast with her tomorrow at Toast. Then they'd be opening a few presents here at Aunt Effie's in the evening, saving the rest for Christmas morning.

Before they knew it, each boy had gone to sleep on Ethan. Jane was exhausted. She knew her brother had to be. It was almost eleven. They arranged the presents under the tree, hiding the hard case Ethan had brought with him to give to Andy. Finally, they woke the boys enough to get them upstairs and in bed.

Ethan went into the yellow room, the room he always slept in as a child when his Aunt Effie was alive. It now had a king sized bed in it and had the same feel as the decor Jane had used in his New York apartment. He laid there wondering where Charlotte could be, as he had every night since her abrupt departure. He resolved the very next time he laid eyes on her, he'd ask her to marry him, not just wear Aunt Effie's ring. Charlotte had changed his life for the better.

He was irrevocably in love with her. Ethan didn't care where they lived, as long as he was with her. Maybe they could find a place for the store in Charleston. That was the last thought he had before sleep claimed him.

Ethan woke up to a quiet room. No car alarms, no horns from taxi cabs, or sirens wailing. Quiet. It was disconcerting until he remembered where he was. Quiet. He liked that. After finding his glasses, he got up, dressing before breakfast. The harbor finally issued noise, the blaring sound of a cargo ship passing by in the channel, faintly presenting itself to the room.

Andy wandered down the hall knocking on the bedroom door until Ethan told him to enter. "Morning. You wear glasses? How long are you going to stay here? Have you heard from Aunt Charlotte?"

"Good morning to you too, Andy. Not a peep from her yet." Ethan chuckled at the inquisition, buttoning up the pink gingham shirt he had on. "I don't know how long I'll stay. Should I wear them today?" He pulled them off long enough to pull a winter white sweater over his head, the edge falling at his hip, covering the top of his jeans.

Andy nodded affirmatively. "I think they're cool."

Ethan put them back on, pushing them up his nose. "Cool huh?" He chuckled.

"Yeah, like Clark Kent."

Andy is a Superman fan? Ethan thought he had some of the original Superman comics in Aunt Effie's attic. He'd try and get up there later and put them under the tree for Andy.

Margaret was seated inside Toast at a table in the back. There was a line down the block to get inside. She was glad to know the owner so well. They'd saved them a table. So many tourists were enjoying Charleston over Christmas right now. It seemed they were eager to taste the popular destination's faire. She waved Jane and the boys on over once they came inside. *Who is this man with them?* Her heart fluttered as she squealed like a school girl. *That was positively undignified. Oh, who cares!* Margaret came out of her seat eagerly hugging her son. "I don't know what possessed you to come home for Christmas but I'm so happy to see you. I didn't know you in the glasses!"

Breakfast passed quickly, everyone eating and enjoying themselves. The bread basket was filled twice with cathead biscuits, now empty again. They had eaten their fill, paid the bill, and walked outside.

Ethan looked down the street. The Market was overflowing with visitors. Then his gaze fixed on the Planter's Inn. He remembered Charlotte saying her family always spent Christmas there. He wondered if they were there now. Jane saw his face and decided she needed a walk after eating that much. Besides, she had a surprise to show them.

They walked over to King Street, bustling with tourists and locals alike. There was a shop nearby that Jane liked, Vieuxtemps. Ethan thought he might wander into Williams Sonoma for some peppermint bark. He was sad to see that Heirloom, The Literature of Food vintage cookbook store, had closed, but the sign in the window said you could still order online. People were getting in last minute shopping. Jane stopped in front of an empty building. Ethan recognized it immediately from all the pictures she'd sent him over the last few months. She held up a large key in front of herself.

"All mine! Finally!"

Ethan picked his baby sister up, spinning her around. "Congratulations!"

"Thank you. I'm going to need your help." Jane looked right at their mother. "The boys have lots of obligations and lessons. If I'm with a client, I might need you to pick them up or take them around for me."

"Let me know. I don't have to buy a mini-van do I?" She winked at her. "I'm so excited for you, Jane. I've never had a job I loved so much it wasn't work. Then again, I've never had a job." Margaret looked up at the three story historic property. "Can we go in?"

Ethan looked at the moulding on the façade as he followed them all inside. The details on the interior, like built in shelves and marble tiles were features Charlotte would appreciate. It's exactly what she was looking for in New York. She could have even been talking about this building when she had mentioned finding a place in Charleston she had liked since it appeared as though New York just wasn't in the cards.

"There are fifteen hundred square feet on each of the top two floors that are usable. The shop here on the bottom has seventeen hundred counting the store room. The top floor would be perfect for painting. Wait until you see the light, Ethan! It's incredible. The acoustics are phenomenal. You could play or give the boys a lesson up there. There's enough room for a large office area. I'm going to put my office on the back half of the second floor. I can use the front half for samples and spread plans out on a…" Jane's words fell off when she saw Ethan's face. He wore a pained expression.

Margaret turned to see what was wrong. She knew the moment she saw the ornate chandeliers hanging from the high ceiling, light pink crystals dangling from their tiers. "She'd love it, wouldn't she?"

Ethan couldn't say a word for fear of losing it, right there. He turned, breathing in and out, trying to control the emotions inside of him that were threatening to spill over. The cell in his pocket began buzzing. It was a text from Charlotte.

Jane walked over to where their mother stood, the boys had run up the stairs. She knew in her heart it was Charlotte. "Is she alright?"

The relief on his face said it all. *Safe and sound and on the ground, in Charleston at the Planters Inn. Christmas with family first. What are you doing New Year's, Mr. Cooper? I seem to recall we had a date.*

Ethan didn't realize he'd been holding his breath until now. He began breathing short breaths of excitement as he realized she was only a few blocks away from him. "She's here! She's in Charleston at the Planters Inn with her family. They come here every year for Christmas."

"Well don't just stand there!" Margaret winked at her son. "Invite her over for the Christmas Eve festivities."

The idea hit him. "Jane, I want to rent your shop space."

"For what?" She was completely puzzled.

"My new company with Charlotte, Bourbon and Bacon, Finely Southern."

CHAPTER TWENTY-TWO

"Okay." She looked at Margaret, still confused. "I like the name."

"I'll meet you back here in a few minutes. I think. Maybe more than a few. Stay here." Ethan practically ran the distance between King and North Market, closing the distance as fast as his legs would carry him. He slowed to a walk as his full stomach began to object to the jostling. By the time he pulled the front door open at the Inn, his breathing had calmed down along with his stomach. *Wow! I need to work on my cardio.*

There she was, standing at the front counter hugging someone. The family resemblance was easy to see. Tall and striking, just like Charlotte. This had to be her brother William. She let him go, her eyes focusing farther away.

Then she saw him. Her breath hitched. Standing there inside the front door, his eyes were fixated on her like a sidewinder missile.

"Ethan." His name came from lips like a prayer.

William turned to see where she was looking. "Who?"

Charlotte closed the distance between them in a few quick steps. "I can't believe you're here!" She kissed him taking his breath completely before he could utter a word.

More of Charlotte's family were now around William, sharing the same question. Who was Charlotte kissing?

Ethan needed air and broke away from her, his glasses all fogged up. "Marry me. That's what I'm doing New Year's. Do we have still have a date?"

Charlotte's eyes lit up issuing a blinding smile. She pulled off his glasses. "Yes, Mr. Cooper. We have a date." Charlotte turned around, leading him toward her family. She handed him the glasses, now clear again. "Everyone, this is Ethan Cooper, my fiancé."

The words rang happily in his ears. Ethan felt the spotlight on him as her family was introduced. Mother, father, brother William, sister-in-law Jennifer, and two nephews Tyler and Lee, all tall and welcoming. They chatted for several minutes, inviting him to lunch with them for shrimp and grits, to which he agreed. They finally excused themselves to leave the two of them alone. Ethan helped her to her room, rolling her luggage inside. His lips met hers, once more, in a lingering kiss before hugging her to him. Several minutes passed in silence before he spoke.

"Oh, I've missed you." He rested his head against her hair, exhaling, closing his eyes to breathe in her familiar scent.

She squeezed him gently. "I've missed you too. I was wondering how fast I could get away from my family and get back to you. I could hear myself saying something ridiculous. 'Sorry y'all. I know it's Christmas, but there's this guy in New York City.' I was wondering how I was going to explain you."

He felt her body move with light laughter. "I suppose you won't have to worry about that now."

"What are you doing in Charleston? I thought you never came home." She pulled back to look at him.

"I couldn't stay in New York for Christmas if you weren't going to be there. I wanted to be near Jane and the boys at least and maybe Mother. I have a lot to tell you." Ethan's face wrinkled up when he mentioned his mother. He still wasn't sure Margaret the

Hun wasn't going to return. "I could stand here and just hold you, all day, but I need you to come with me, right now."

"Where are we going?" Charlotte was entirely curious.

"My family is waiting. I have something to show you." He led her toward the door, picking up her purse as they left the room.

"Am I dressed appropriately?" Her eyebrows raised with the question.

"Perfect. You're even wearing flats. We have some walking to do." He passed her bag over as they approached the elevator.

They walked hand-in-hand back to King Street. Ethan paused in front of Jane's building, allowing Charlotte to take in the details outside. He opened the door to the shop, pulling her inside. He could hear his family talking somewhere upstairs. "Welcome to the new home of Bourbon and Bacon, Finely Southern, our new venture. The shop space is ours, as of today."

Charlotte saw the moulding, the built-in shelves that would house books and stationery. Then her eyes drifted to the sales counter, and finally to the pink crystals on the chandeliers. She stepped forward, kissing him with all that she was. "It's perfect."

Christmas Eve was passing by in a blur. The sky was growing dim as the day waited patiently to kiss the night sky. Margaret knocked on the door to her late sister Effie's home, now occupied by all that remained of her family. This would be the first Christmas she'd had with both her children in years. She had resolved to take in every smile, every laugh, and give as many hugs as she could get by with. She'd lived by herself for far too long. Embracing life had become a glorious revelation.

Andy opened the door. "Hey Granny! Come on in." He took the gifts she was holding on over to the tree with her. "Do we get to open these tonight?"

Margaret ruffled his hair. "Perhaps."

Andy's chin dropped in obvious disappointment.

She put her index finger under his chin, lifting it up. "Only if I can stay and watch you open them and enjoy them."

"Yes, ma'am!" His face lit up. "Do you want me to put your purse in the kitchen or on the foyer table?"

"Let's leave it on the sofa. It sounds like the party is in the kitch-en." Margaret walked with Andy toward the voices and Christmas music emanating from the kitchen.

There was food spread out on the island. Spiced bread was cook-ing in the oven. Margaret detected the familiar scent. Olives, several kinds of meat, cheeses, figs, apricots, nuts, sugar cookies, and fudge.

Charlotte was laughing at something while she helped Nic cut into a cake of some sort. Jane was indulging in fudge. Ethan was sitting in a chair at the kitchen table, strumming a guitar along with a Christmas song playing on Nic's portable speaker. *It's going to be a great Christmas*, Margaret thought, as she took in the scene.

"You're here!" Charlotte's eyes lit up, greeting Margaret.

"You made it to our little fete. Merry Christmas, Charlotte."

"Merry Christmas, Margaret. Would you like a piece of bourbon fruit cake?" Charlotte's eyes twinkled at the word 'bourbon.'

Andy grabbed a plate and stuck it out for a slice of the cake. "I want one!"

Margaret was pleasantly surprised as she sunk her teeth into a bite. The cake was shaped like a pound cake, baked in a festive pan, but was no ordinary cake." I have never had a fruit cake like this. This is actually very good."

Jane laughed, "I know what you mean. I didn't quite know what to think when the boys started helping her make it a little while ago. Chopped apricots, pistachios, bourbon sauce once it came out. Fruit cakes have never been my favorite, but this is the exception. It's delicious, Charlotte. I need the recipe."

"I'll give it to you."

Ethan put the guitar down and stepped beside Charlotte at the island. "I want a bite, please." Charlotte lifted her fork to his mouth. A moment later and he tried to take her piece away.

"Get your own!" She smacked his hands away playfully before cutting him a piece.

Andy put the glass dome over the cake once everyone had been served. "This is so good. I see why you like bourbon so much, Uncle E."

"The taste is there but the alcohol cooks out when you make the sauce. I don't want you drinking anything until you're old enough." Ethan winked at Andy as he finished off the small piece of cake.

"Keep the dome over it after you cut a slice off. It will dry out and we can't have that." Charlotte smiled at him as Ethan pulled the dome off to get another slice for himself.

Margaret put her plate down and asked Ethan to join her in the living room. He followed, puzzled. She reached into her bag and pulled out a velvet jewelry box, handing it to him. "Give these to Charlotte. They shouldn't be separated from that ring any longer."

Ethan opened the box although he knew what was inside. It had been many years since he'd seen the diamond earrings that perfectly matched Aunt Effie's ring, worn on Charlotte's finger. He put the box into his pocket and leaned forward, hugging his mother tightly. "I love you, Mom."

Tears welled up almost immediately in Margaret's eyes. Hearing those words from Ethan had been a long time coming. For so long she didn't deserve them. He had called her mom instead of mother. "I love you too, Son."

Healing came in many forms. Tonight it came in the form of a hug, something rarely seen over the years between the two of them.

The family chatted, munched, chatted more, and finally settled in the living room around the tree.

With Andy's help, Margaret handed out the gifts she'd brought with her. She'd be sleeping in tomorrow and seeing them all later in the day. "Now boys, there are more at my house for you, but these are for tonight."

Andy and Nic tore into small boxes that held a gift card for each boy. "Thank you, Granny!" Each boy took their turn hugging her for their media cards that could be used for gaming, music, or videos.

Jane stopped them from disappearing immediately to find their pads and load the cards. "You can go in a minute. Uncle Ethan has something first, so sit down, please."

Margaret prompted Jane to open the wrapped gift in front of her.

"Oh, it's just as beautiful as I remember! Thank you!" Jane hopped up and hugged Margaret before resuming her seat. The string of large South-Sea pearls hung perfectly around Jane's neck, matching the earrings she now wore. She was grinning broadly.

"You always admired them as a child. I remember chastising you for playing in my jewelry. Forgive me. Enjoy them."

"I will. Thank you, Mom."

Margaret's heart swelled even more. *Another Mom. I'm not going to cry. I'm not going to cry!* She inhaled and exhaled, trying to let the moisture subside. "Ethan?"

He took the cue to pull out the box from his pocket. He opened the box, presenting it to Charlotte. The slightly pink pear shaped diamond earrings reflected the lights on the Christmas tree, sending spots of light onto everything nearby in the room. She gasped, removing the box from his hand to inspect the contents more closely. "They're beautiful!"

Margaret spoke up as she watched the delight on Charlotte's face echoed in her son's as well. "A thing of beauty is a joy forever only if it's enjoyed. Those were given to me the same night Effie received the ring. Our father had them made for us. I rarely wore them. Effie put the ring on and never took it off, well barely." She paused, laughing a bit. "I never enjoyed them nearly as much as she did with her gift. It's time someone had both and delighted in wearing them together. Jane's a pearl girl. And that ring is perfect for you, Charlotte. Enjoy the earrings, please."

Charlotte got up and gave Margaret yet another hug, this one in silence.

"Okay! Photo time. Put your earrings on." Ethan pulled his phone out. They gathered in while Ethan held his phone out as far as possible away from him. "Say Christmas!"

Jane sat back down along with everyone else. She knew the boys were eagerly awaiting the time they could slip away and load their cards to play on the pads.

Ethan stood up and picked up four gifts from under the tree, placing them in front of Jane, the boys, and his mother. Margaret wasted no time in unwrapping her flat, rather large, gift.

She squealed with delight. *I really have to stop doing that!* Before her was a family portrait. She recognized the clothes they wore from the evening of the fundraiser. "I absolutely adore it! I know exactly where I'm going to hang it. I can take down that piece Mary Kay painted last year. It's going in the living room. Thank you so much!" She returned the hug Ethan had given her earlier. "It's just missing my other daughter." Margaret winked at Charlotte.

Jane laughed, "Ethan can paint her in soon enough."

Andy and Nic were also unwrapping their gifts. They usually received something Nancy had picked up and mailed to them, or something Ethan had asked Jane to pick-up for him. Not this year. Andy pulled open the well-worn case of his uncle's silver trumpet. He was at a loss for words. The instrument was expensive but had so much more meaning because it belonged to his uncle. Andy immediately pushed the case away and hugged his uncle.

"Thank you so much. It's perfect! I've always hoped you'd give it to me." Andy sat down on the sofa beside Ethan. "Now I can play it any time and not just when I'm visiting you."

Ethan patted Andy's knee, watching Nic dance around wearing his inherited watch. They were both amused at Nic's antics.

"Thank you, Uncle E! Thank you, thank you, thank you!"

"Wear it and enjoy it. Just don't lose it, okay?"

"I won't. I promise." Nic was showing his gSranny the watch with the blue face he'd admired and voiced his wish for since he was eight. That seemed like forever for him.

Ethan cleared his throat, looking at Andy first, then the others in the room. "I bought out Charles Grey. The firm is mine...and I'm taking a cue from him. I'm choosing Racheal to run it. I can work remotely, when I choose, from here. So Andy, I fully expect to hear you play that often. I'll fly back and forth when I need to, but this is home again. It's where all of you are. That's home."

The group piled onto the sofa for a family hug.

Jane turned around to open her present finally, resuming her seat in the chair. She unwrapped a recipe box, full of cards with familiar handwriting. Her face belied how delighted she was with the gift. "You stinker!" She looked across to Ethan who was grinning broadly. "You made copies of all of Mrs. Icey's recipe cards. Thank you. I've wanted this for years!"

"And now we can cook these recipes together." Ethan rose from the sofa to hug Jane. "Merry Christmas, Carlye Jane."

The boys left the room with their presents. Margaret and Jane went back to the kitchen to make them all a drink. Ethan put his arm Charlotte, squeezing her to him on the sofa. He whispered into her hair, knowing she could easily hear him with the aid of her bionic ears. "Merry Christmas, Charlotte. You're what I wanted for Christmas."

"Same here. And that can't be wrapped under a tree." She turned and kissed him.

23

What Are You Doin' New Years?

New Years Eve came quickly for Charlotte and Ethan. They exchanged vows at St. Phillips earlier that evening with just their families present. Now they were dancing the night away in the courtyard at the Planters Inn, Charlotte in a light blush lacey dress and cashmere wrap, her gifted earrings sparkling in the courtyard lights more visible with her new above-the-shoulder bob haircut. Ethan was clad in a suit and pink tie. They took a break to sit and have a slice of their wedding cake as the clock was about to strike midnight.

Ethan raised a bite of the famous Ultimate Coconut Cake to Charlotte's mouth. She returned the gesture.

"You wouldn't dare eat all that piece would you?" Charlotte smirked at him.

"I wouldn't dream of it. That's why I had them wrap up several pieces to take home with us. We can take them on the road when we drive up to Kentucky for our honeymoon. Of course I am looking forward to spending a few days in Franklin with your family."

"Spending a week on the bourbon trail seems appropriate for us." She took another bite of the cake. "If you like it there, and I know you will, I might not have a house anymore but I still have fifteen acres on Rose Creek. William said we can stay in my old house with them, anytime, because the boys will be away at school. I'll have some back and forth there anyway for the business as we transition to him taking over."

"I think a country house sounds perfect. Besides, having a cooler place to retreat to during the heat of summer will be welcome. And I happen to know someone who can help us decorate it." Ethan kissed his wife with great delight, smearing coconut frosting on her lips. He happily kissed it off.

"Oh you two are just too cute over here!" Racheal brought two glasses of champagne, sitting them down on the table in the warm night air. She and Gabriel had flown down. Gabriel handed her a glass for herself as he retained his, taking a sip.

Racheal raised her glass. "To new beginnings."

The firm had a new managing partner at Cooper Maxwell.

"To new beginnings!"

Ethan reserved drinking from his glass for the moment. "May love always find it's way back to us. To new beginnings, indeed."

Someone opened the door to the courtyard from the Peninsula Grill and started counting down loudly from ten.

Fireworks started exploding over the Cooper River, shot from the Ravenel bridge, sending colored light flashes everywhere. Ethan led Charlotte to the roof to watch the fireworks. He pointed across the river to Patriots Point where they were celebrating on the deck of the USS Yorktown.

"Happy New Year, Mr. Cooper."

Ethan leaned forward and kissed Charlotte. "Happy New Year, Mrs. Cooper. I love you, Pink."

THE END

DID YOU LOVE IT?

*Please follow Monica and
leave a review for Pink at:*
Goodreads.com
Amazon.com
BarnesandNoble.com
Bookbub.com

Your review can be short and sweet, but please leave your great review today. Your help is critical to get this book into the hands of other readers. Tag your social media posts so we can feature you and your Pink photos!

#PinkNovel #PinkChristmas #PinkRomance

Want more Pink?
Visit Monica's website for more about Pink, recipes, anecdotes, and even
Bourbon & Bacon merchandise.

monicacollier.com

Pink was typeset using
Adobe Garamond Pro, 12 pt
for the body, and
Blooming Elegant Monoline
of varying sizes for the main and chapter titles.

Thank you for reading Pink!

CPSIA information can be obtained
at www.ICGtesting.com
Printed in the USA
BVHW032131041121
620855BV00004B/122